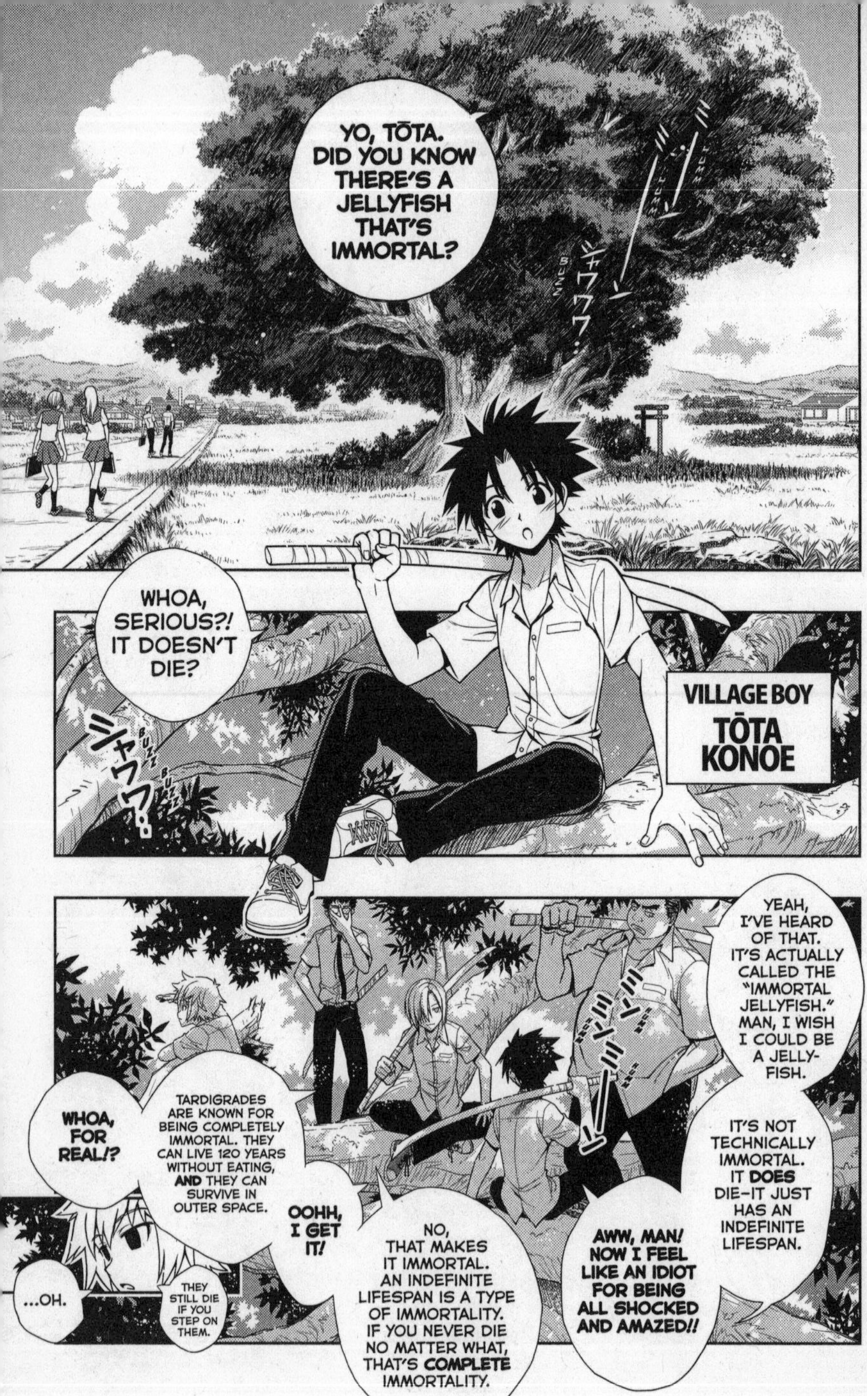
YO, TŌTA. DID YOU KNOW THERE'S A JELLYFISH THAT'S IMMORTAL?
BUZZ
WHOA, SERIOUS?! IT DOESN'T DIE?
VILLAGE BOY TŌTA KONOE
BUZZ BUZZ
YEAH, I'VE HEARD OF THAT. IT'S ACTUALLY CALLED THE "IMMORTAL JELLYFISH." MAN, I WISH I COULD BE A JELLY-FISH.
IT'S NOT TECHNICALLY IMMORTAL. IT **DOES** DIE—IT JUST HAS AN INDEFINITE LIFESPAN.
AWW, MAN! NOW I FEEL LIKE AN IDIOT FOR BEING ALL SHOCKED AND AMAZED!!
NO, THAT MAKES IT IMMORTAL. AN INDEFINITE LIFESPAN IS A TYPE OF IMMORTALITY. IF YOU NEVER DIE NO MATTER WHAT, THAT'S **COMPLETE** IMMORTALITY.
OOHH, I GET IT!
TARDIGRADES ARE KNOWN FOR BEING COMPLETELY IMMORTAL. THEY CAN LIVE 120 YEARS WITHOUT EATING, **AND** THEY CAN SURVIVE IN OUTER SPACE.
WHOA, FOR REAL!?
THEY STILL DIE IF YOU STEP ON THEM.
...OH.

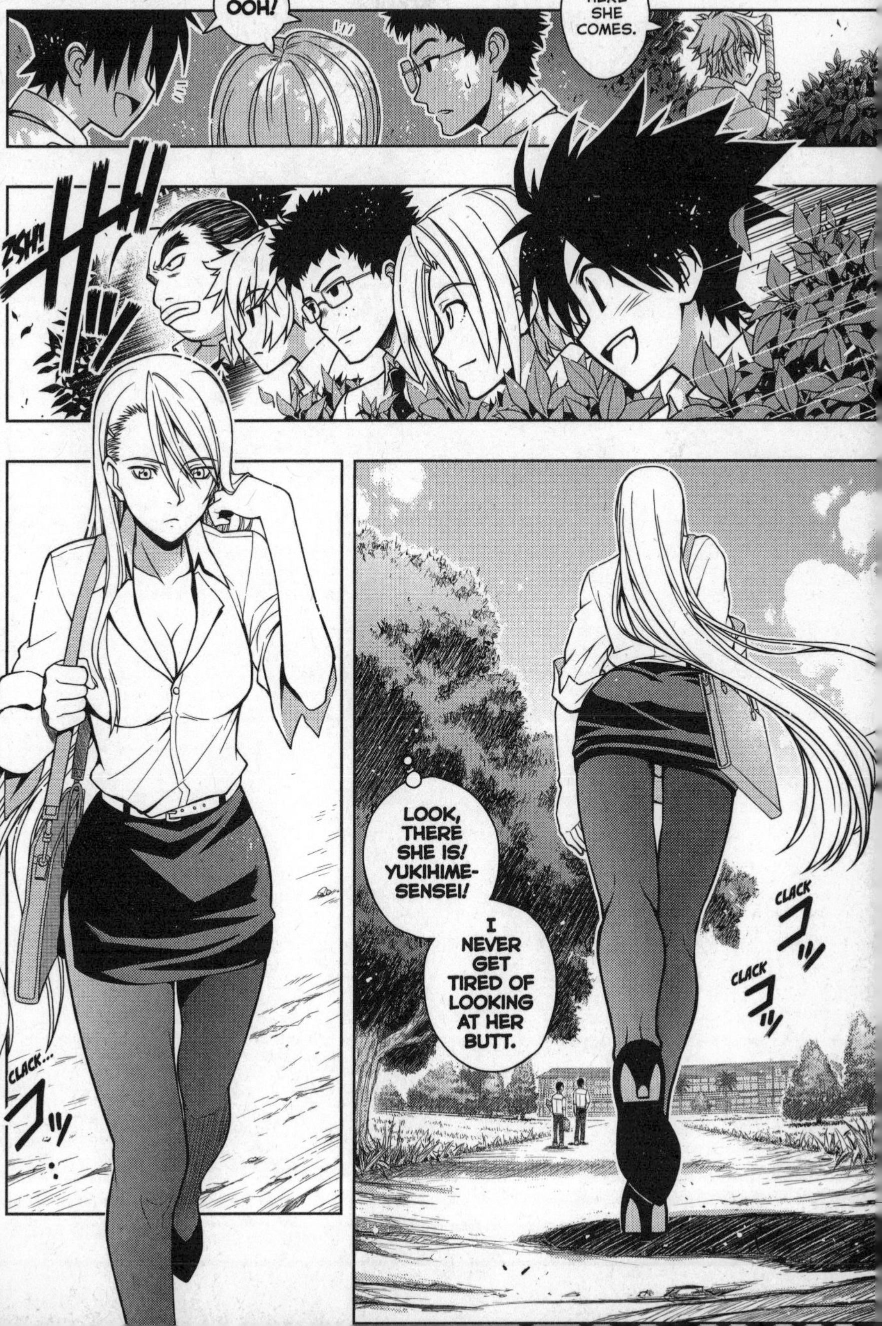
HERE SHE COMES.
OOH!
ZSH!
LOOK, THERE SHE IS! YUKIHIME-SENSEI!
I NEVER GET TIRED OF LOOKING AT HER BUTT.
CLACK
CLACK
CLACK...

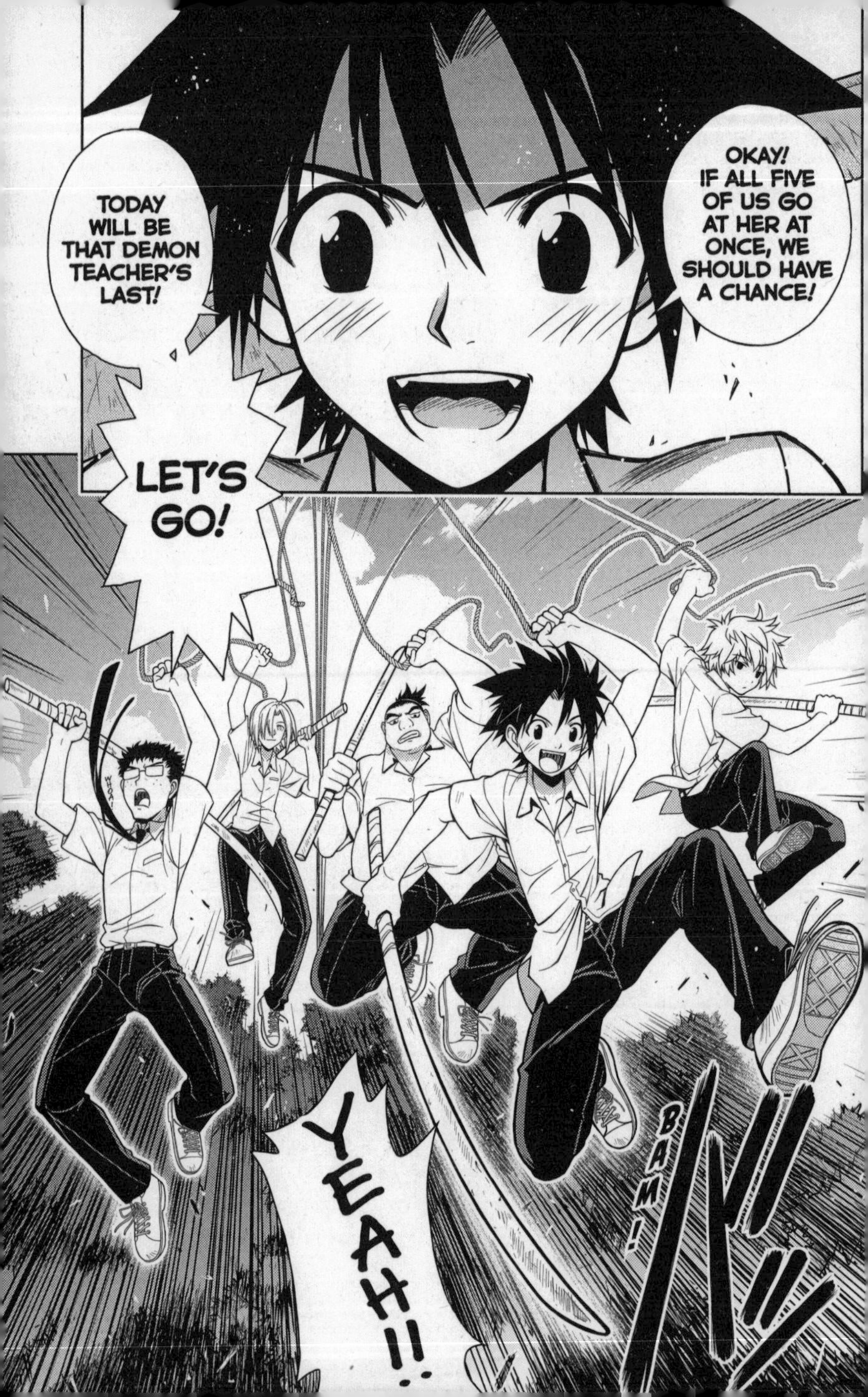
OKAY! IF ALL FIVE OF US GO AT HER AT ONCE, WE SHOULD HAVE A CHANCE!
TODAY WILL BE THAT DEMON TEACHER'S LAST!
LET'S GO!
BAM!
YEAH!!
WHOA!

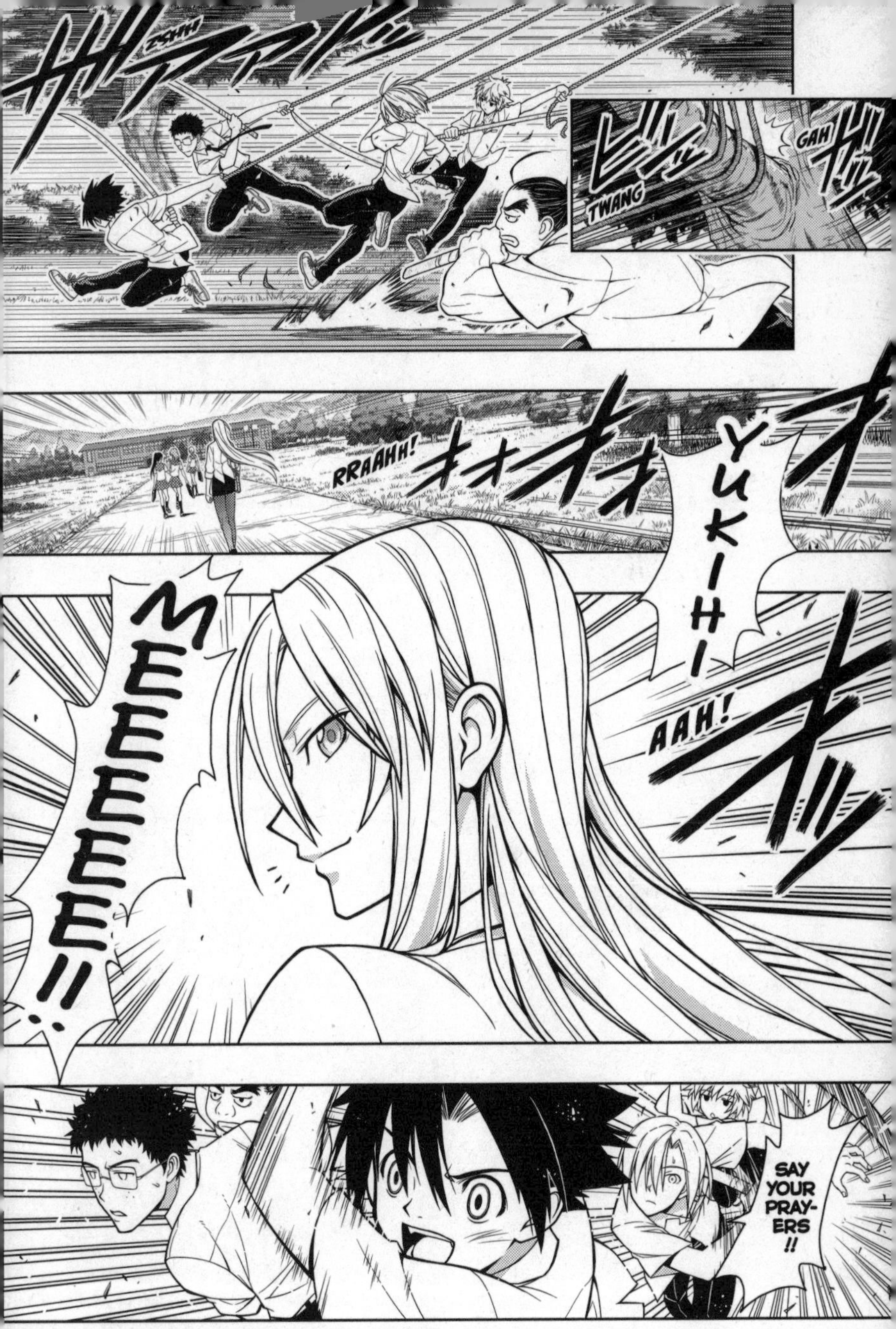

TWANG
GAH
ZSHH
RRAAHH!
YUKIHI-I
AAH!
MEEEEEE!!
SAY YOUR PRAY-ERS!!

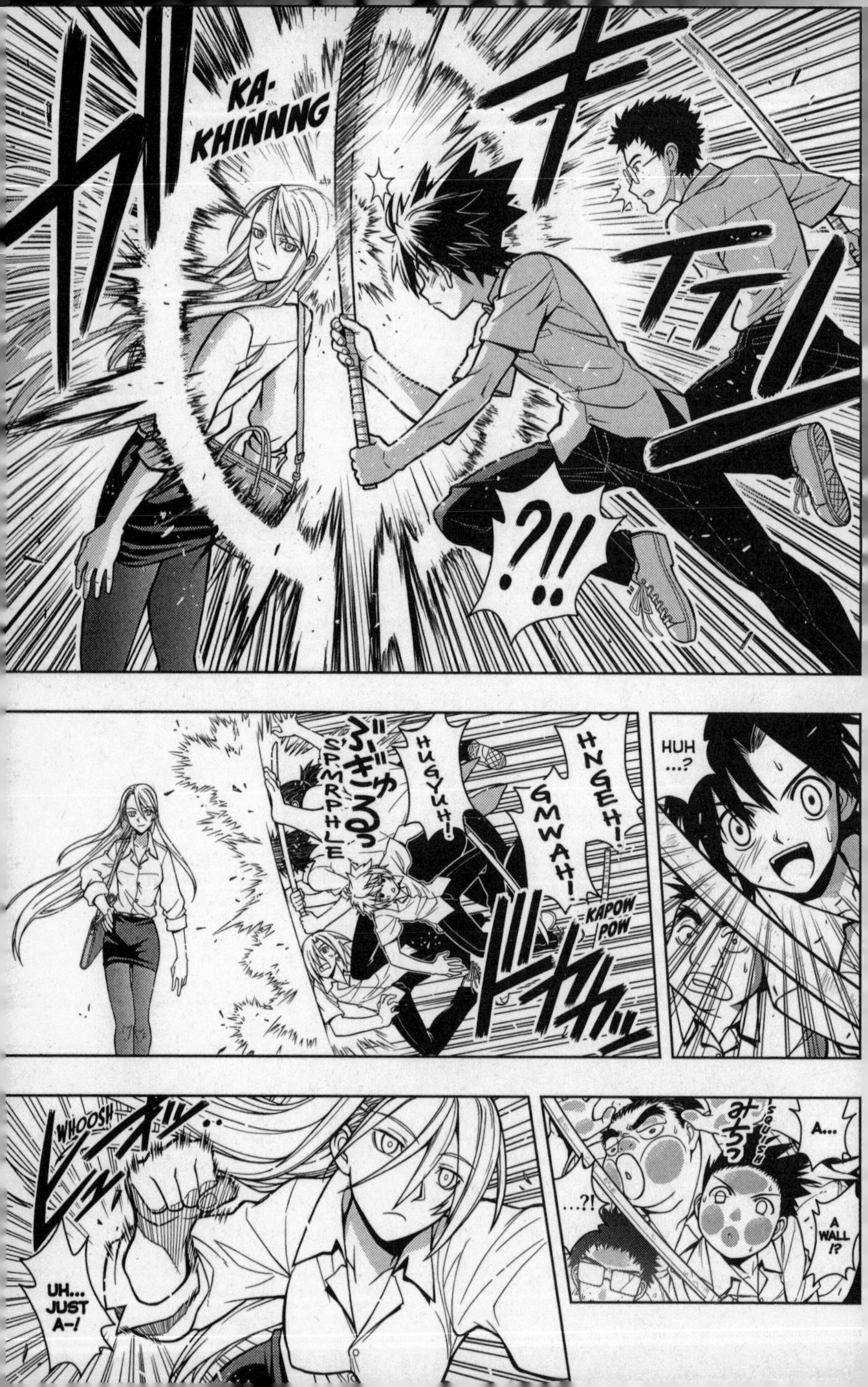
KA-KHINNNG
?!!
HUH ...?
HNGEH!
GMWAH!
HUGYUH!
ぶぎゅるっ
SPMRPHLE
KAPOW POW
A...
みちっ
SQUISH
A WALL !?
...?!
WHOOSH
UH... JUST A-!

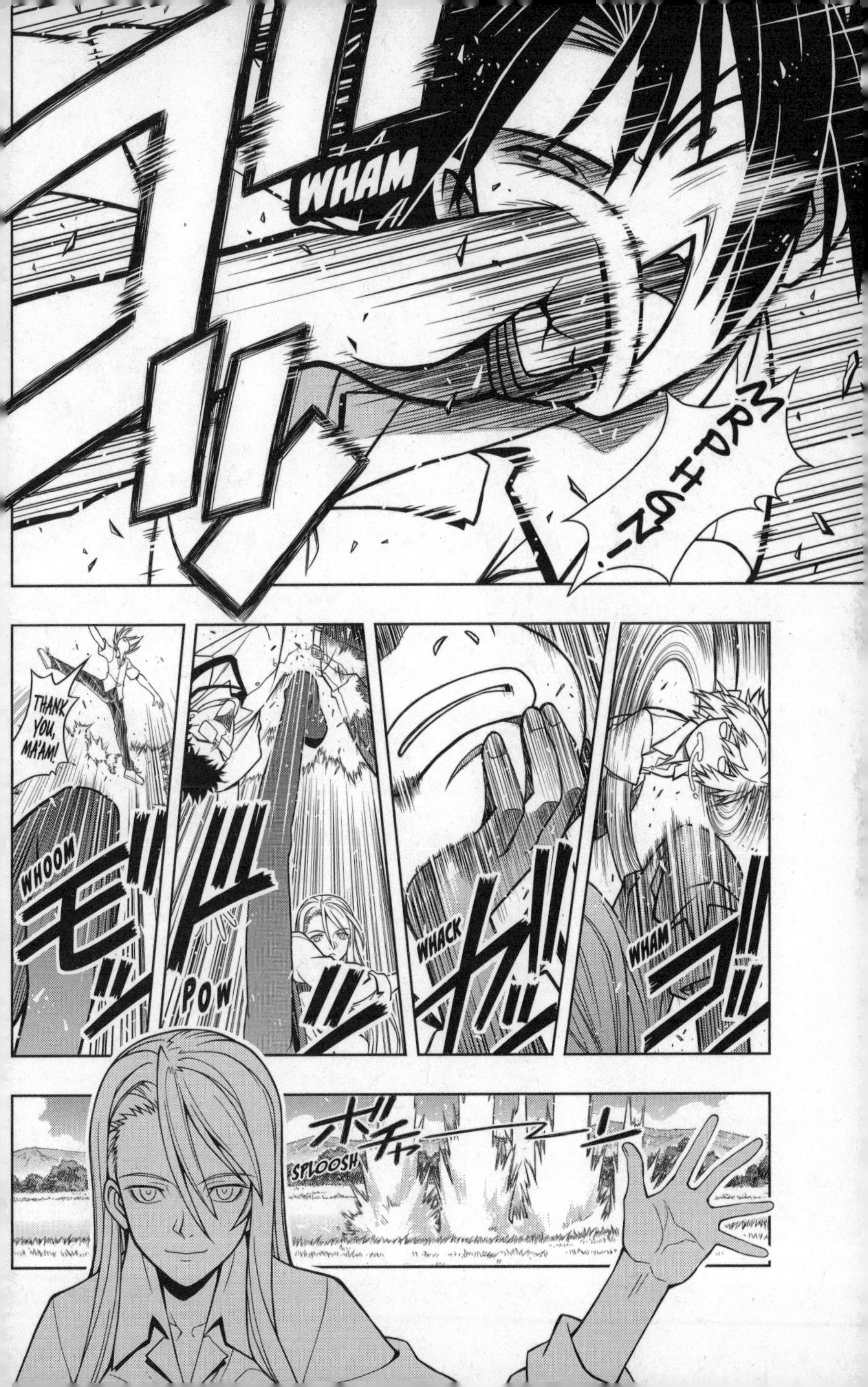
WHAM
MRPHSN—!
WHAM
WHACK
POW
THANK YOU, MA'AM!
WHOOM
SPLOOSH

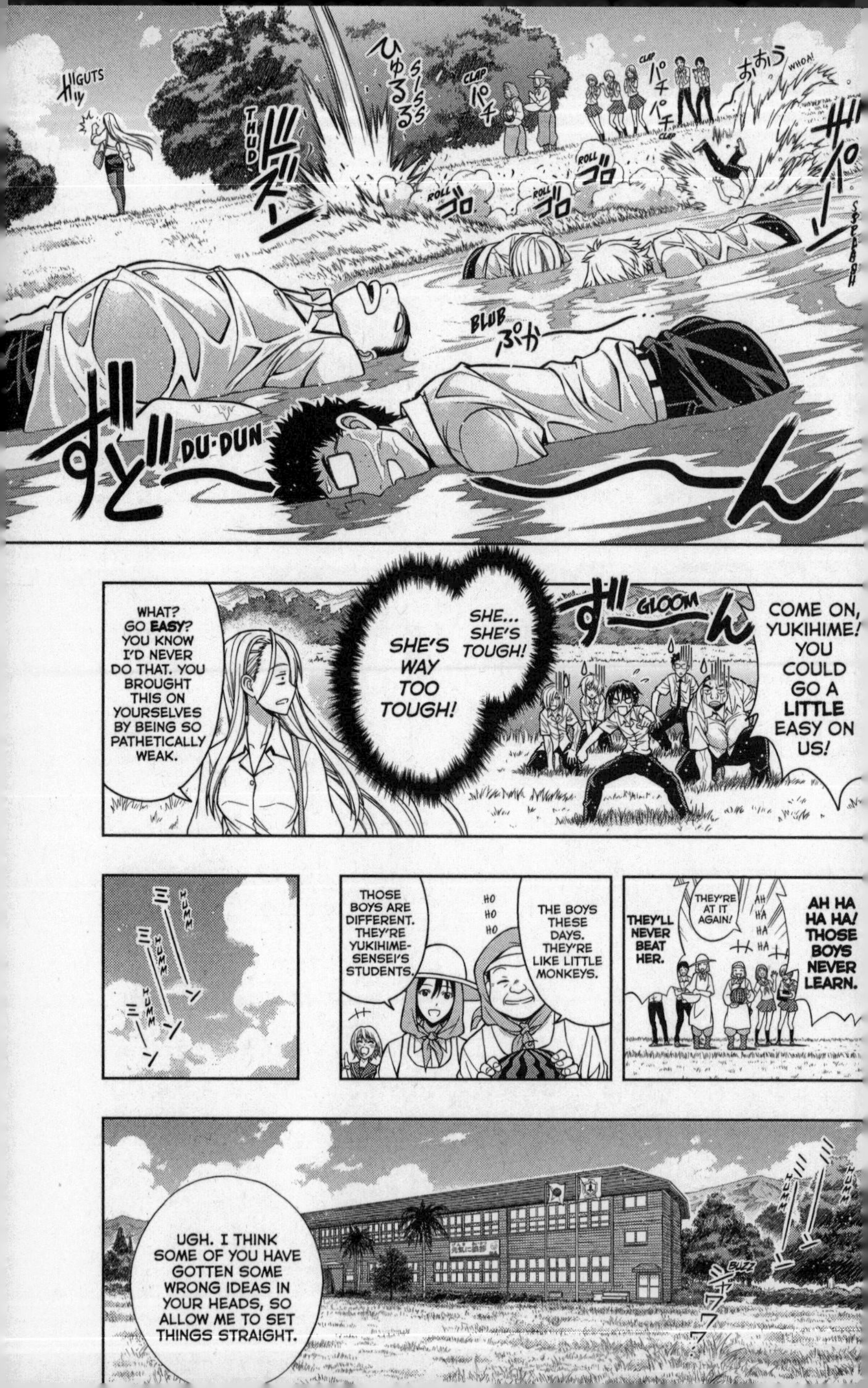
ザパーン SPLASH
おおう WHOA!
パチパチ CLAP CLAP
パチ CLAP
ゴロ ROLL
ゴロ ROLL
ゴロ ROLL
ひゅるる S-S-S
ドズン THUD
ガッ GUTS
ぷか BLUB
ずど〜ん DU-DUN
COME ON, YUKIHIME! YOU COULD GO A LITTLE EASY ON US!
ずーん GLOOM
SHE... SHE'S TOUGH!
SHE'S WAY TOO TOUGH!
WHAT? GO EASY? YOU KNOW I'D NEVER DO THAT. YOU BROUGHT THIS ON YOURSELVES BY BEING SO PATHETICALLY WEAK.
AH HA HA HA! THOSE BOYS NEVER LEARN.
AH HA HA HA
THEY'RE AT IT AGAIN!
THEY'LL NEVER BEAT HER.
THE BOYS THESE DAYS. THEY'RE LIKE LITTLE MONKEYS.
HO HO HO
THOSE BOYS ARE DIFFERENT. THEY'RE YUKIHIME-SENSEI'S STUDENTS.
ミーン HUMM
ミーン HUMM
ミーン HUMM
ミーン HUMM
ミーン HUMM
ジワワ BUZZ
UGH. I THINK SOME OF YOU HAVE GOTTEN SOME WRONG IDEAS IN YOUR HEADS, SO ALLOW ME TO SET THINGS STRAIGHT.

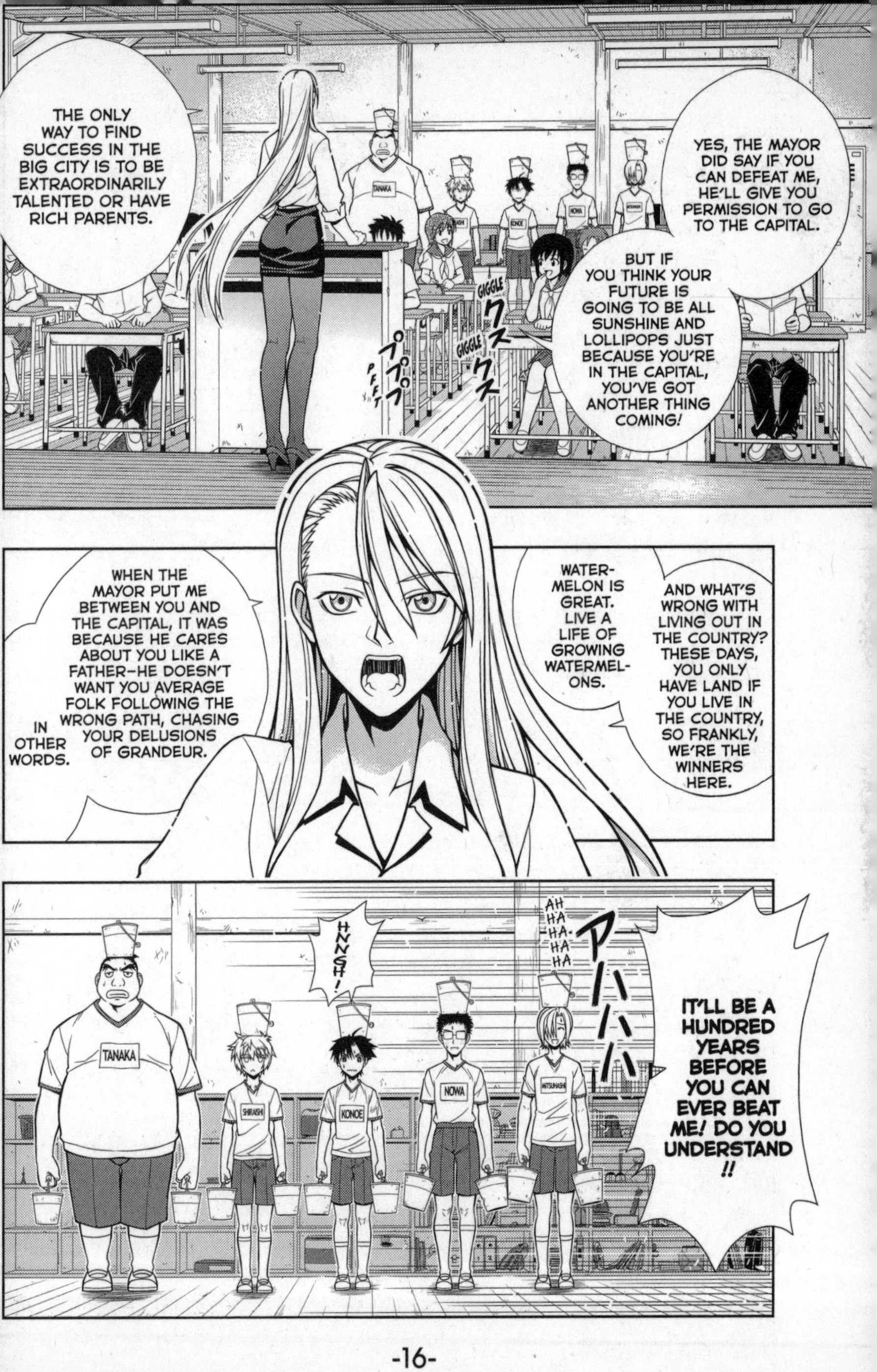
YES, THE MAYOR DID SAY IF YOU CAN DEFEAT ME, HE'LL GIVE YOU PERMISSION TO GO TO THE CAPITAL.
BUT IF YOU THINK YOUR FUTURE IS GOING TO BE ALL SUNSHINE AND LOLLIPOPS JUST BECAUSE YOU'RE IN THE CAPITAL, YOU'VE GOT ANOTHER THING COMING!
GIGGLE クス
GIGGLE クス
PFFT ププ
THE ONLY WAY TO FIND SUCCESS IN THE BIG CITY IS TO BE EXTRAORDINARILY TALENTED OR HAVE RICH PARENTS.
AND WHAT'S WRONG WITH LIVING OUT IN THE COUNTRY? THESE DAYS, YOU ONLY HAVE LAND IF YOU LIVE IN THE COUNTRY, SO FRANKLY, WE'RE THE WINNERS HERE.
WATER-MELON IS GREAT. LIVE A LIFE OF GROWING WATERMEL-ONS.
IN OTHER WORDS.
WHEN THE MAYOR PUT ME BETWEEN YOU AND THE CAPITAL, IT WAS BECAUSE HE CARES ABOUT YOU LIKE A FATHER–HE DOESN'T WANT YOU AVERAGE FOLK FOLLOWING THE WRONG PATH, CHASING YOUR DELUSIONS OF GRANDEUR.
AH HA HA HA HA アハハハ
IT'LL BE A HUNDRED YEARS BEFORE YOU CAN EVER BEAT ME! DO YOU UNDERSTAND!!
HNNGH!
TANAKA
KONOE
NOWA
MITSUHASHI

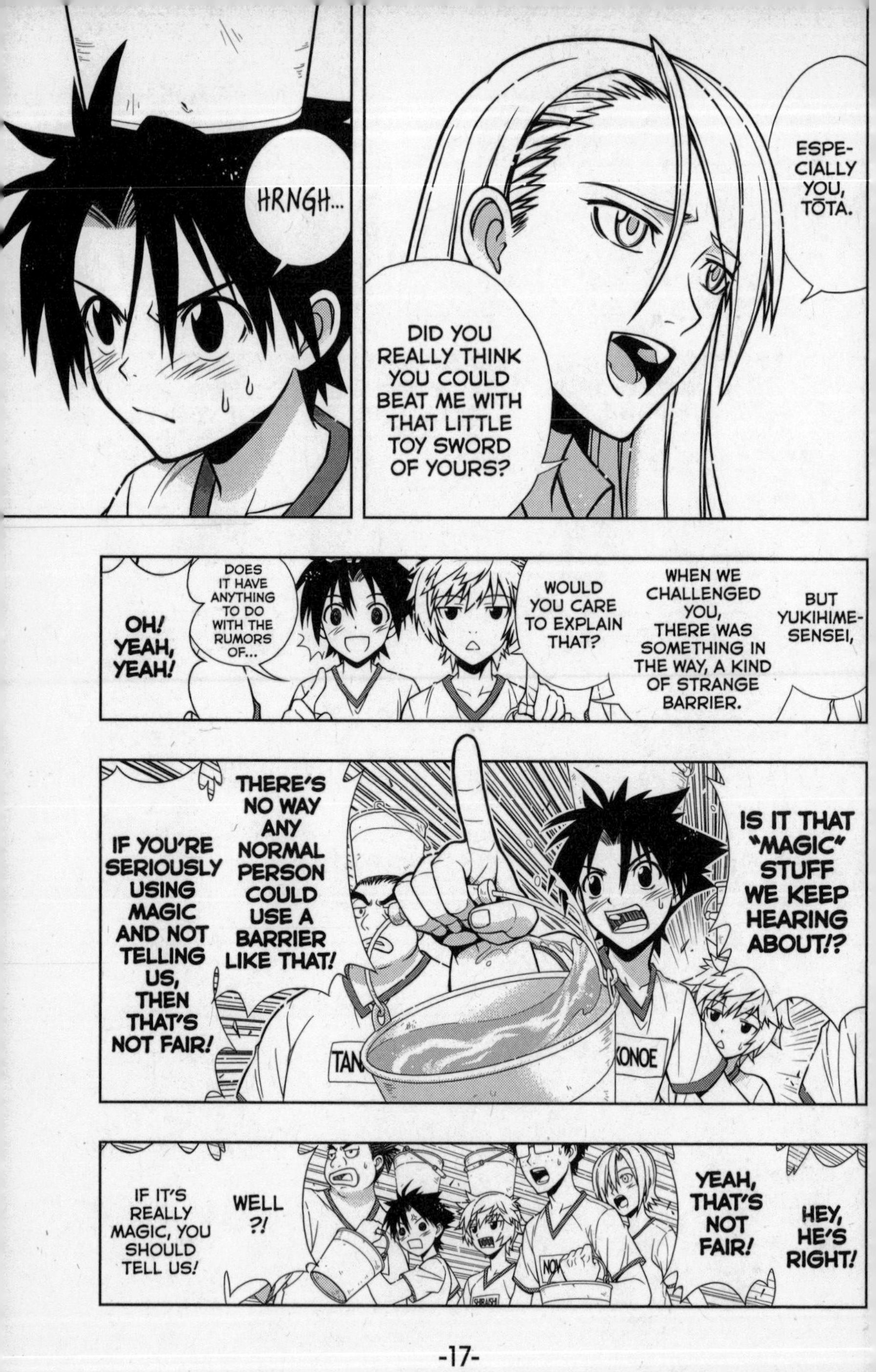
ESPECIALLY YOU, TŌTA.
DID YOU REALLY THINK YOU COULD BEAT ME WITH THAT LITTLE TOY SWORD OF YOURS?
HRNGH...
BUT YUKIHIME-SENSEI,
WHEN WE CHALLENGED YOU, THERE WAS SOMETHING IN THE WAY, A KIND OF STRANGE BARRIER.
WOULD YOU CARE TO EXPLAIN THAT?
DOES IT HAVE ANYTHING TO DO WITH THE RUMORS OF...
OH! YEAH, YEAH!
IS IT THAT "MAGIC" STUFF WE KEEP HEARING ABOUT!?
THERE'S NO WAY ANY NORMAL PERSON COULD USE A BARRIER LIKE THAT!
IF YOU'RE SERIOUSLY USING MAGIC AND NOT TELLING US, THEN THAT'S NOT FAIR!
KONOE
HEY, HE'S RIGHT!
YEAH, THAT'S NOT FAIR!
WELL?!
IF IT'S REALLY MAGIC, YOU SHOULD TELL US!

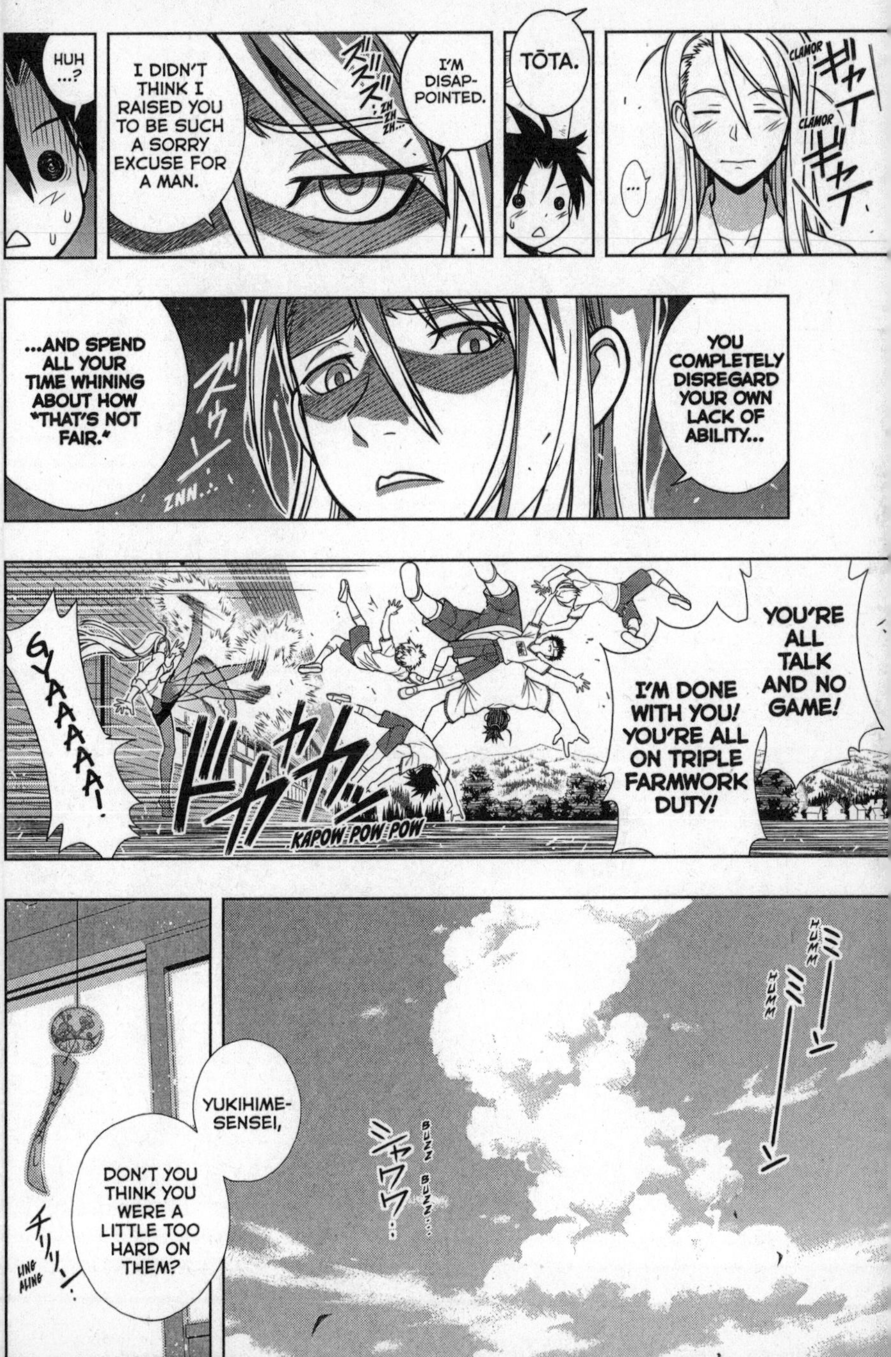
CLAMOR
CLAMOR
...
TŌTA.
I'M DISAPPOINTED.
ZH ZH ZH...
I DIDN'T THINK I RAISED YOU TO BE SUCH A SORRY EXCUSE FOR A MAN.
HUH ...?
YOU COMPLETELY DISREGARD YOUR OWN LACK OF ABILITY...
ZNN...
...AND SPEND ALL YOUR TIME WHINING ABOUT HOW "THAT'S NOT FAIR."
YOU'RE ALL TALK AND NO GAME!
I'M DONE WITH YOU! YOU'RE ALL ON TRIPLE FARMWORK DUTY!
KAPOW POW POW
GYAAAAA!
HUMM
HUMM
BUZZ BUZZ...
YUKIHIME-SENSEI,
DON'T YOU THINK YOU WERE A LITTLE TOO HARD ON THEM?
LING ALING

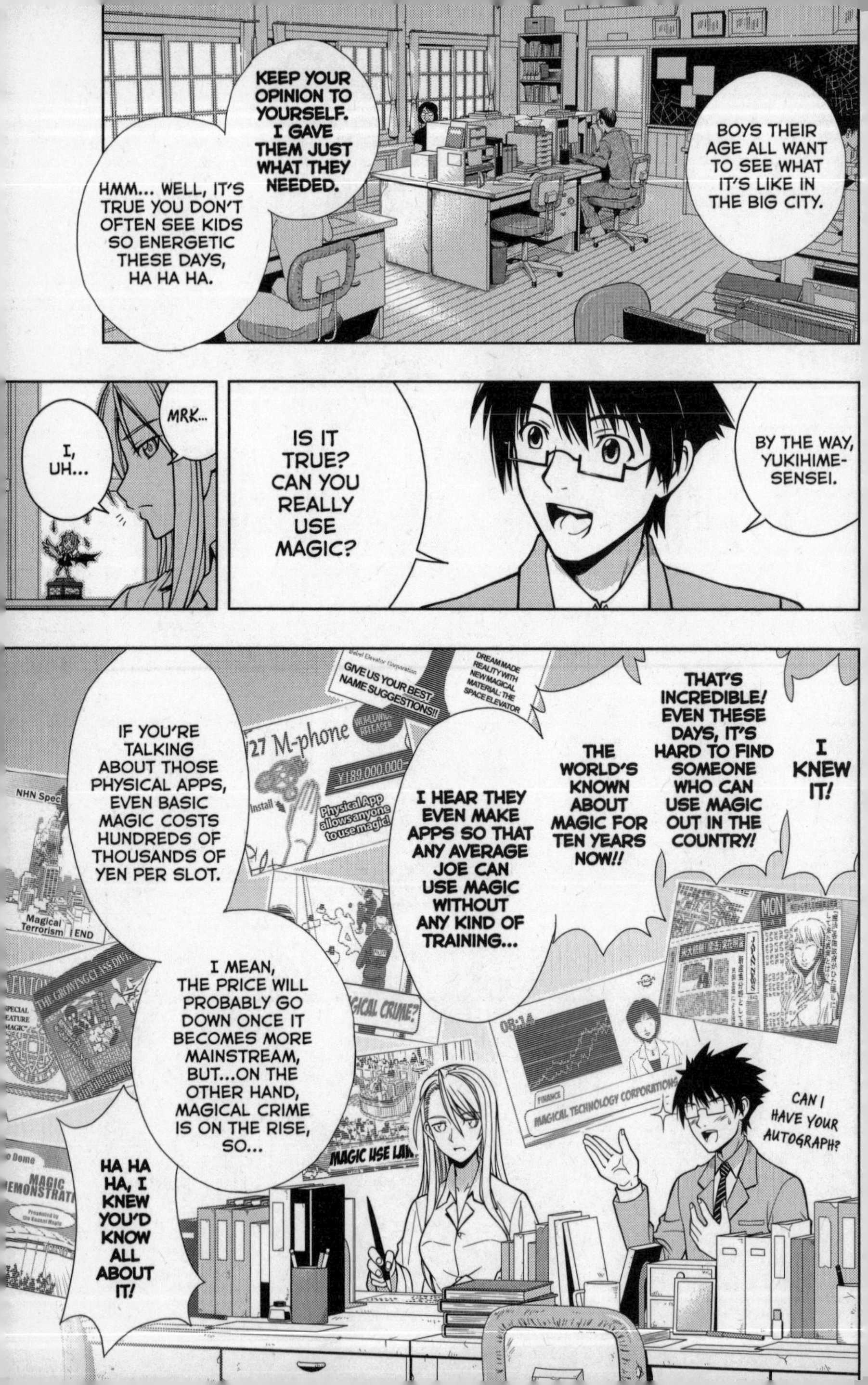
BOYS THEIR AGE ALL WANT TO SEE WHAT IT'S LIKE IN THE BIG CITY.
KEEP YOUR OPINION TO YOURSELF. I GAVE THEM JUST WHAT THEY NEEDED.
HMM... WELL, IT'S TRUE YOU DON'T OFTEN SEE KIDS SO ENERGETIC THESE DAYS, HA HA HA.
BY THE WAY, YUKIHIME-SENSEI.
IS IT TRUE? CAN YOU REALLY USE MAGIC?
MRK...
I, UH...
I KNEW IT!
THAT'S INCREDIBLE! EVEN THESE DAYS, IT'S HARD TO FIND SOMEONE WHO CAN USE MAGIC OUT IN THE COUNTRY!
THE WORLD'S KNOWN ABOUT MAGIC FOR TEN YEARS NOW!!
DREAM MADE REALITY WITH NEW MAGICAL MATERIAL: THE SPACE ELEVATOR
GIVE US YOUR BEST NAME SUGGESTIONS!!
I HEAR THEY EVEN MAKE APPS SO THAT ANY AVERAGE JOE CAN USE MAGIC WITHOUT ANY KIND OF TRAINING...
'27 M-phone
Physical App allows anyone to use magic!
IF YOU'RE TALKING ABOUT THOSE PHYSICAL APPS, EVEN BASIC MAGIC COSTS HUNDREDS OF THOUSANDS OF YEN PER SLOT.
Magical Terrorism END
FINANCE
MAGICAL TECHNOLOGY CORPORATIONS
CAN I HAVE YOUR AUTOGRAPH?
MAGICAL CRIME?
I MEAN, THE PRICE WILL PROBABLY GO DOWN ONCE IT BECOMES MORE MAINSTREAM, BUT...ON THE OTHER HAND, MAGICAL CRIME IS ON THE RISE, SO...
MAGIC USE LAW
HA HA HA, I KNEW YOU'D KNOW ALL ABOUT IT!

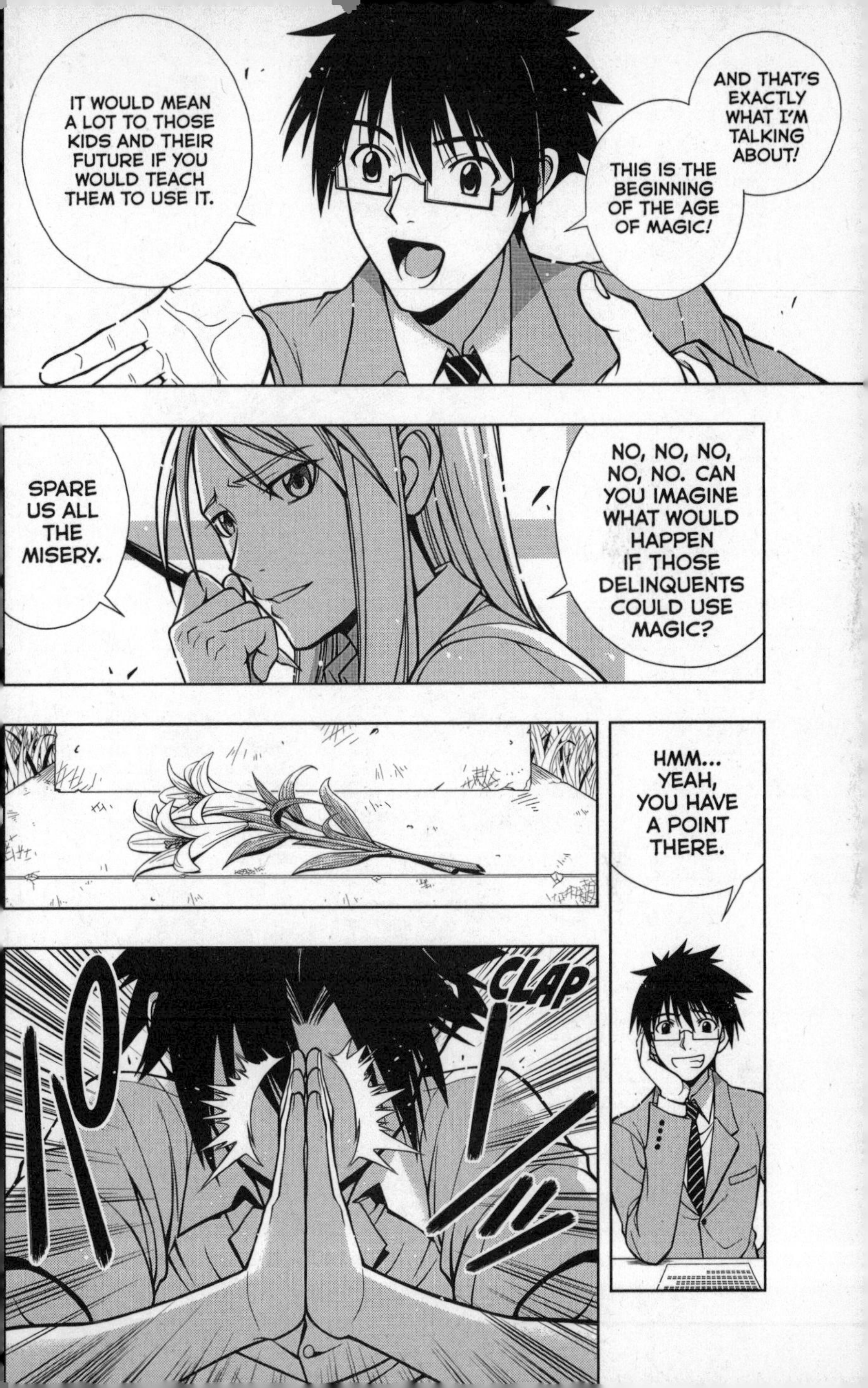
AND THAT'S EXACTLY WHAT I'M TALKING ABOUT!
THIS IS THE BEGINNING OF THE AGE OF MAGIC!
IT WOULD MEAN A LOT TO THOSE KIDS AND THEIR FUTURE IF YOU WOULD TEACH THEM TO USE IT.
NO, NO, NO, NO, NO. CAN YOU IMAGINE WHAT WOULD HAPPEN IF THOSE DELINQUENTS COULD USE MAGIC?
SPARE US ALL THE MISERY.
HMM... YEAH, YOU HAVE A POINT THERE.
CLAP

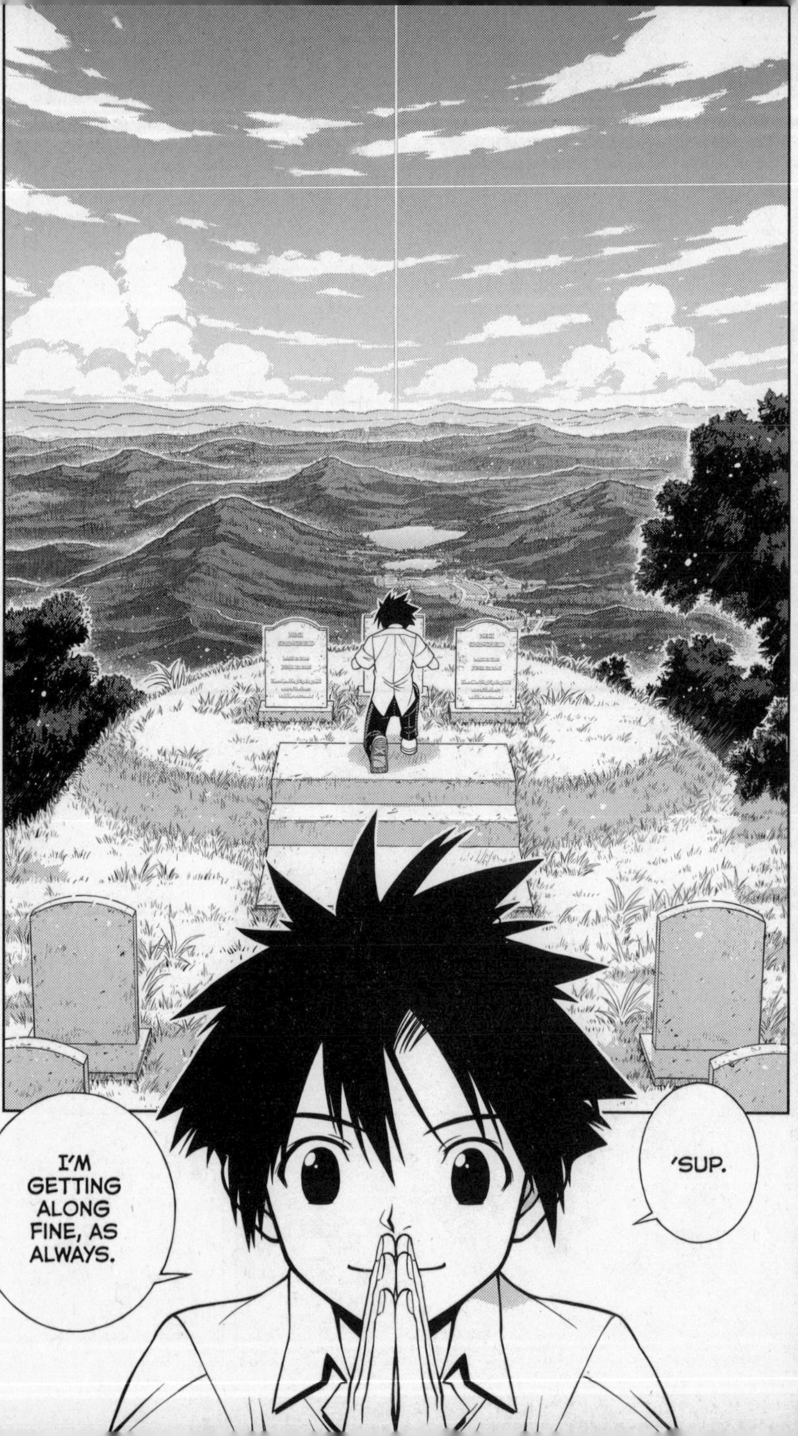
'SUP.
I'M GETTING ALONG FINE, AS ALWAYS.

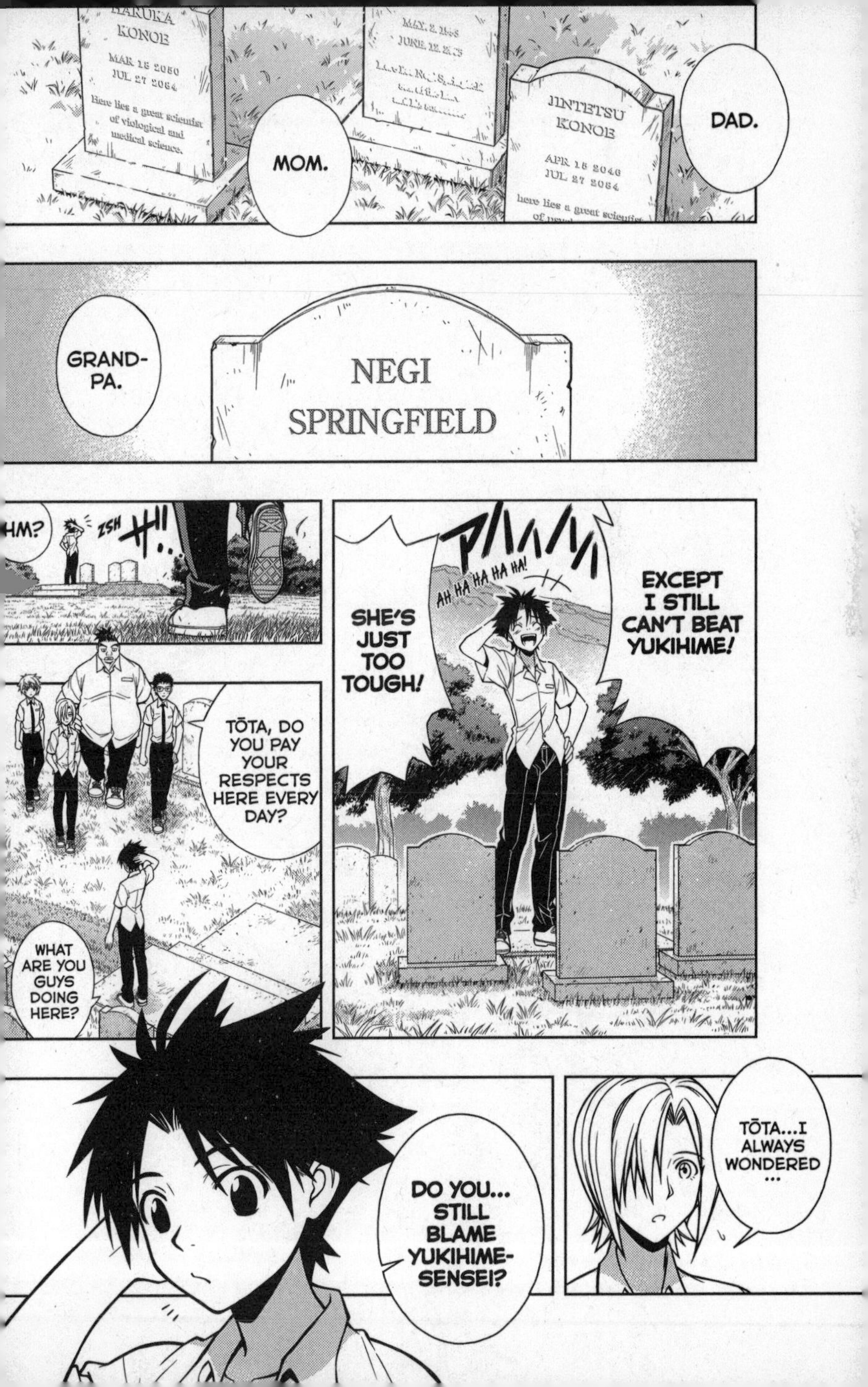
DAD.
JINTETSU KONOE
MOM.
KONOE
Here lies a great scientist of viological and medical science.
GRAND-PA.
NEGI SPRINGFIELD
HM?
ZSH
EXCEPT I STILL CAN'T BEAT YUKIHIME!
AH HA HA HA HA!
SHE'S JUST TOO TOUGH!
TŌTA, DO YOU PAY YOUR RESPECTS HERE EVERY DAY?
WHAT ARE YOU GUYS DOING HERE?
TŌTA...I ALWAYS WONDERED...
DO YOU... STILL BLAME YUKIHIME-SENSEI?

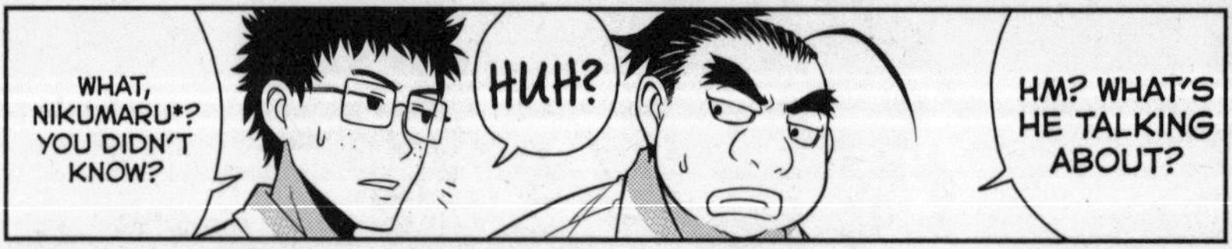
HM? WHAT'S HE TALKING ABOUT?
HUH?
WHAT, NIKUMARU*? YOU DIDN'T KNOW?

*Whether this is his real name or a nickname, it means, roughly, "meatball."

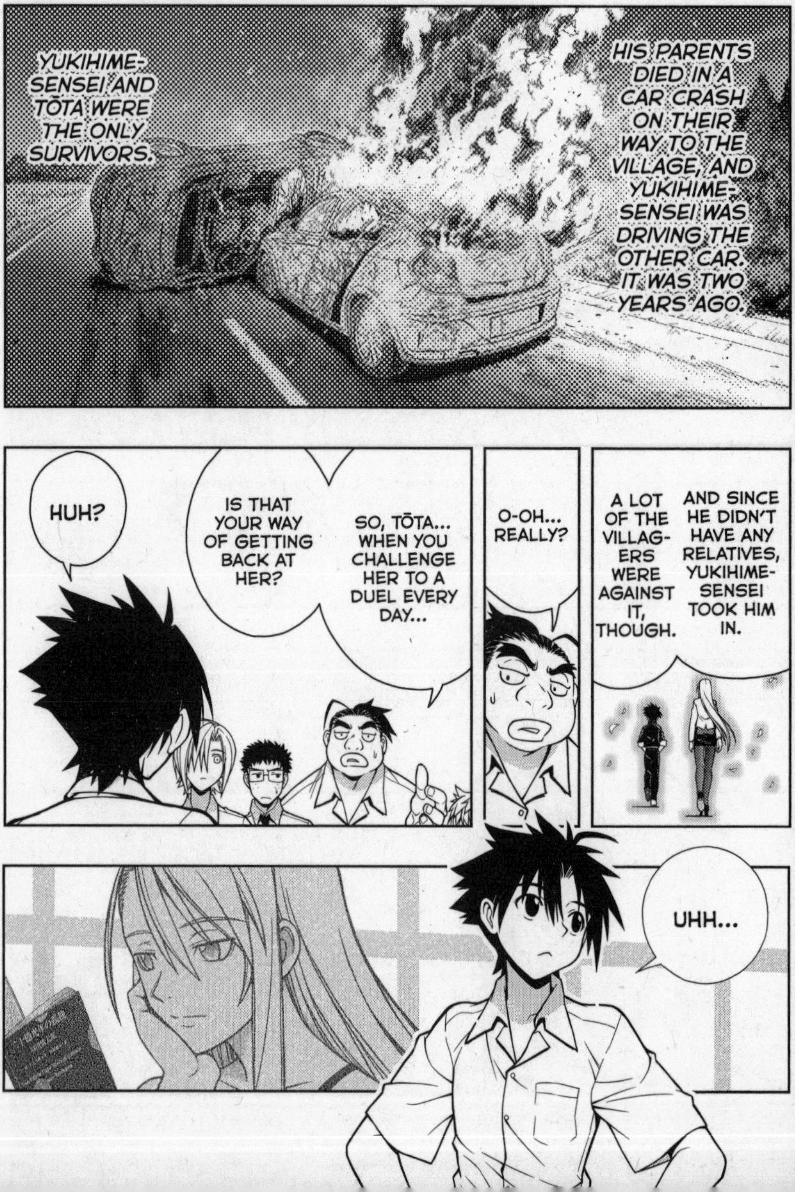
HIS PARENTS DIED IN A CAR CRASH ON THEIR WAY TO THE VILLAGE, AND YUKIHIME-SENSEI WAS DRIVING THE OTHER CAR. IT WAS TWO YEARS AGO.
YUKIHIME-SENSEI AND TŌTA WERE THE ONLY SURVIVORS.
AND SINCE HE DIDN'T HAVE ANY RELATIVES, YUKIHIME-SENSEI TOOK HIM IN.
A LOT OF THE VILLAGERS WERE AGAINST IT, THOUGH.
O-OH... REALLY?
SO, TŌTA... WHEN YOU CHALLENGE HER TO A DUEL EVERY DAY...
IS THAT YOUR WAY OF GETTING BACK AT HER?
HUH?
UHH...

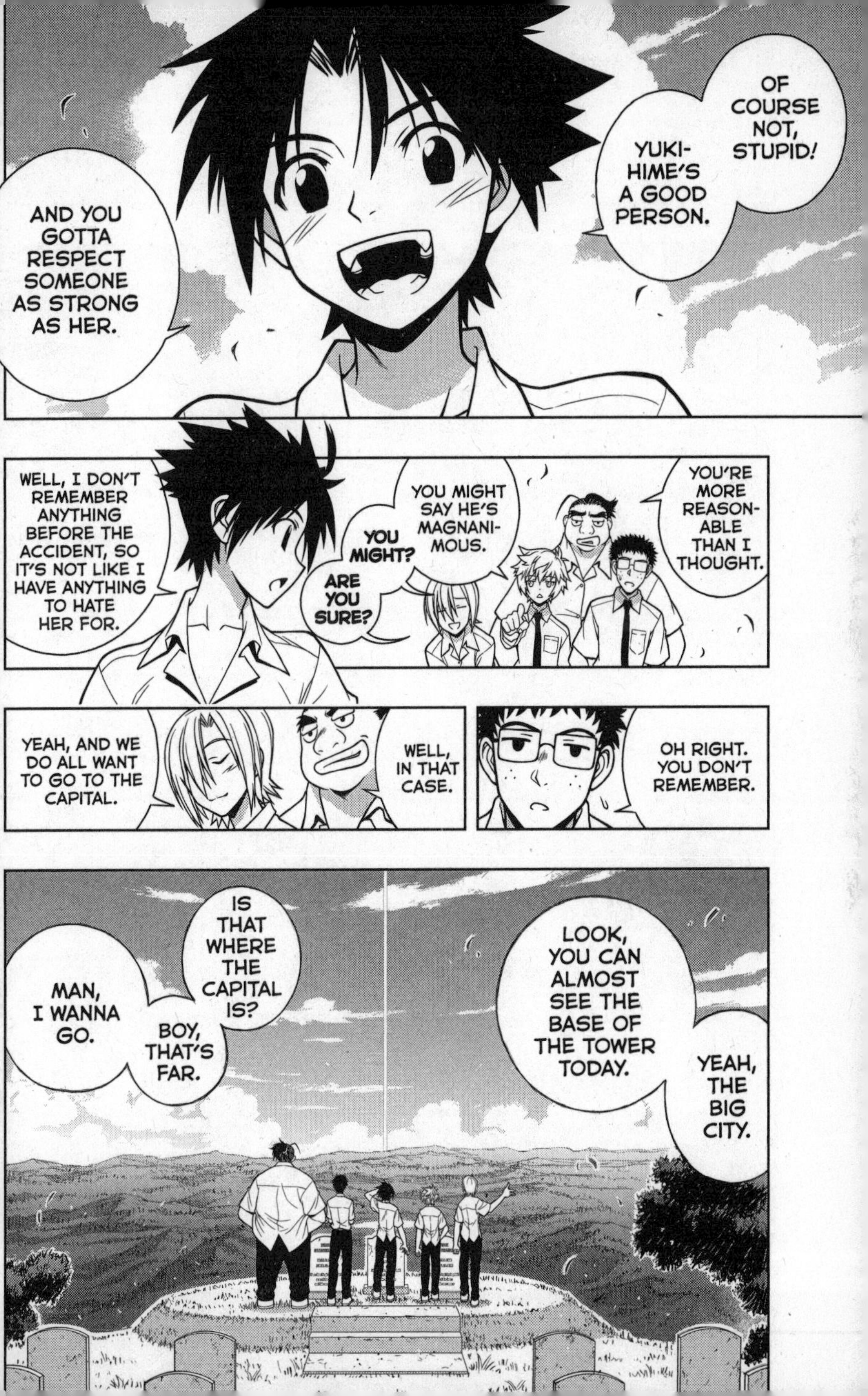
OF COURSE NOT, STUPID!
YUKI-HIME'S A GOOD PERSON.
AND YOU GOTTA RESPECT SOMEONE AS STRONG AS HER.
YOU'RE MORE REASON-ABLE THAN I THOUGHT.
YOU MIGHT SAY HE'S MAGNANI-MOUS.
YOU MIGHT?
ARE YOU SURE?
WELL, I DON'T REMEMBER ANYTHING BEFORE THE ACCIDENT, SO IT'S NOT LIKE I HAVE ANYTHING TO HATE HER FOR.
OH RIGHT. YOU DON'T REMEMBER.
WELL, IN THAT CASE.
YEAH, AND WE DO ALL WANT TO GO TO THE CAPITAL.
LOOK, YOU CAN ALMOST SEE THE BASE OF THE TOWER TODAY.
YEAH, THE BIG CITY.
IS THAT WHERE THE CAPITAL IS?
BOY, THAT'S FAR.
MAN, I WANNA GO.

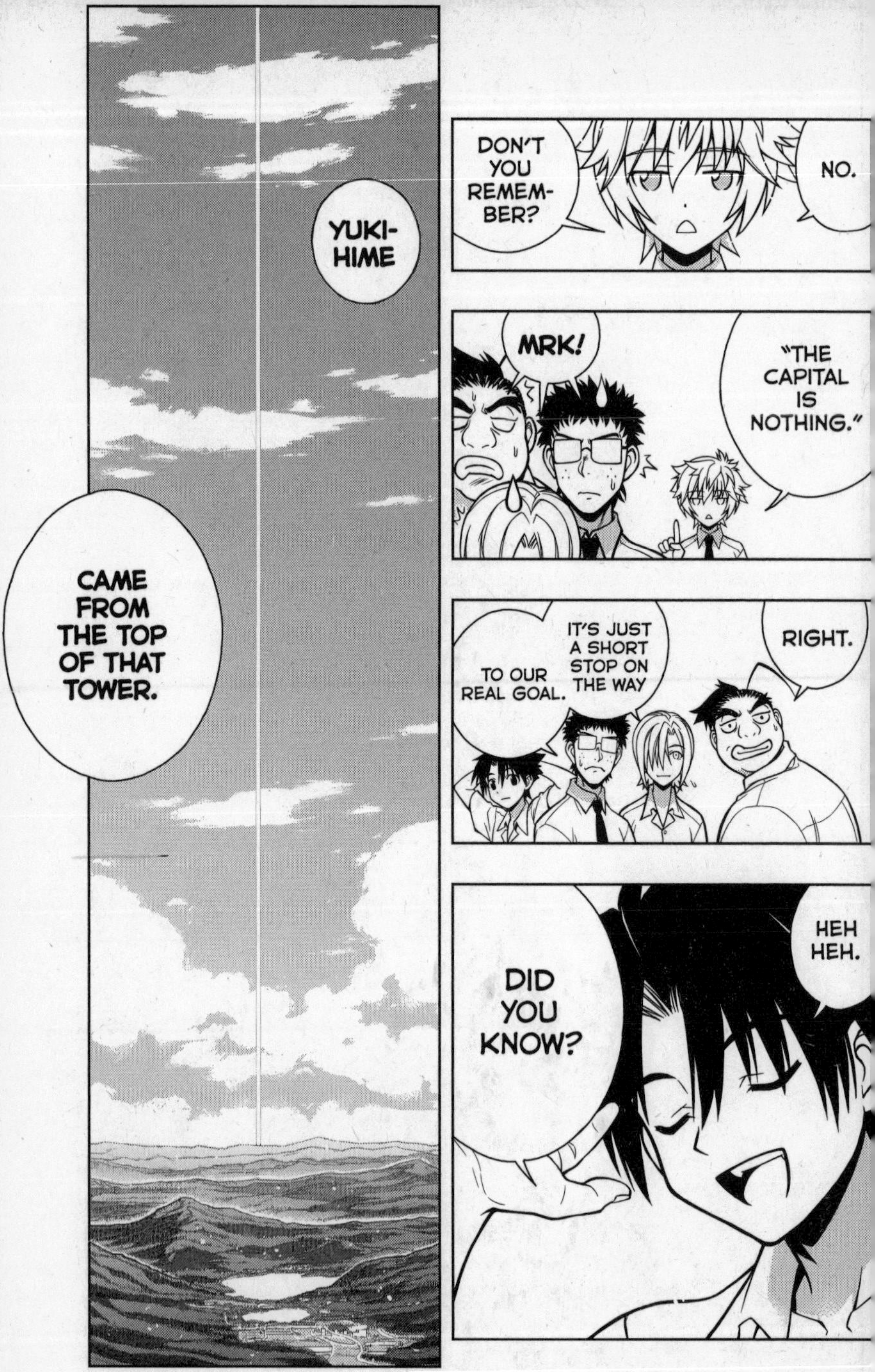
NO.
DON'T YOU REMEMBER?
"THE CAPITAL IS NOTHING."
MRK!
RIGHT.
IT'S JUST A SHORT STOP ON THE WAY
TO OUR REAL GOAL.
HEH HEH.
DID YOU KNOW?
YUKI-HIME
CAME FROM THE TOP OF THAT TOWER.

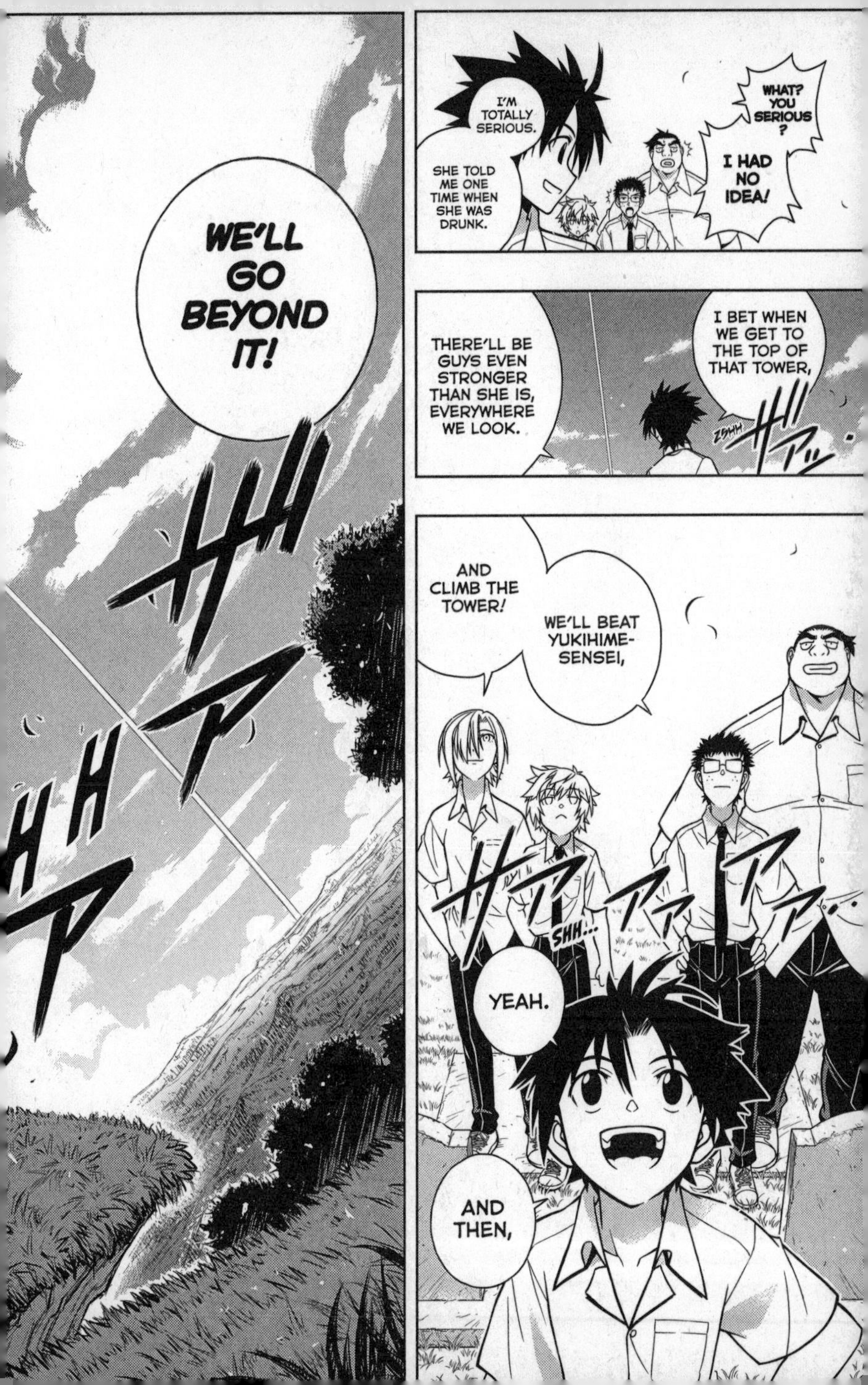
WHAT? YOU SERIOUS?
I HAD NO IDEA!
I'M TOTALLY SERIOUS.
SHE TOLD ME ONE TIME WHEN SHE WAS DRUNK.
I BET WHEN WE GET TO THE TOP OF THAT TOWER,
ZSHH
THERE'LL BE GUYS EVEN STRONGER THAN SHE IS, EVERYWHERE WE LOOK.
WE'LL BEAT YUKIHIME-SENSEI,
AND CLIMB THE TOWER!
SHH...
YEAH.
AND THEN,
WE'LL GO BEYOND IT!

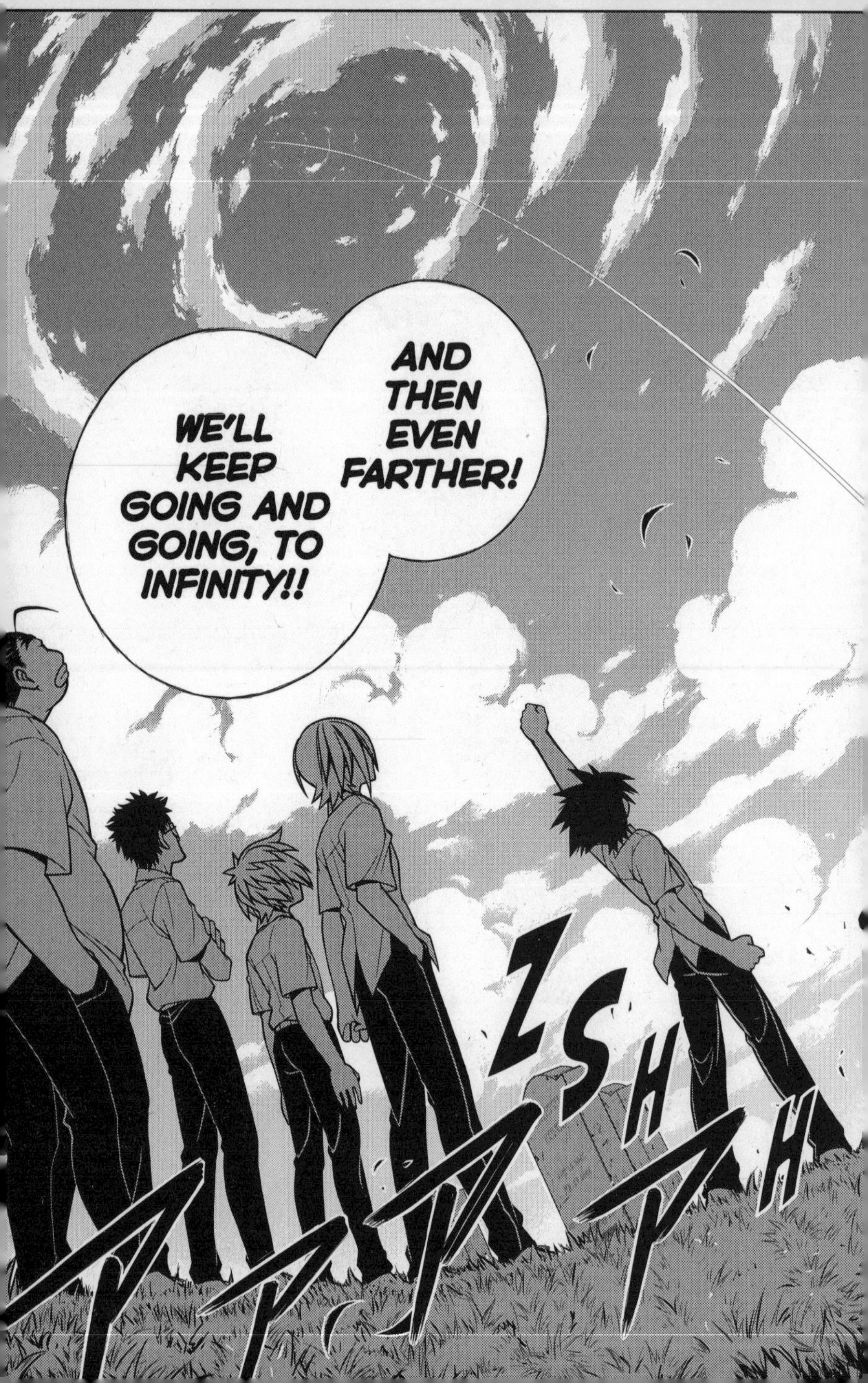
AND THEN EVEN FARTHER!
WE'LL KEEP GOING AND GOING, TO INFINITY!!
ZSH
ZSHHH

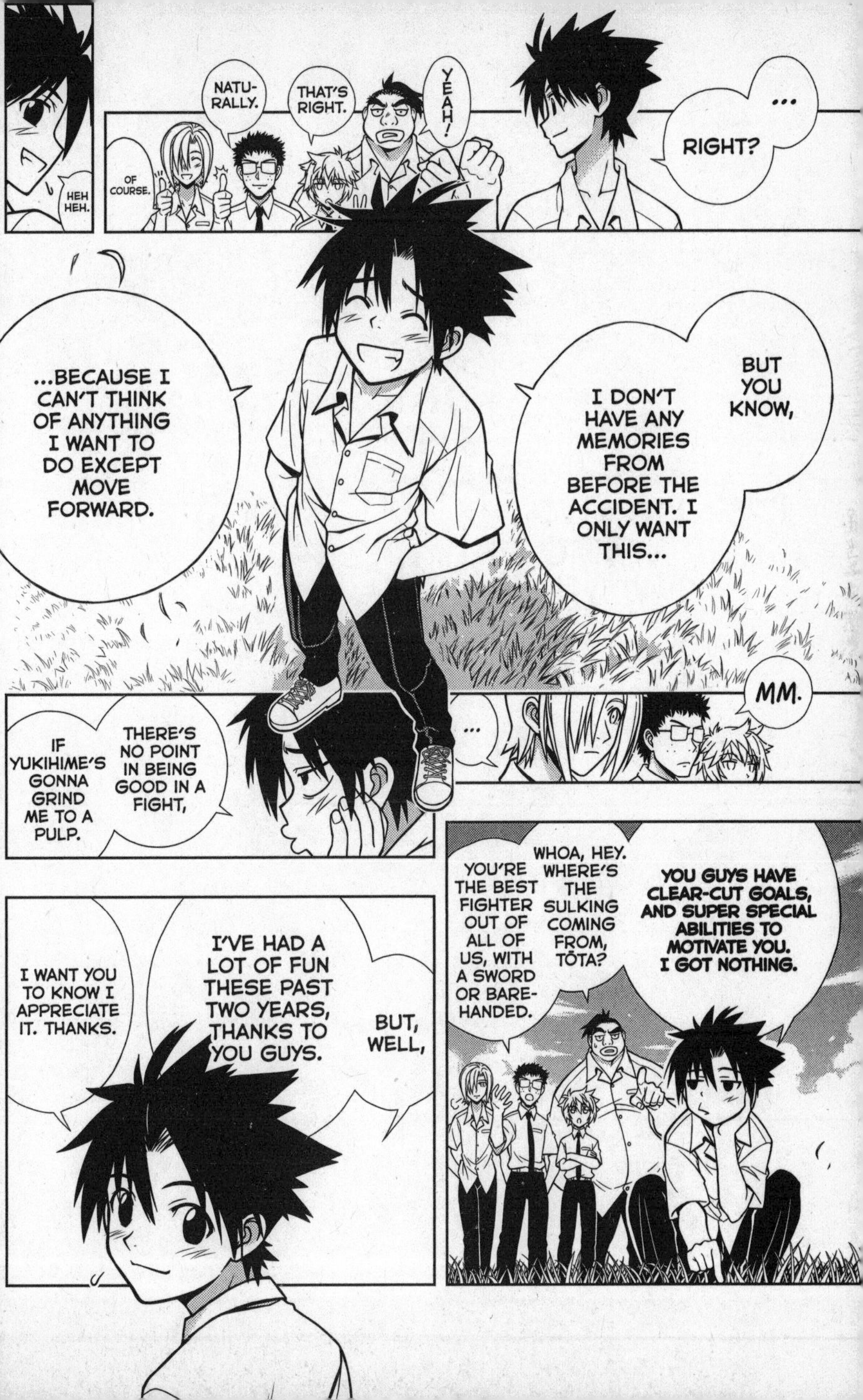
...
RIGHT?
YEAH!
THAT'S RIGHT.
NATU-RALLY.
OF COURSE.
HEH HEH.
BUT YOU KNOW,
I DON'T HAVE ANY MEMORIES FROM BEFORE THE ACCIDENT. I ONLY WANT THIS...
...BECAUSE I CAN'T THINK OF ANYTHING I WANT TO DO EXCEPT MOVE FORWARD.
MM.
...
THERE'S NO POINT IN BEING GOOD IN A FIGHT,
IF YUKIHIME'S GONNA GRIND ME TO A PULP.
YOU GUYS HAVE CLEAR-CUT GOALS, AND SUPER SPECIAL ABILITIES TO MOTIVATE YOU. I GOT NOTHING.
WHOA, HEY. WHERE'S THE SULKING COMING FROM, TŌTA?
YOU'RE THE BEST FIGHTER OUT OF ALL OF US, WITH A SWORD OR BARE-HANDED.
BUT, WELL,
I'VE HAD A LOT OF FUN THESE PAST TWO YEARS, THANKS TO YOU GUYS.
I WANT YOU TO KNOW I APPRECIATE IT. THANKS.

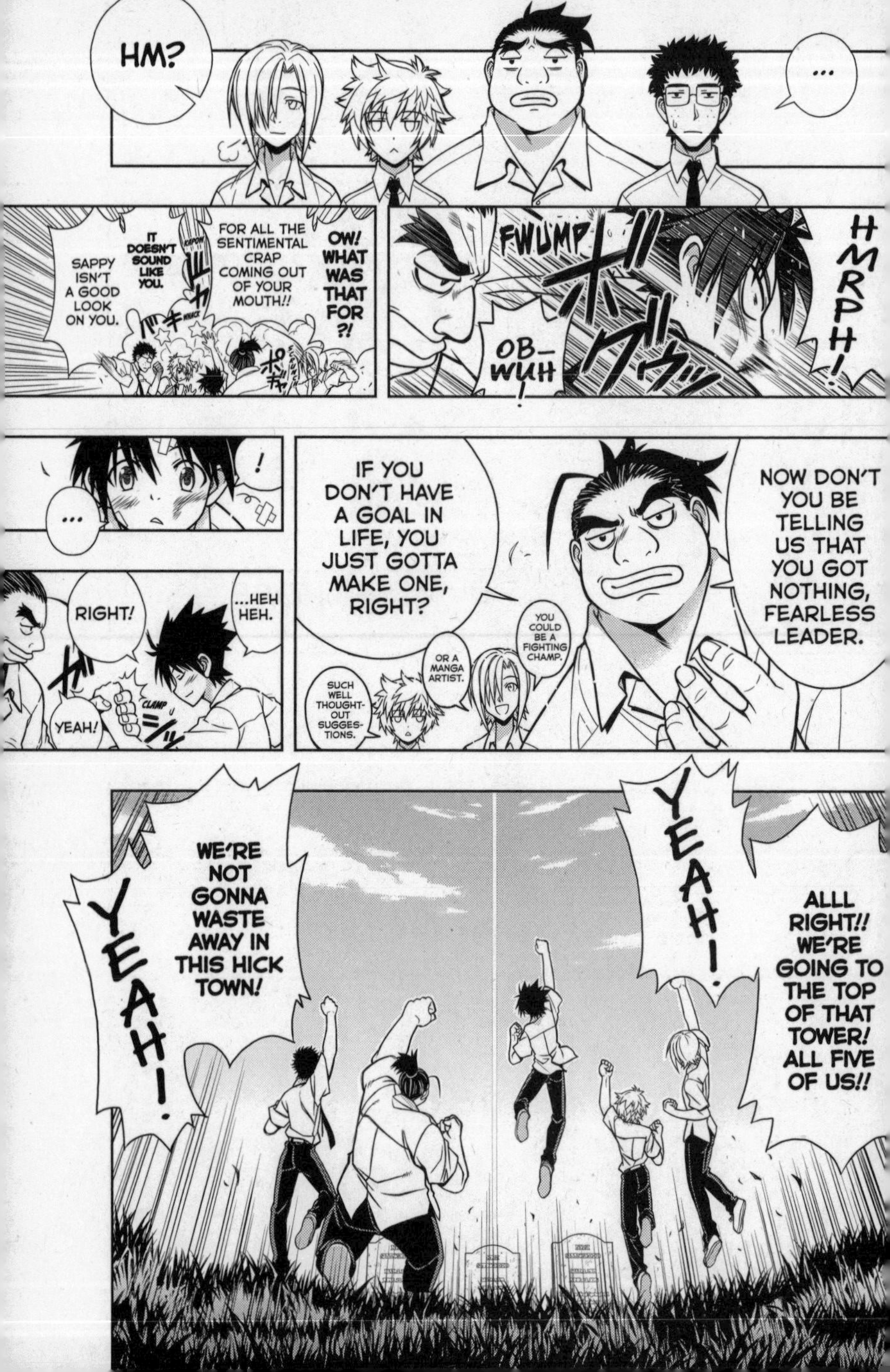
...
HM?
HMRPH!
FWUMP
OB-WUH!
OW! WHAT WAS THAT FOR?!
FOR ALL THE SENTIMENTAL CRAP COMING OUT OF YOUR MOUTH!!
KAPON
WHACK
IT DOESN'T SOUND LIKE YOU.
SAPPY ISN'T A GOOD LOOK ON YOU.
NOW DON'T YOU BE TELLING US THAT YOU GOT NOTHING, FEARLESS LEADER.
IF YOU DON'T HAVE A GOAL IN LIFE, YOU JUST GOTTA MAKE ONE, RIGHT?
YOU COULD BE A FIGHTING CHAMP.
OR A MANGA ARTIST.
SUCH WELL THOUGHT-OUT SUGGESTIONS.
!
...
...HEH HEH.
RIGHT!
CLAMP
YEAH!
ALLL RIGHT!! WE'RE GOING TO THE TOP OF THAT TOWER! ALL FIVE OF US!!
YEAH!
WE'RE NOT GONNA WASTE AWAY IN THIS HICK TOWN!
YEAH!

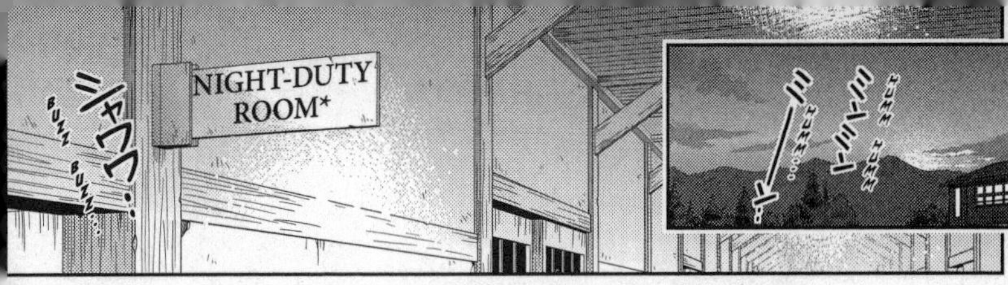
HUMM HUMM
HUMM...
NIGHT-DUTY ROOM*
BUZZ BUZZ...

*For teachers staying at the school overnight. In this case, it appears to be Yukihime's home.

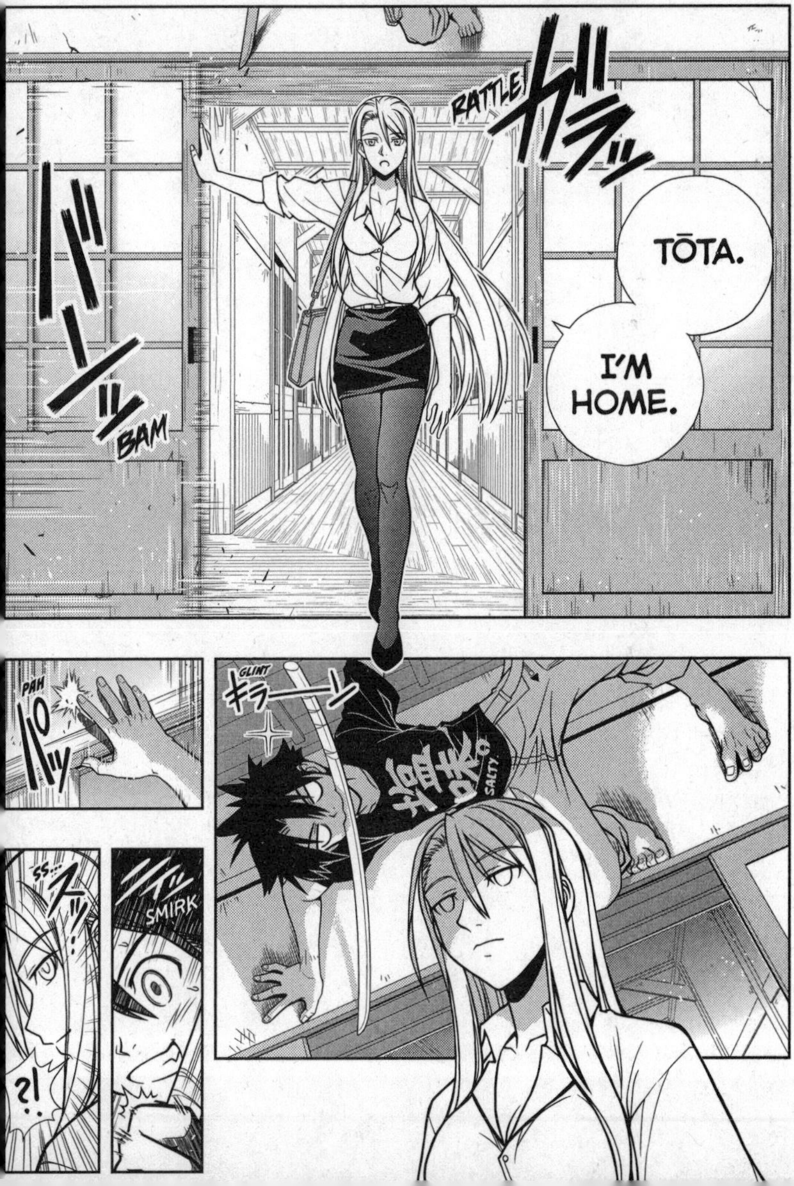
RATTLE
BAM
TŌTA.
I'M HOME.
GLINT
SALTY
PAH
SMIRK
SS...
?!

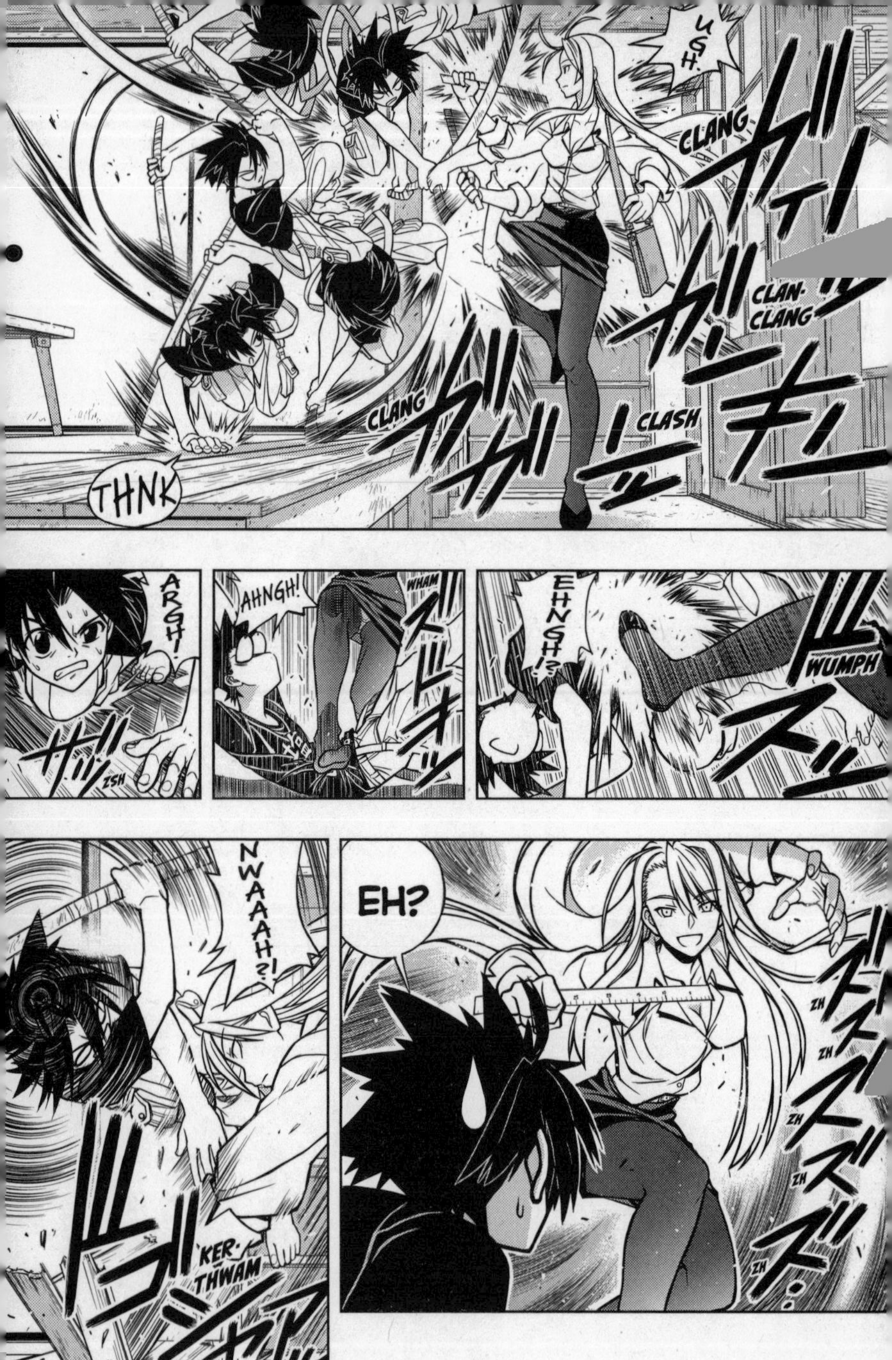
UGH.
CLANG
CLAN-CLANG
CLASH
CLANG
THNK
EHNGH!?
WUMPH
AHNGH!
WHAM
ARGH!
ZSH
EH?
ZH
ZH
ZH
ZH
ZH
NWAAAAH?!
KER-THWAM

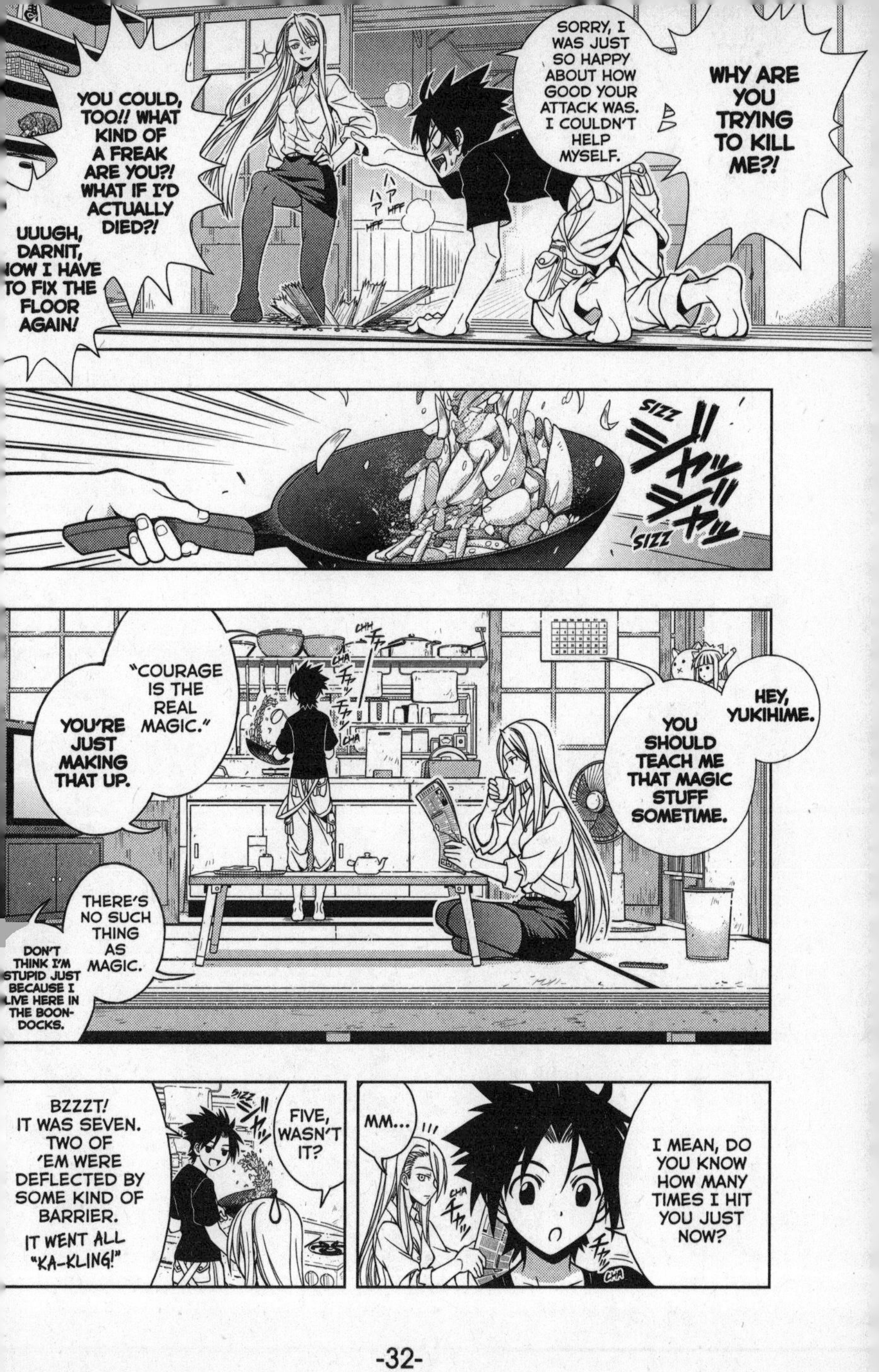
WHY ARE YOU TRYING TO KILL ME?!
SORRY, I WAS JUST SO HAPPY ABOUT HOW GOOD YOUR ATTACK WAS. I COULDN'T HELP MYSELF.
HFF HFF
YOU COULD, TOO!! WHAT KIND OF A FREAK ARE YOU?! WHAT IF I'D ACTUALLY DIED?!
UUUGH, DARNIT, NOW I HAVE TO FIX THE FLOOR AGAIN!
SIZZ
SIZZ
HEY, YUKIHIME.
YOU SHOULD TEACH ME THAT MAGIC STUFF SOMETIME.
CHH
CHA
CHA
"COURAGE IS THE REAL MAGIC."
YOU'RE JUST MAKING THAT UP.
THERE'S NO SUCH THING AS MAGIC.
DON'T THINK I'M STUPID JUST BECAUSE I LIVE HERE IN THE BOON-DOCKS.
I MEAN, DO YOU KNOW HOW MANY TIMES I HIT YOU JUST NOW?
MM...
CHA
CHA
FIVE, WASN'T IT?
SIZZ
BZZZT! IT WAS SEVEN. TWO OF 'EM WERE DEFLECTED BY SOME KIND OF BARRIER.
IT WENT ALL "KA-KLING!"

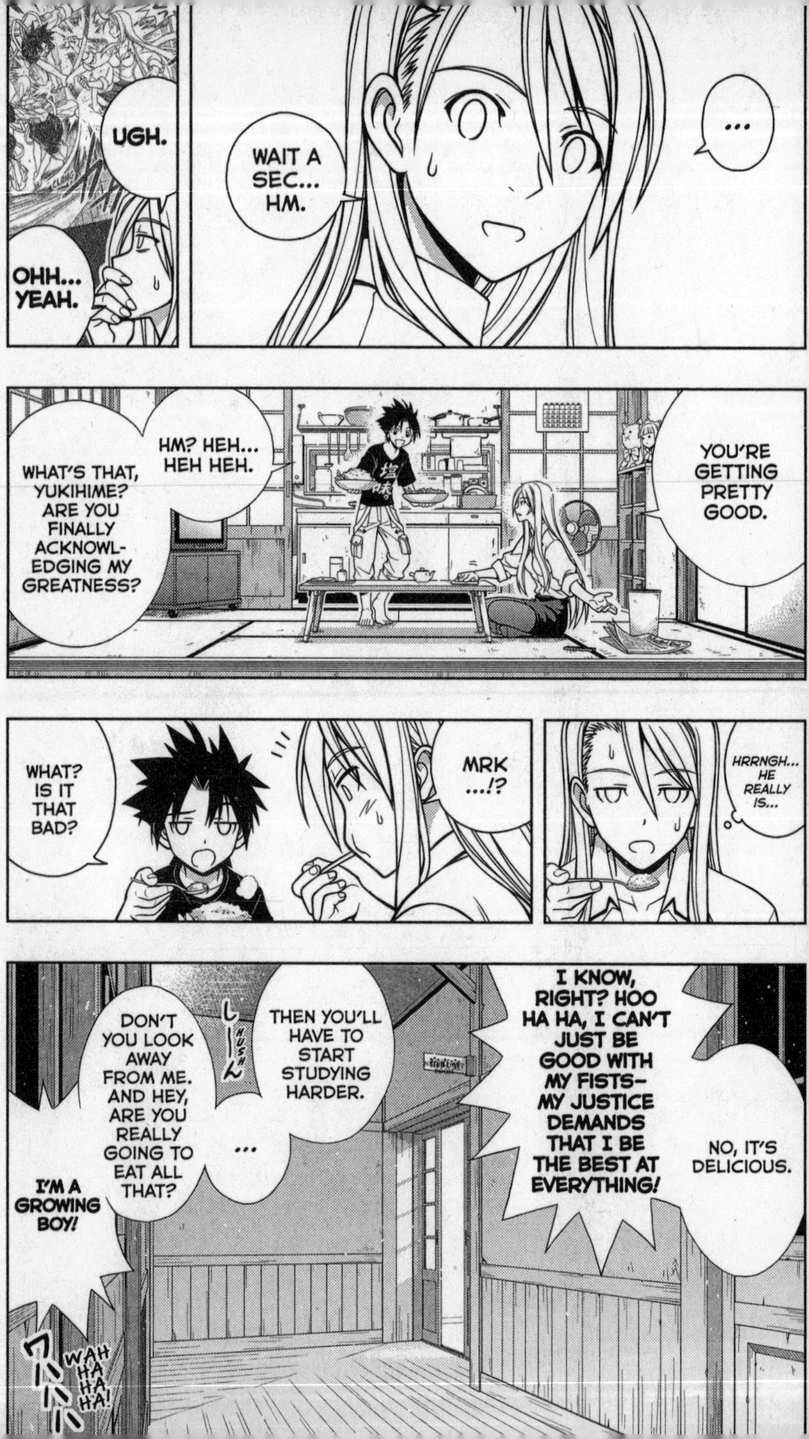
...
WAIT A SEC... HM.
UGH.
OHH... YEAH.
YOU'RE GETTING PRETTY GOOD.
HM? HEH... HEH HEH.
WHAT'S THAT, YUKIHIME? ARE YOU FINALLY ACKNOWL-EDGING MY GREATNESS?
HRRNGH... HE REALLY IS...
MRK ...!?
WHAT? IS IT THAT BAD?
NO, IT'S DELICIOUS.
I KNOW, RIGHT? HOO HA HA, I CAN'T JUST BE GOOD WITH MY FISTS— MY JUSTICE DEMANDS THAT I BE THE BEST AT EVERYTHING!
THEN YOU'LL HAVE TO START STUDYING HARDER.
しーん HUSH
...
DON'T YOU LOOK AWAY FROM ME. AND HEY, ARE YOU REALLY GOING TO EAT ALL THAT?
I'M A GROWING BOY!
ワハハハ WAH HA HA HA!

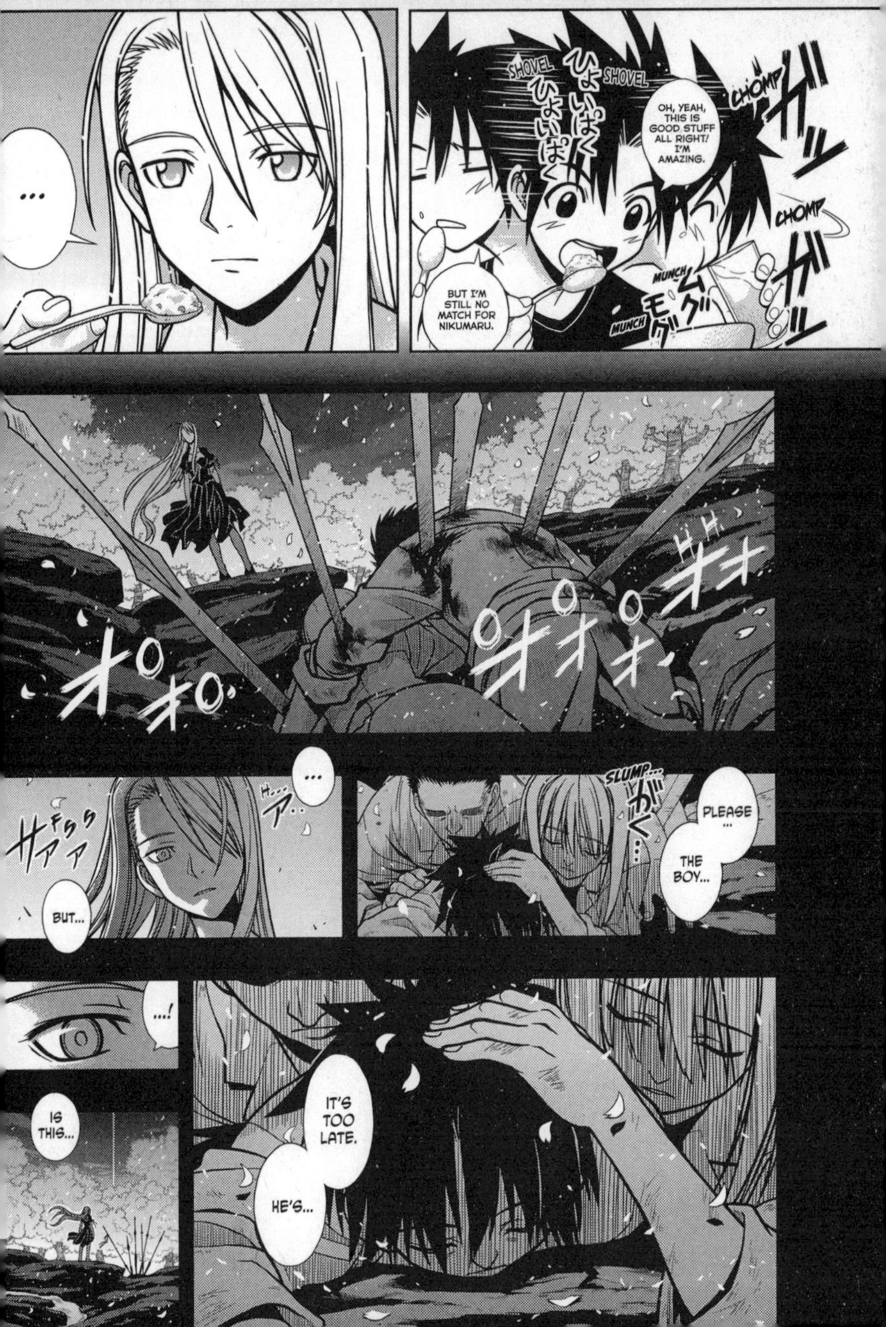
CHOMP ガッ
CHOMP ガッ
OH, YEAH, THIS IS GOOD STUFF ALL RIGHT! I'M AMAZING.
SHOVEL ひょいぱく SHOVEL ひょいぱく
MUNCH ムグ MUNCH モグ
BUT I'M STILL NO MATCH FOR NIKUMARU.
...
SLUMP... がく...
PLEASE ...
THE BOY...
...
H... ア..
FSSS サアア
BUT...
IT'S TOO LATE.
HE'S...
...!
IS THIS...

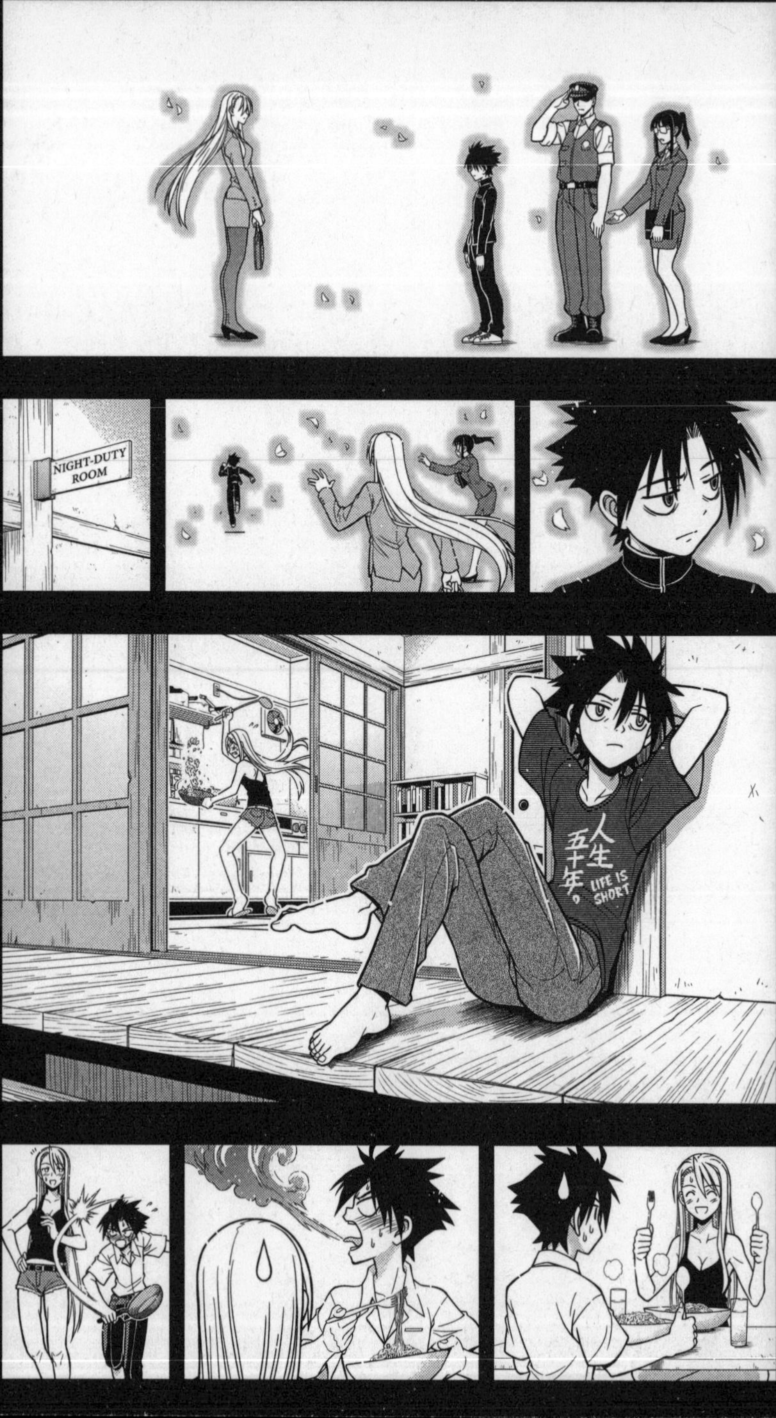
NIGHT-DUTY ROOM
人生五十年。
LIFE IS SHORT

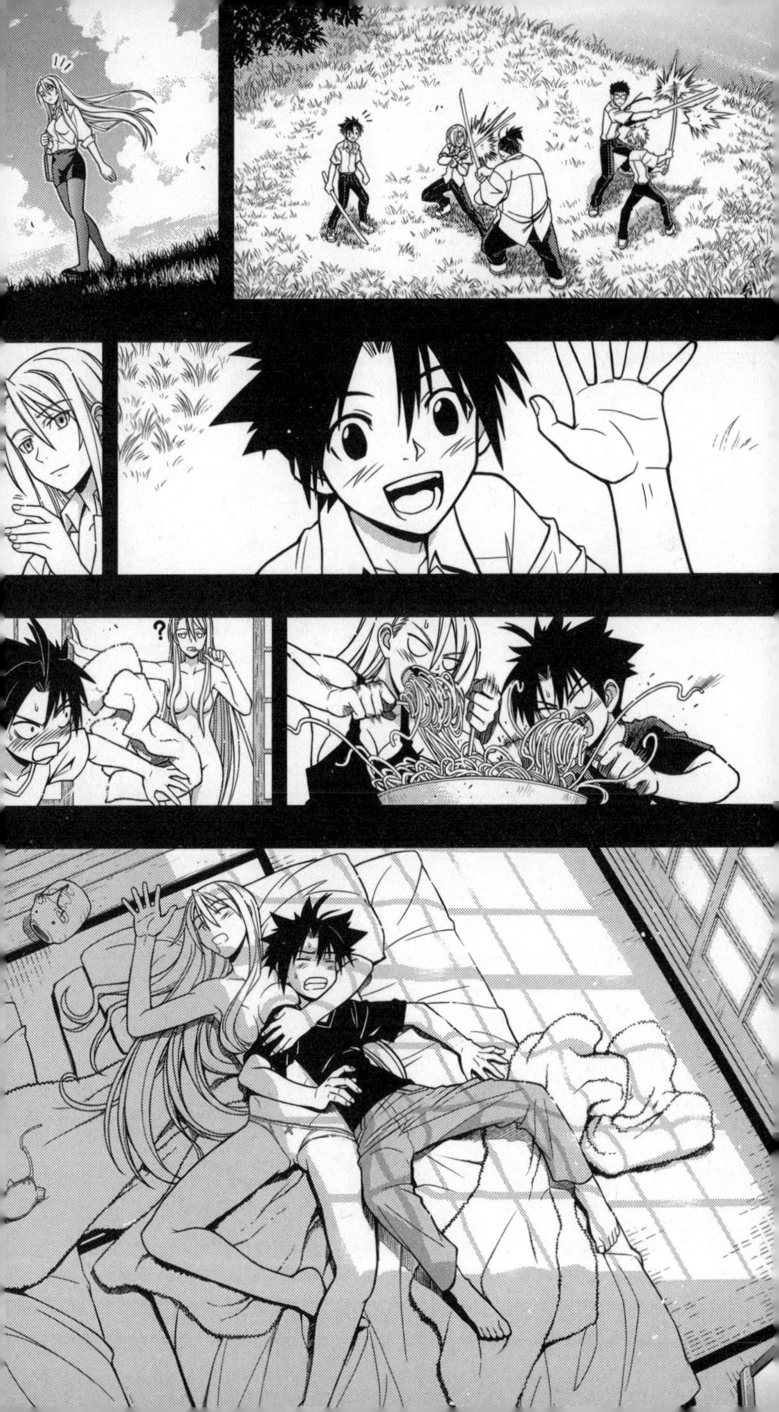

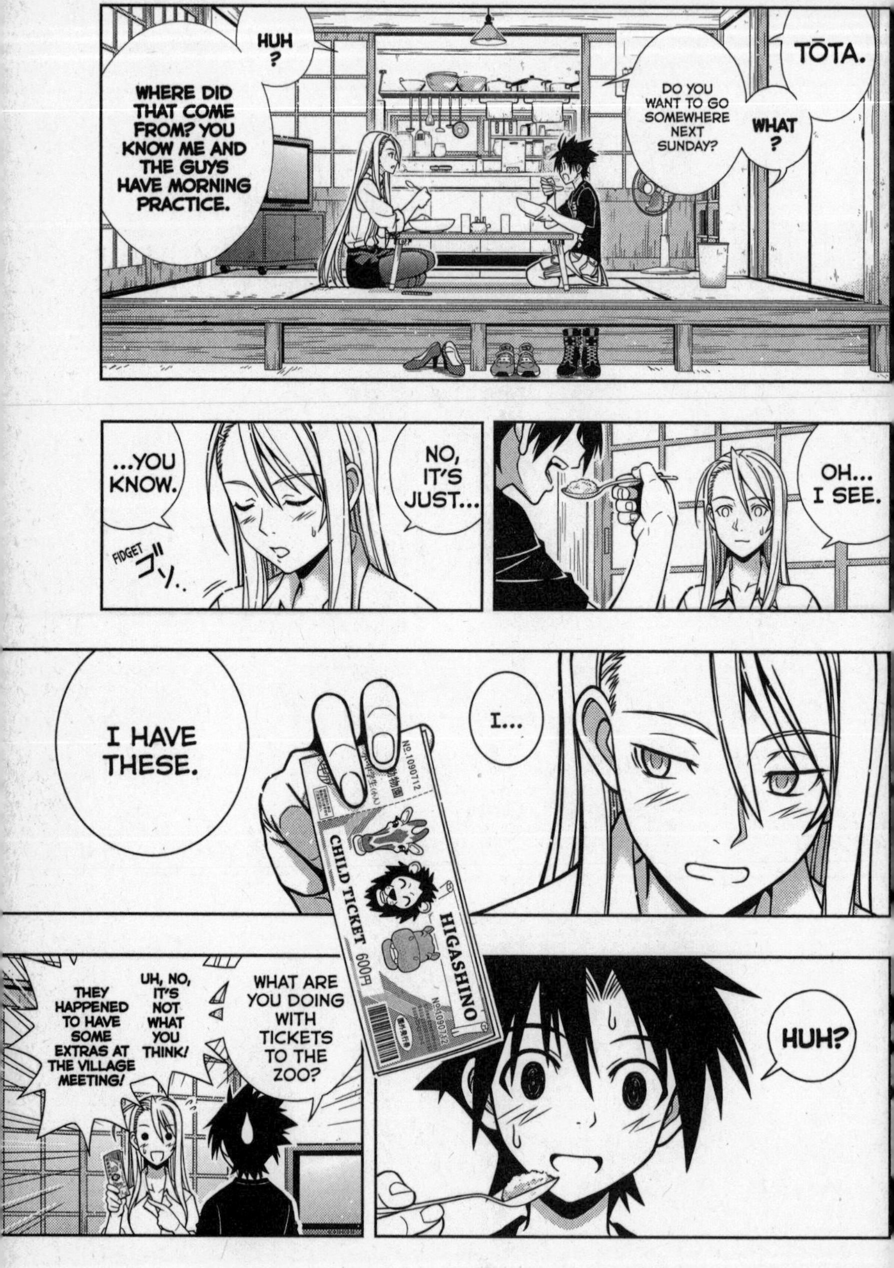
TŌTA.
WHAT?
DO YOU WANT TO GO SOMEWHERE NEXT SUNDAY?
HUH?
WHERE DID THAT COME FROM? YOU KNOW ME AND THE GUYS HAVE MORNING PRACTICE.
OH... I SEE.
NO, IT'S JUST...
...YOU KNOW.
FIDGET
I...
I HAVE THESE.
HIGASHINO
CHILD TICKET 600円
HUH?
WHAT ARE YOU DOING WITH TICKETS TO THE ZOO?
UH, NO, IT'S NOT WHAT YOU THINK!
THEY HAPPENED TO HAVE SOME EXTRAS AT THE VILLAGE MEETING!

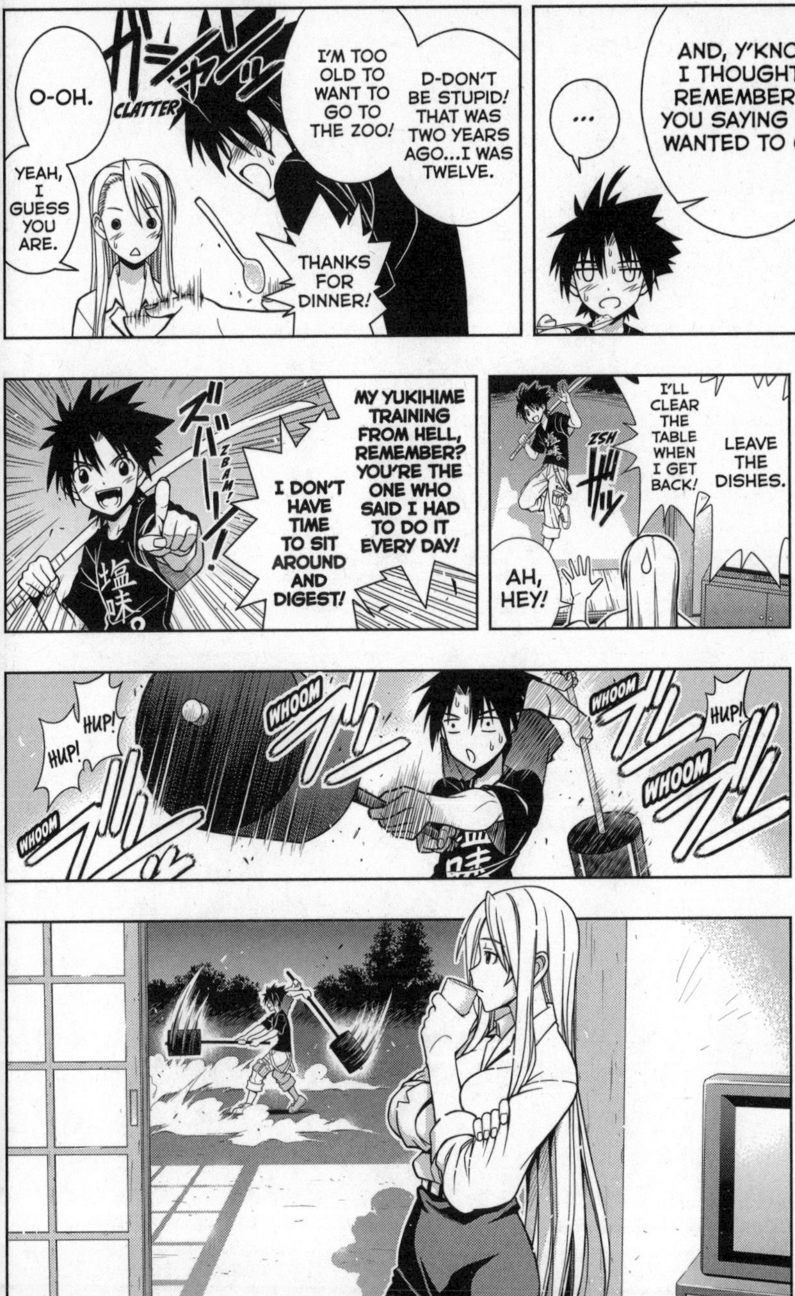

AND, Y'KNOW, I THOUGHT I REMEMBERED YOU SAYING YOU WANTED TO GO.
...
D-DON'T BE STUPID! THAT WAS TWO YEARS AGO...I WAS TWELVE.
I'M TOO OLD TO WANT TO GO TO THE ZOO!
CLATTER
O-OH.
THANKS FOR DINNER!
YEAH, I GUESS YOU ARE.
LEAVE THE DISHES.
I'LL CLEAR THE TABLE WHEN I GET BACK!
ZSH
AH, HEY!
MY YUKIHIME TRAINING FROM HELL, REMEMBER? YOU'RE THE ONE WHO SAID I HAD TO DO IT EVERY DAY!
ZBAM!
I DON'T HAVE TIME TO SIT AROUND AND DIGEST!
HUP!
WHOOM
WHOOM
WHOOM
HUP!
HUP!
WHOOM

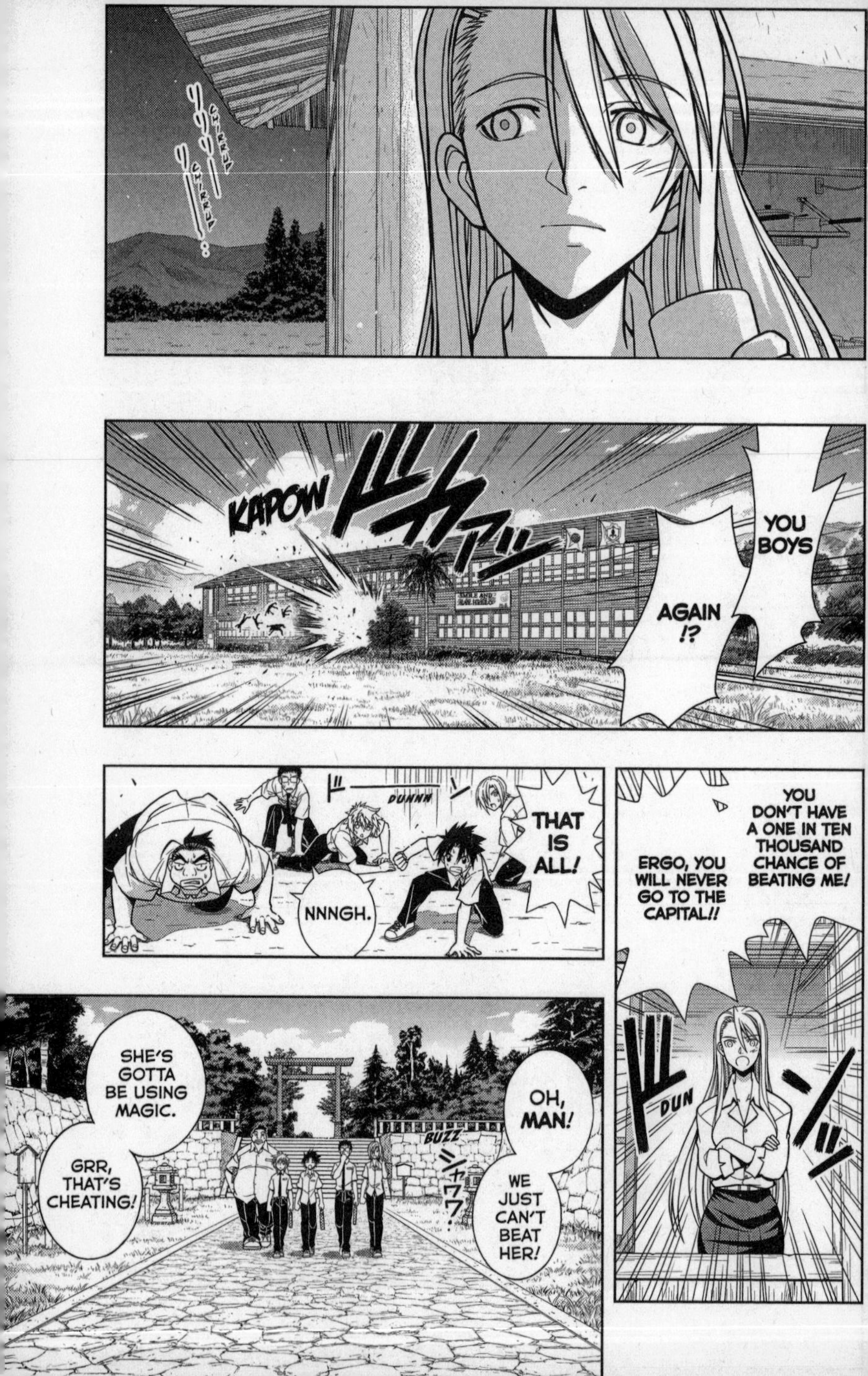
CHIRRUP
CHIRRUP
リリリー
リー…
YOU BOYS AGAIN!?
KAPOW
ドカアッ
YOU DON'T HAVE A ONE IN TEN THOUSAND CHANCE OF BEATING ME!
ERGO, YOU WILL NEVER GO TO THE CAPITAL!!
DUN
ドン
ドー
DUNNN
THAT IS ALL!
NNNGH.
OH, MAN!
WE JUST CAN'T BEAT HER!
BUZZ
ジャワワ
SHE'S GOTTA BE USING MAGIC.
GRR, THAT'S CHEATING!

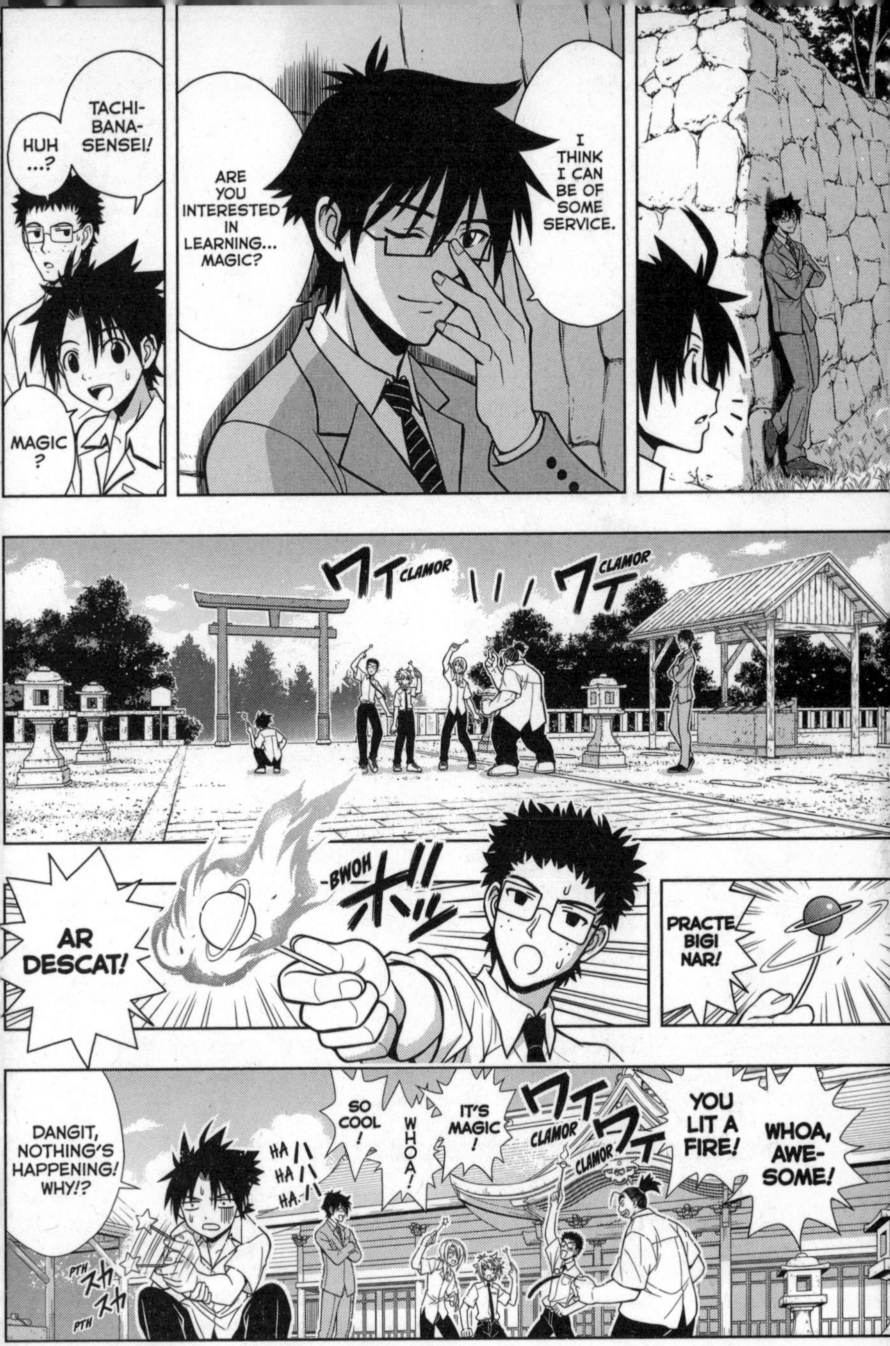
I THINK I CAN BE OF SOME SERVICE.
ARE YOU INTERESTED IN LEARNING... MAGIC?
TACHIBANA-SENSEI!
HUH ...?
MAGIC ?
ワイ CLAMOR
ワイ CLAMOR
PRACTE BIGI NAR!
BWOH ボッ
AR DESCAT!
WHOA, AWE-SOME!
YOU LIT A FIRE!
ワイ CLAMOR
ワイ CLAMOR
IT'S MAGIC !
WHOA!
SO COOL !
HA HA HA ハハハ
DANGIT, NOTHING'S HAPPENING! WHY!?
PTH スカ
PTH スカ

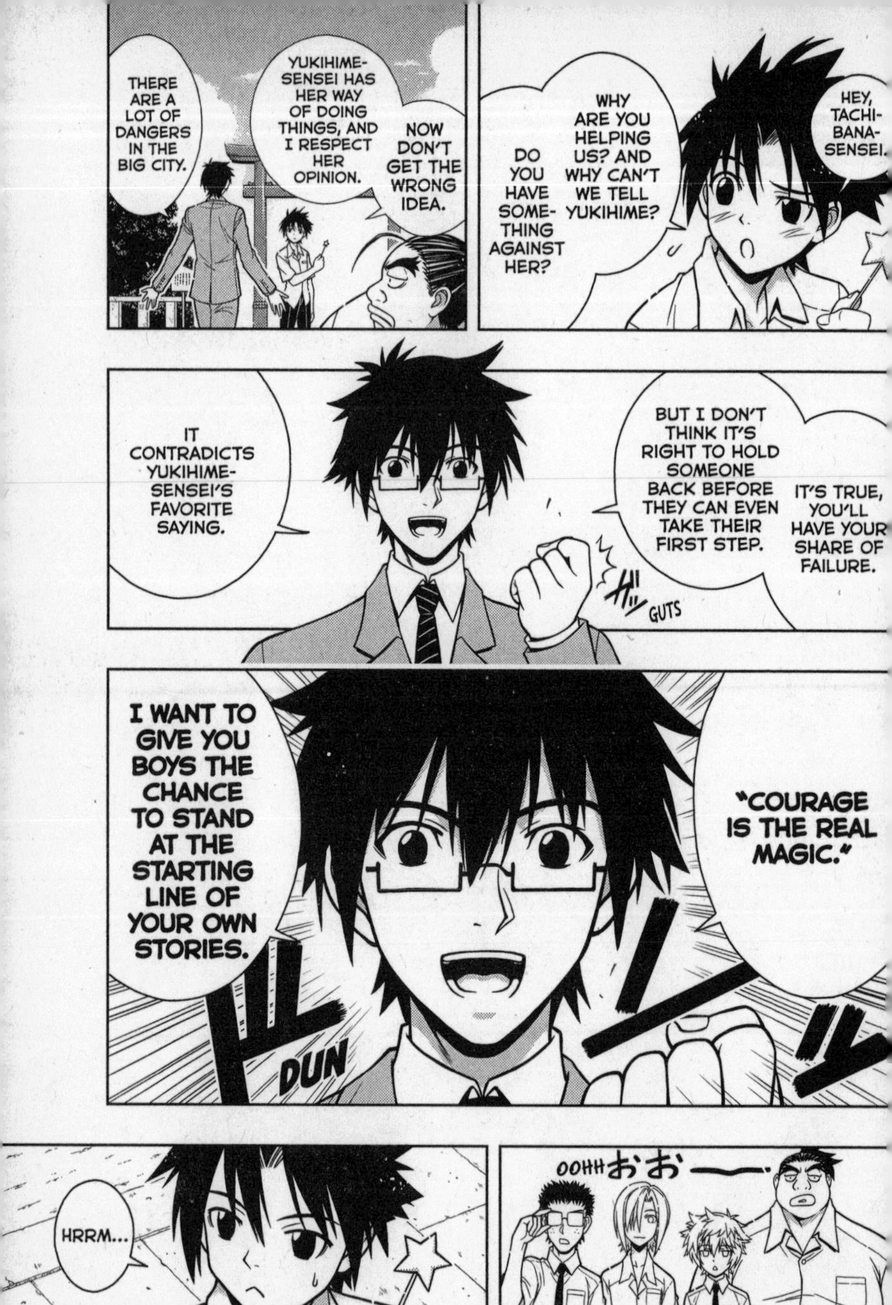
HEY, TACHIBANA-SENSEI.
WHY ARE YOU HELPING US? AND WHY CAN'T WE TELL YUKIHIME?
DO YOU HAVE SOMETHING AGAINST HER?
NOW DON'T GET THE WRONG IDEA.
YUKIHIME-SENSEI HAS HER WAY OF DOING THINGS, AND I RESPECT HER OPINION.
THERE ARE A LOT OF DANGERS IN THE BIG CITY.
IT'S TRUE, YOU'LL HAVE YOUR SHARE OF FAILURE.
BUT I DON'T THINK IT'S RIGHT TO HOLD SOMEONE BACK BEFORE THEY CAN EVEN TAKE THEIR FIRST STEP.
GUTS
IT CONTRADICTS YUKIHIME-SENSEI'S FAVORITE SAYING.
"COURAGE IS THE REAL MAGIC."
I WANT TO GIVE YOU BOYS THE CHANCE TO STAND AT THE STARTING LINE OF YOUR OWN STORIES.
DUN
OOHH おおーー
HRRM...

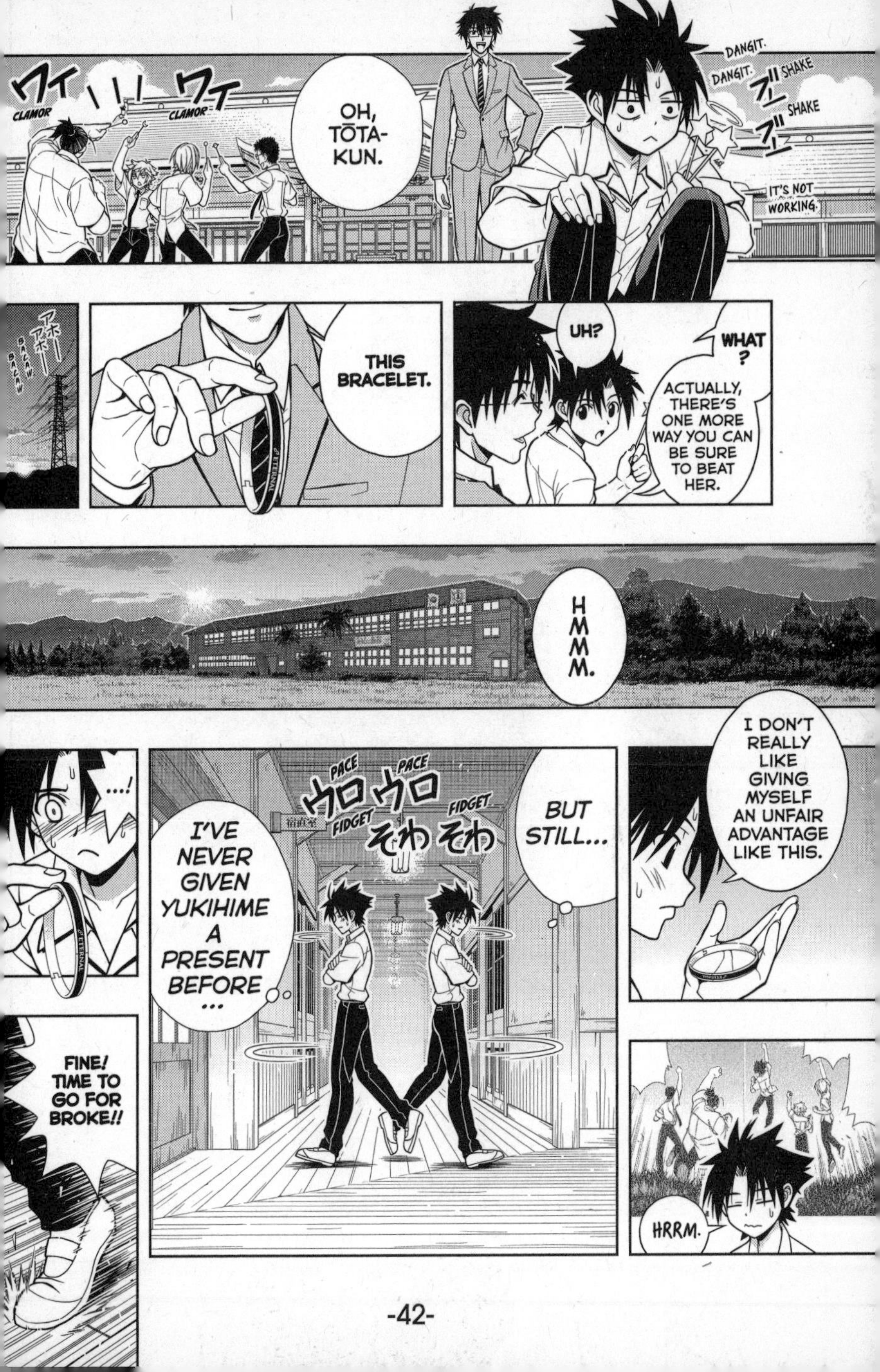
DANGIT.
DANGIT.
SHAKE
SHAKE
IT'S NOT WORKING.
OH, TŌTA-KUN.
ワイワイ
CLAMOR
ワイワイ
CLAMOR
UH?
WHAT?
ACTUALLY, THERE'S ONE MORE WAY YOU CAN BE SURE TO BEAT HER.
THIS BRACELET.
アホー
BA-CAW
アホー
BA-CAW
HMMM.
I DON'T REALLY LIKE GIVING MYSELF AN UNFAIR ADVANTAGE LIKE THIS.
HRRM.
BUT STILL...
ウロウロ
PACE PACE
そわそわ
FIDGET FIDGET
I'VE NEVER GIVEN YUKIHIME A PRESENT BEFORE...
...!
FINE! TIME TO GO FOR BROKE!!

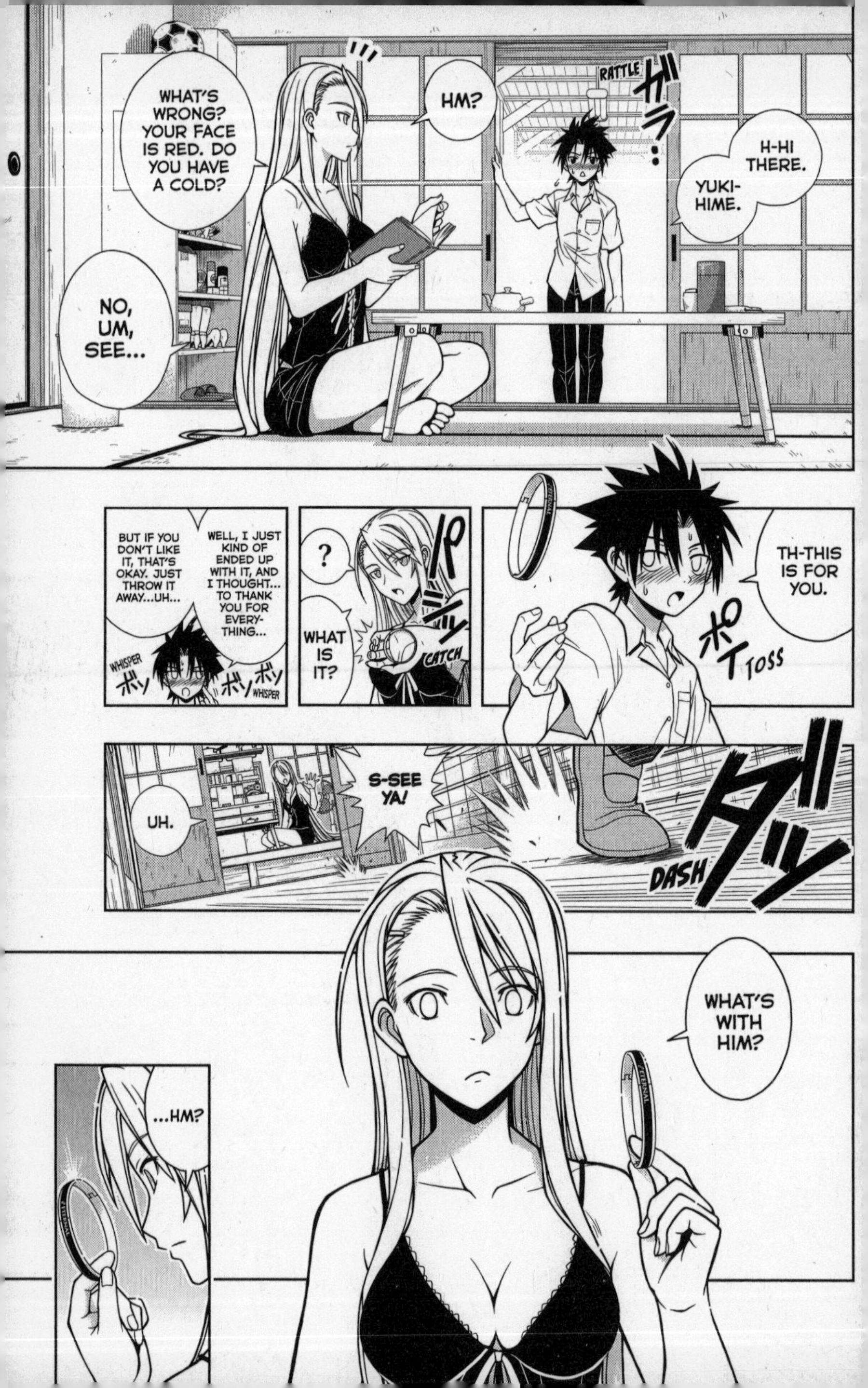

RATTLE
ガラ
H-HI THERE.
YUKI-HIME.
HM?
WHAT'S WRONG? YOUR FACE IS RED. DO YOU HAVE A COLD?
NO, UM, SEE...
TH-THIS IS FOR YOU.
TOSS
?
WHAT IS IT?
CATCH
WELL, I JUST KIND OF ENDED UP WITH IT, AND I THOUGHT... TO THANK YOU FOR EVERYTHING...
BUT IF YOU DON'T LIKE IT, THAT'S OKAY. JUST THROW IT AWAY...UH...
WHISPER
WHISPER
DASH
S-SEE YA!
UH.
WHAT'S WITH HIM?
...HM?

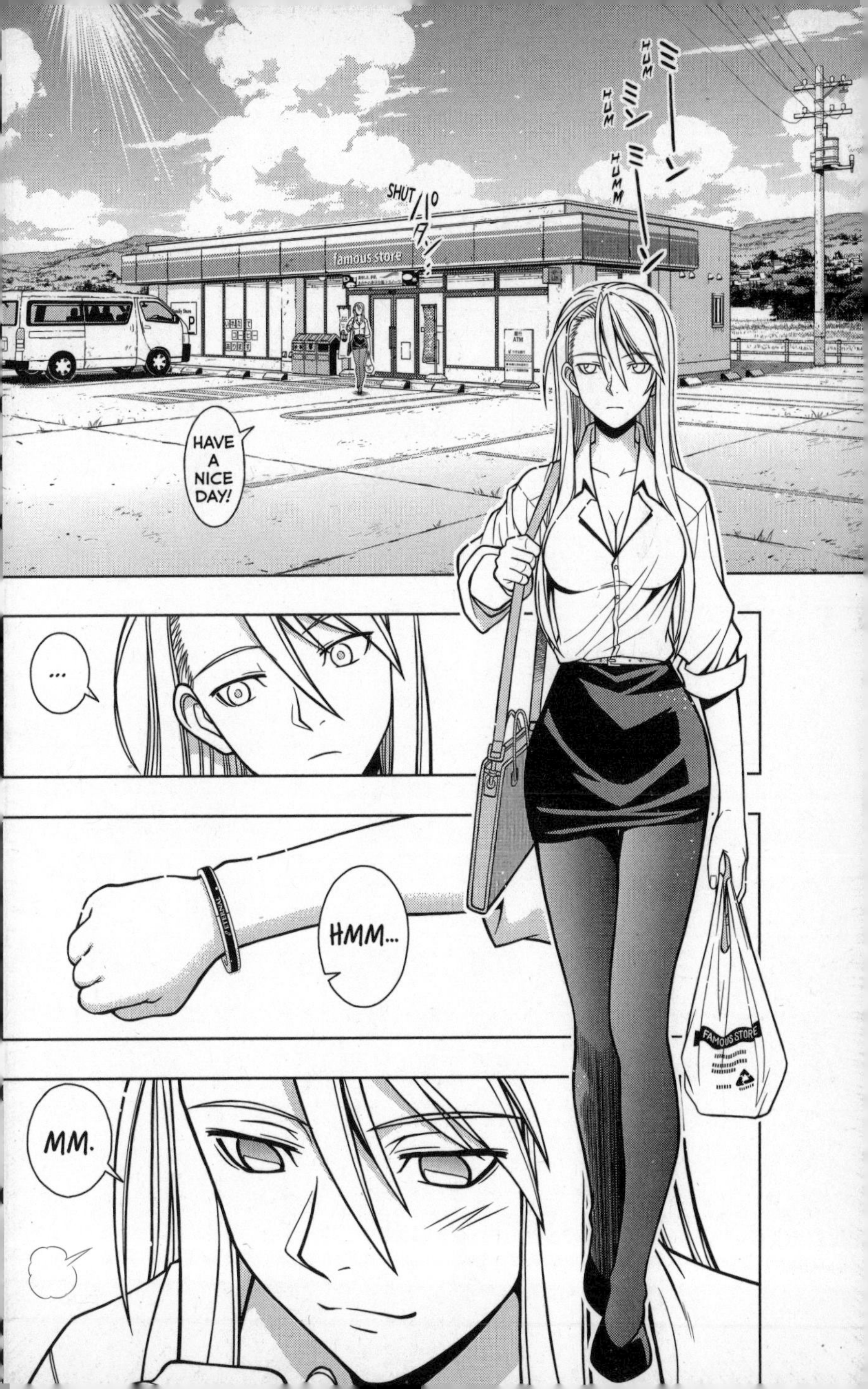
HUM HUM HUM HUMM
ミーン ミンミーン
famous store
SHUT
バタン
HAVE A NICE DAY!
ATM
...
HMM...
FAMOUS STORE
MM.

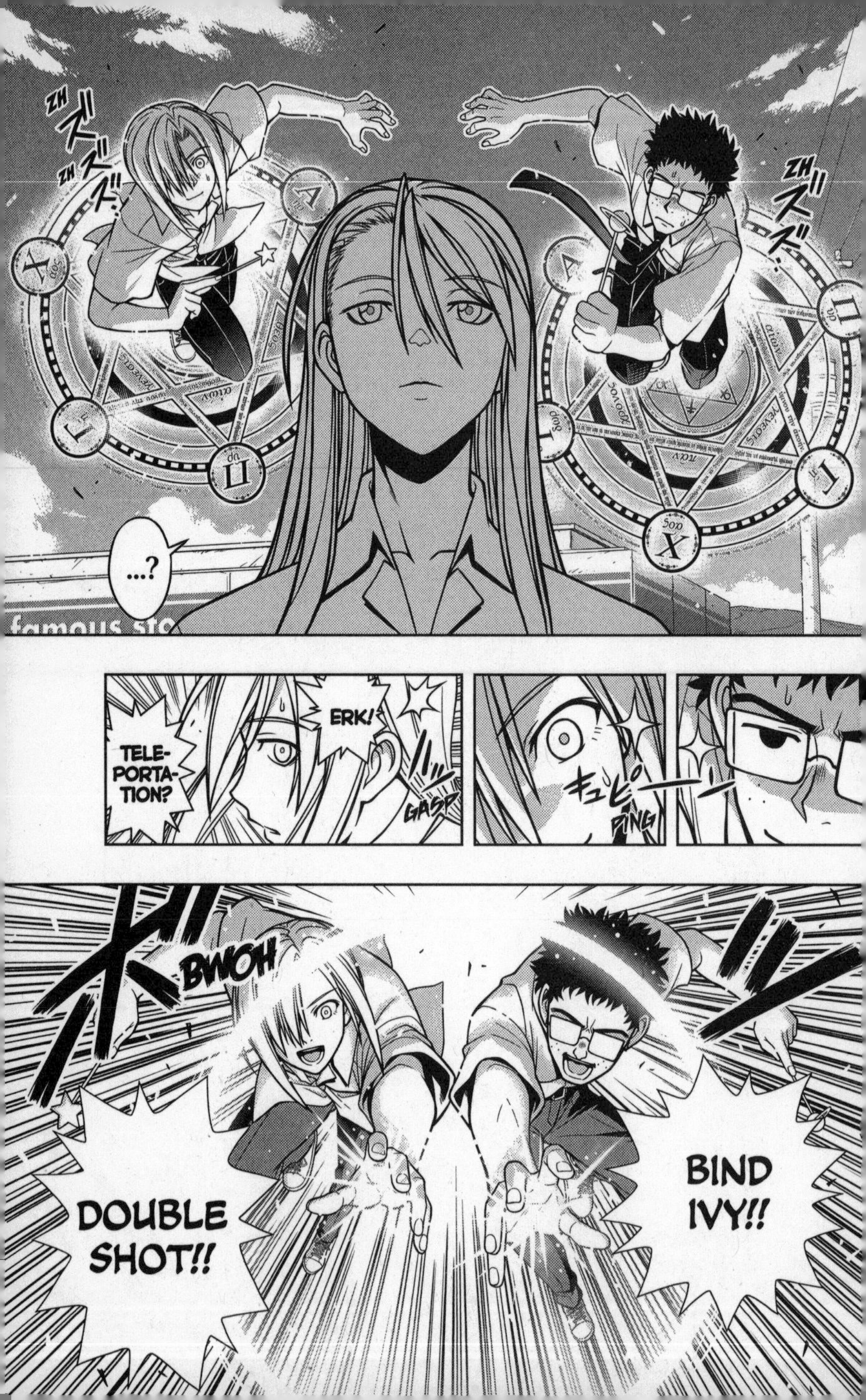

ZH
ZH
ZH
ZH
...?
ERK!
TELE-PORTA-TION?
GASP
PING
BWOH
BIND IVY!!
DOUBLE SHOT!!

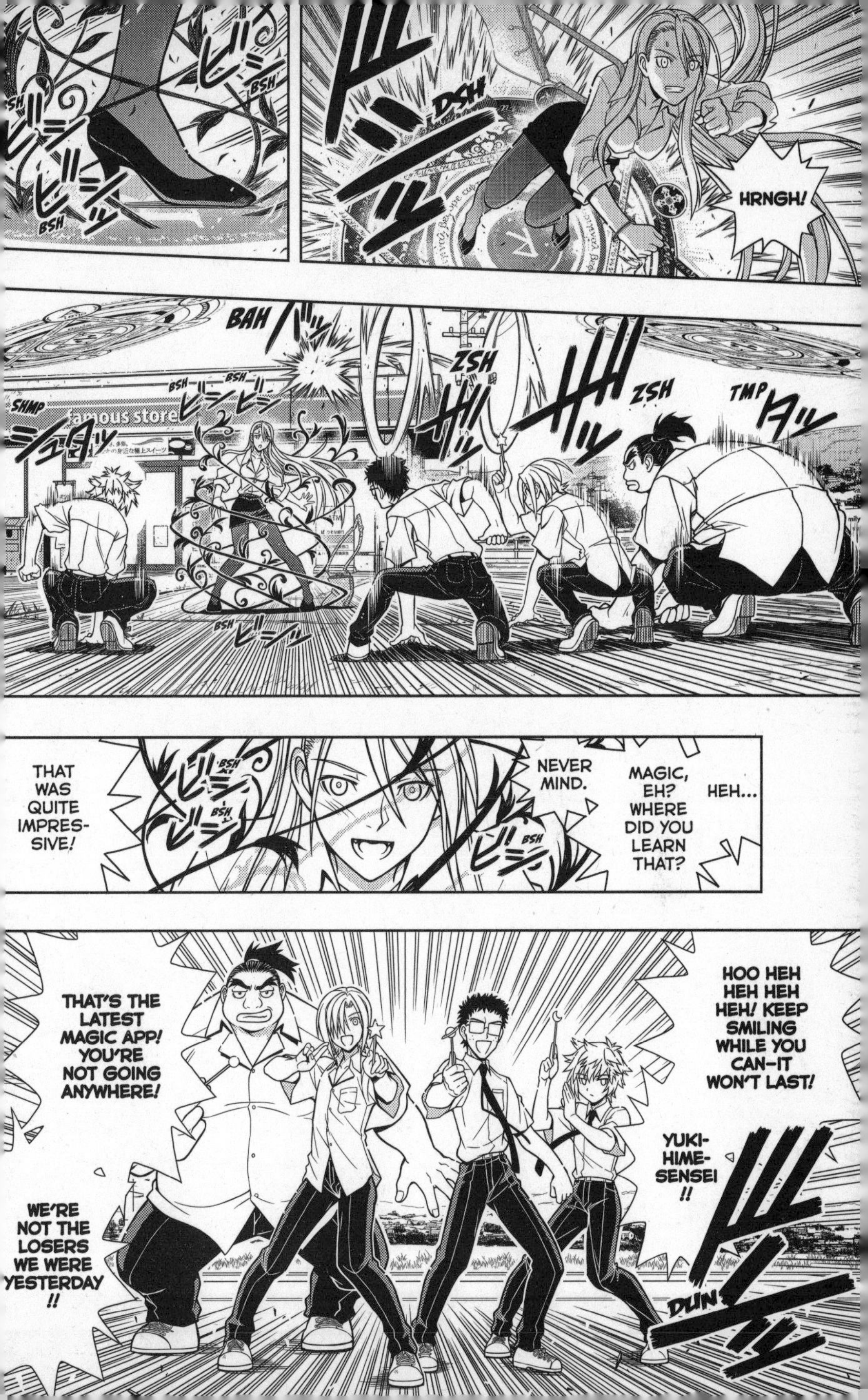

HRNGH!
DSH
BSH
BSH
BSH
TMP
ZSH
ZSH
BAH
BSH
BSH
SHMP
famous store
BSH
HEH...
MAGIC, EH? WHERE DID YOU LEARN THAT?
NEVER MIND.
BSH
BSH
BSH
THAT WAS QUITE IMPRESSIVE!
HOO HEH HEH HEH HEH! KEEP SMILING WHILE YOU CAN—IT WON'T LAST!
YUKI-HIME-SENSEI!!
THAT'S THE LATEST MAGIC APP! YOU'RE NOT GOING ANYWHERE!
WE'RE NOT THE LOSERS WE WERE YESTERDAY!!
DUN

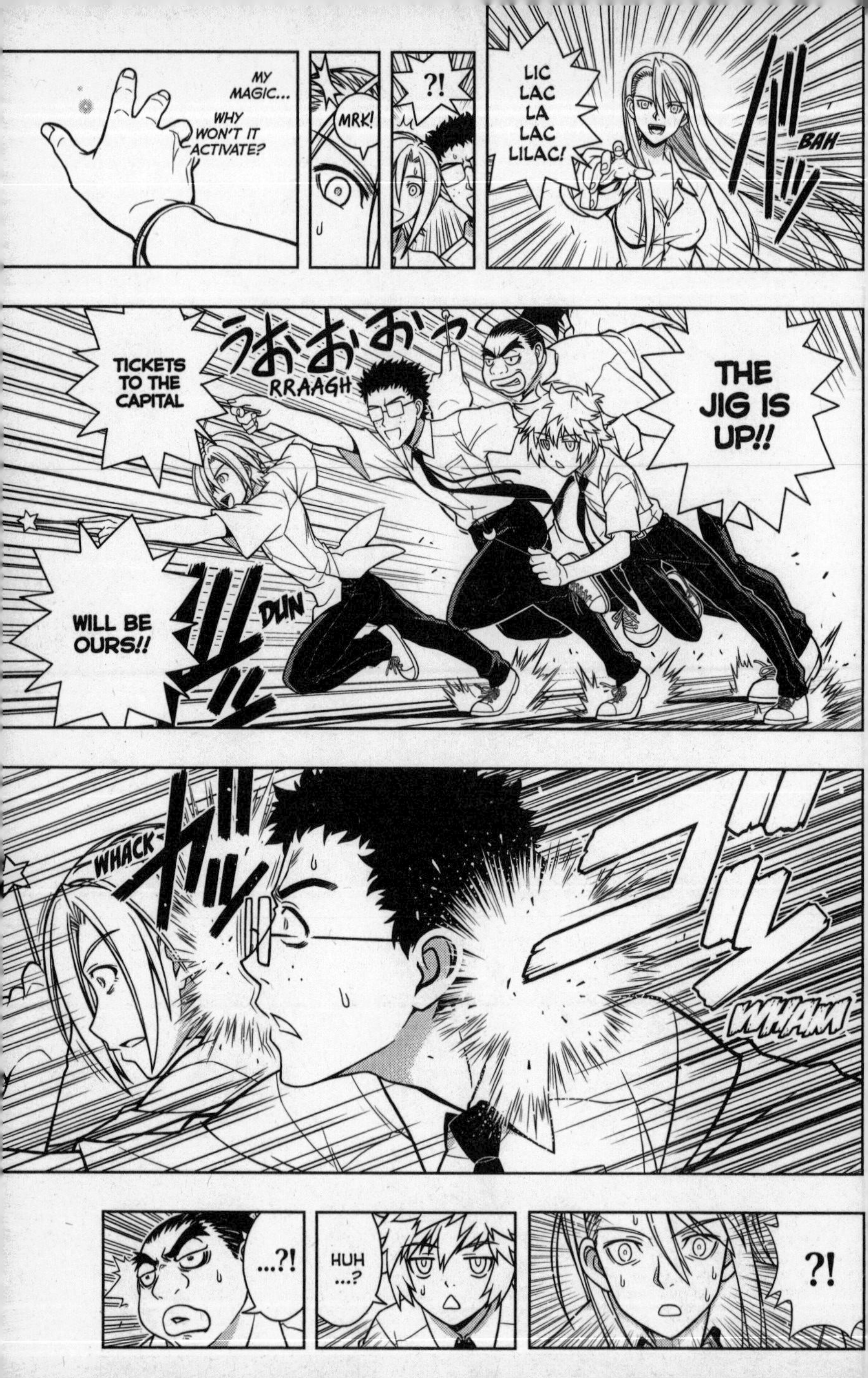
LIC LAC LA LAC LILAC!
BAH
?!
MRK!
MY MAGIC...
WHY WON'T IT ACTIVATE?
THE JIG IS UP!!
うおおおっ
RRAAGH
TICKETS TO THE CAPITAL
WILL BE OURS!!
DUN
WHAM
WHACK
?!
HUH ...?
...?!

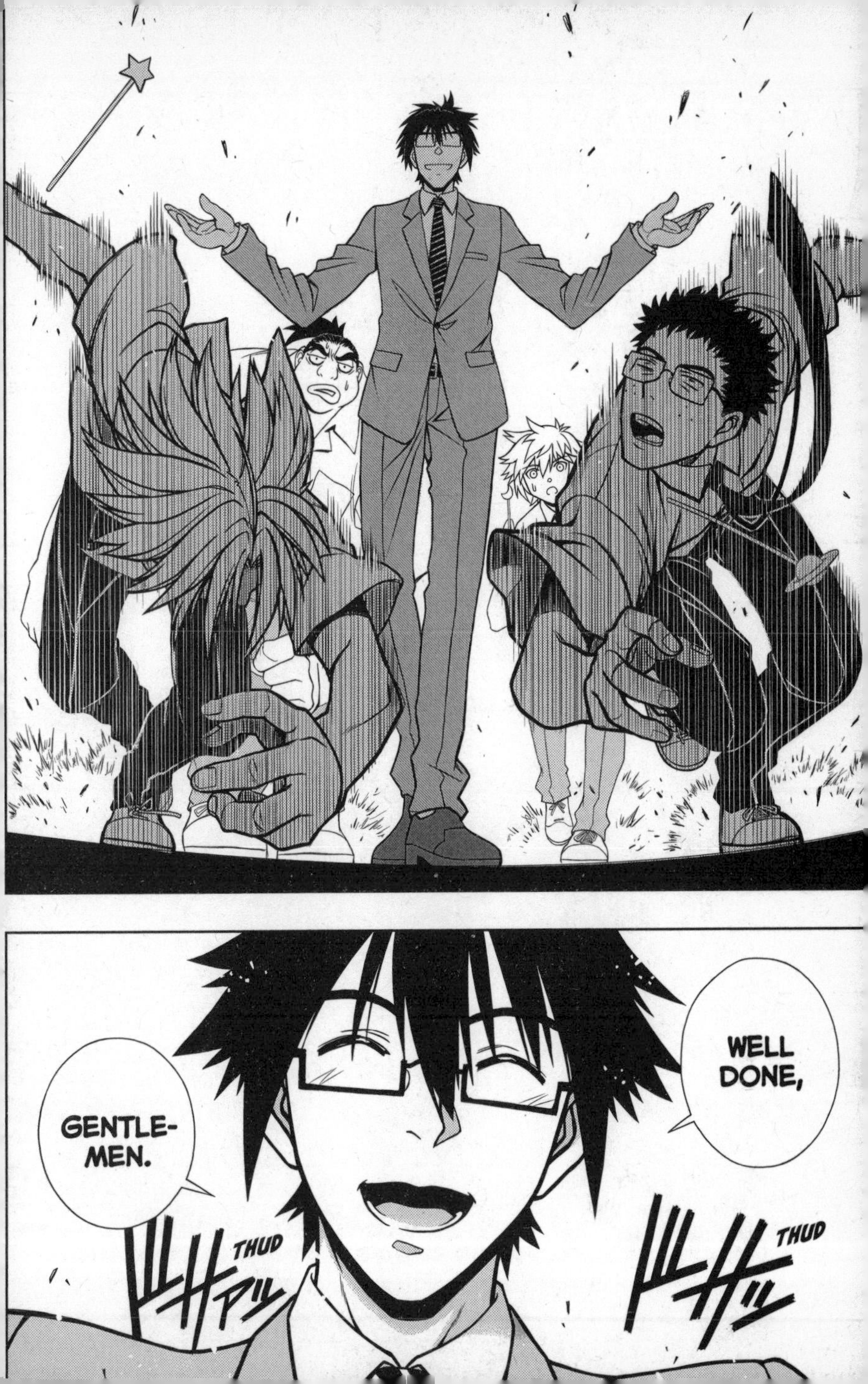
WELL DONE,
GENTLE-MEN.
THUD
THUD

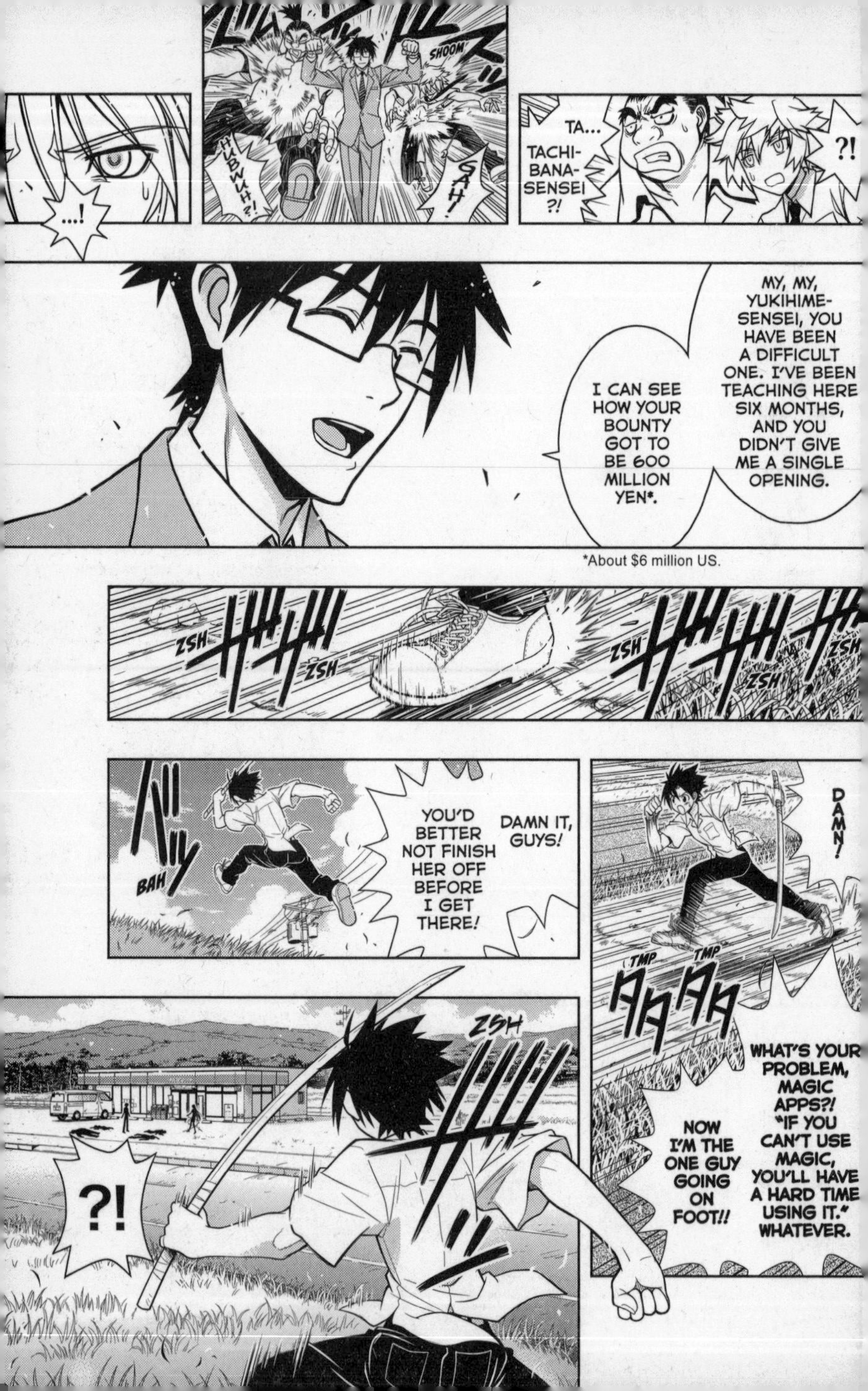
TA... TACHIBANA-SENSEI?!
?!
SHOOM
HUBWUH?!
GAH!
...!
MY, MY, YUKIHIME-SENSEI, YOU HAVE BEEN A DIFFICULT ONE. I'VE BEEN TEACHING HERE SIX MONTHS, AND YOU DIDN'T GIVE ME A SINGLE OPENING.
I CAN SEE HOW YOUR BOUNTY GOT TO BE 600 MILLION YEN*.
ZSH
ZSH
ZSH
ZSH
ZSH
DAMN!
TMP TMP
WHAT'S YOUR PROBLEM, MAGIC APPS?! "IF YOU CAN'T USE MAGIC, YOU'LL HAVE A HARD TIME USING IT." WHATEVER.
NOW I'M THE ONE GUY GOING ON FOOT!!
DAMN IT, GUYS!
YOU'D BETTER NOT FINISH HER OFF BEFORE I GET THERE!
BAH
ZSH
?!

*About $6 million US.

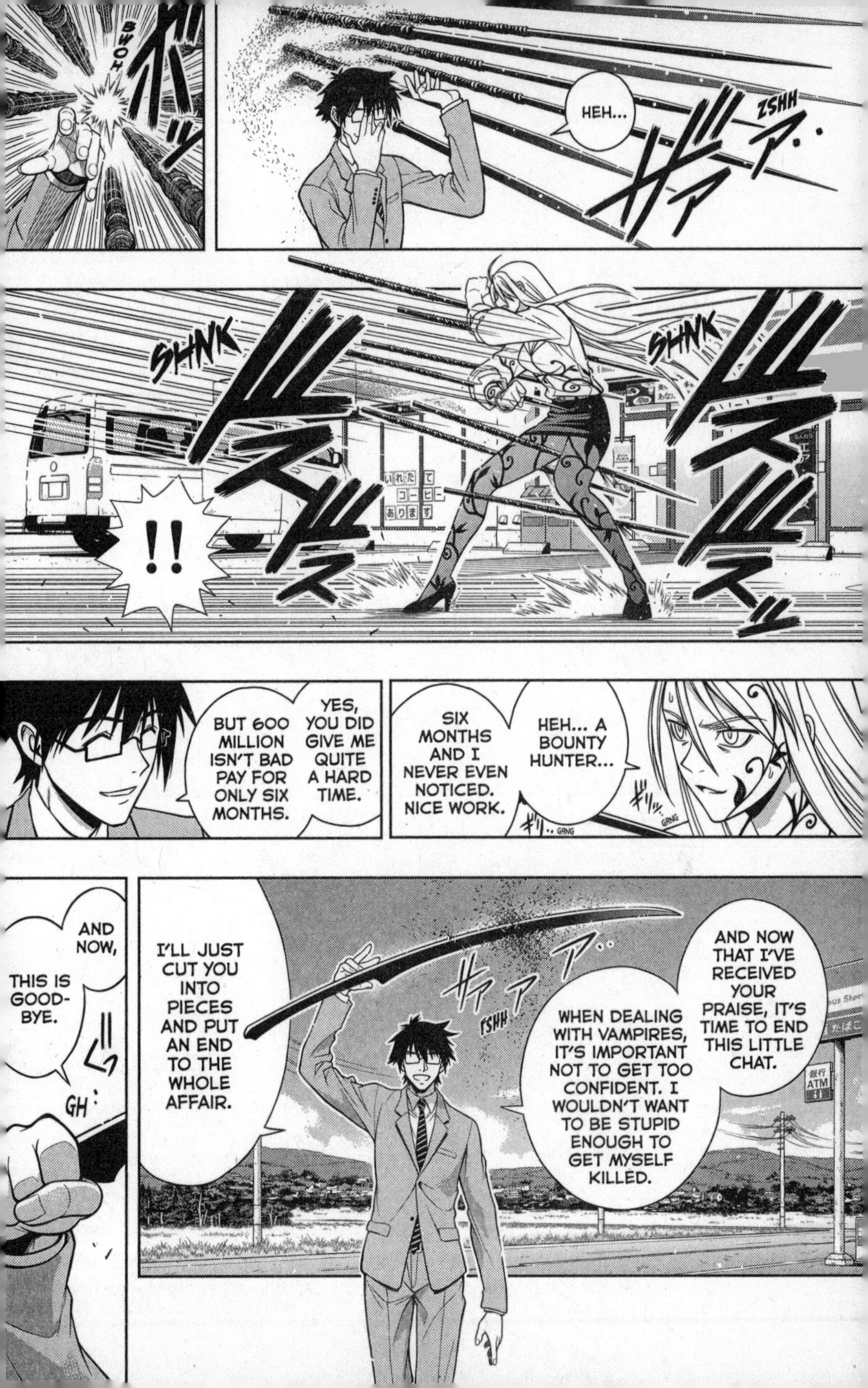
HEH...
ZSHH
BWOH
SHNK
SHNK
!!
HEH... A BOUNTY HUNTER...
SIX MONTHS AND I NEVER EVEN NOTICED. NICE WORK.
GRNG
GRNG
YES, YOU DID GIVE ME QUITE A HARD TIME.
BUT 600 MILLION ISN'T BAD PAY FOR ONLY SIX MONTHS.
AND NOW THAT I'VE RECEIVED YOUR PRAISE, IT'S TIME TO END THIS LITTLE CHAT.
WHEN DEALING WITH VAMPIRES, IT'S IMPORTANT NOT TO GET TOO CONFIDENT. I WOULDN'T WANT TO BE STUPID ENOUGH TO GET MYSELF KILLED.
TSHH
I'LL JUST CUT YOU INTO PIECES AND PUT AN END TO THE WHOLE AFFAIR.
AND NOW,
THIS IS GOOD-BYE.
GH:

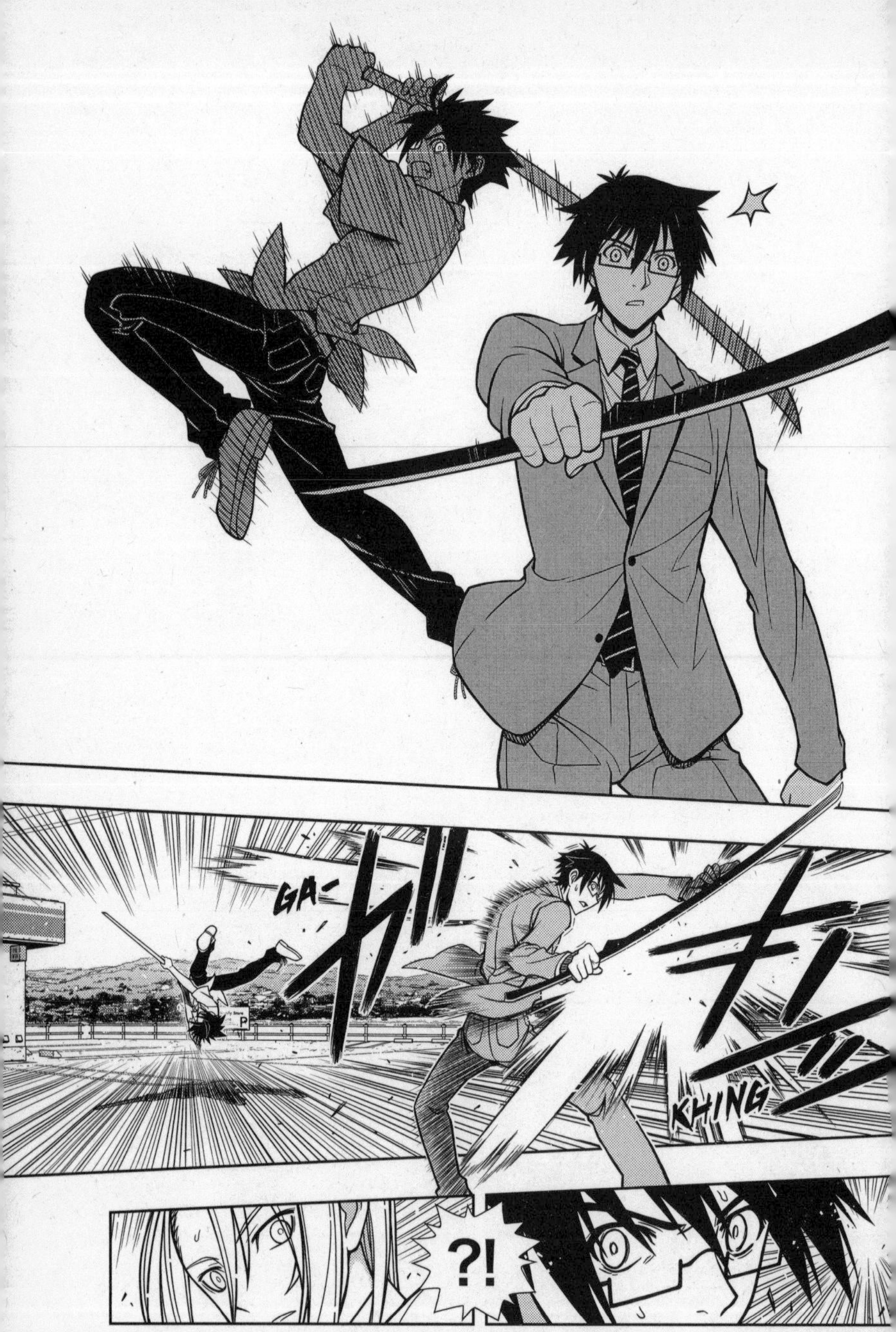
KHING
GA-
?!

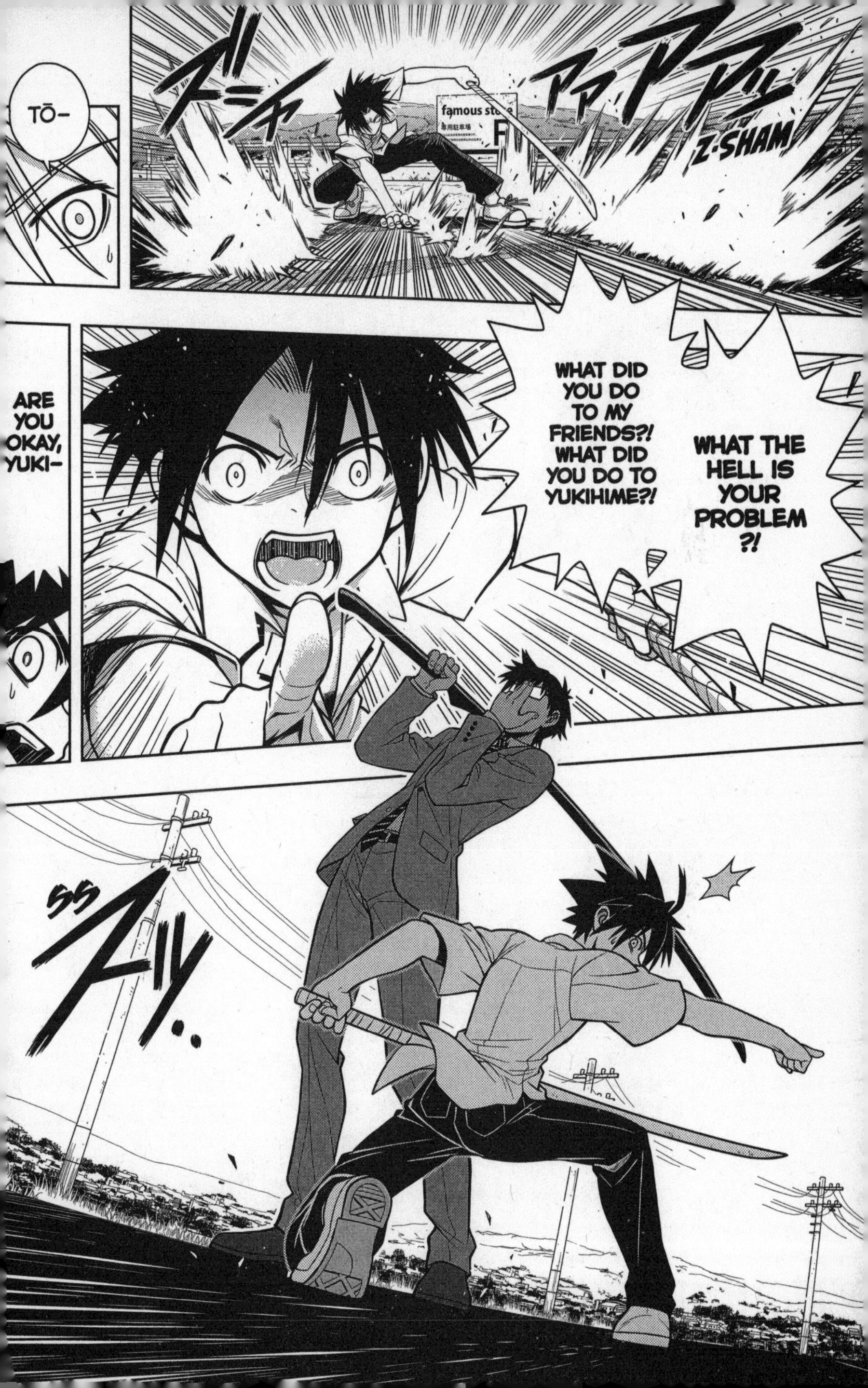
Z-SHAM
TŌ-
WHAT THE HELL IS YOUR PROBLEM?!
WHAT DID YOU DO TO MY FRIENDS?! WHAT DID YOU DO TO YUKIHIME?!
ARE YOU OKAY, YUKI-
SS

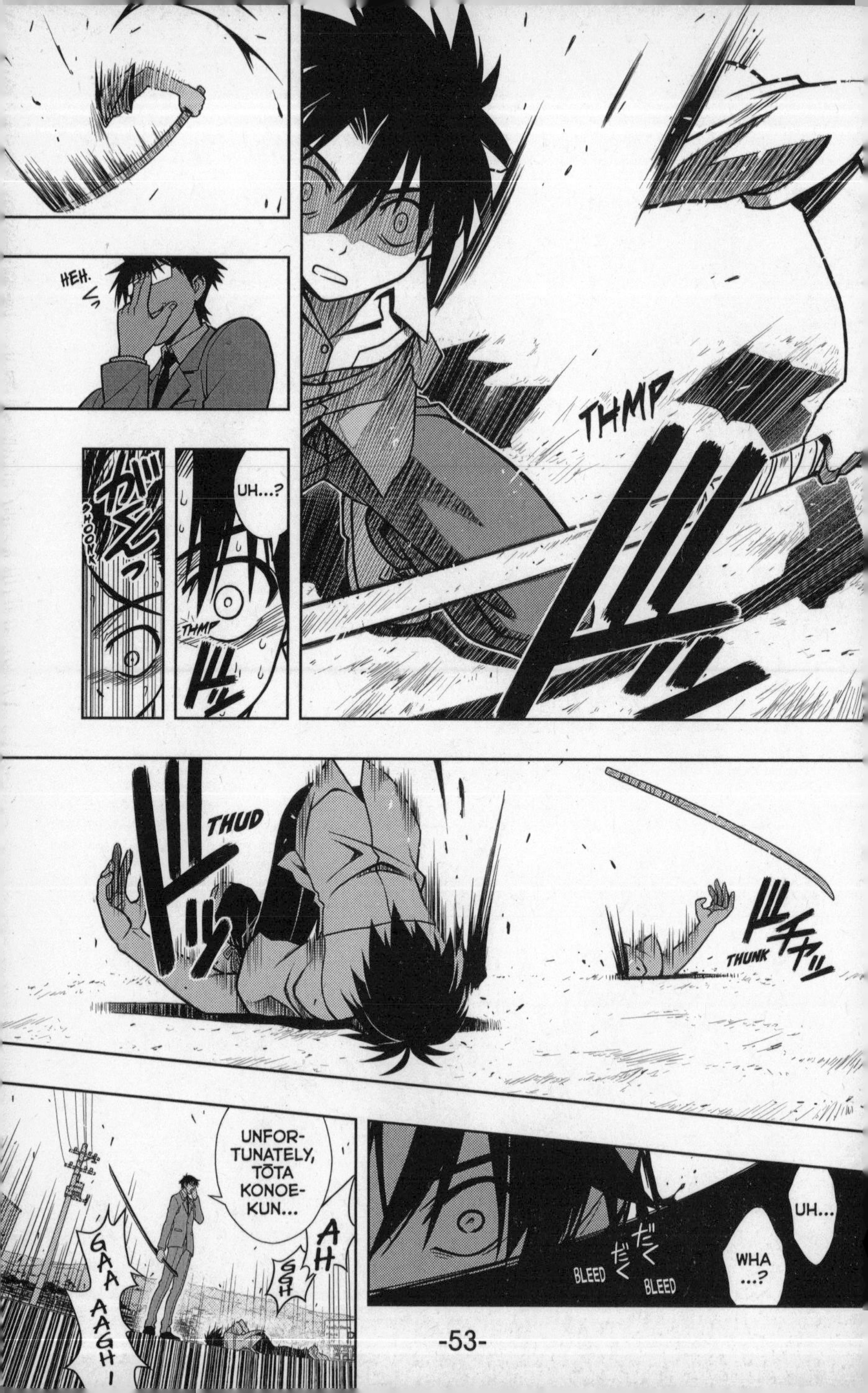
THMP
HEH.
UH...?
THMP
GHOONK
THUD
THUNK
UH...
WHA ...?
BLEED
だく
だく
BLEED
UNFORTUNATELY, TŌTA KONOE-KUN...
AH GGH
GAA AAGH!

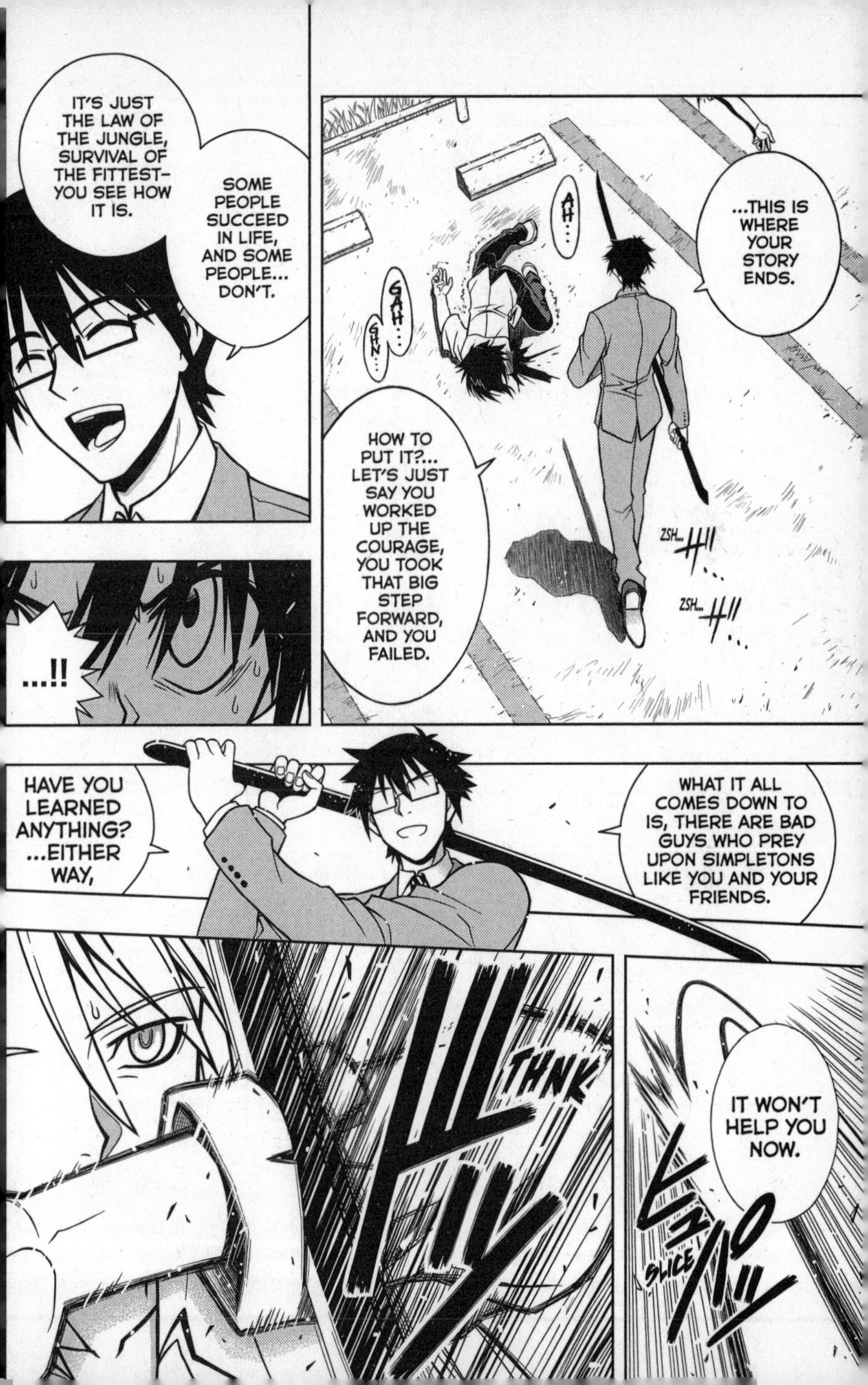
...THIS IS WHERE YOUR STORY ENDS.
AH...
GAH...
GHN...
HOW TO PUT IT?... LET'S JUST SAY YOU WORKED UP THE COURAGE, YOU TOOK THAT BIG STEP FORWARD, AND YOU FAILED.
ZSH...
ZSH...
SOME PEOPLE SUCCEED IN LIFE, AND SOME PEOPLE... DON'T.
IT'S JUST THE LAW OF THE JUNGLE, SURVIVAL OF THE FITTEST- YOU SEE HOW IT IS.
...!!
WHAT IT ALL COMES DOWN TO IS, THERE ARE BAD GUYS WHO PREY UPON SIMPLETONS LIKE YOU AND YOUR FRIENDS.
HAVE YOU LEARNED ANYTHING? ...EITHER WAY,
IT WON'T HELP YOU NOW.
SLICE
THNK

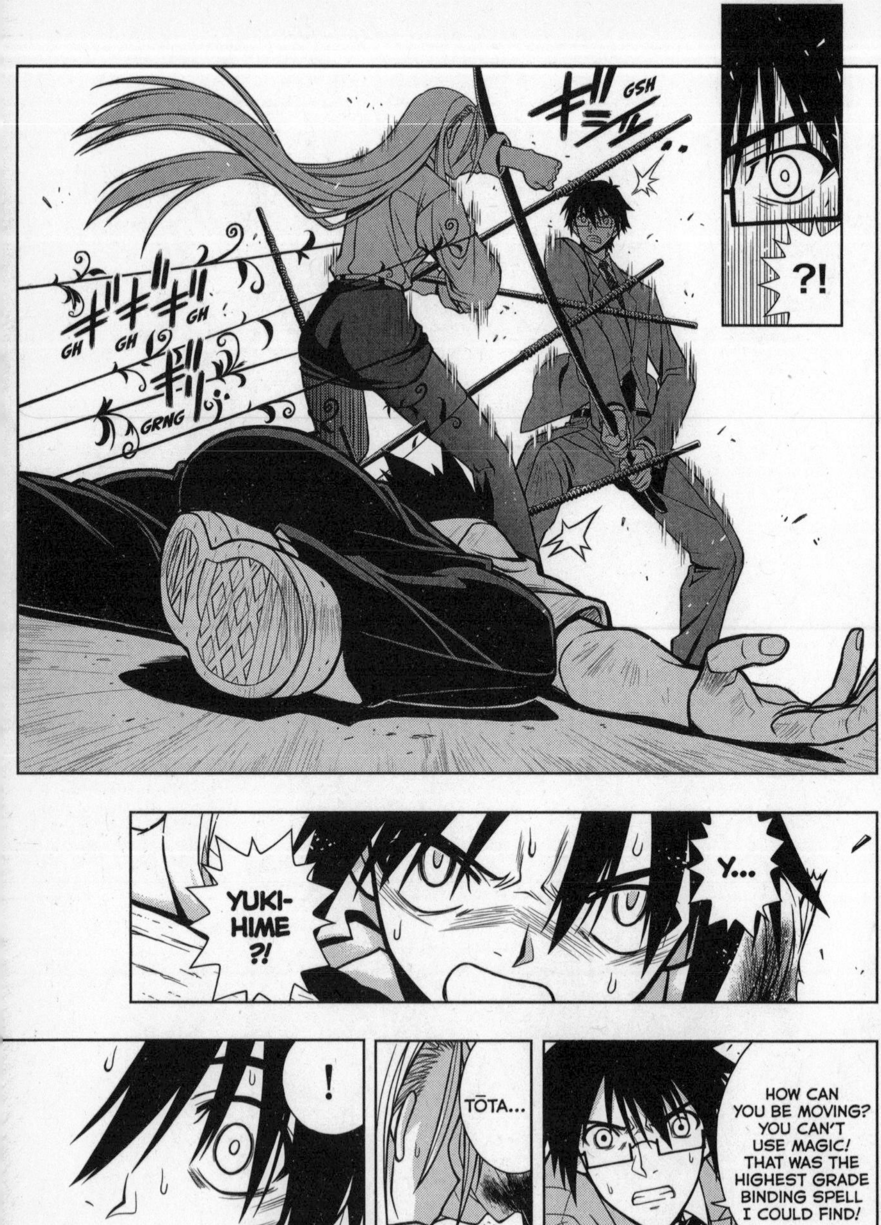
?!
GSH
GH
GH
GH
GRNG
Y...
YUKI-HIME ?!
HOW CAN YOU BE MOVING? YOU CAN'T USE MAGIC! THAT WAS THE HIGHEST GRADE BINDING SPELL I COULD FIND!
TŌTA...
!

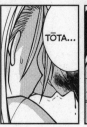

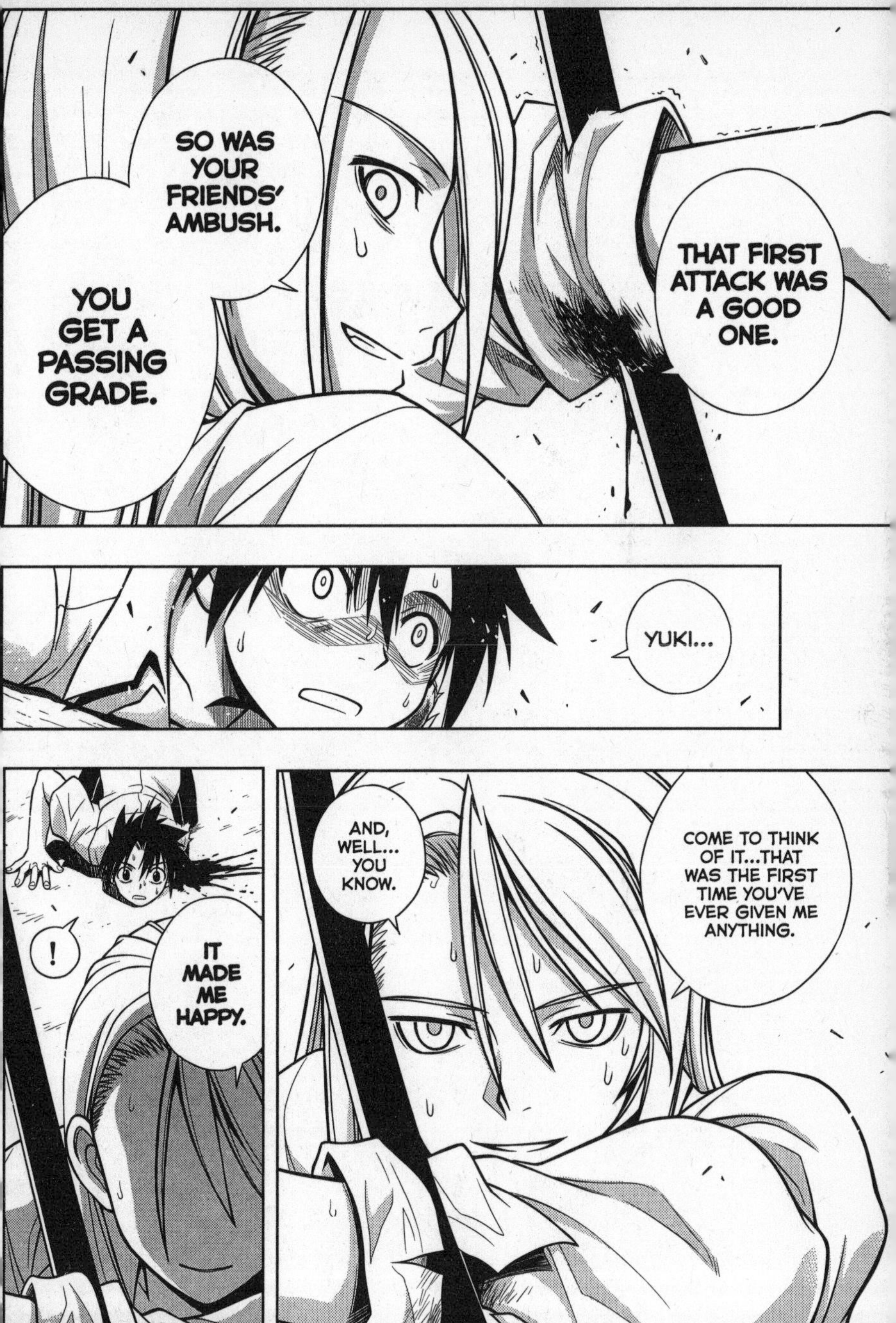
THAT FIRST ATTACK WAS A GOOD ONE.
SO WAS YOUR FRIENDS' AMBUSH.
YOU GET A PASSING GRADE.
YUKI...
COME TO THINK OF IT...THAT WAS THE FIRST TIME YOU'VE EVER GIVEN ME ANYTHING.
AND, WELL... YOU KNOW.
!
IT MADE ME HAPPY.

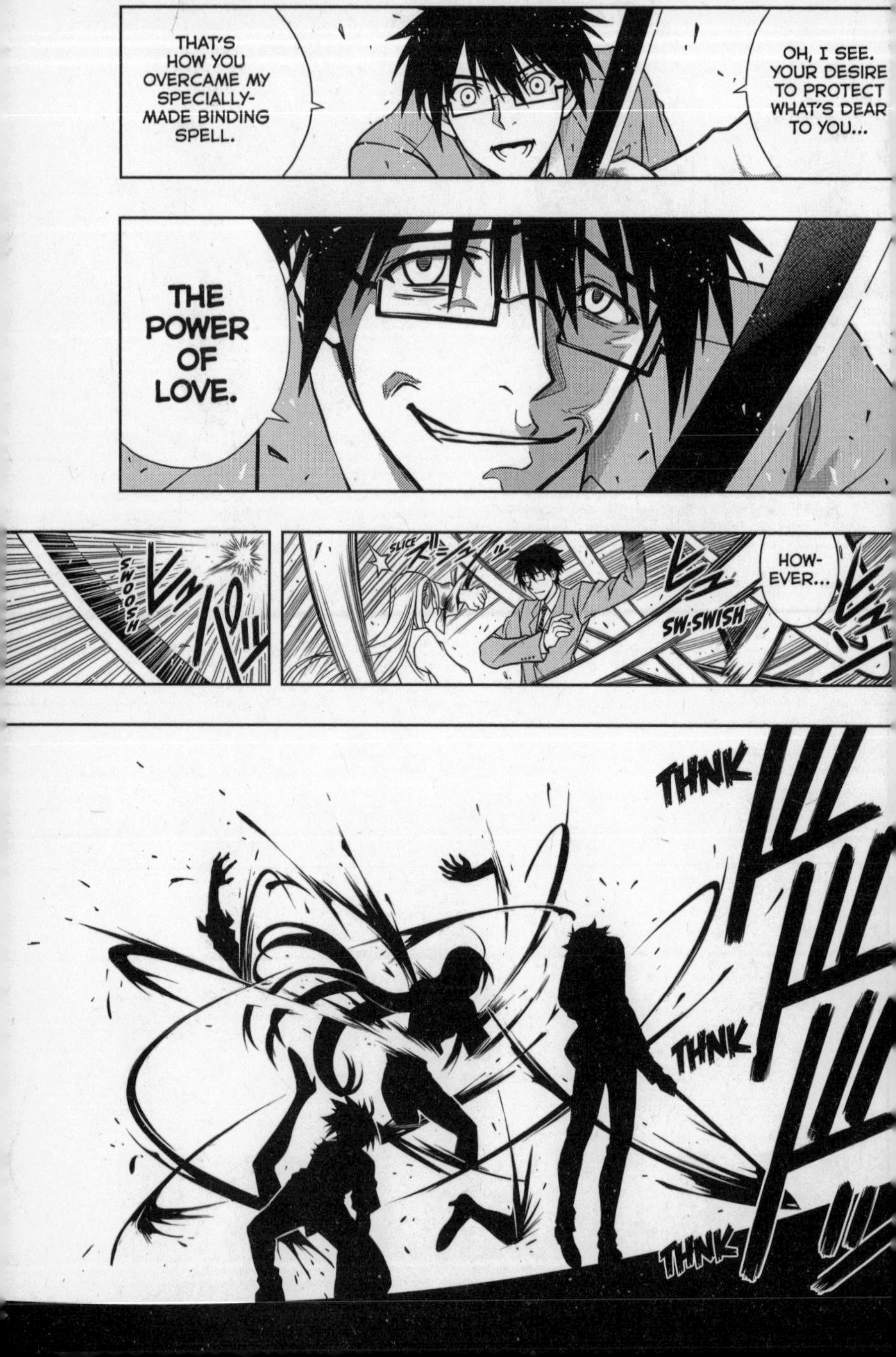
OH, I SEE. YOUR DESIRE TO PROTECT WHAT'S DEAR TO YOU...
THAT'S HOW YOU OVERCAME MY SPECIALLY-MADE BINDING SPELL.
THE POWER OF LOVE.
HOW-EVER...
SW-SWISH
SLICE
SWOOSH
THNK
THNK
THNK

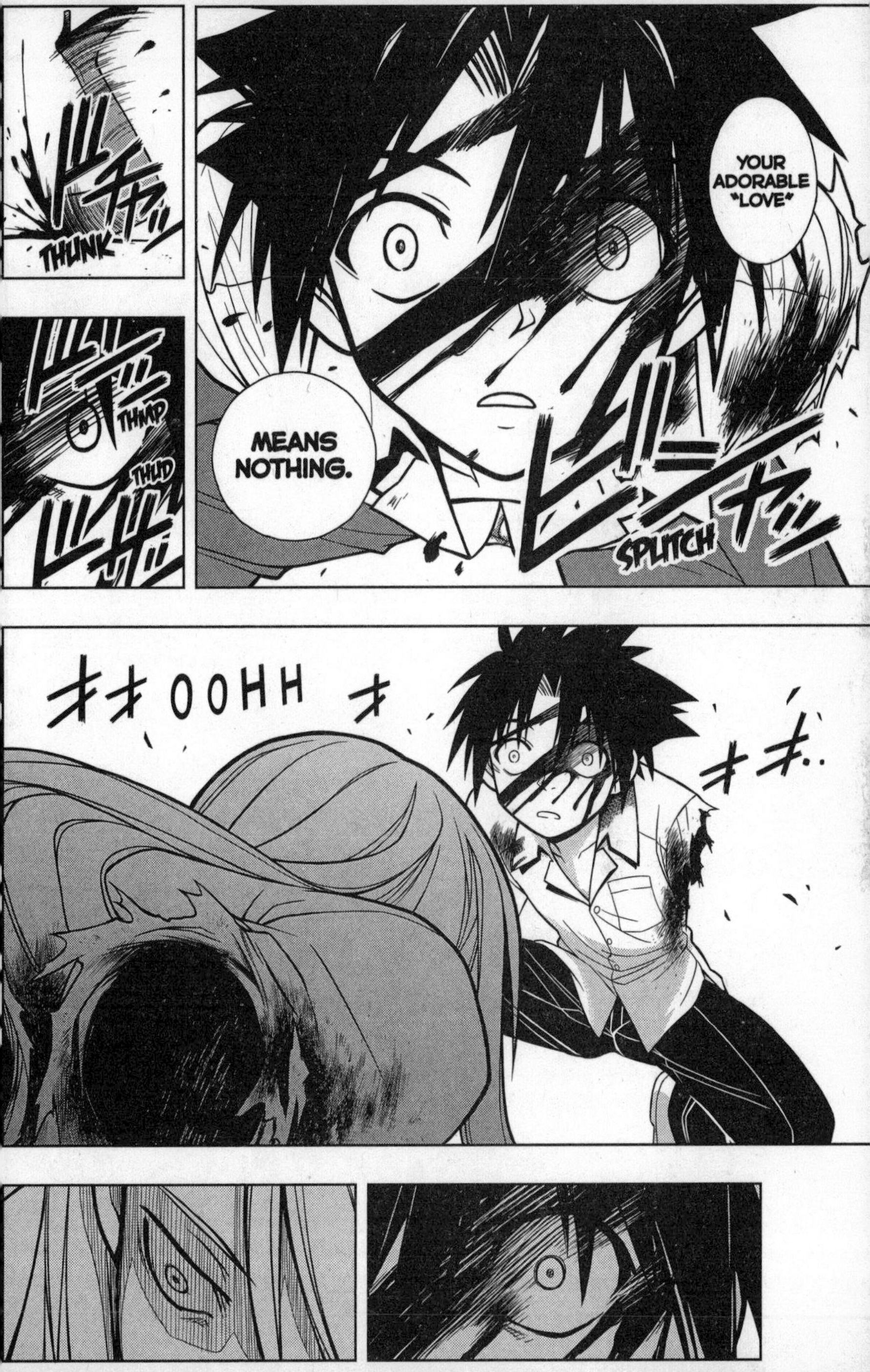
YOUR ADORABLE "LOVE"
MEANS NOTHING.
SPLITCH
THUNK
THMP
THUD
OOHH

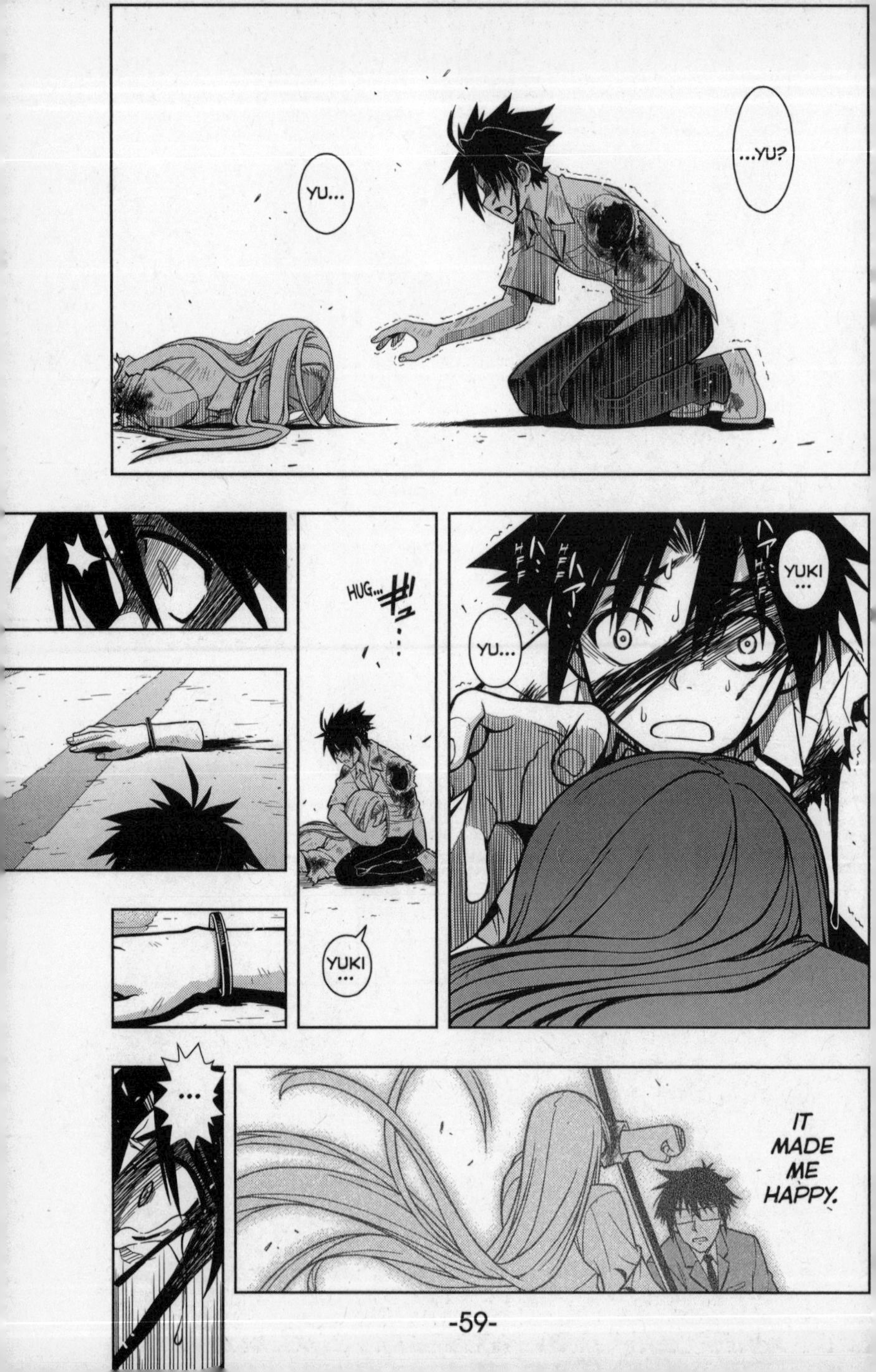
...YU?
YU...
YUKI ...
HFF
HFF
HFF
YU...
HUG...
YUKI ...
IT MADE ME HAPPY.
...

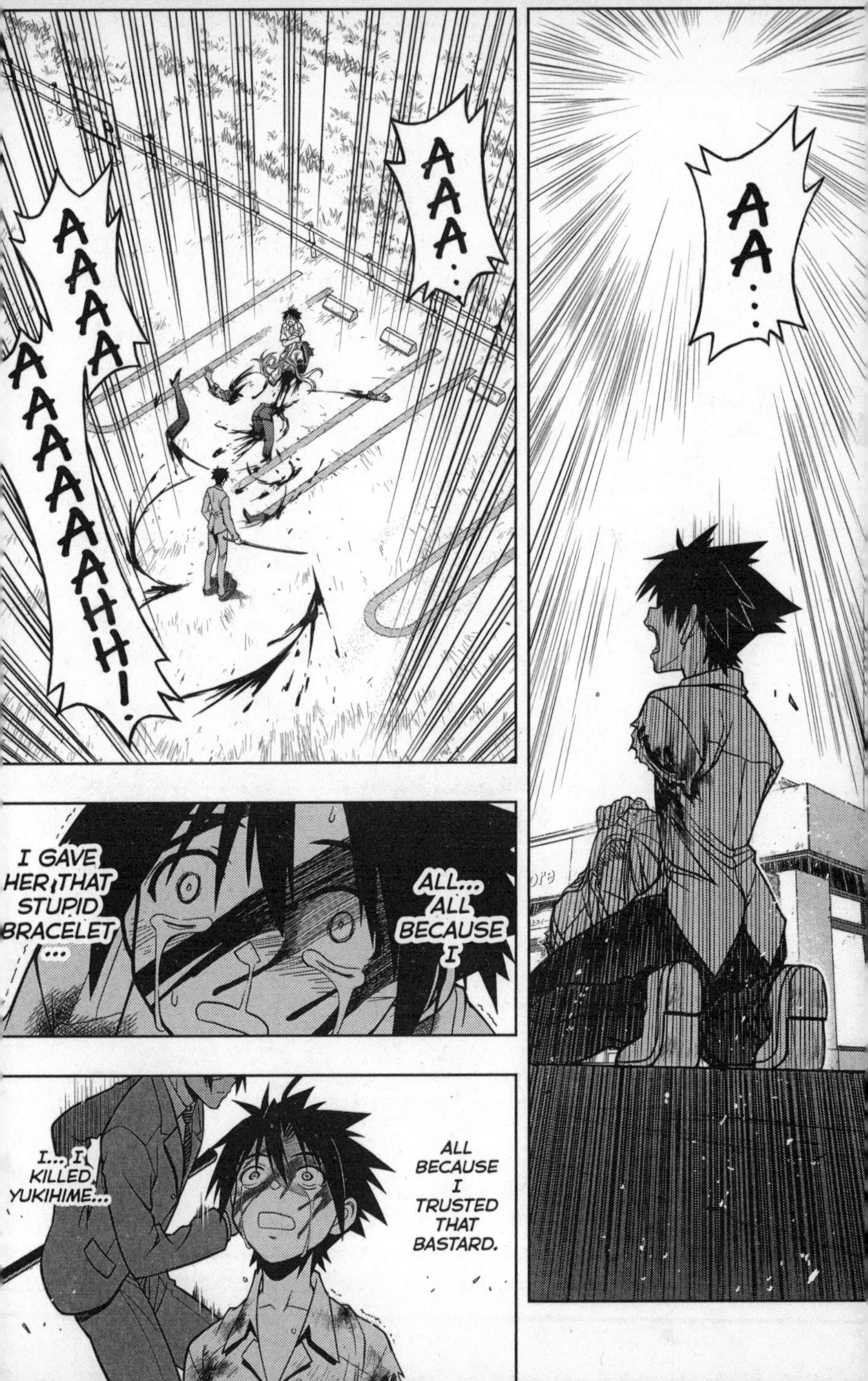
AA...
AAA...
AAAAAAAAAAHH!
ALL... ALL BECAUSE I
I GAVE HER THAT STUPID BRACELET...
ALL BECAUSE I TRUSTED THAT BASTARD.
I... I KILLED YUKIHIME...

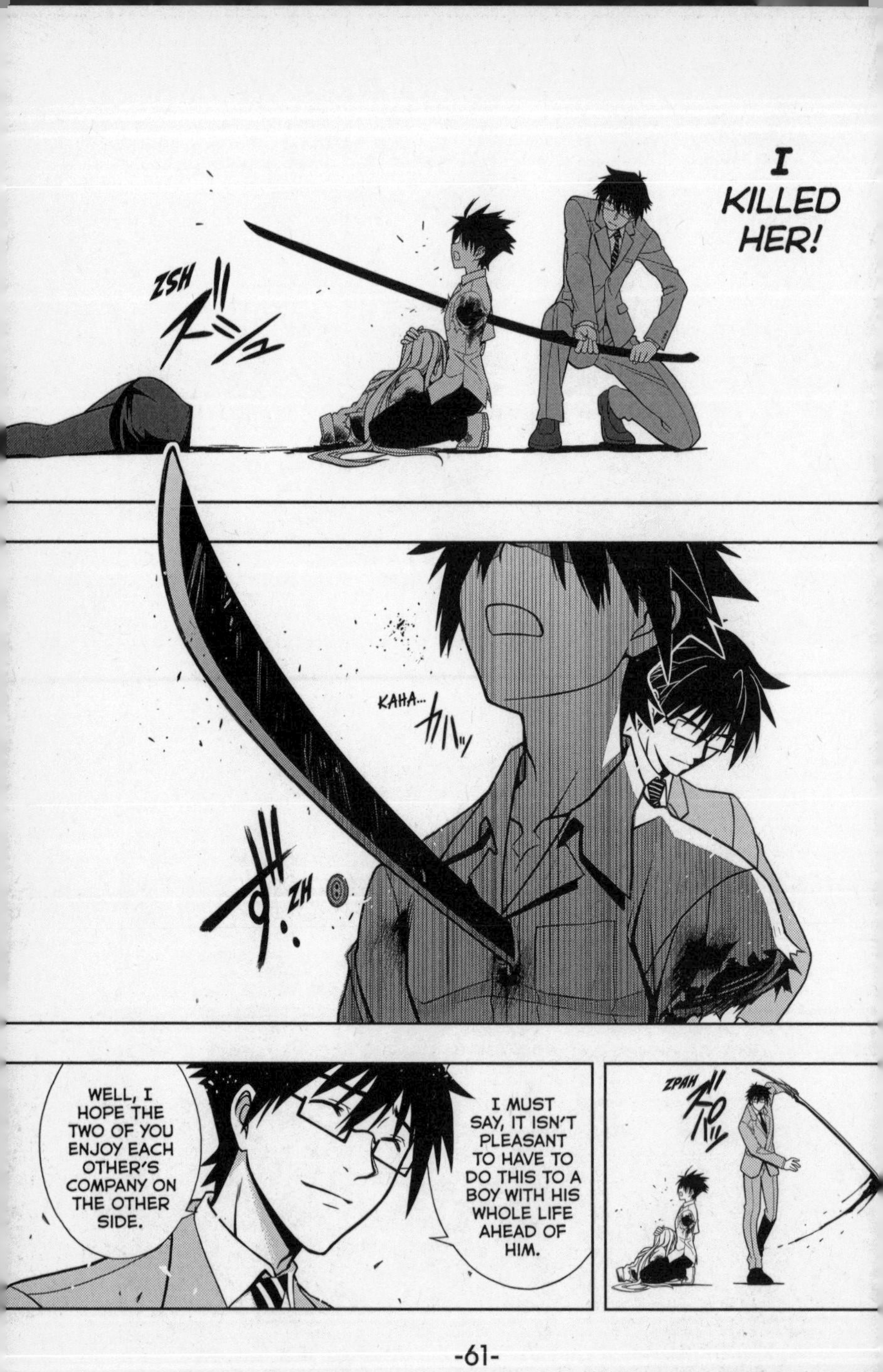

I KILLED HER!
ZSH
ズシュ
KAHA...
カハッ
ZH
ず
ZPAH
ズパッ
I MUST SAY, IT ISN'T PLEASANT TO HAVE TO DO THIS TO A BOY WITH HIS WHOLE LIFE AHEAD OF HIM.
WELL, I HOPE THE TWO OF YOU ENJOY EACH OTHER'S COMPANY ON THE OTHER SIDE.

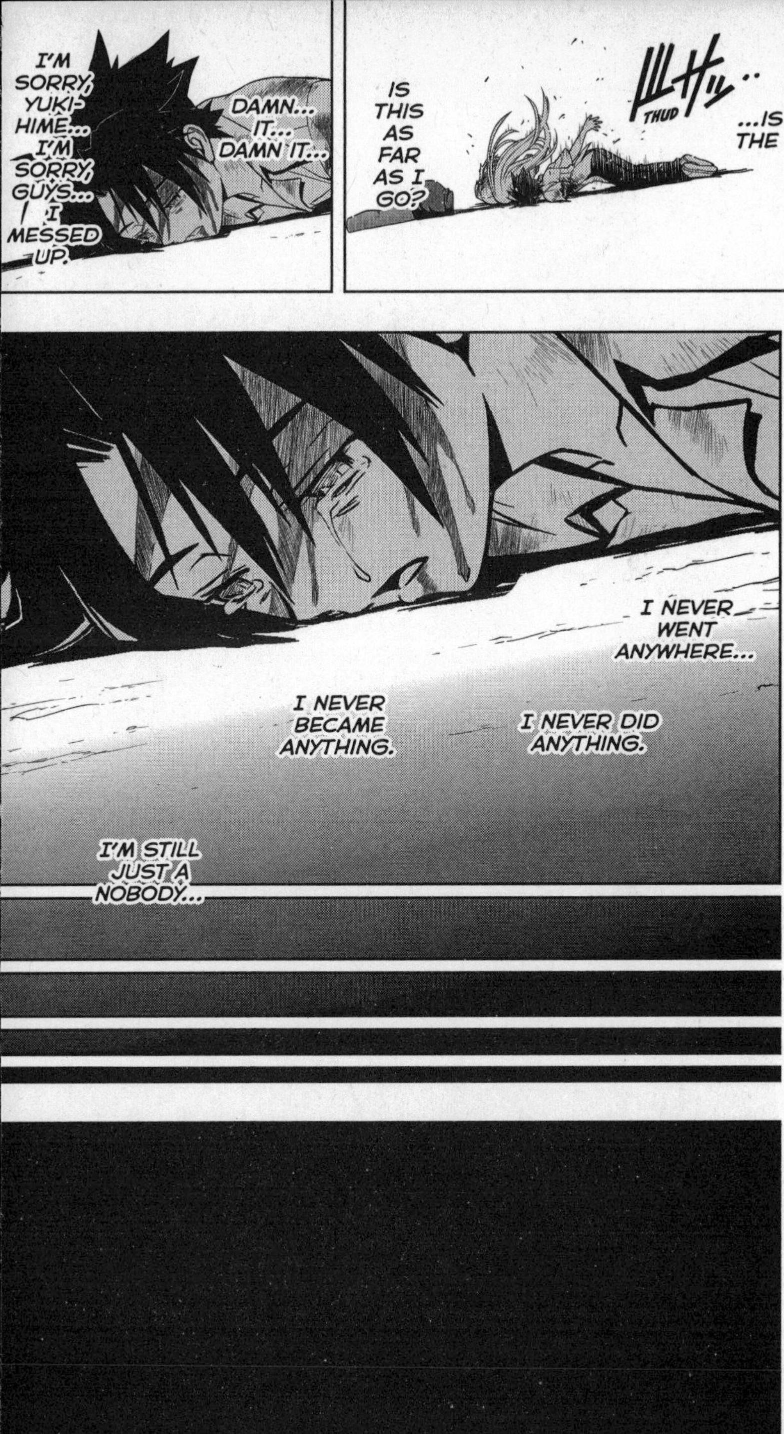
...IS THIS THE END?
THUD
IS THIS AS FAR AS I GO?
DAMN... IT... DAMN IT...
I'M SORRY, YUKI-HIME... I'M SORRY, GUYS... I MESSED UP.
I NEVER WENT ANYWHERE...
I NEVER DID ANYTHING.
I NEVER BECAME ANYTHING.
I'M STILL JUST A NOBODY...

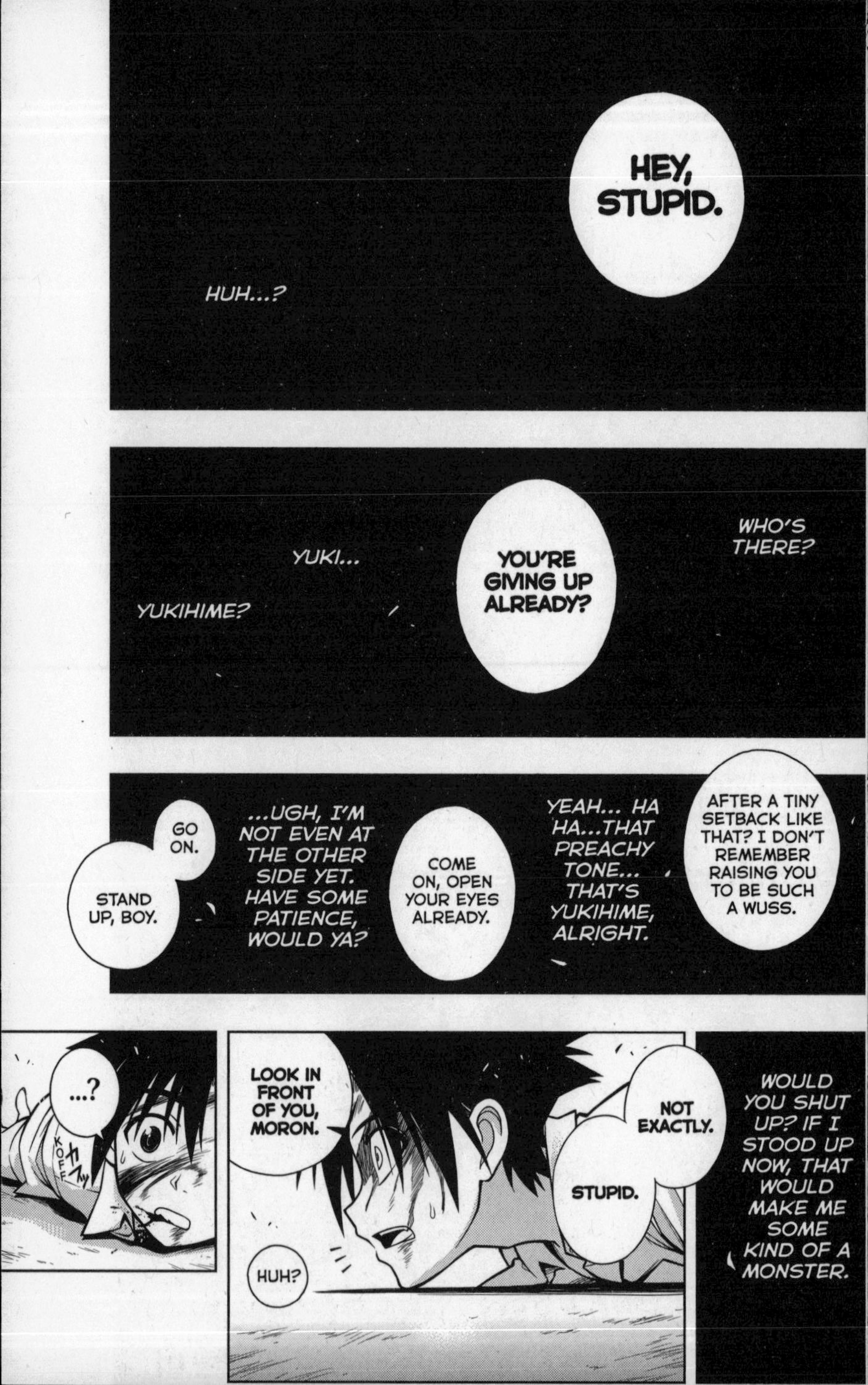
HEY, STUPID.
HUH...?
WHO'S THERE?
YOU'RE GIVING UP ALREADY?
YUKI...
YUKIHIME?
AFTER A TINY SETBACK LIKE THAT? I DON'T REMEMBER RAISING YOU TO BE SUCH A WUSS.
YEAH... HA HA...THAT PREACHY TONE... THAT'S YUKIHIME, ALRIGHT.
COME ON, OPEN YOUR EYES ALREADY.
...UGH, I'M NOT EVEN AT THE OTHER SIDE YET. HAVE SOME PATIENCE, WOULD YA?
GO ON.
STAND UP, BOY.
WOULD YOU SHUT UP? IF I STOOD UP NOW, THAT WOULD MAKE ME SOME KIND OF A MONSTER.
NOT EXACTLY.
STUPID.
LOOK IN FRONT OF YOU, MORON.
HUH?
...?
KOFF

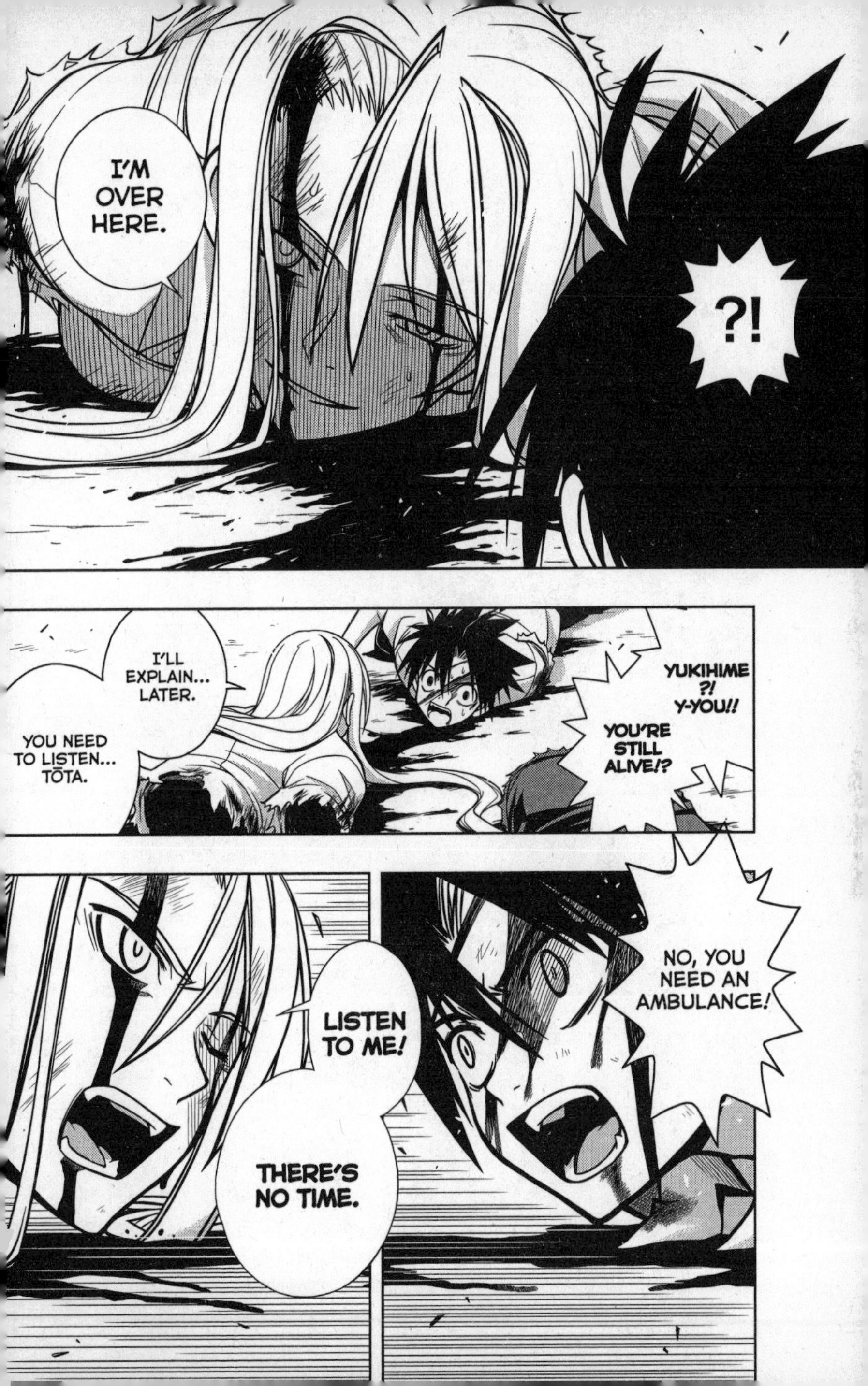
I'M OVER HERE.
?!
YUKIHIME ?! Y-YOU!!
YOU'RE STILL ALIVE!?
I'LL EXPLAIN... LATER.
YOU NEED TO LISTEN... TŌTA.
NO, YOU NEED AN AMBULANCE!
LISTEN TO ME!
THERE'S NO TIME.

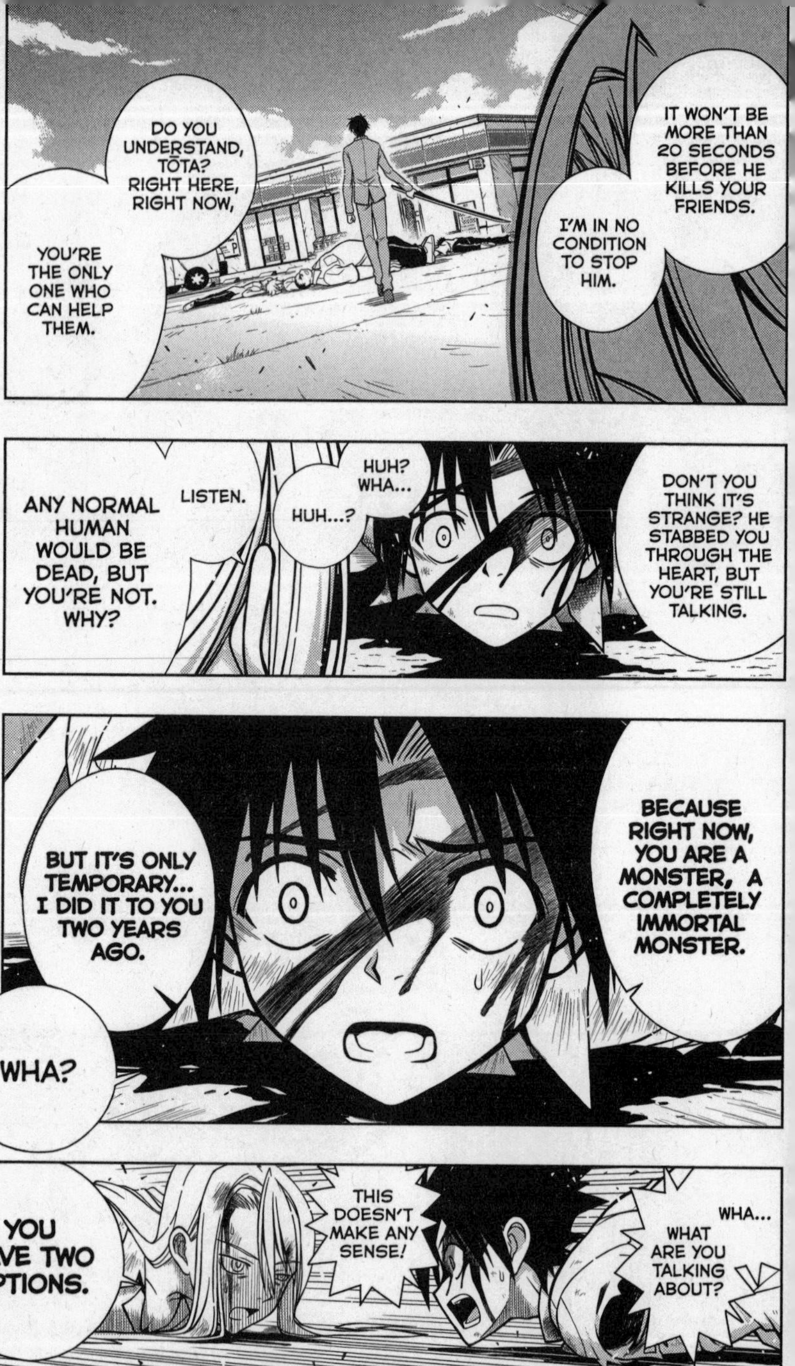
IT WON'T BE MORE THAN 20 SECONDS BEFORE HE KILLS YOUR FRIENDS.
I'M IN NO CONDITION TO STOP HIM.
DO YOU UNDERSTAND, TŌTA? RIGHT HERE, RIGHT NOW,
YOU'RE THE ONLY ONE WHO CAN HELP THEM.
DON'T YOU THINK IT'S STRANGE? HE STABBED YOU THROUGH THE HEART, BUT YOU'RE STILL TALKING.
HUH? WHA...
HUH...?
LISTEN.
ANY NORMAL HUMAN WOULD BE DEAD, BUT YOU'RE NOT. WHY?
BECAUSE RIGHT NOW, YOU ARE A MONSTER, A COMPLETELY IMMORTAL MONSTER.
BUT IT'S ONLY TEMPORARY... I DID IT TO YOU TWO YEARS AGO.
WHA?
WHA... WHAT ARE YOU TALKING ABOUT?
THIS DOESN'T MAKE ANY SENSE!
YOU HAVE TWO OPTIONS.

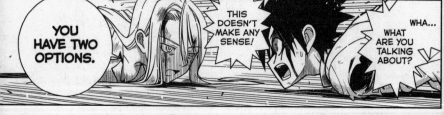

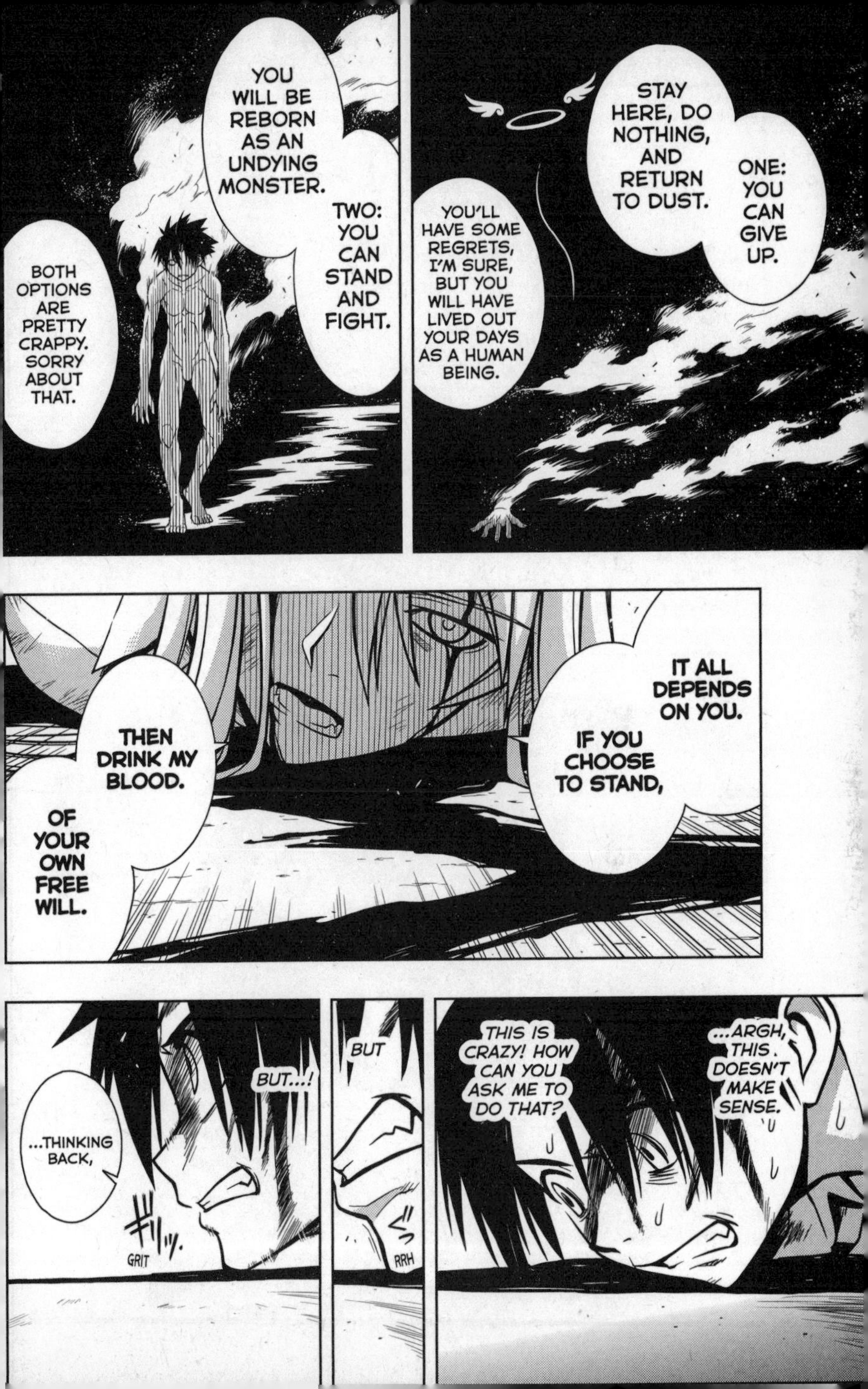
ONE: YOU CAN GIVE UP.
STAY HERE, DO NOTHING, AND RETURN TO DUST.
YOU'LL HAVE SOME REGRETS, I'M SURE, BUT YOU WILL HAVE LIVED OUT YOUR DAYS AS A HUMAN BEING.
TWO: YOU CAN STAND AND FIGHT.
YOU WILL BE REBORN AS AN UNDYING MONSTER.
BOTH OPTIONS ARE PRETTY CRAPPY. SORRY ABOUT THAT.
IT ALL DEPENDS ON YOU.
IF YOU CHOOSE TO STAND,
THEN DRINK MY BLOOD.
OF YOUR OWN FREE WILL.
...ARGH, THIS DOESN'T MAKE SENSE.
THIS IS CRAZY! HOW CAN YOU ASK ME TO DO THAT?
BUT
RRH
BUT...!
...THINKING BACK,
GRIT

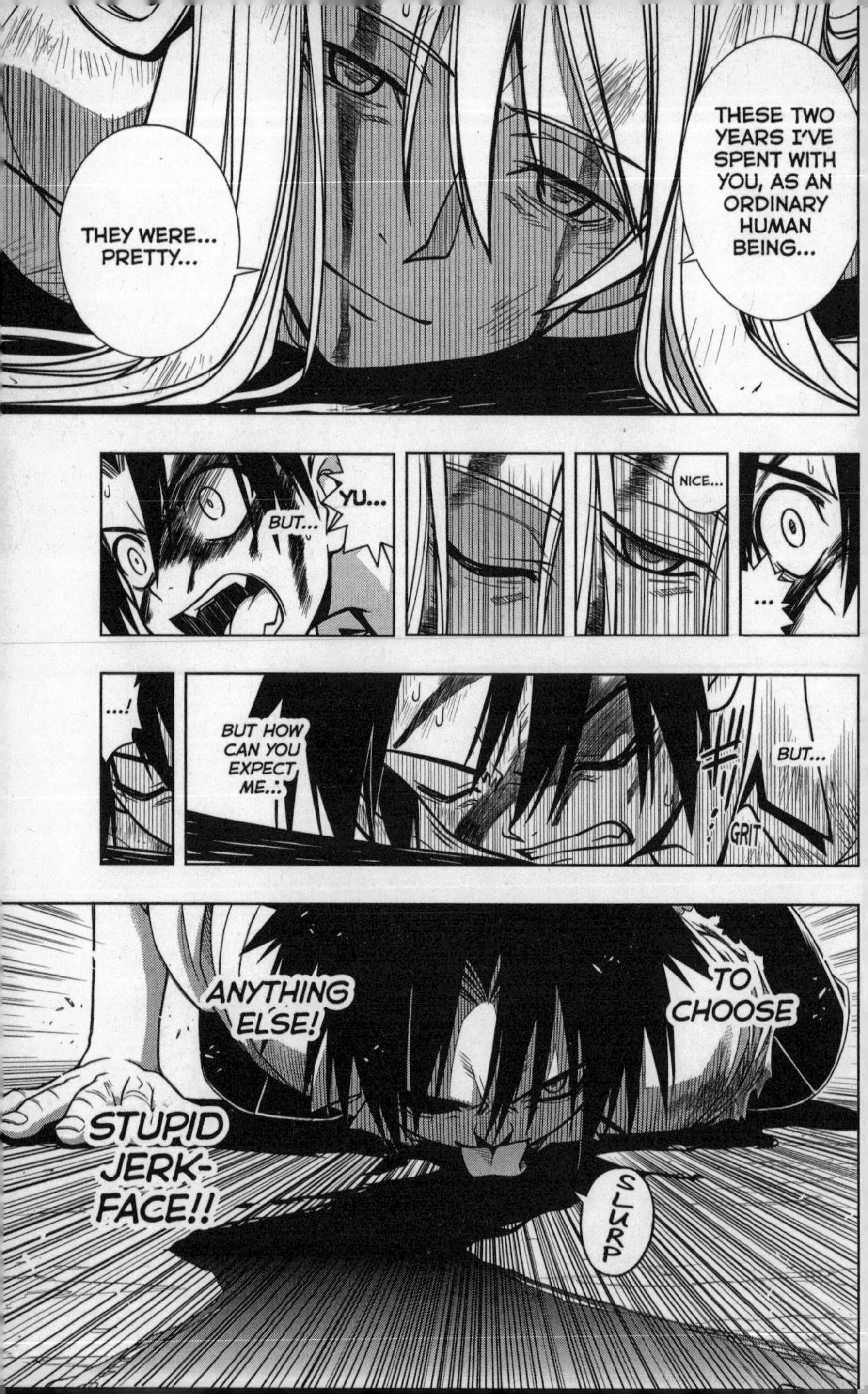
THESE TWO YEARS I'VE SPENT WITH YOU, AS AN ORDINARY HUMAN BEING...
THEY WERE... PRETTY...
...
NICE...
YU...
BUT...
BUT...
GRIT
BUT HOW CAN YOU EXPECT ME...
...!
TO CHOOSE
ANYTHING ELSE!
SLURP
STUPID JERK-FACE!!

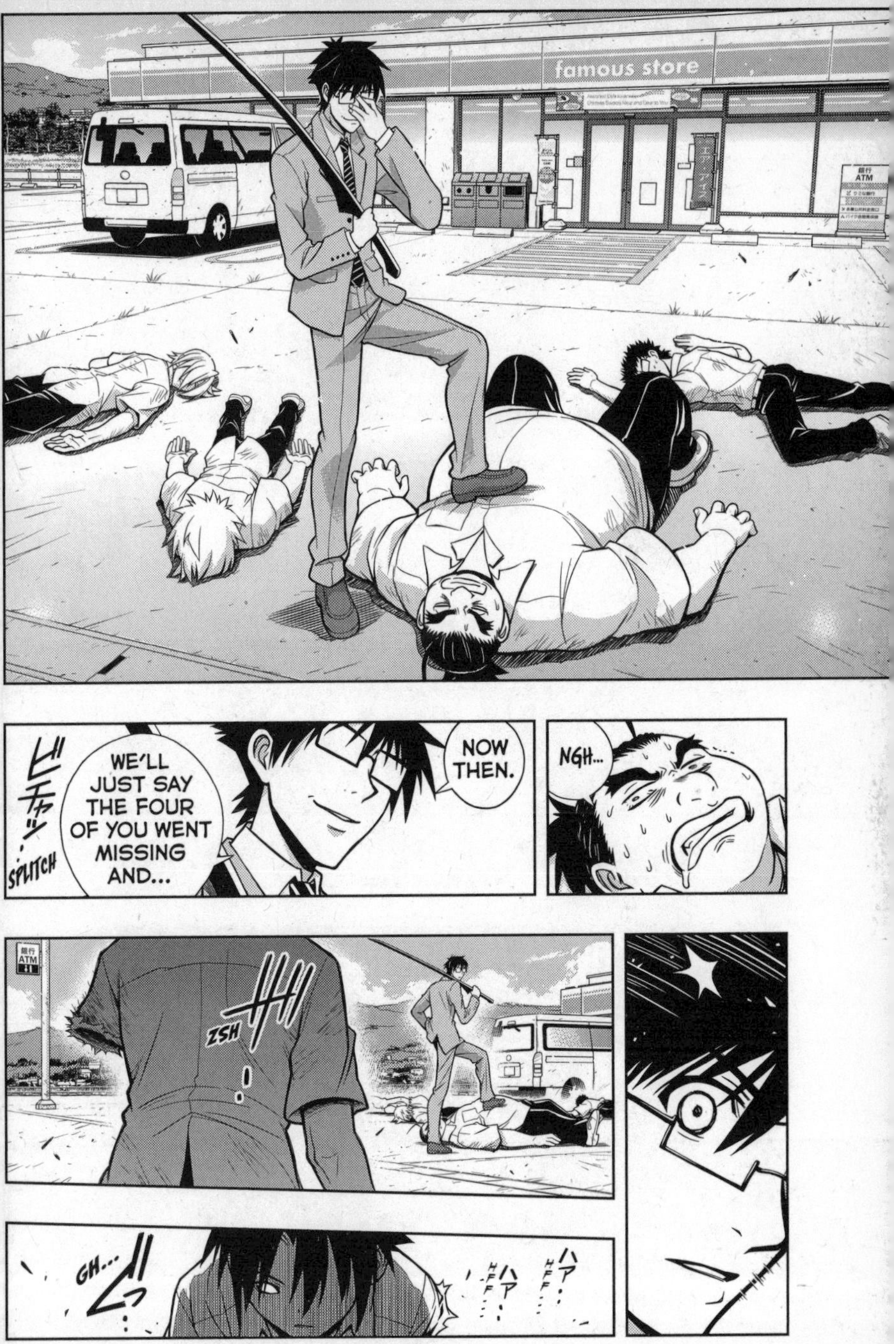
famous store
銀行
ATM
NGH...
NOW THEN.
WE'LL JUST SAY THE FOUR OF YOU WENT MISSING AND...
ビチャッ
SPLITCH
銀行
ATM
ZSH
ハア
HFF...
ハア
HFF...
GH...
ぐっ

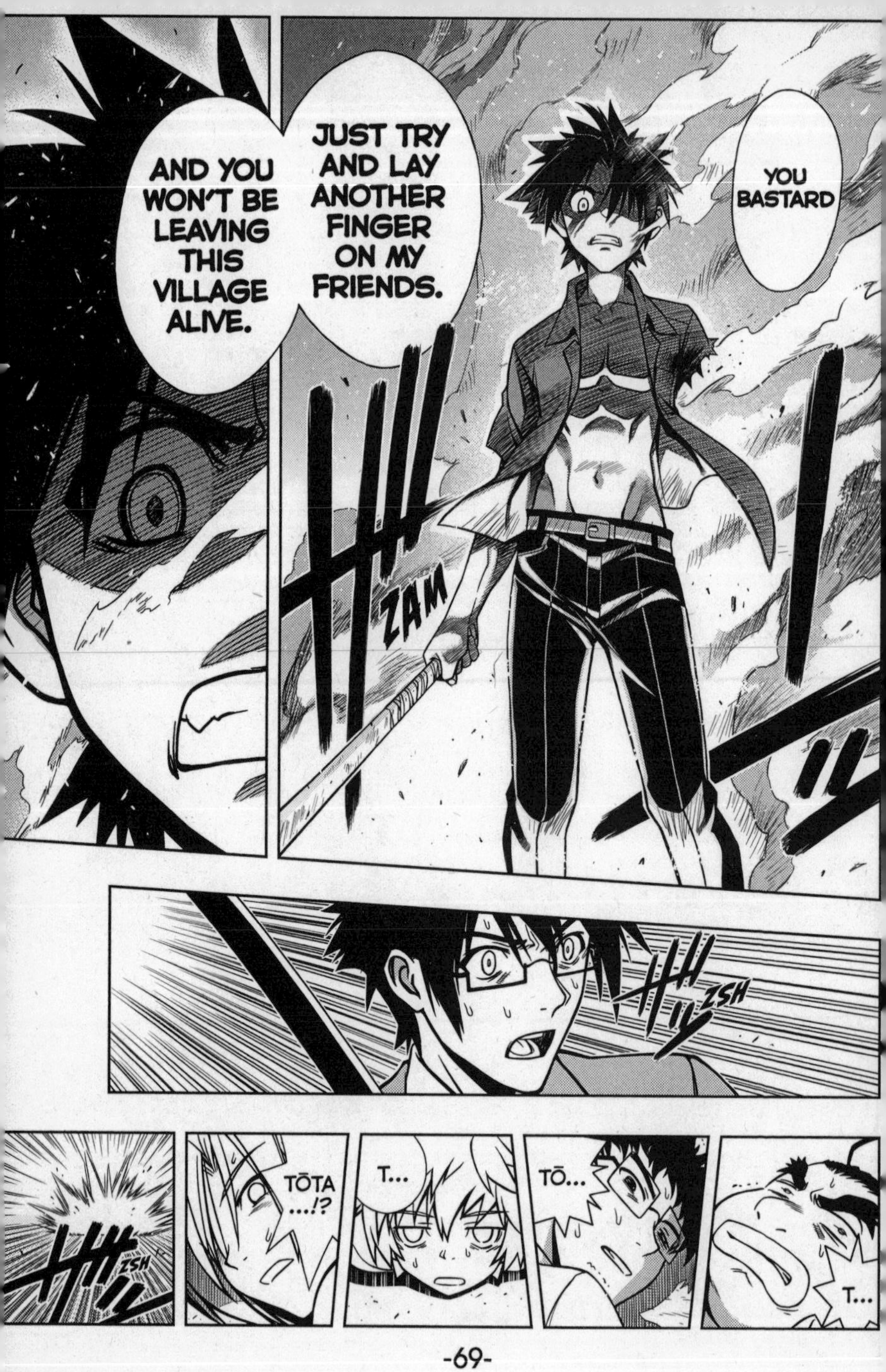
YOU BASTARD
JUST TRY AND LAY ANOTHER FINGER ON MY FRIENDS.
AND YOU WON'T BE LEAVING THIS VILLAGE ALIVE.
ZAM
ZSH
...
T...
TŌ...
T...
TŌTA ...!?
ZSH

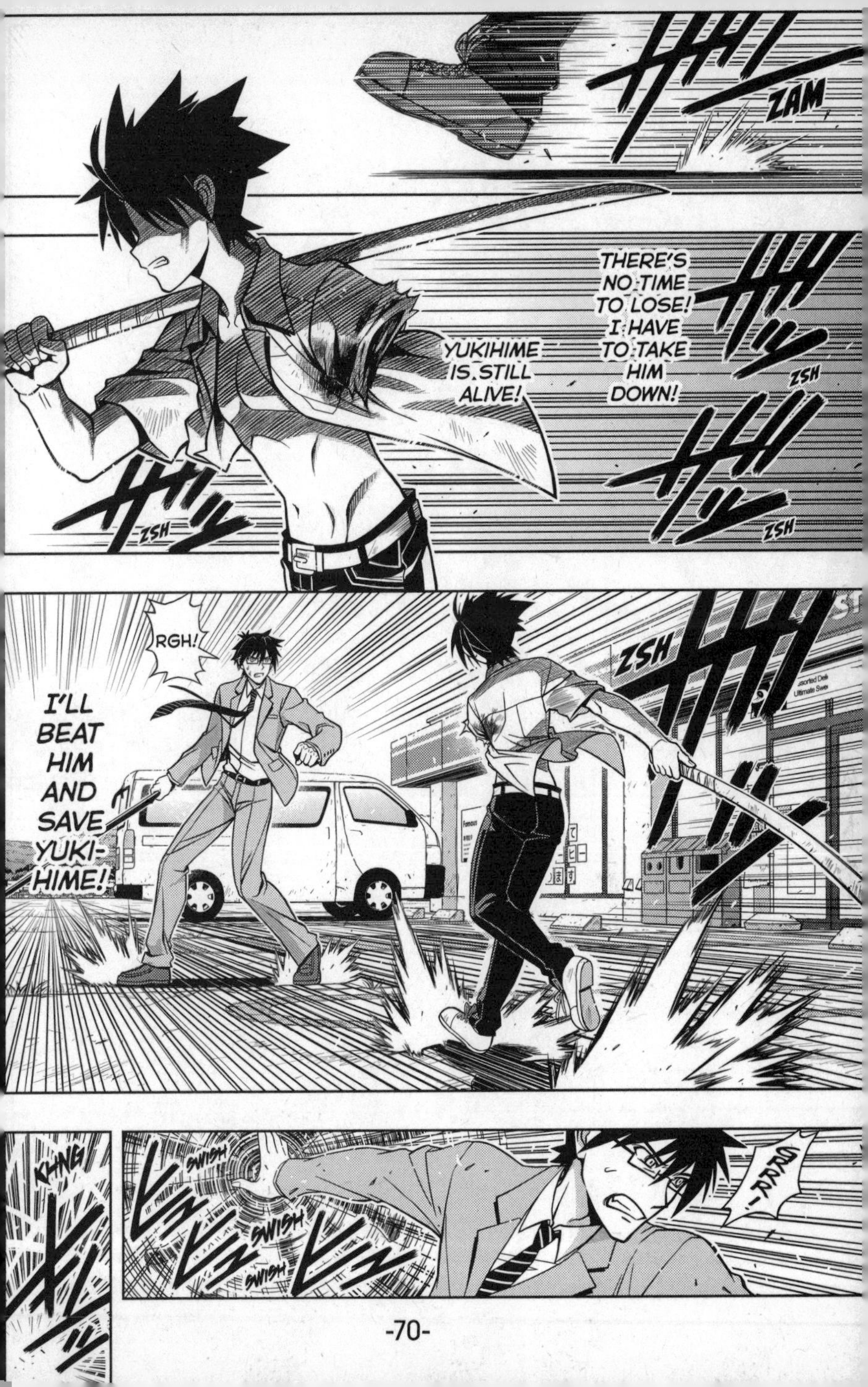
ZAM
THERE'S NO TIME TO LOSE! I HAVE TO TAKE HIM DOWN!
ZSH
ZSH
YUKIHIME IS STILL ALIVE!
ZSH
ZSH
RGH!
I'LL BEAT HIM AND SAVE YUKI-HIME!
GRRR!
SWISH
SWISH
SWISH
KLING

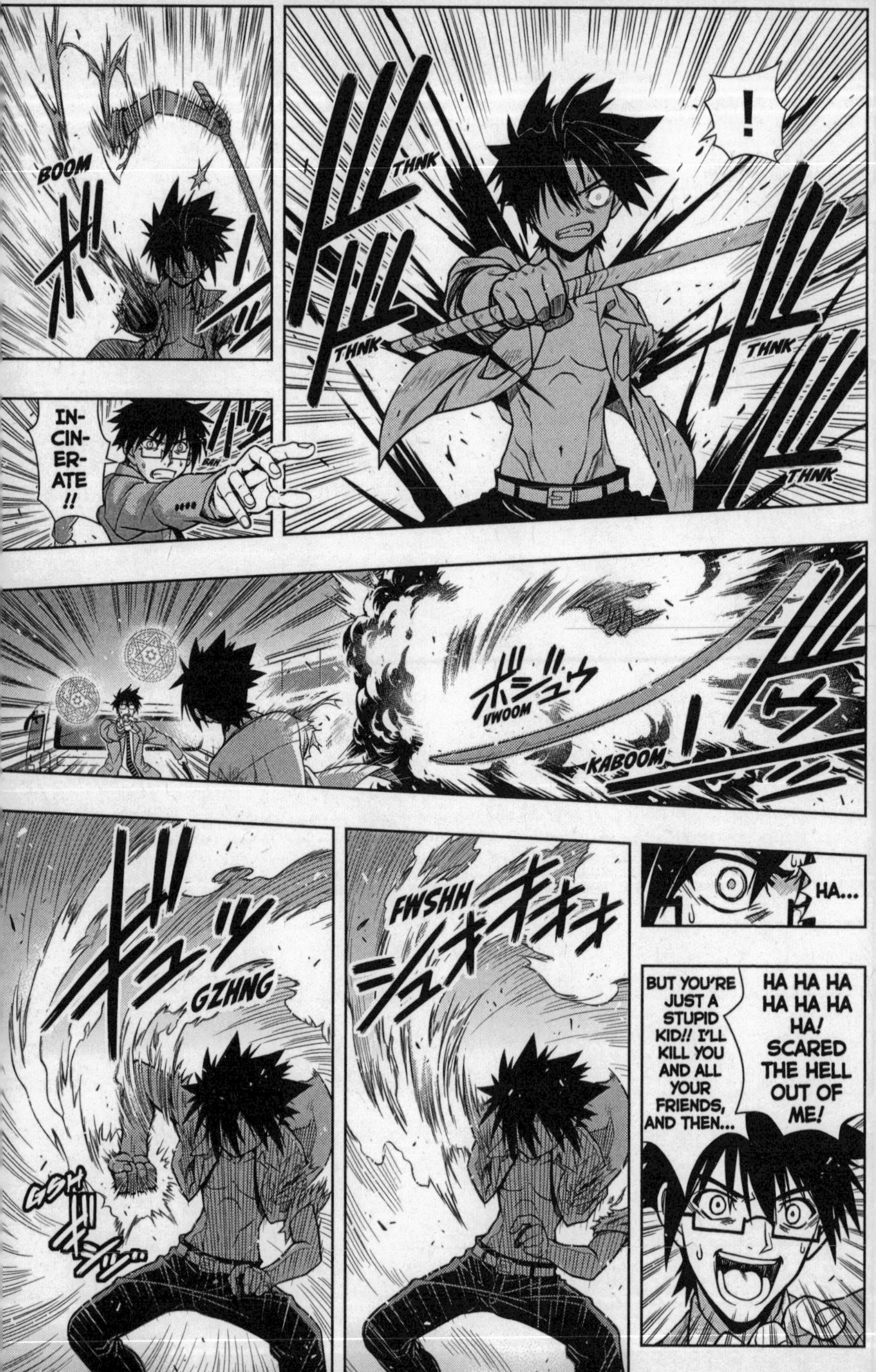

!
THNK
THNK
THNK
THNK
BOOM
!!
IN-CIN-ER-ATE!!
BAH
VWOOM
KABOOM
HA...
HA HA HA HA HA HA HA! SCARED THE HELL OUT OF ME!
BUT YOU'RE JUST A STUPID KID!! I'LL KILL YOU AND ALL YOUR FRIENDS, AND THEN...
FWSHH
GZHNG
GSH

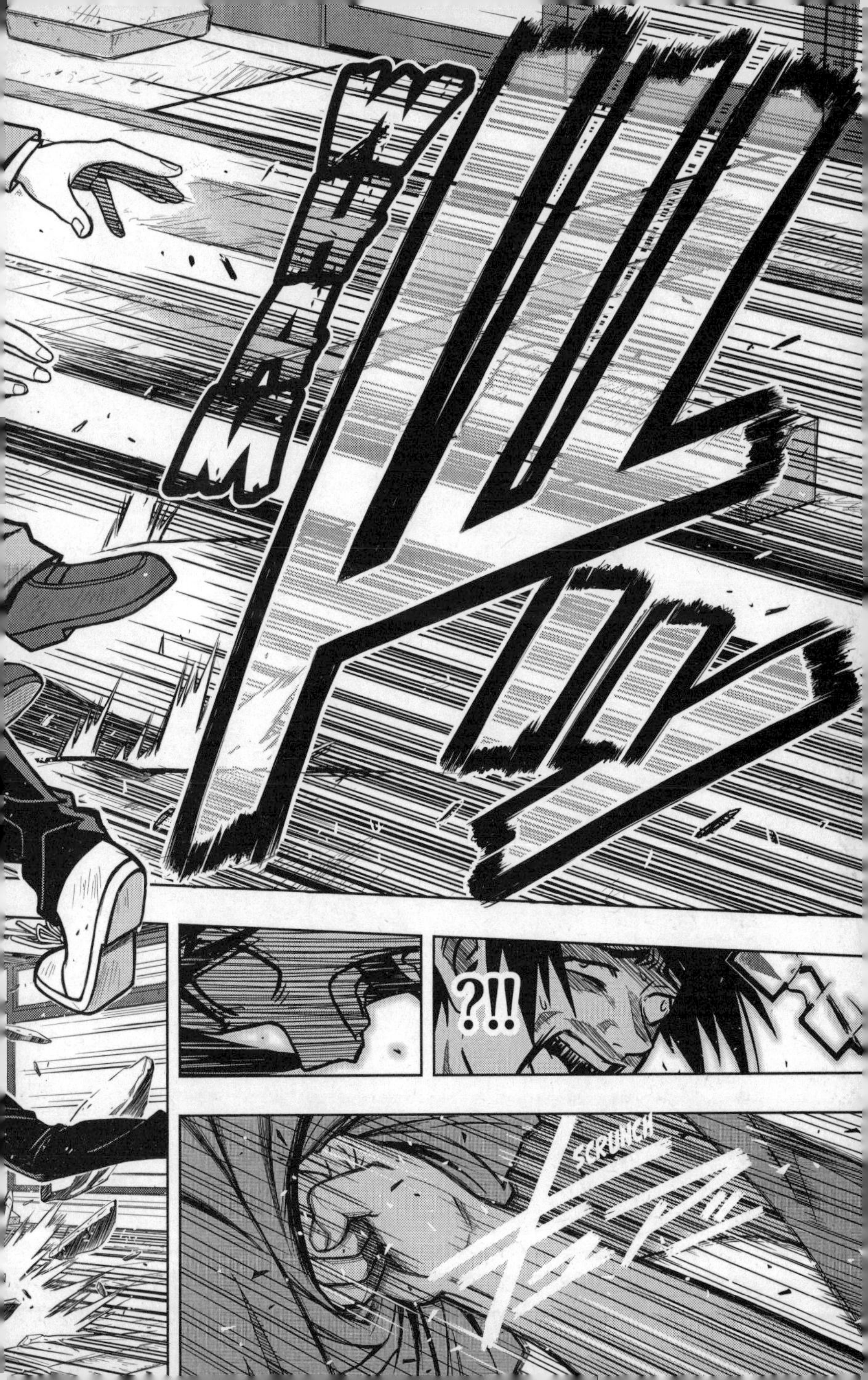
WHAM
?!!
SCRUNCH

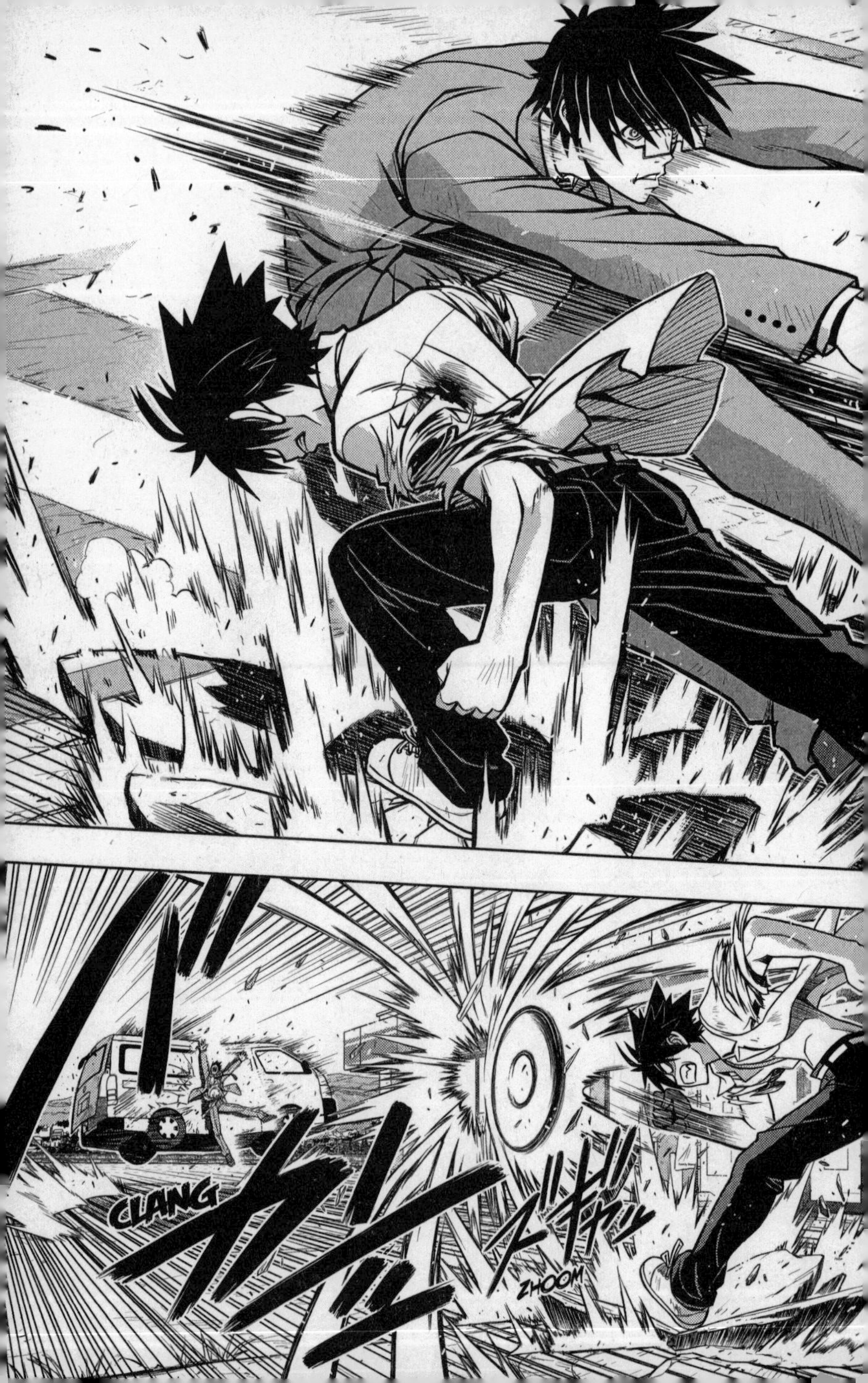

....
CLANG
ZHOOM

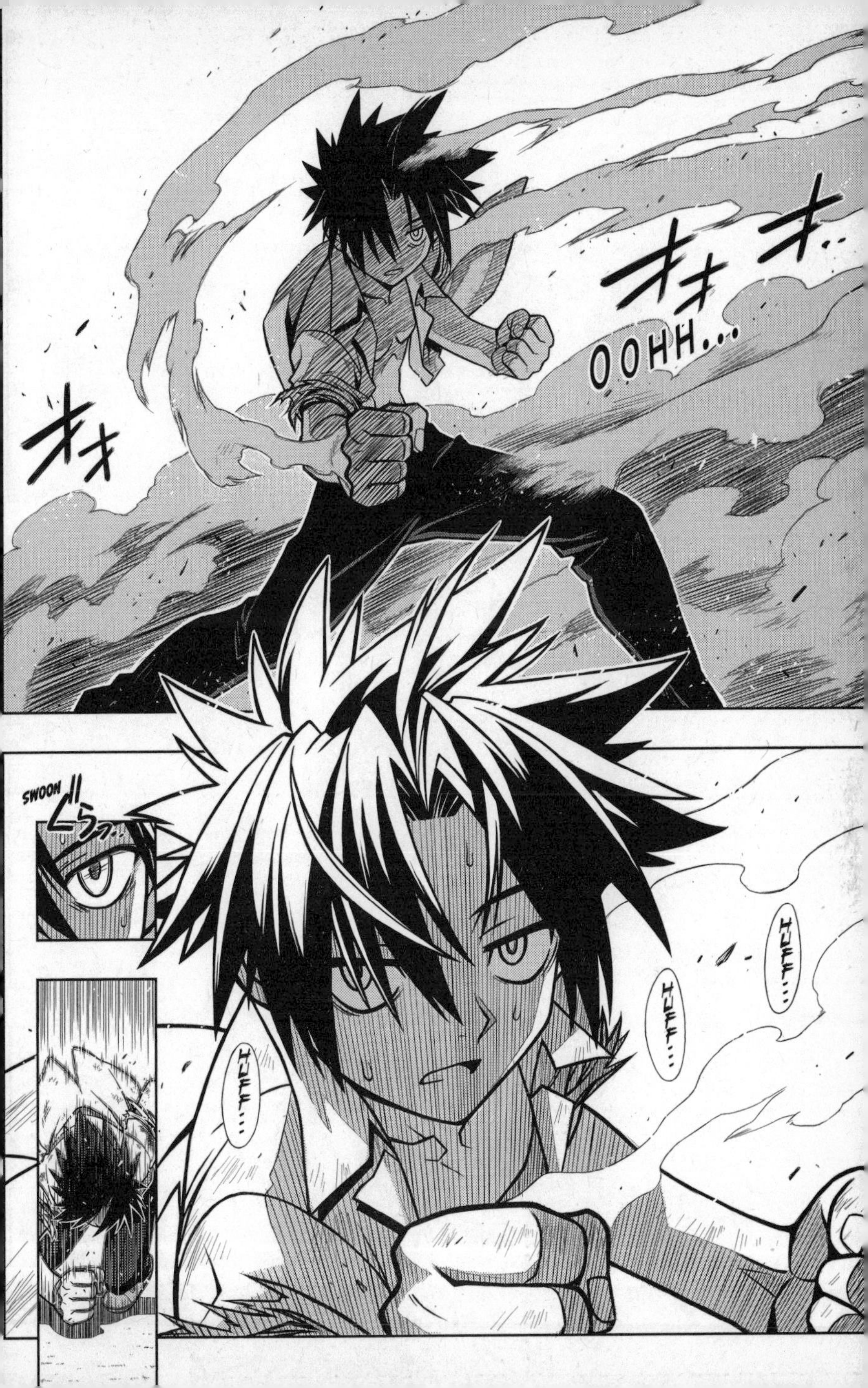
オォォ…
OOHH...
オォ
HUFF...
HUFF...
HUFF...
SWOON
くらっ…

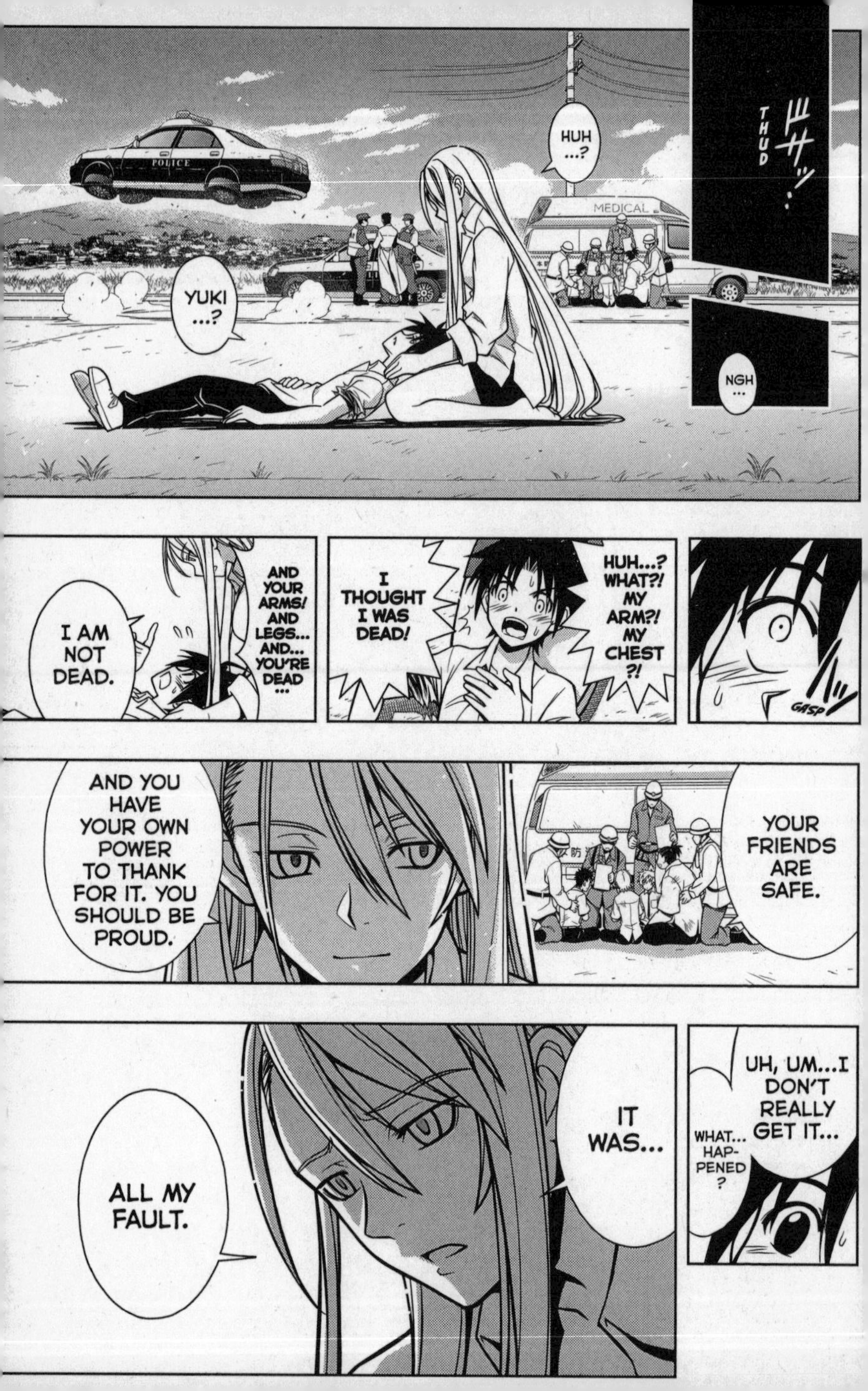
ドサッ
THUD
NGH...
HUH ...?
MEDICAL
POLICE
YUKI ...?
GASP
HUH...? WHAT?! MY ARM?! MY CHEST ?!
I THOUGHT I WAS DEAD!
AND YOUR ARMS! AND LEGS... AND... YOU'RE DEAD ...
I AM NOT DEAD.
YOUR FRIENDS ARE SAFE.
AND YOU HAVE YOUR OWN POWER TO THANK FOR IT. YOU SHOULD BE PROUD.
UH, UM...I DON'T REALLY GET IT...
WHAT... HAP-PENED ?
IT WAS...
ALL MY FAULT.

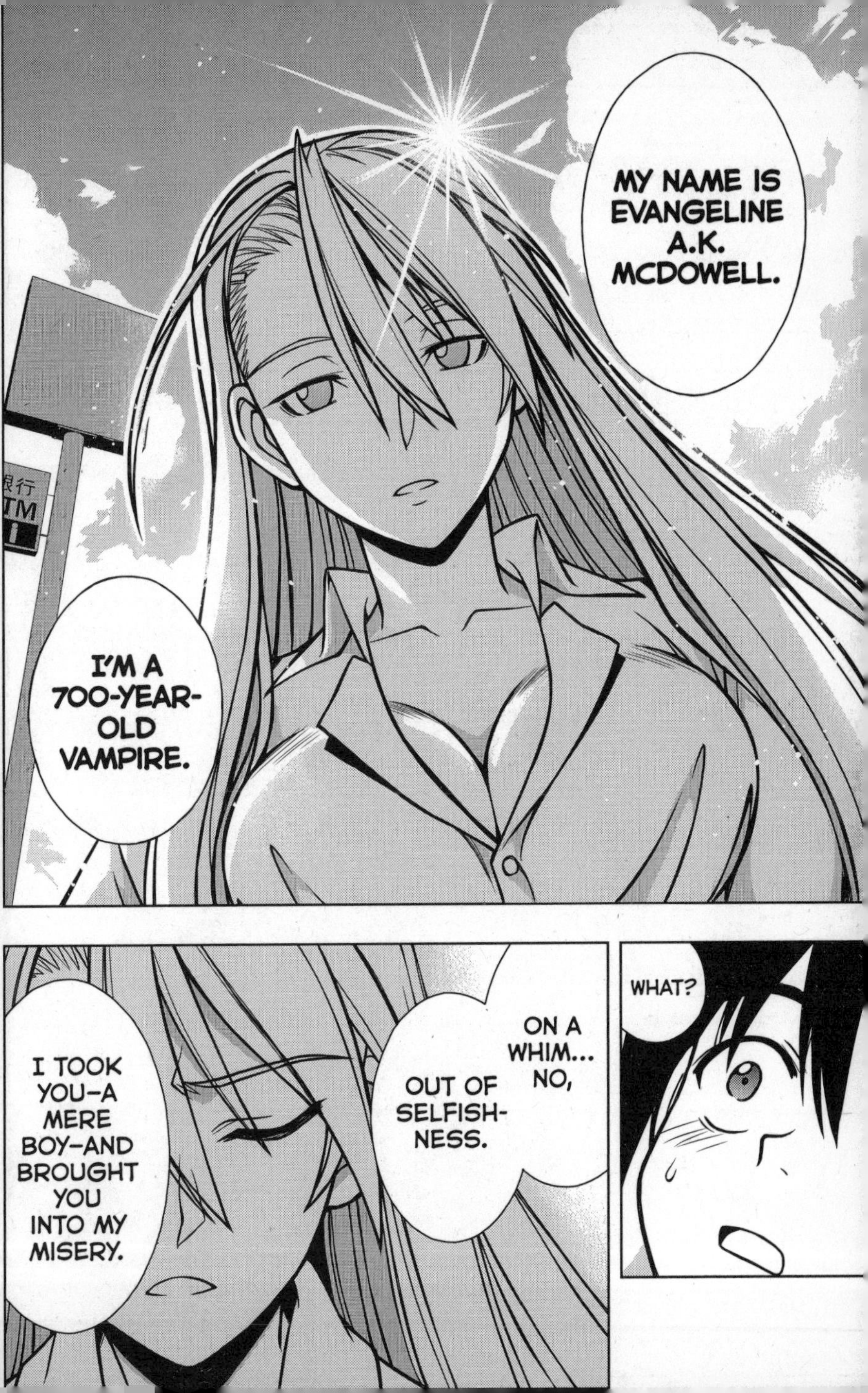
MY NAME IS EVANGELINE A.K. MCDOWELL.
I'M A 700-YEAR-OLD VAMPIRE.
WHAT?
ON A WHIM... NO,
OUT OF SELFISH-NESS.
I TOOK YOU—A MERE BOY—AND BROUGHT YOU INTO MY MISERY.

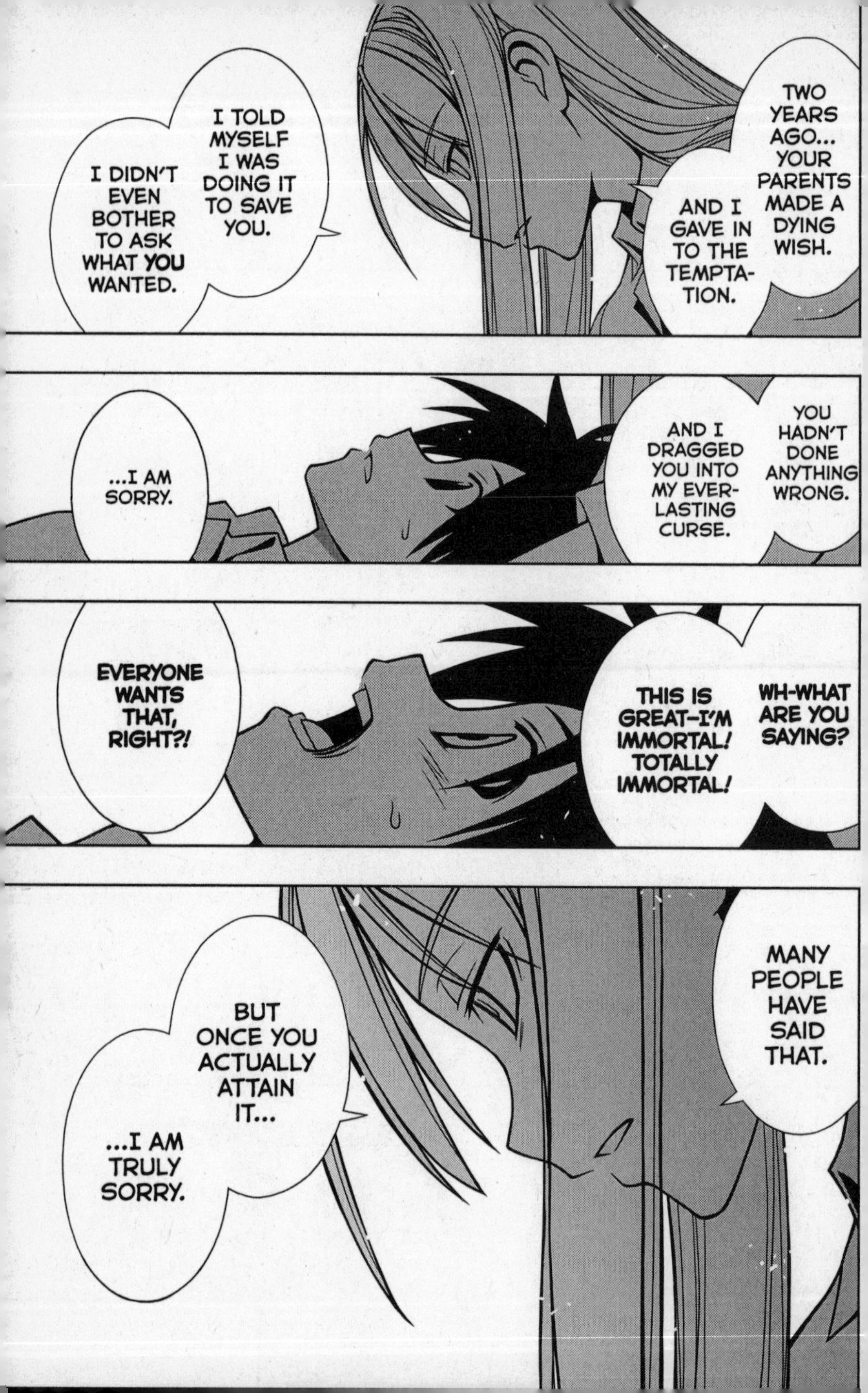
TWO YEARS AGO... YOUR PARENTS MADE A DYING WISH.
AND I GAVE IN TO THE TEMPTATION.
I TOLD MYSELF I WAS DOING IT TO SAVE YOU.
I DIDN'T EVEN BOTHER TO ASK WHAT YOU WANTED.
YOU HADN'T DONE ANYTHING WRONG.
AND I DRAGGED YOU INTO MY EVERLASTING CURSE.
...I AM SORRY.
WH-WHAT ARE YOU SAYING?
THIS IS GREAT—I'M IMMORTAL! TOTALLY IMMORTAL!
EVERYONE WANTS THAT, RIGHT?!
MANY PEOPLE HAVE SAID THAT.
BUT ONCE YOU ACTUALLY ATTAIN IT...
...I AM TRULY SORRY.

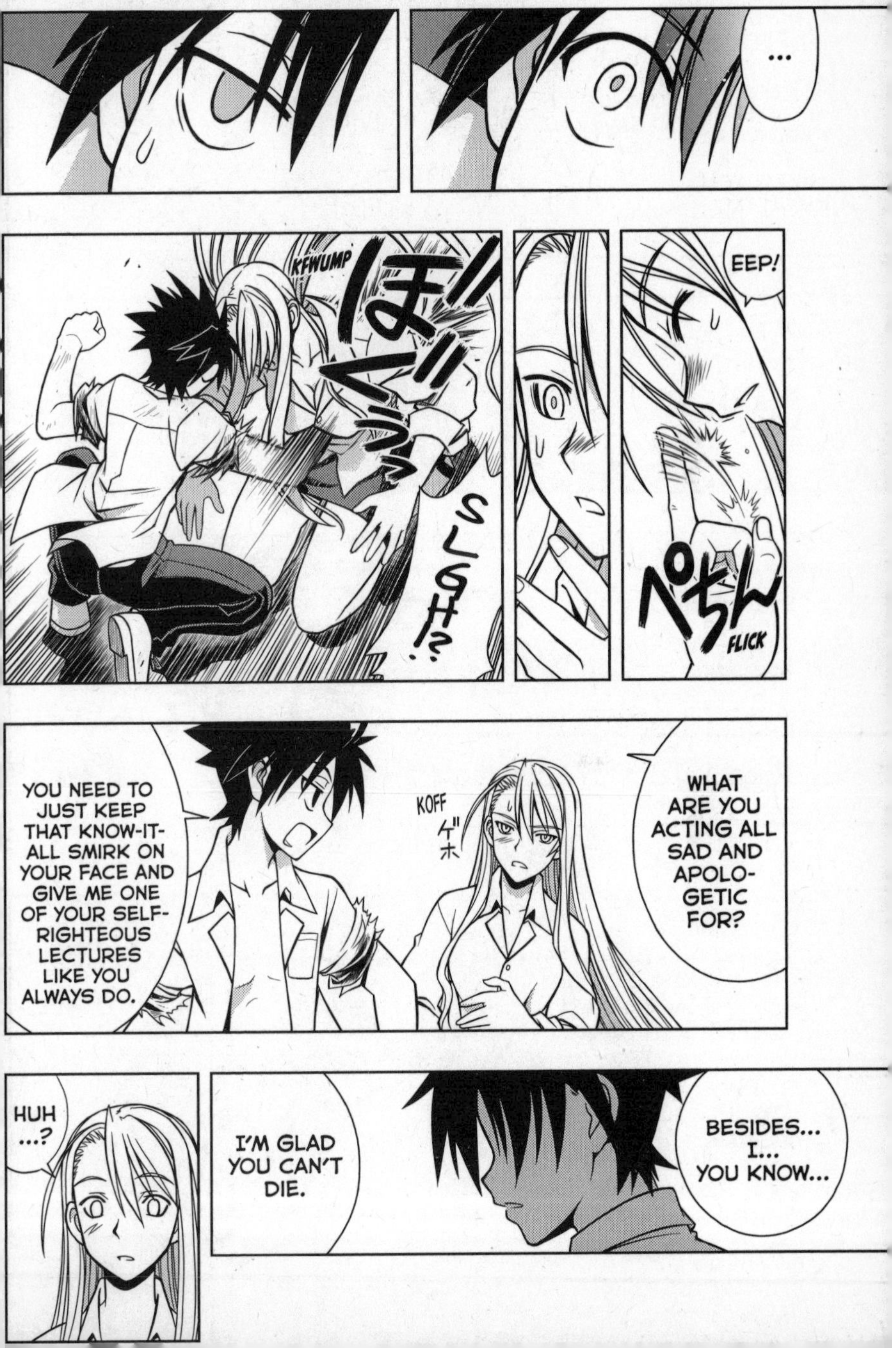
...
EEP!
ぺちん
FLICK
KFWUMP
ぼくぅっ
SLGH!?
WHAT ARE YOU ACTING ALL SAD AND APOLO-GETIC FOR?
KOFF
ゲホ
YOU NEED TO JUST KEEP THAT KNOW-IT-ALL SMIRK ON YOUR FACE AND GIVE ME ONE OF YOUR SELF-RIGHTEOUS LECTURES LIKE YOU ALWAYS DO.
BESIDES... I... YOU KNOW...
I'M GLAD YOU CAN'T DIE.
HUH ...?

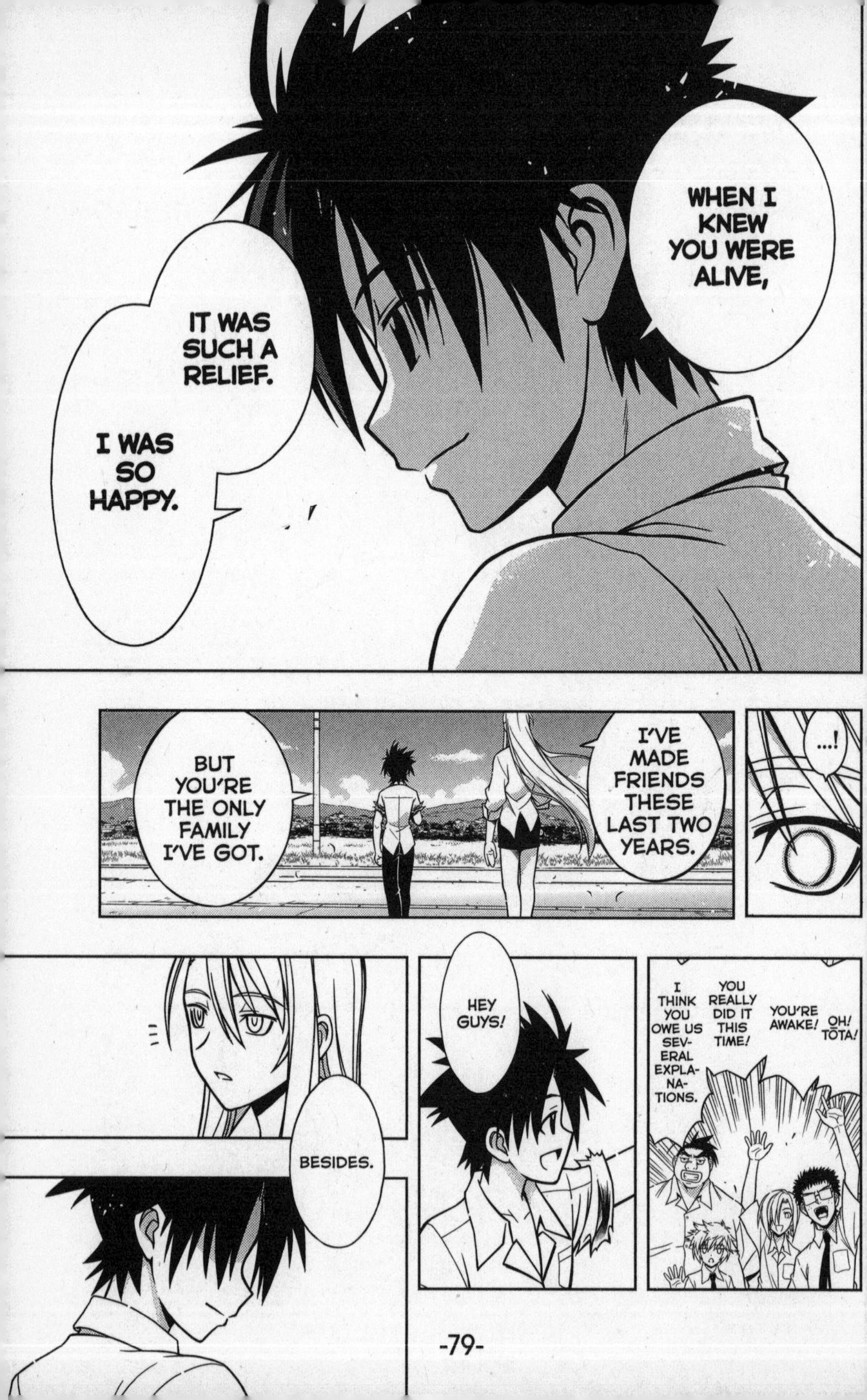
WHEN I KNEW YOU WERE ALIVE,
IT WAS SUCH A RELIEF.
I WAS SO HAPPY.
...!
I'VE MADE FRIENDS THESE LAST TWO YEARS.
BUT YOU'RE THE ONLY FAMILY I'VE GOT.
OH! TŌTA!
YOU'RE AWAKE!
YOU REALLY DID IT THIS TIME!
I THINK YOU OWE US SEV-ERAL EXPLA-NA-TIONS.
HEY GUYS!
BESIDES.

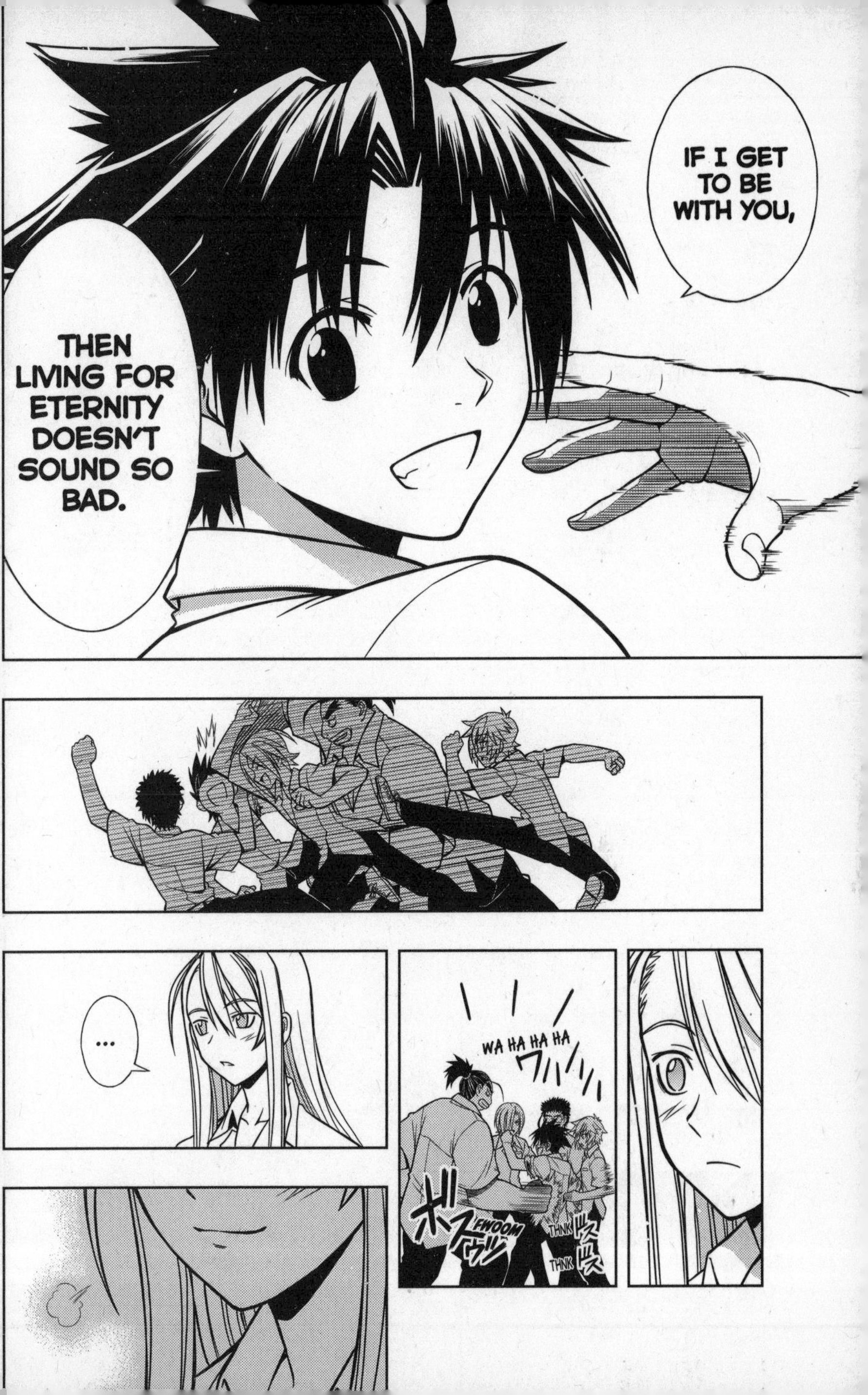
IF I GET TO BE WITH YOU,
THEN LIVING FOR ETERNITY DOESN'T SOUND SO BAD.
WA HA HA HA
FWOOM
THNK
THNK
...

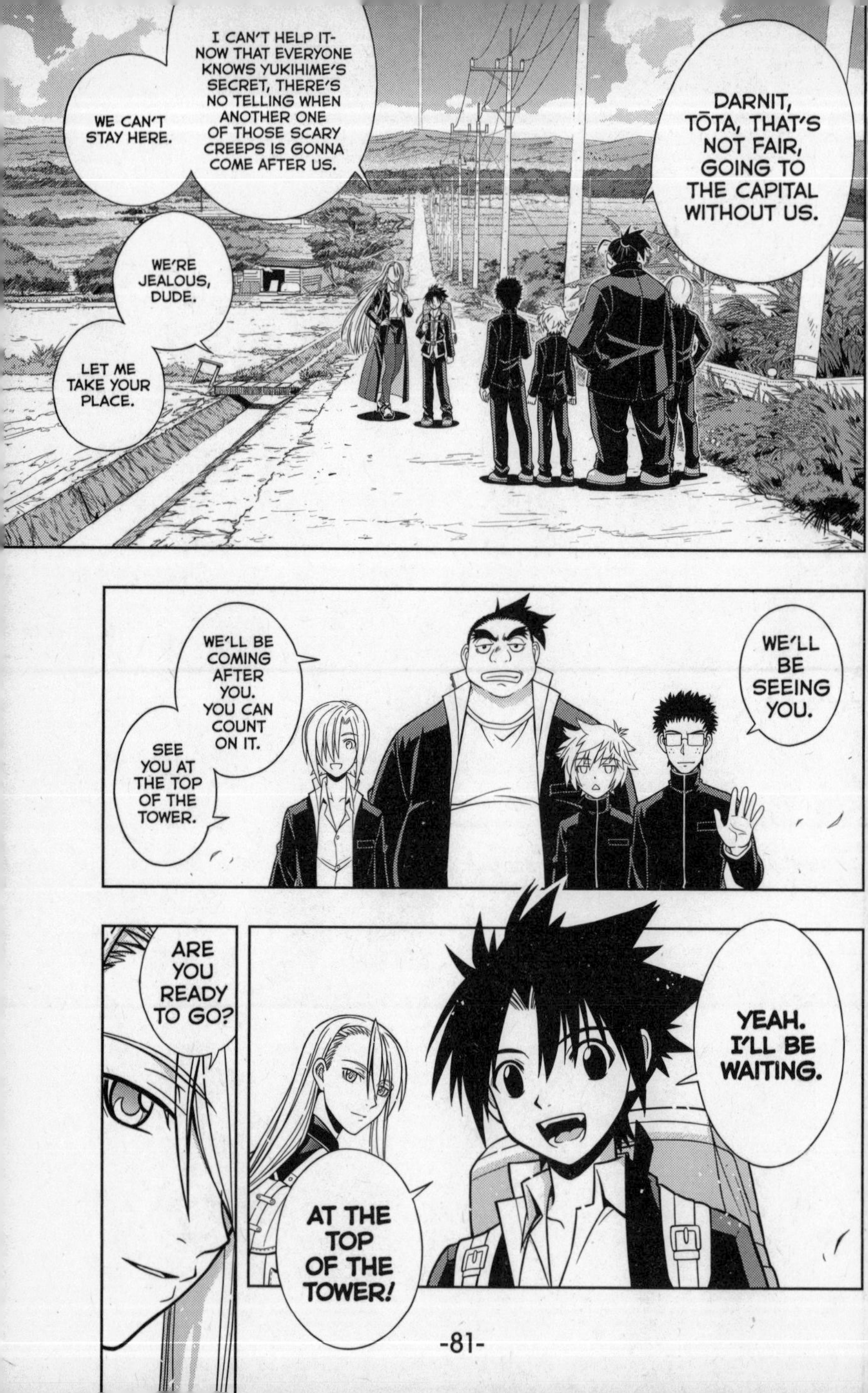
DARNIT, TŌTA, THAT'S NOT FAIR, GOING TO THE CAPITAL WITHOUT US.
I CAN'T HELP IT- NOW THAT EVERYONE KNOWS YUKIHIME'S SECRET, THERE'S NO TELLING WHEN ANOTHER ONE OF THOSE SCARY CREEPS IS GONNA COME AFTER US.
WE CAN'T STAY HERE.
WE'RE JEALOUS, DUDE.
LET ME TAKE YOUR PLACE.
WE'LL BE SEEING YOU.
WE'LL BE COMING AFTER YOU. YOU CAN COUNT ON IT.
SEE YOU AT THE TOP OF THE TOWER.
YEAH. I'LL BE WAITING.
AT THE TOP OF THE TOWER!
ARE YOU READY TO GO?

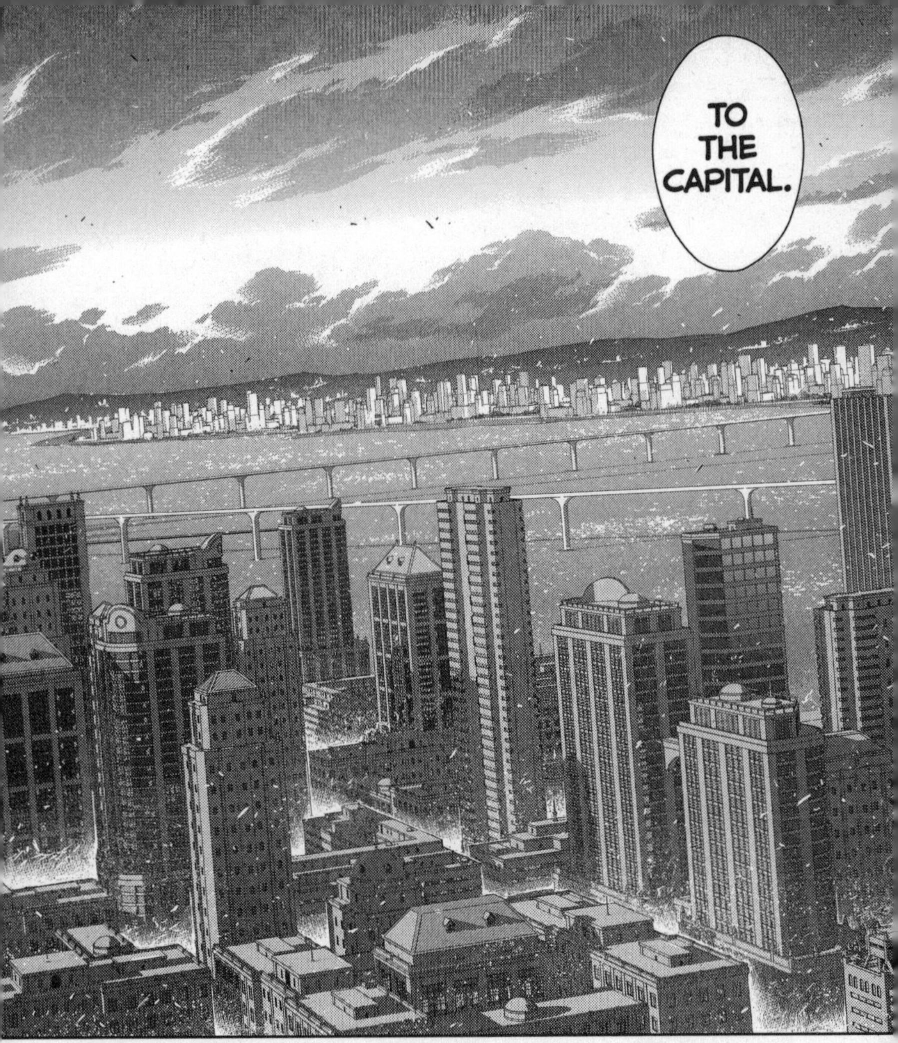
TO THE CAPITAL.

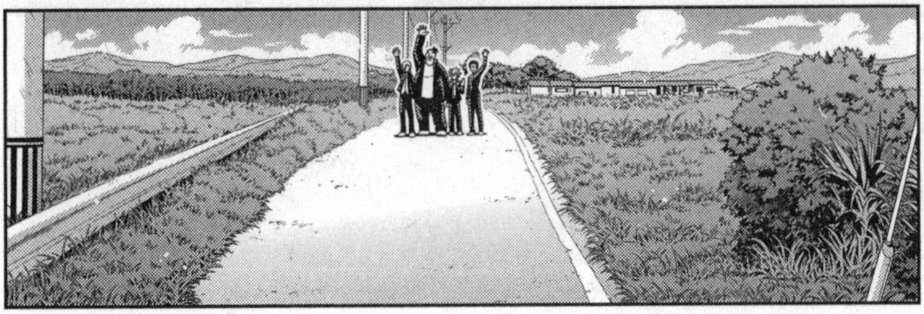

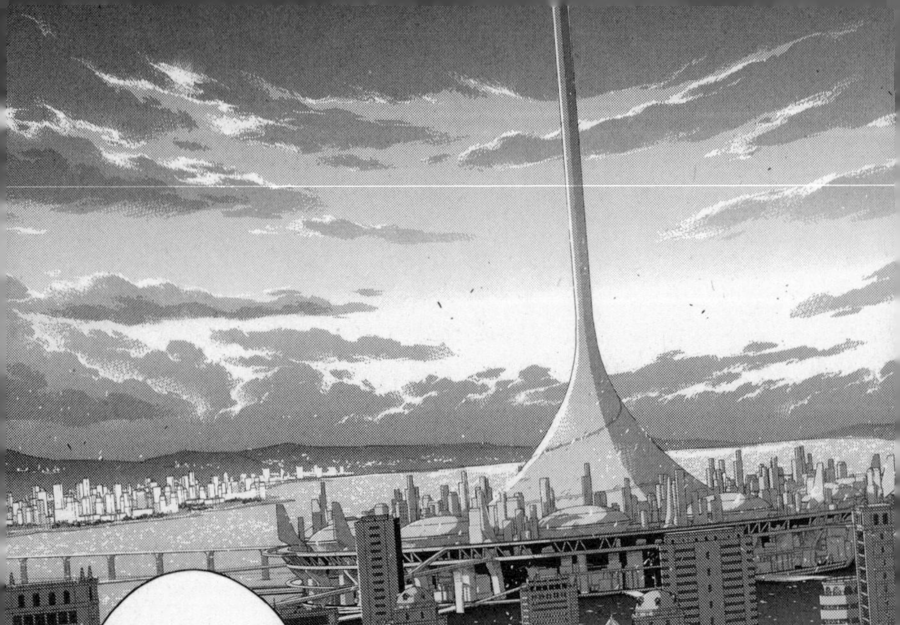
TO AMANO-MIHASHIRA, SHIN-TOKYO*.

*Heaven's Pillar, New Tokyo

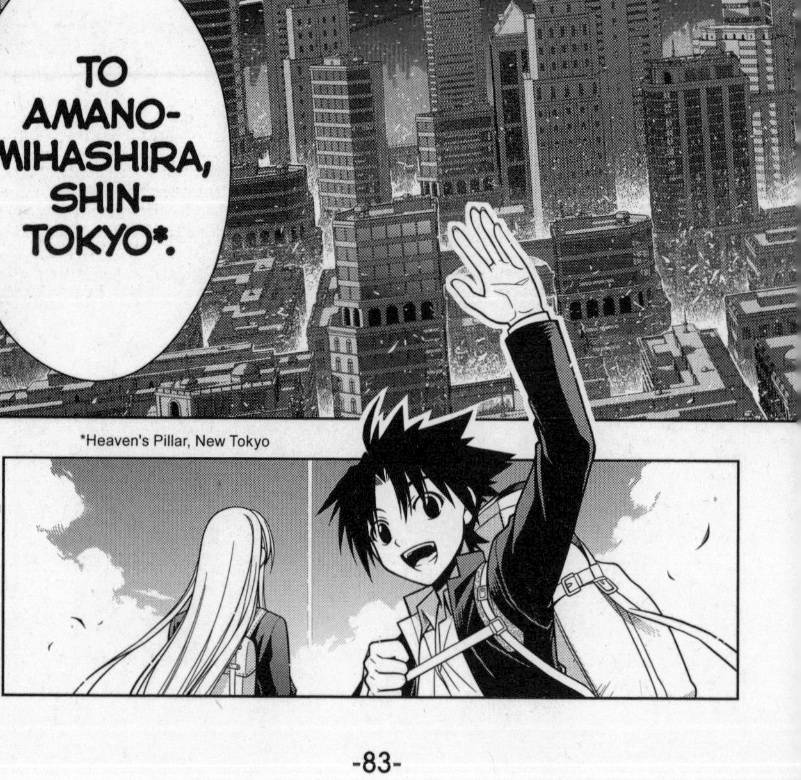

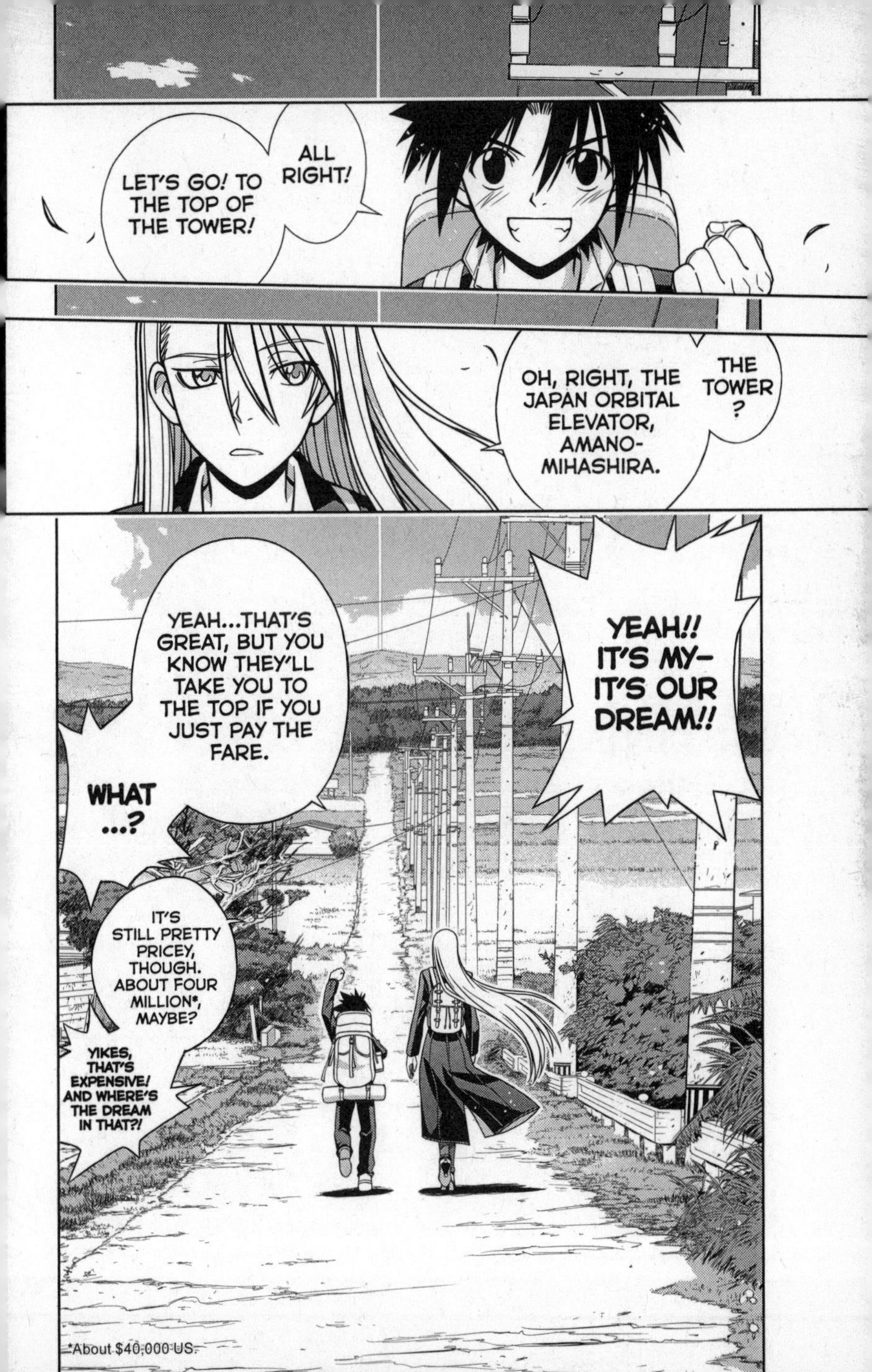
ALL RIGHT!
LET'S GO! TO THE TOP OF THE TOWER!
THE TOWER?
OH, RIGHT, THE JAPAN ORBITAL ELEVATOR, AMANO-MIHASHIRA.
YEAH!! IT'S MY— IT'S OUR DREAM!!
YEAH...THAT'S GREAT, BUT YOU KNOW THEY'LL TAKE YOU TO THE TOP IF YOU JUST PAY THE FARE.
WHAT ...?
IT'S STILL PRETTY PRICEY, THOUGH. ABOUT FOUR MILLION*, MAYBE?
YIKES, THAT'S EXPENSIVE! AND WHERE'S THE DREAM IN THAT?!

*About $40,000 US.

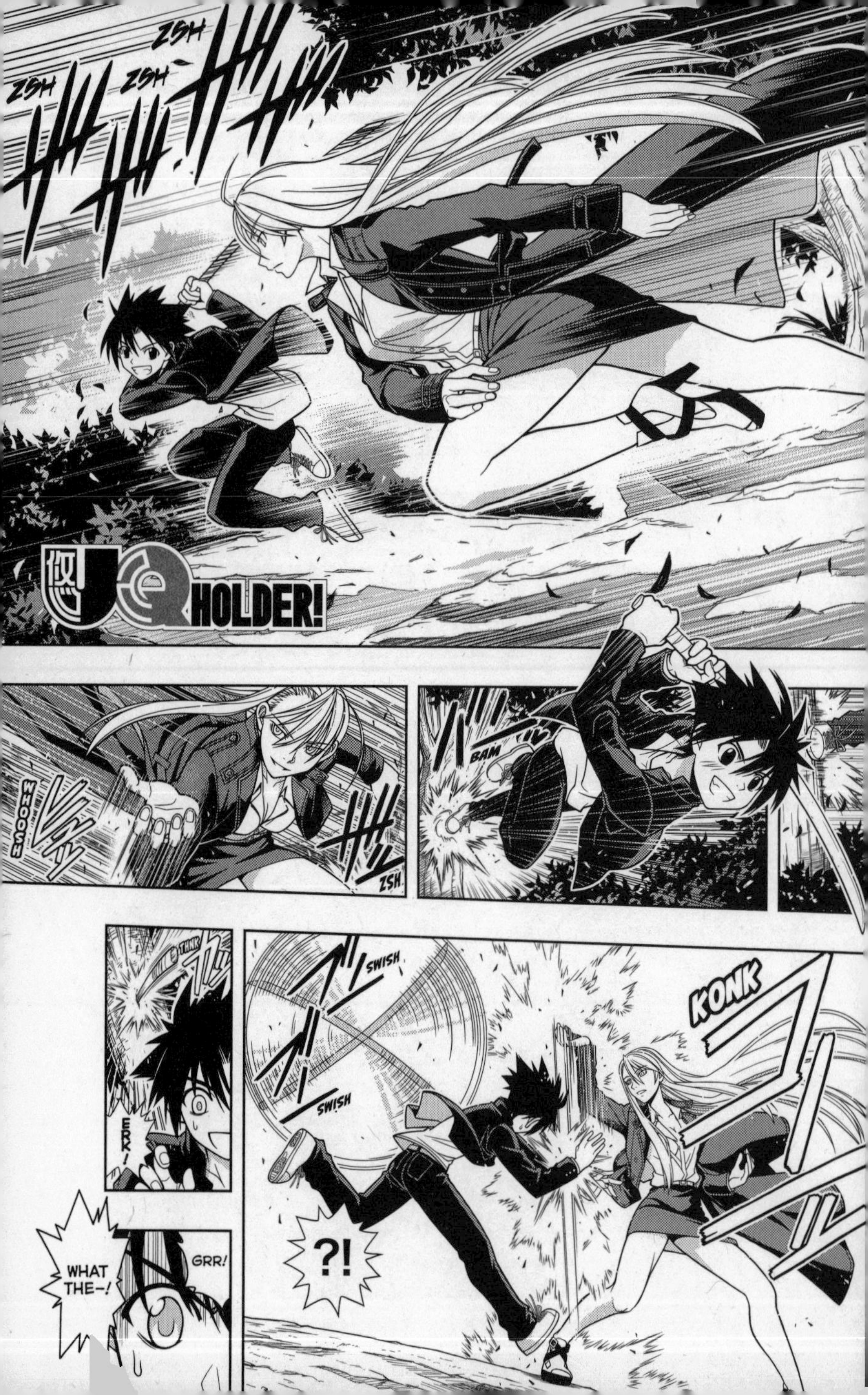
ZSH
ZSH
ZSH
UQ HOLDER!
BAM
WHOOSH
ZSH
KONK
SWISH
SWISH
?!
THNK
ERK!
GRR!
WHAT THE-!

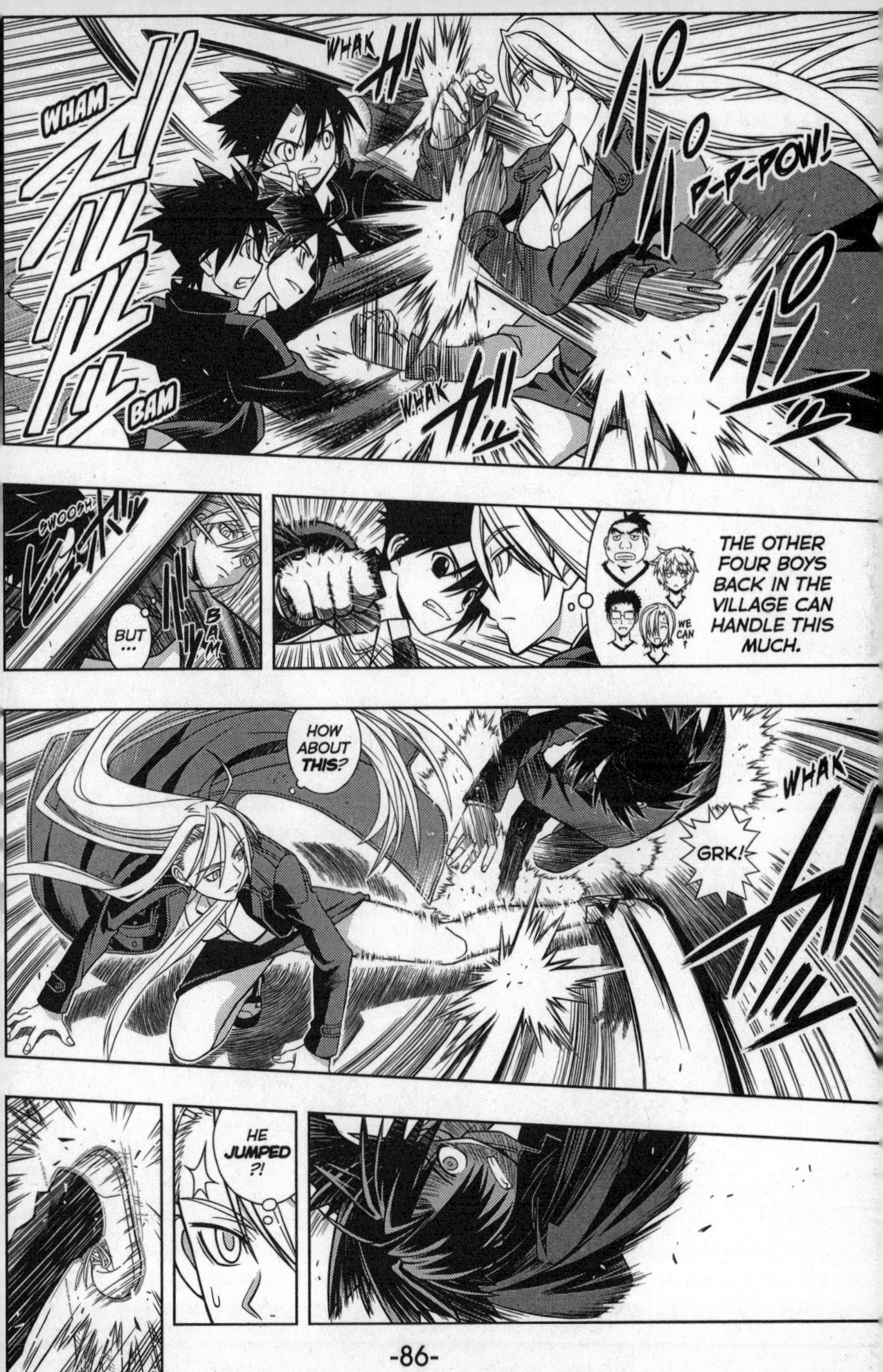
P-P-POW!
WHAK
WHAM
BAM
WHAK
THE OTHER FOUR BOYS BACK IN THE VILLAGE CAN HANDLE THIS MUCH.
WE CAN?
SWOOSH
BAM
BUT ...
WHAK
GRK!
HOW ABOUT THIS?
HE JUMPED ?!

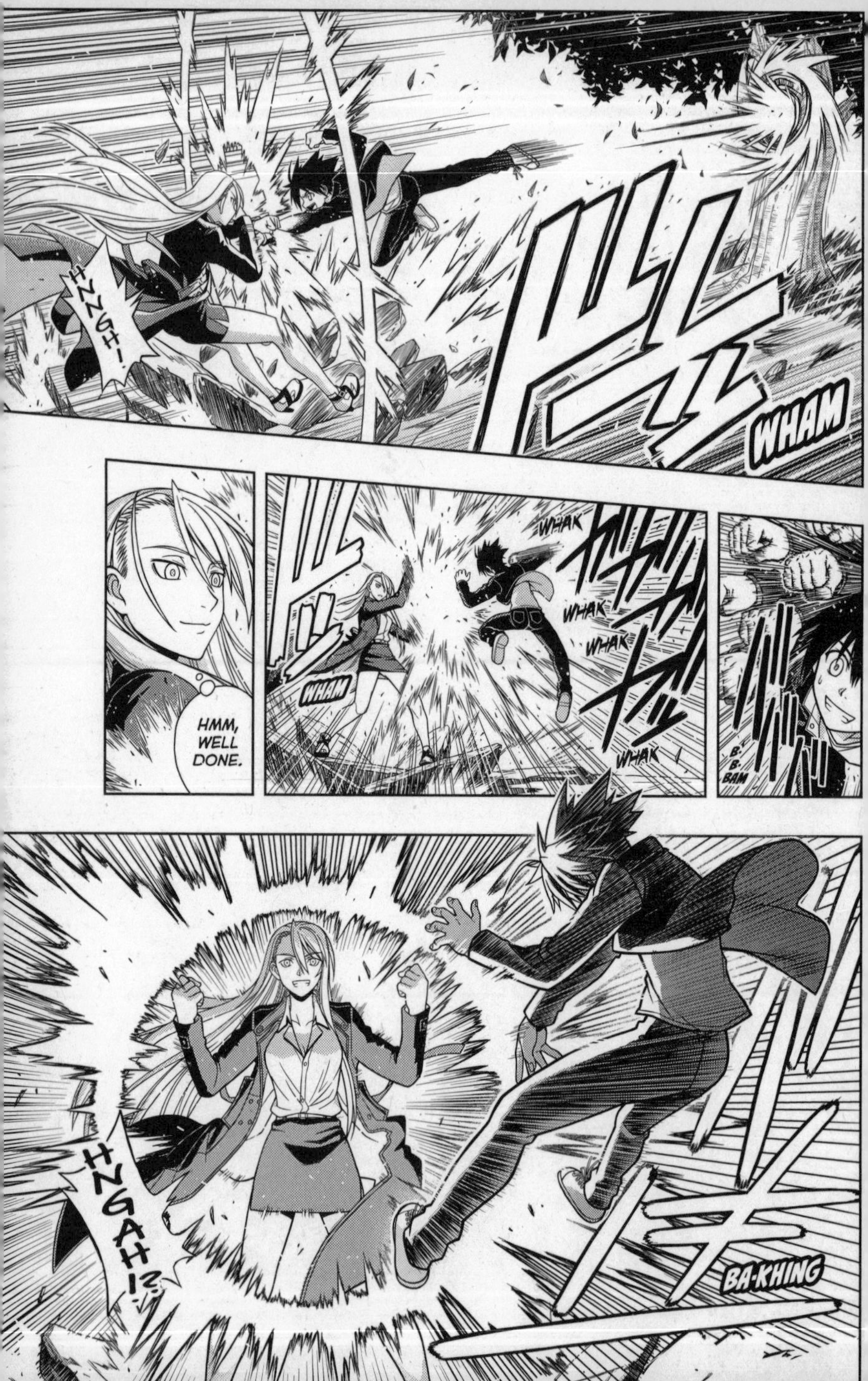
WHAM
HNNGH!
B-B-BAM
WHAK
WHAK
WHAK
WHAK
WHAM
HMM, WELL DONE.
BA-KHING
HNGAH!?

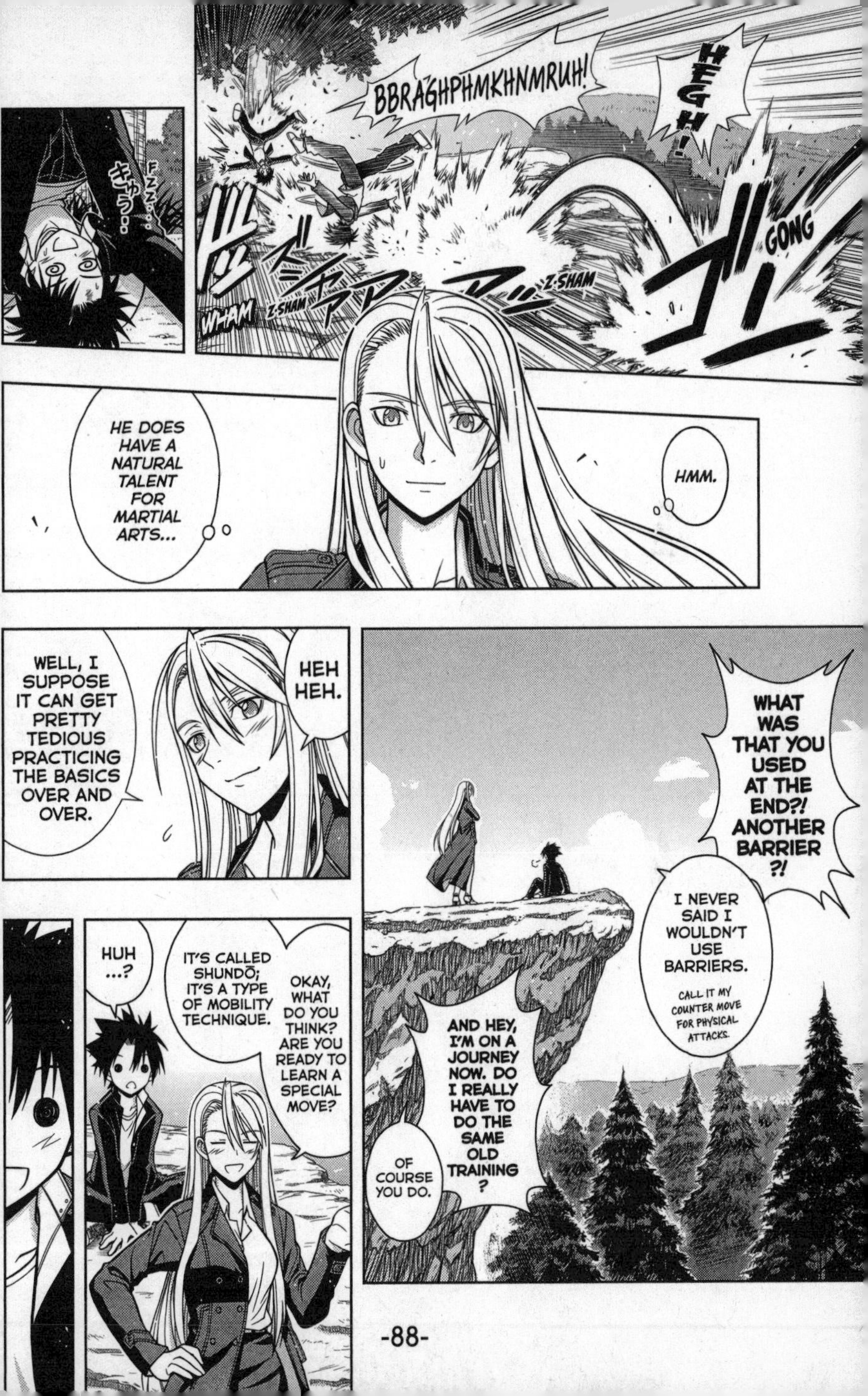
BBRAGHPHMKHNMRUH!
HEGH!
GONG
Z-SHAM
Z-SHAM
WHAM
FZZZ...
きゅう…
HMM.
HE DOES HAVE A NATURAL TALENT FOR MARTIAL ARTS...
WHAT WAS THAT YOU USED AT THE END?! ANOTHER BARRIER?!
I NEVER SAID I WOULDN'T USE BARRIERS.
CALL IT MY COUNTER MOVE FOR PHYSICAL ATTACKS.
AND HEY, I'M ON A JOURNEY NOW. DO I REALLY HAVE TO DO THE SAME OLD TRAINING?
OF COURSE YOU DO.
HEH HEH.
WELL, I SUPPOSE IT CAN GET PRETTY TEDIOUS PRACTICING THE BASICS OVER AND OVER.
OKAY, WHAT DO YOU THINK? ARE YOU READY TO LEARN A SPECIAL MOVE?
IT'S CALLED SHUNDŌ; IT'S A TYPE OF MOBILITY TECHNIQUE.
HUH...?

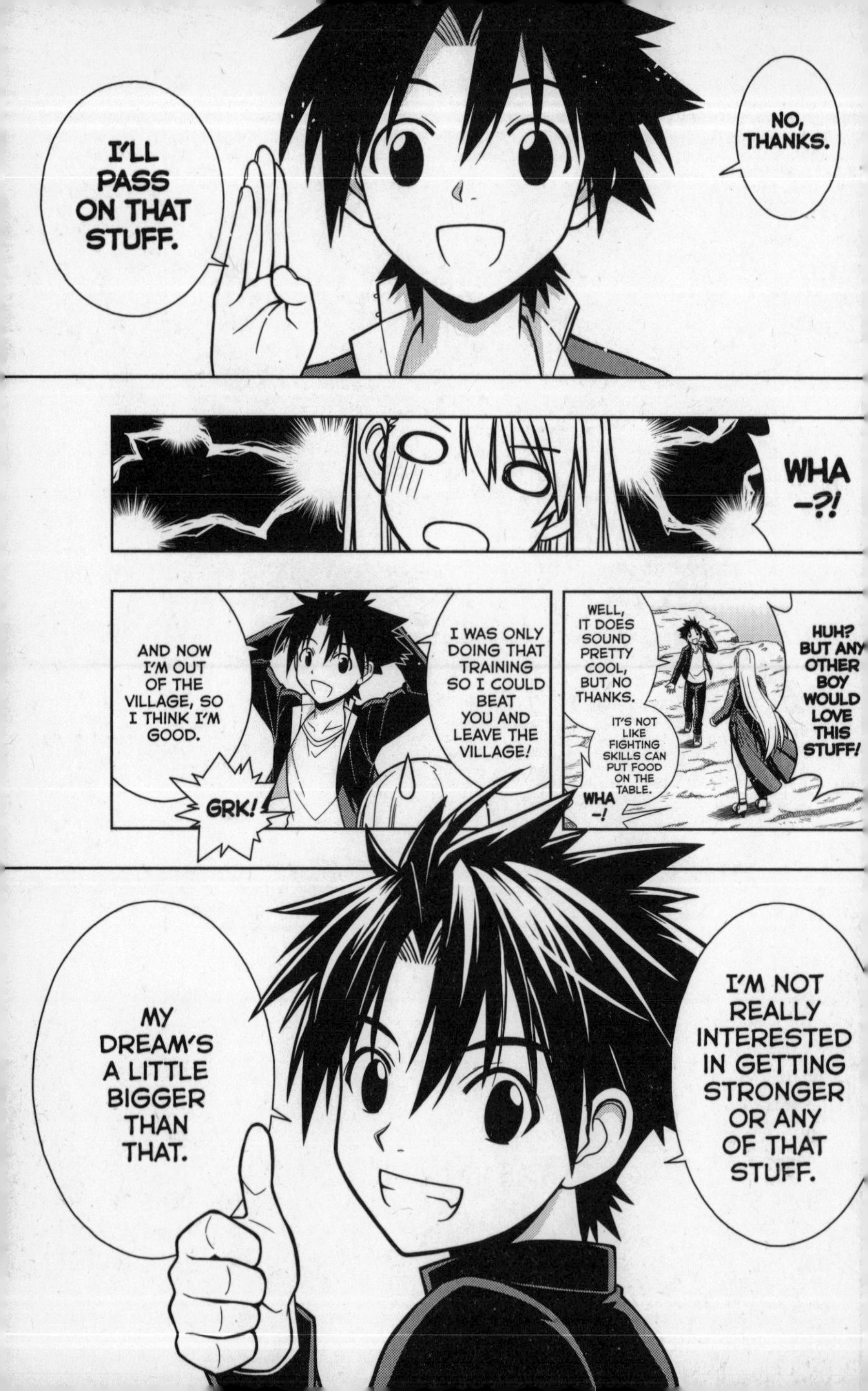
NO, THANKS.
I'LL PASS ON THAT STUFF.
WHA-?!
HUH? BUT ANY OTHER BOY WOULD LOVE THIS STUFF!
WELL, IT DOES SOUND PRETTY COOL, BUT NO THANKS.
IT'S NOT LIKE FIGHTING SKILLS CAN PUT FOOD ON THE TABLE.
WHA-!
I WAS ONLY DOING THAT TRAINING SO I COULD BEAT YOU AND LEAVE THE VILLAGE!
AND NOW I'M OUT OF THE VILLAGE, SO I THINK I'M GOOD.
GRK!
I'M NOT REALLY INTERESTED IN GETTING STRONGER OR ANY OF THAT STUFF.
MY DREAM'S A LITTLE BIGGER THAN THAT.

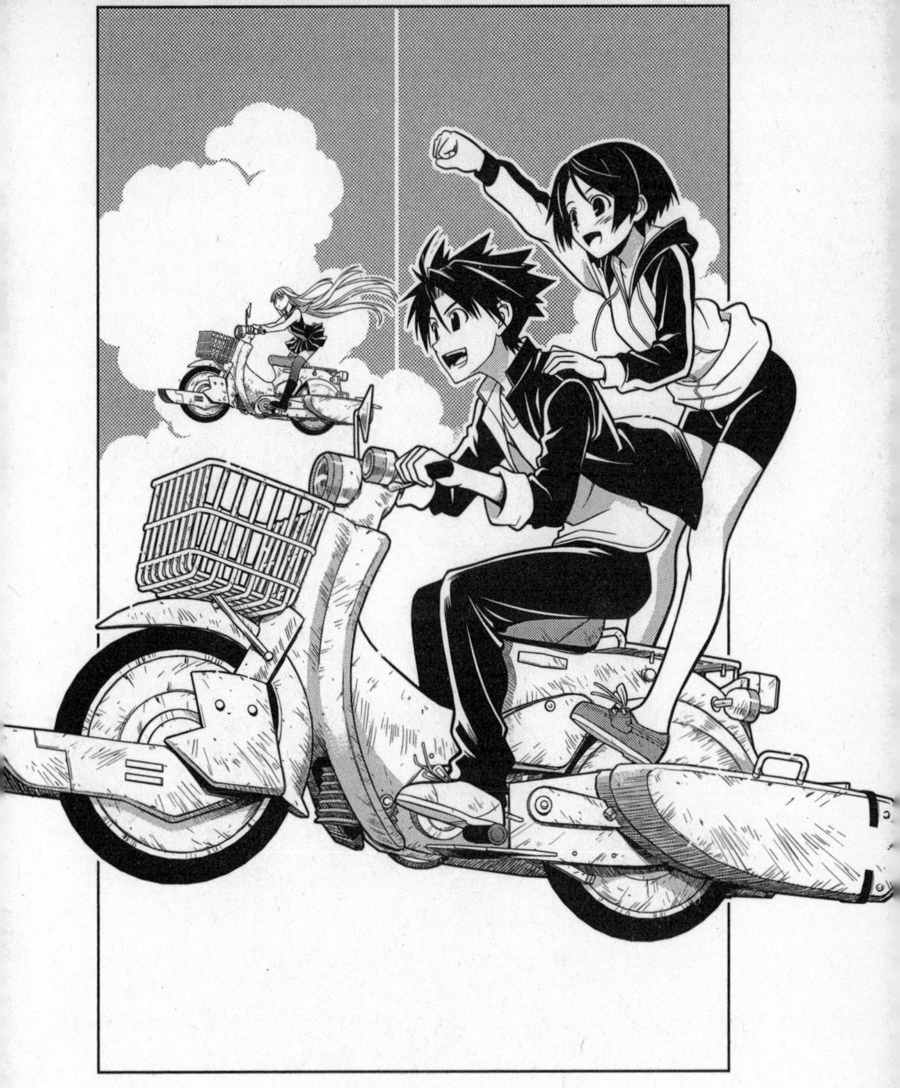

STAGE 2: STUPID IMMORTALITY!

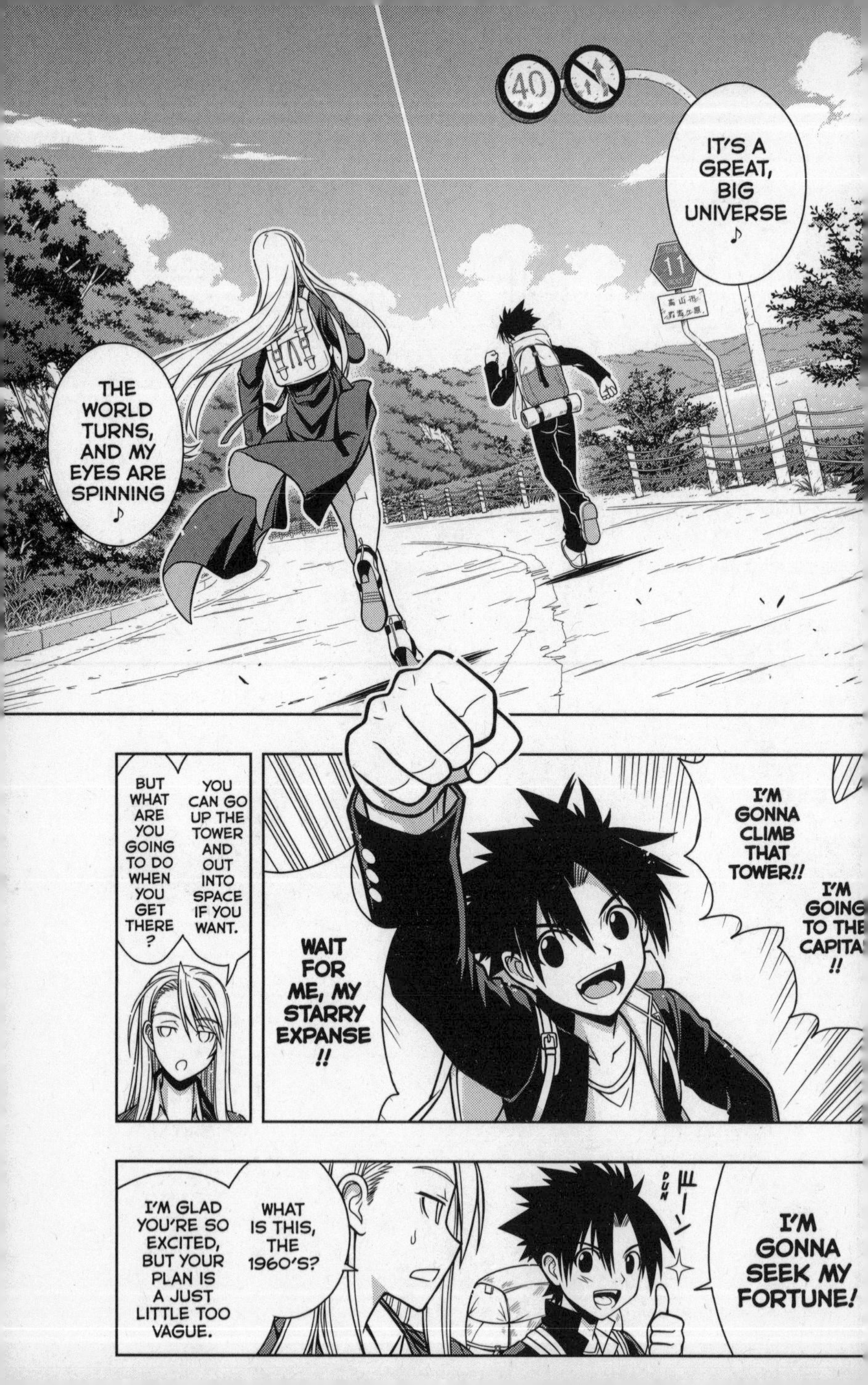
IT'S A GREAT, BIG UNIVERSE ♪
THE WORLD TURNS, AND MY EYES ARE SPINNING ♪
40
11
I'M GOING TO THE CAPITA !!
I'M GONNA CLIMB THAT TOWER!!
WAIT FOR ME, MY STARRY EXPANSE !!
YOU CAN GO UP THE TOWER AND OUT INTO SPACE IF YOU WANT.
BUT WHAT ARE YOU GOING TO DO WHEN YOU GET THERE ?
I'M GONNA SEEK MY FORTUNE!
DUN
WHAT IS THIS, THE 1960'S?
I'M GLAD YOU'RE SO EXCITED, BUT YOUR PLAN IS A JUST LITTLE TOO VAGUE.

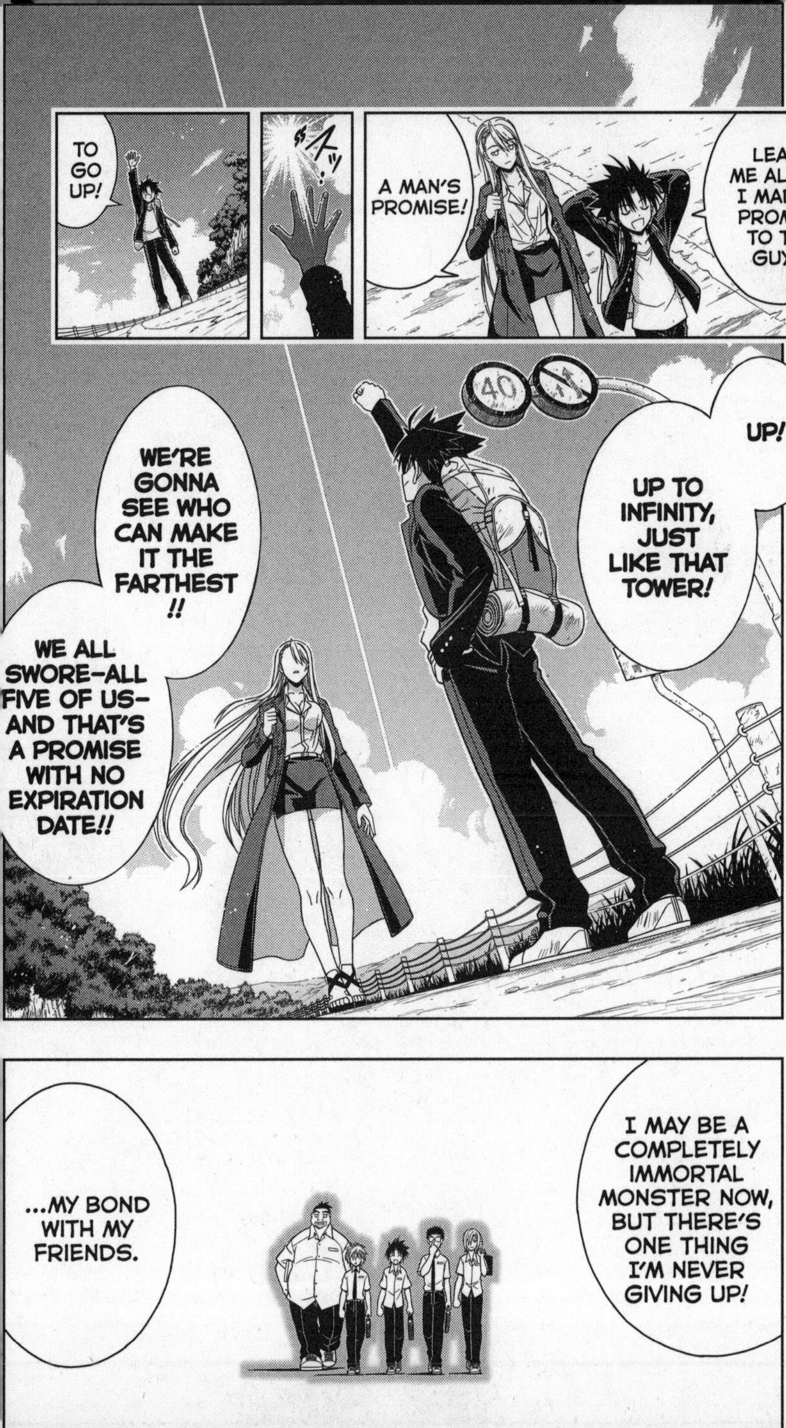
LEAVE ME ALONE. I MADE A PROMISE TO THE GUYS.
A MAN'S PROMISE!
TO GO UP!
UP!
UP TO INFINITY, JUST LIKE THAT TOWER!
WE'RE GONNA SEE WHO CAN MAKE IT THE FARTHEST!!
WE ALL SWORE—ALL FIVE OF US—AND THAT'S A PROMISE WITH NO EXPIRATION DATE!!
I MAY BE A COMPLETELY IMMORTAL MONSTER NOW, BUT THERE'S ONE THING I'M NEVER GIVING UP!
...MY BOND WITH MY FRIENDS.

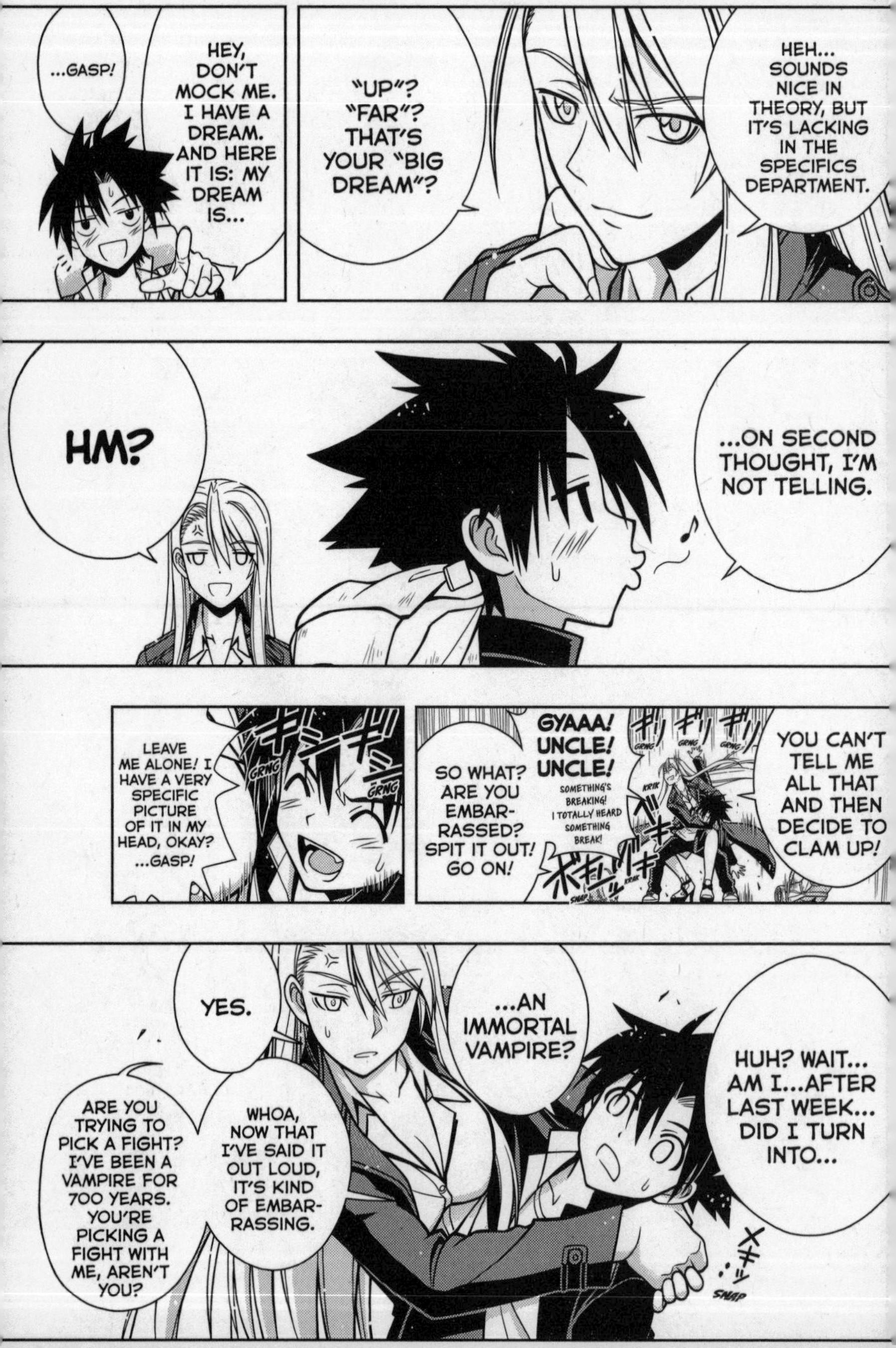
HEH... SOUNDS NICE IN THEORY, BUT IT'S LACKING IN THE SPECIFICS DEPARTMENT.
"UP"? "FAR"? THAT'S YOUR "BIG DREAM"?
HEY, DON'T MOCK ME. I HAVE A DREAM. AND HERE IT IS: MY DREAM IS...
...GASP!
...ON SECOND THOUGHT, I'M NOT TELLING.
HM?
YOU CAN'T TELL ME ALL THAT AND THEN DECIDE TO CLAM UP!
GRNG GRNG GRNG
GYAAA! UNCLE! UNCLE!
SOMETHING'S BREAKING! I TOTALLY HEARD SOMETHING BREAK!
KRIK
KRAK
SNAP
SO WHAT? ARE YOU EMBARRASSED? SPIT IT OUT! GO ON!
GRNG
GRNG
LEAVE ME ALONE! I HAVE A VERY SPECIFIC PICTURE OF IT IN MY HEAD, OKAY? ...GASP!
HUH? WAIT... AM I...AFTER LAST WEEK... DID I TURN INTO...
...AN IMMORTAL VAMPIRE?
YES.
WHOA, NOW THAT I'VE SAID IT OUT LOUD, IT'S KIND OF EMBARRASSING.
ARE YOU TRYING TO PICK A FIGHT? I'VE BEEN A VAMPIRE FOR 700 YEARS. YOU'RE PICKING A FIGHT WITH ME, AREN'T YOU?
SNAP

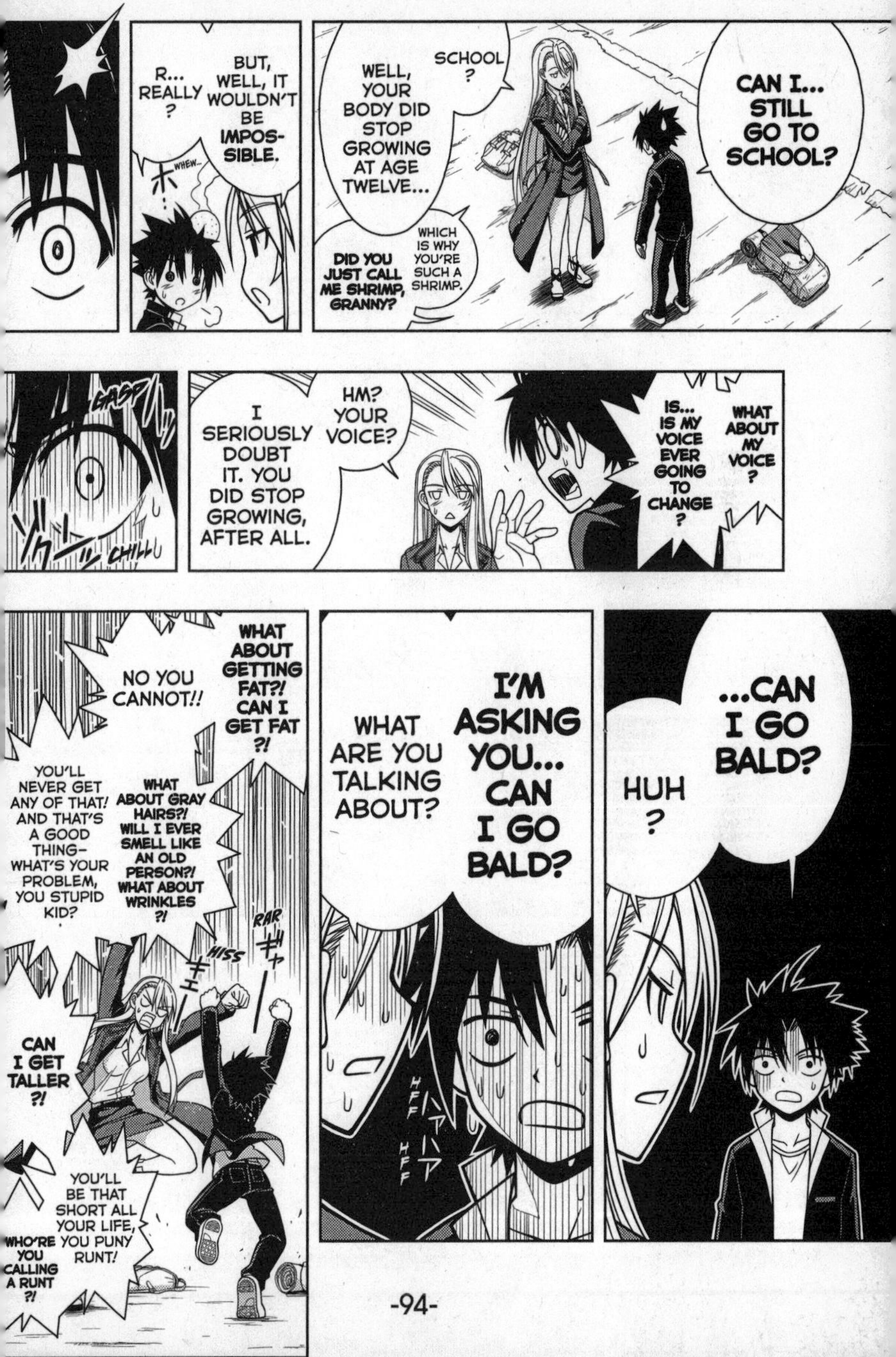
CAN I... STILL GO TO SCHOOL?
SCHOOL?
WELL, YOUR BODY DID STOP GROWING AT AGE TWELVE...
WHICH IS WHY YOU'RE SUCH A SHRIMP.
DID YOU JUST CALL ME SHRIMP, GRANNY?
BUT, WELL, IT WOULDN'T BE IMPOSSIBLE.
WHEW...
R... REALLY?
WHAT ABOUT MY VOICE?
IS... IS MY VOICE EVER GOING TO CHANGE?
HM? YOUR VOICE?
I SERIOUSLY DOUBT IT. YOU DID STOP GROWING, AFTER ALL.
GASP
CHILL
...CAN I GO BALD?
HUH?
I'M ASKING YOU... CAN I GO BALD?
WHAT ARE YOU TALKING ABOUT?
HFF
HFF
WHAT ABOUT GETTING FAT?! CAN I GET FAT?!
NO YOU CANNOT!!
WHAT ABOUT GRAY HAIRS?! WILL I EVER SMELL LIKE AN OLD PERSON?! WHAT ABOUT WRINKLES?!
YOU'LL NEVER GET ANY OF THAT! AND THAT'S A GOOD THING– WHAT'S YOUR PROBLEM, YOU STUPID KID?
RAR
HISS
CAN I GET TALLER?!
YOU'LL BE THAT SHORT ALL YOUR LIFE, YOU PUNY RUNT!
WHO'RE YOU CALLING A RUNT?!

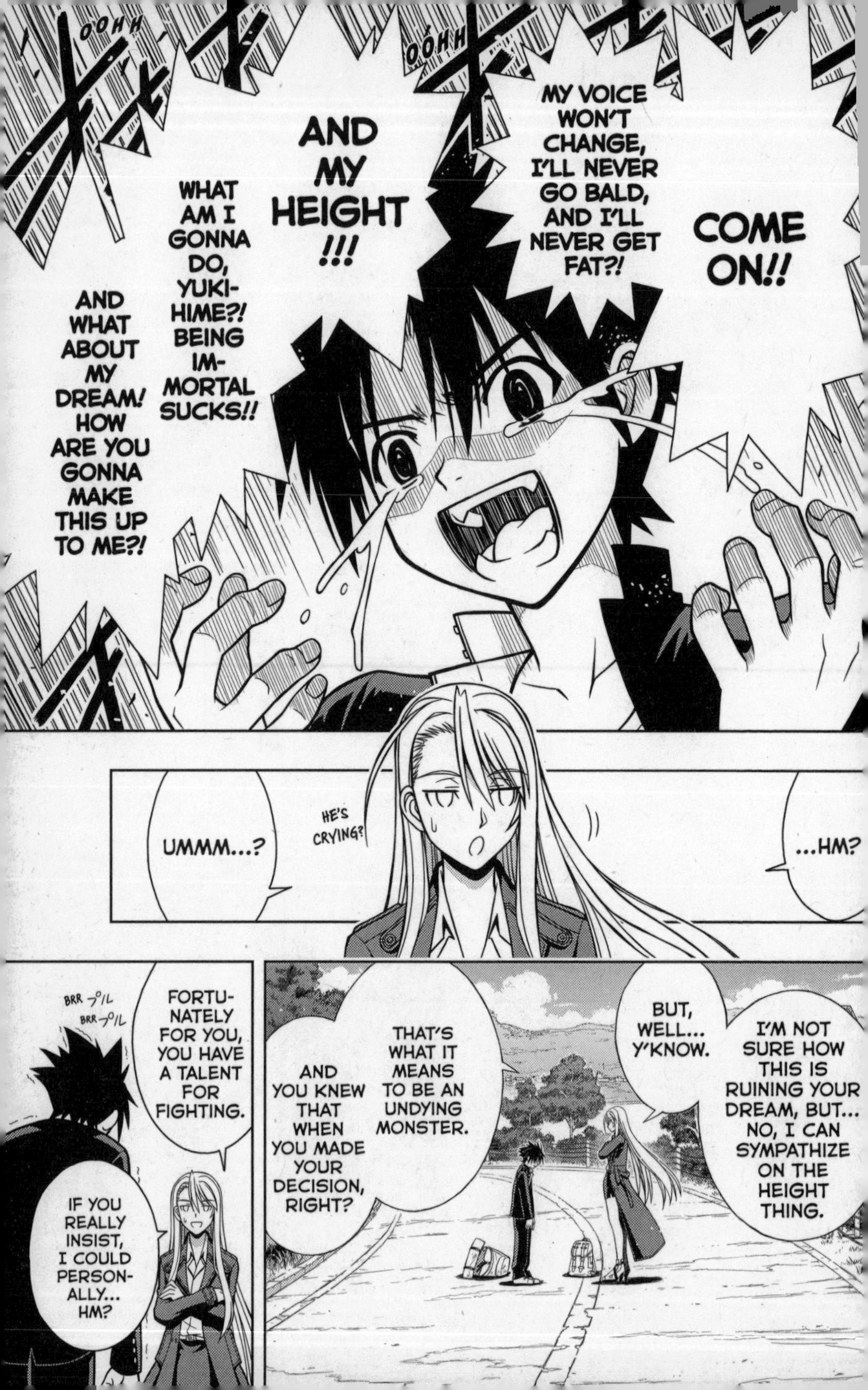
OOHH
OOHH
COME ON!!
MY VOICE WON'T CHANGE, I'LL NEVER GO BALD, AND I'LL NEVER GET FAT?!
AND MY HEIGHT!!!
WHAT AM I GONNA DO, YUKI-HIME?! BEING IM-MORTAL SUCKS!!
AND WHAT ABOUT MY DREAM! HOW ARE YOU GONNA MAKE THIS UP TO ME?!
...HM?
HE'S CRYING?
UMMM...?
I'M NOT SURE HOW THIS IS RUINING YOUR DREAM, BUT... NO, I CAN SYMPATHIZE ON THE HEIGHT THING.
BUT, WELL... Y'KNOW.
THAT'S WHAT IT MEANS TO BE AN UNDYING MONSTER.
AND YOU KNEW THAT WHEN YOU MADE YOUR DECISION, RIGHT?
FORTU-NATELY FOR YOU, YOU HAVE A TALENT FOR FIGHTING.
BRR プル
BRR プル
IF YOU REALLY INSIST, I COULD PERSON-ALLY... HM?

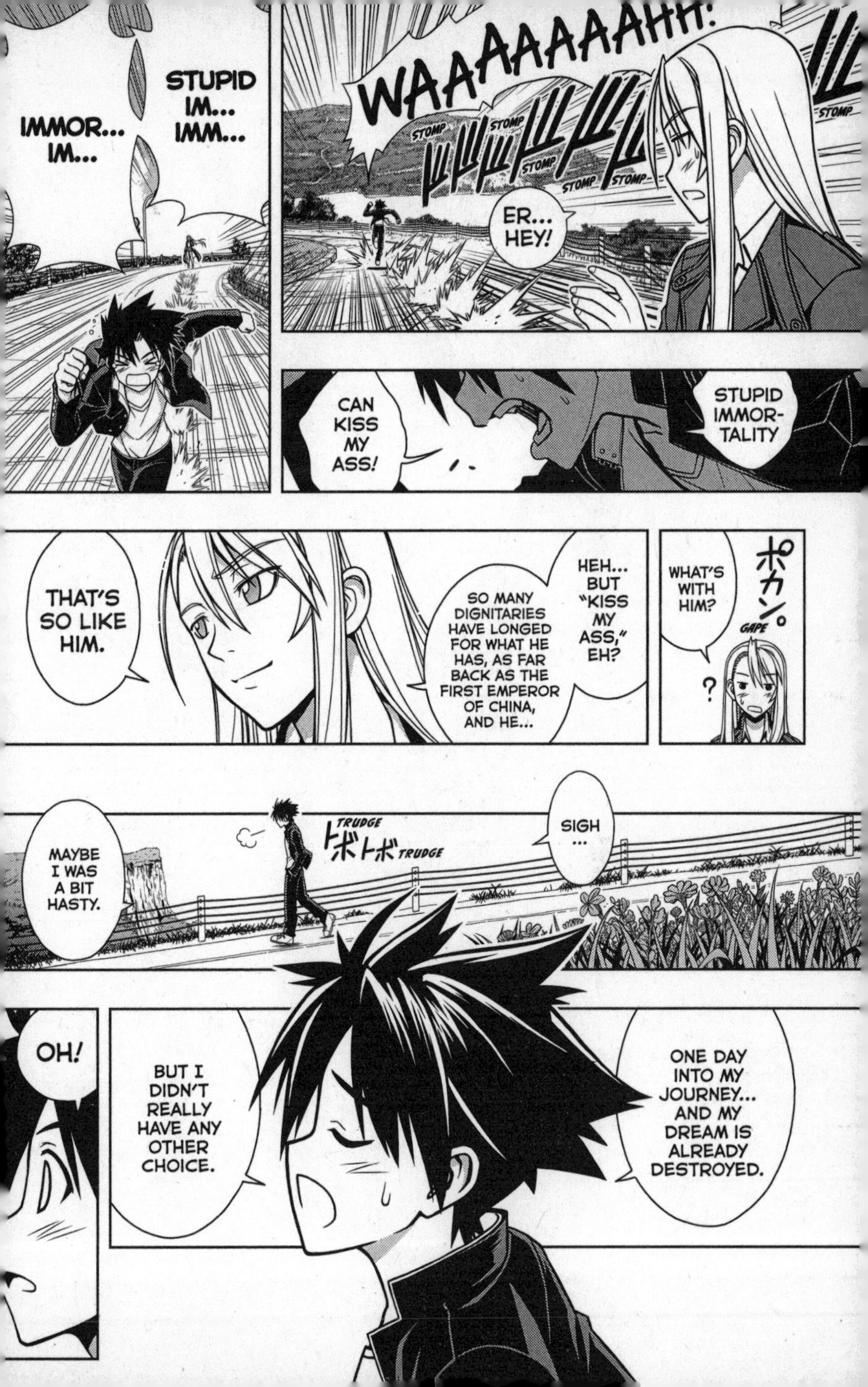
WAAAAAAAHH!
STOMP STOMP STOMP STOMP STOMP STOMP
ER... HEY!
STUPID IMMORTALITY
CAN KISS MY ASS!
STUPID IM... IMM...
IMMOR... IM...
ポカン。
GAPE
WHAT'S WITH HIM?
?
HEH... BUT "KISS MY ASS," EH?
SO MANY DIGNITARIES HAVE LONGED FOR WHAT HE HAS, AS FAR BACK AS THE FIRST EMPEROR OF CHINA, AND HE...
THAT'S SO LIKE HIM.
SIGH ...
TRUDGE トボトボ TRUDGE
MAYBE I WAS A BIT HASTY.
ONE DAY INTO MY JOURNEY... AND MY DREAM IS ALREADY DESTROYED.
BUT I DIDN'T REALLY HAVE ANY OTHER CHOICE.
OH!

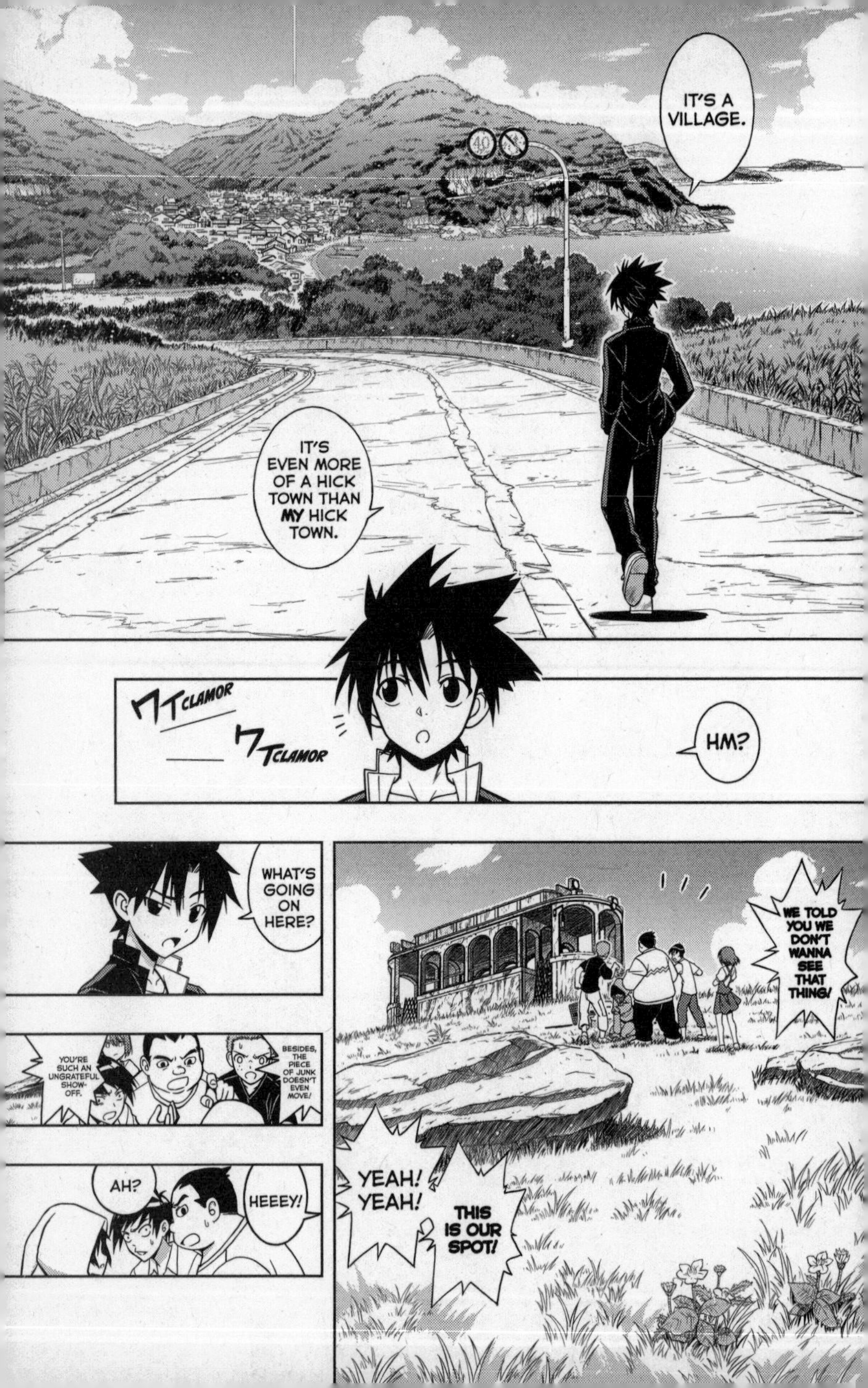

IT'S A VILLAGE.
IT'S EVEN MORE OF A HICK TOWN THAN MY HICK TOWN.
CLAMOR
CLAMOR
HM?
WE TOLD YOU WE DON'T WANNA SEE THAT THING!
YEAH! YEAH!
THIS IS OUR SPOT!
WHAT'S GOING ON HERE?
BESIDES, THE PIECE OF JUNK DOESN'T EVEN MOVE!
YOU'RE SUCH AN UNGRATEFUL SHOW-OFF.
HEEEY!
AH?

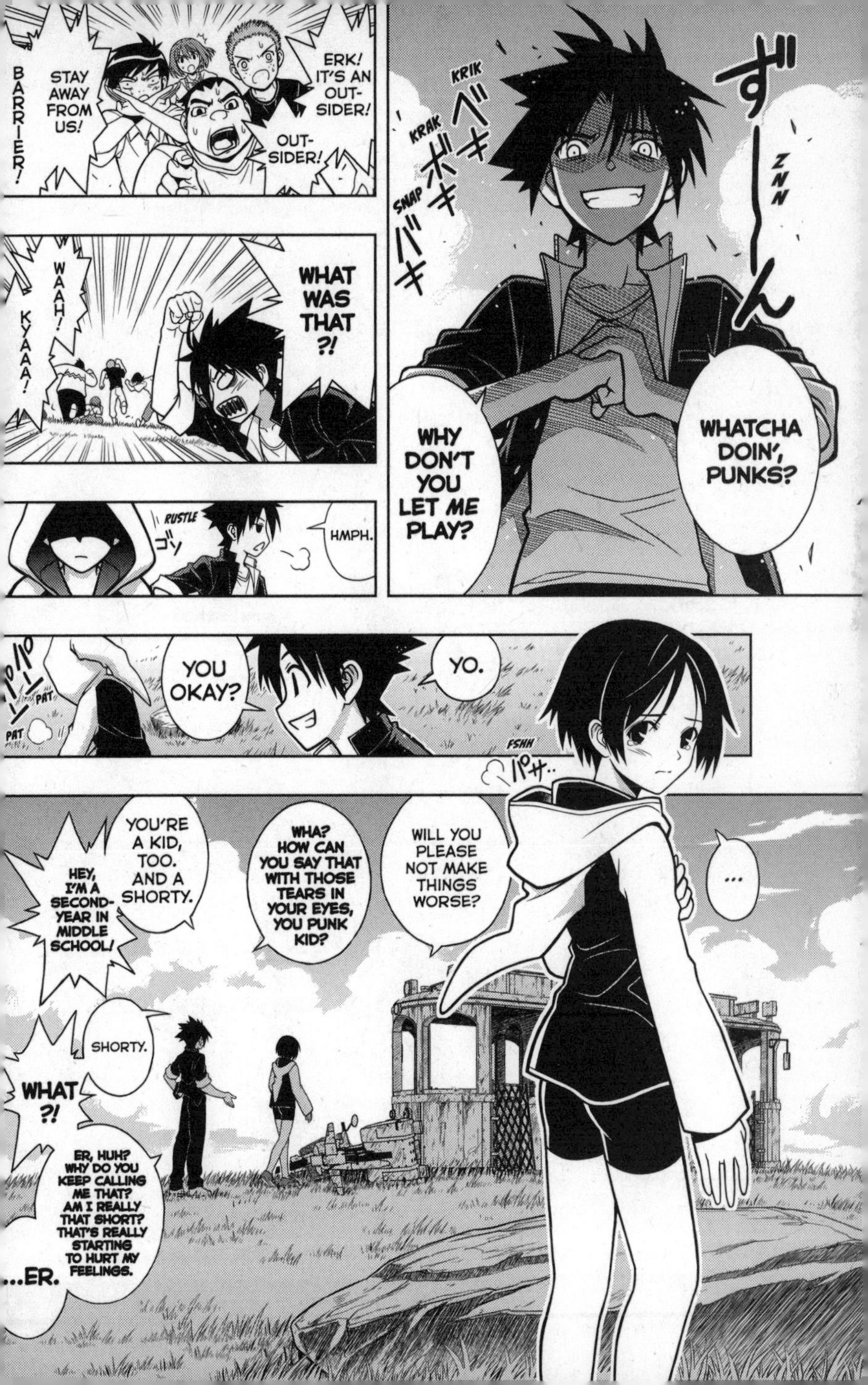
ずーん
ZNN
KRIK
ベキ
KRAK
ボキ
SNAP
バキ
WHATCHA DOIN', PUNKS?
WHY DON'T YOU LET ME PLAY?
ERK! IT'S AN OUT-SIDER!
OUT-SIDER!
STAY AWAY FROM US!
BARRIER!
WHAT WAS THAT?!
WAAH!
KYAAA!
HMPH.
RUSTLE
ゴソ
YO.
YOU OKAY?
PAT
PAT
FSHH
パサ..
...
WILL YOU PLEASE NOT MAKE THINGS WORSE?
WHA? HOW CAN YOU SAY THAT WITH THOSE TEARS IN YOUR EYES, YOU PUNK KID?
YOU'RE A KID, TOO. AND A SHORTY.
HEY, I'M A SECOND-YEAR IN MIDDLE SCHOOL!
SHORTY.
WHAT?!
ER, HUH? WHY DO YOU KEEP CALLING ME THAT? AM I REALLY THAT SHORT? THAT'S REALLY STARTING TO HURT MY FEELINGS.
...ER.

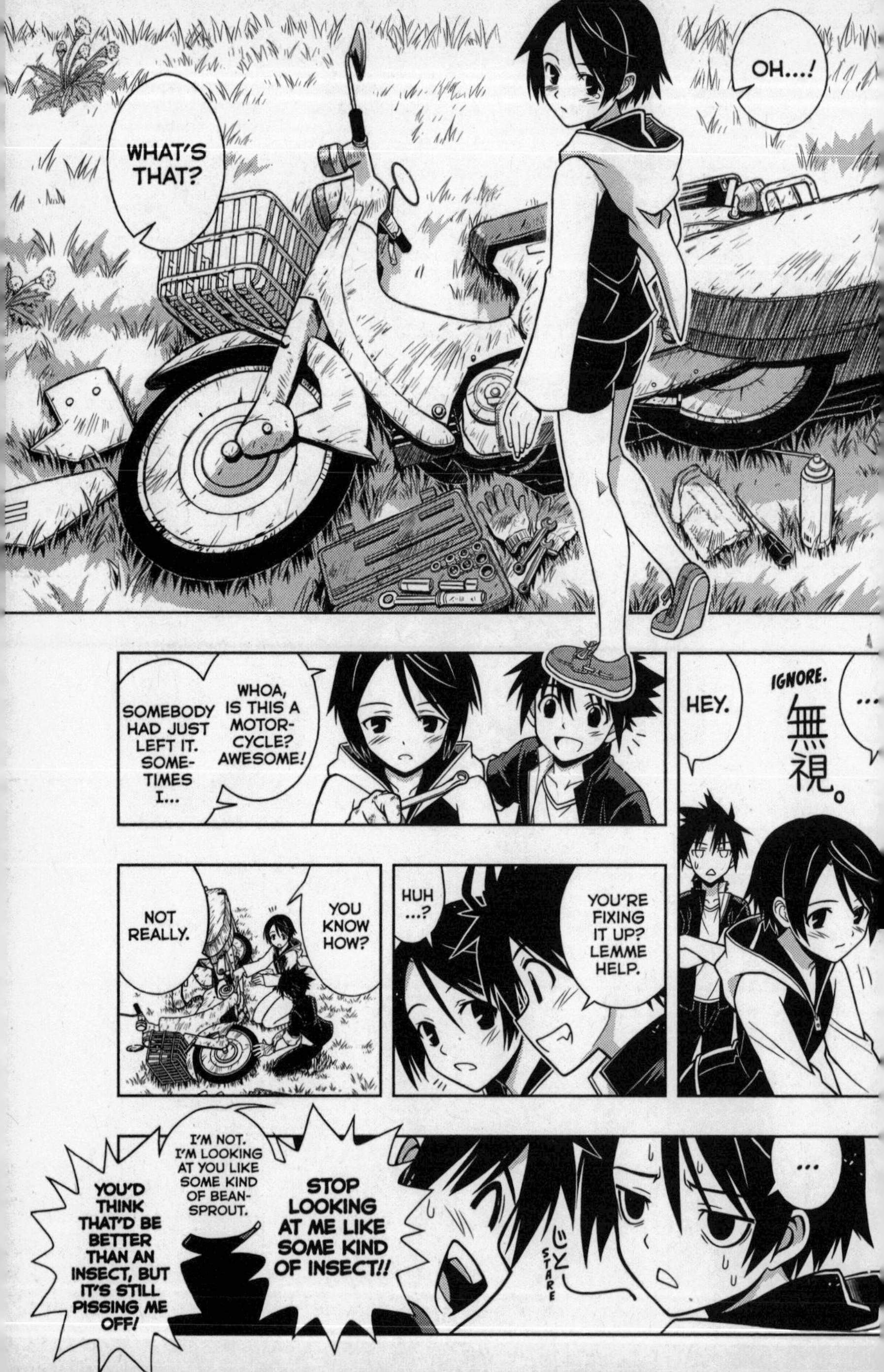
OH...!
WHAT'S THAT?
...
IGNORE.
無視。
HEY.
WHOA, IS THIS A MOTOR-CYCLE? AWESOME!
SOMEBODY HAD JUST LEFT IT. SOME-TIMES I...
YOU'RE FIXING IT UP? LEMME HELP.
HUH ...?
YOU KNOW HOW?
NOT REALLY.
...
STARE
STOP LOOKING AT ME LIKE SOME KIND OF INSECT!!
I'M NOT. I'M LOOKING AT YOU LIKE SOME KIND OF BEAN-SPROUT.
YOU'D THINK THAT'D BE BETTER THAN AN INSECT, BUT IT'S STILL PISSING ME OFF!

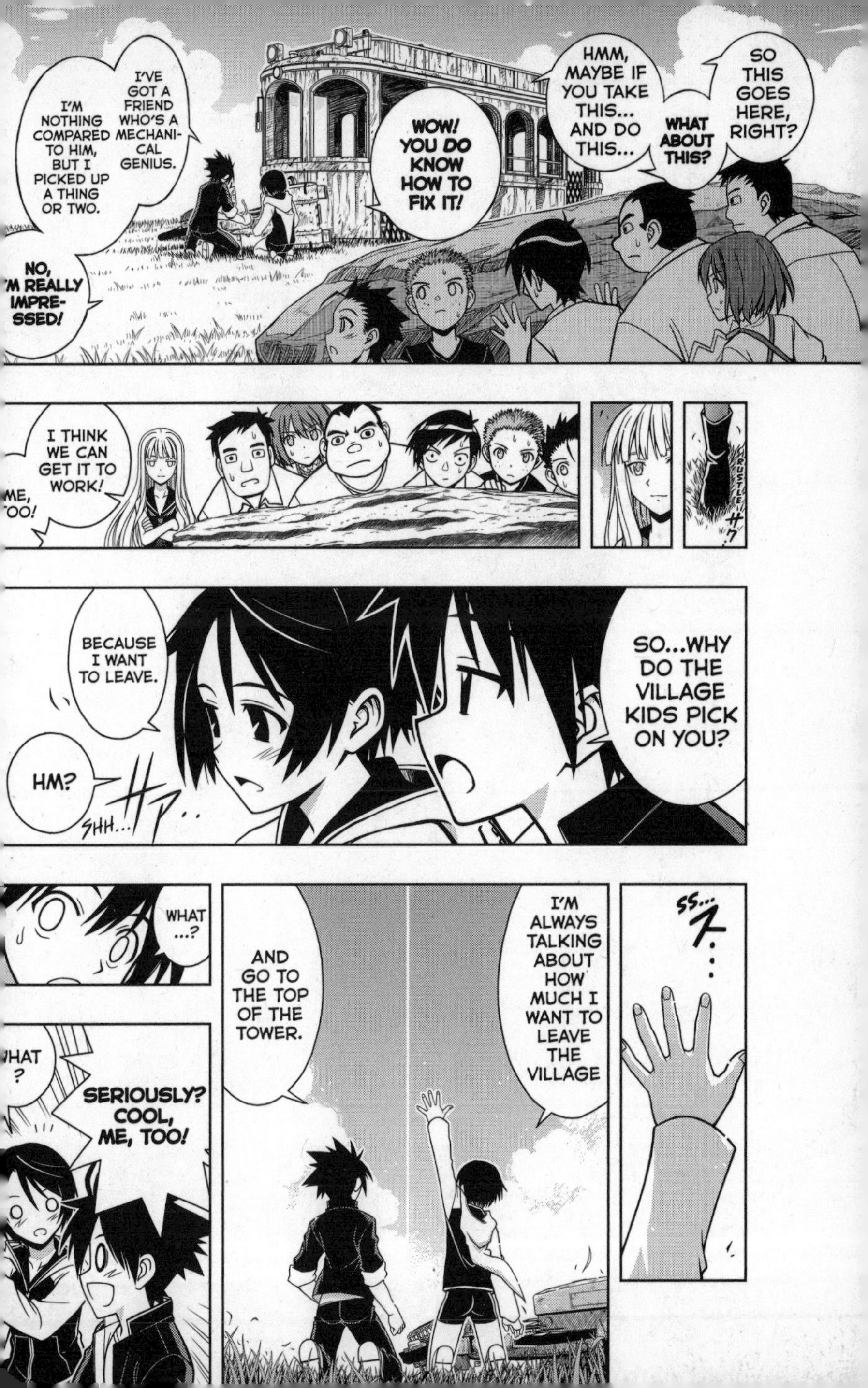
SO THIS GOES HERE, RIGHT?
WHAT ABOUT THIS?
HMM, MAYBE IF YOU TAKE THIS... AND DO THIS...
WOW! YOU DO KNOW HOW TO FIX IT!
I'VE GOT A FRIEND WHO'S A MECHANICAL GENIUS.
I'M NOTHING COMPARED TO HIM, BUT I PICKED UP A THING OR TWO.
NO, 'M REALLY IMPRESSED!
RUSTLE
I THINK WE CAN GET IT TO WORK!
ME, OO!
SO...WHY DO THE VILLAGE KIDS PICK ON YOU?
BECAUSE I WANT TO LEAVE.
HM?
SHH...
SS...
I'M ALWAYS TALKING ABOUT HOW MUCH I WANT TO LEAVE THE VILLAGE
AND GO TO THE TOP OF THE TOWER.
WHAT ...?
WHAT ?
SERIOUSLY? COOL, ME, TOO!

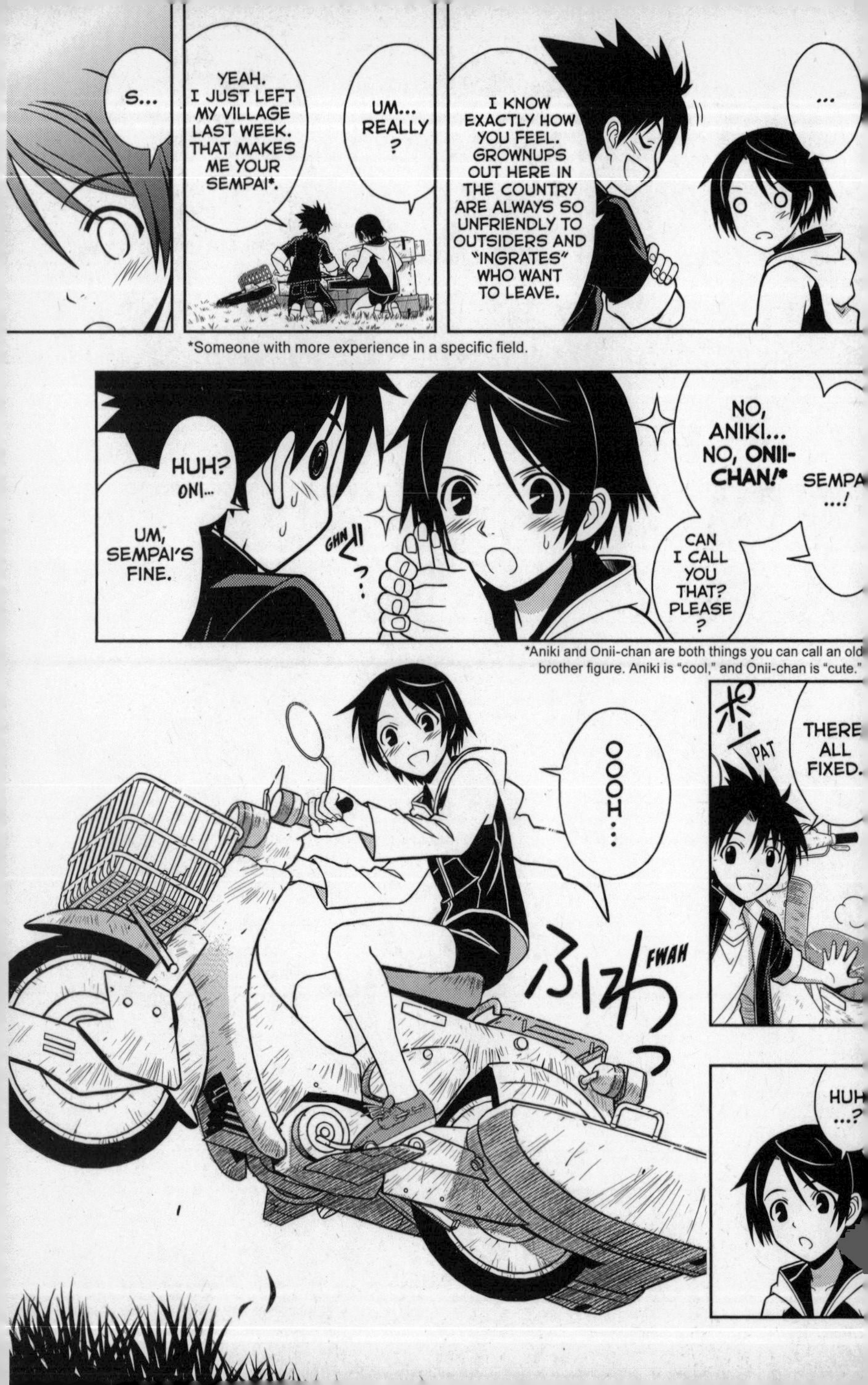
...
I KNOW EXACTLY HOW YOU FEEL. GROWNUPS OUT HERE IN THE COUNTRY ARE ALWAYS SO UNFRIENDLY TO OUTSIDERS AND "INGRATES" WHO WANT TO LEAVE.
UM... REALLY?
YEAH. I JUST LEFT MY VILLAGE LAST WEEK. THAT MAKES ME YOUR SEMPAI*.
S...
SEMPA ...!
NO, ANIKI... NO, ONII-CHAN!*
CAN I CALL YOU THAT? PLEASE?
GHN
HUH? ONI...
UM, SEMPAI'S FINE.
PAT
THERE ALL FIXED.
HUH ...?
OOOH...
FWAH

*Someone with more experience in a specific field.

*Aniki and Onii-chan are both things you can call an old brother figure. Aniki is "cool," and Onii-chan is "cute."

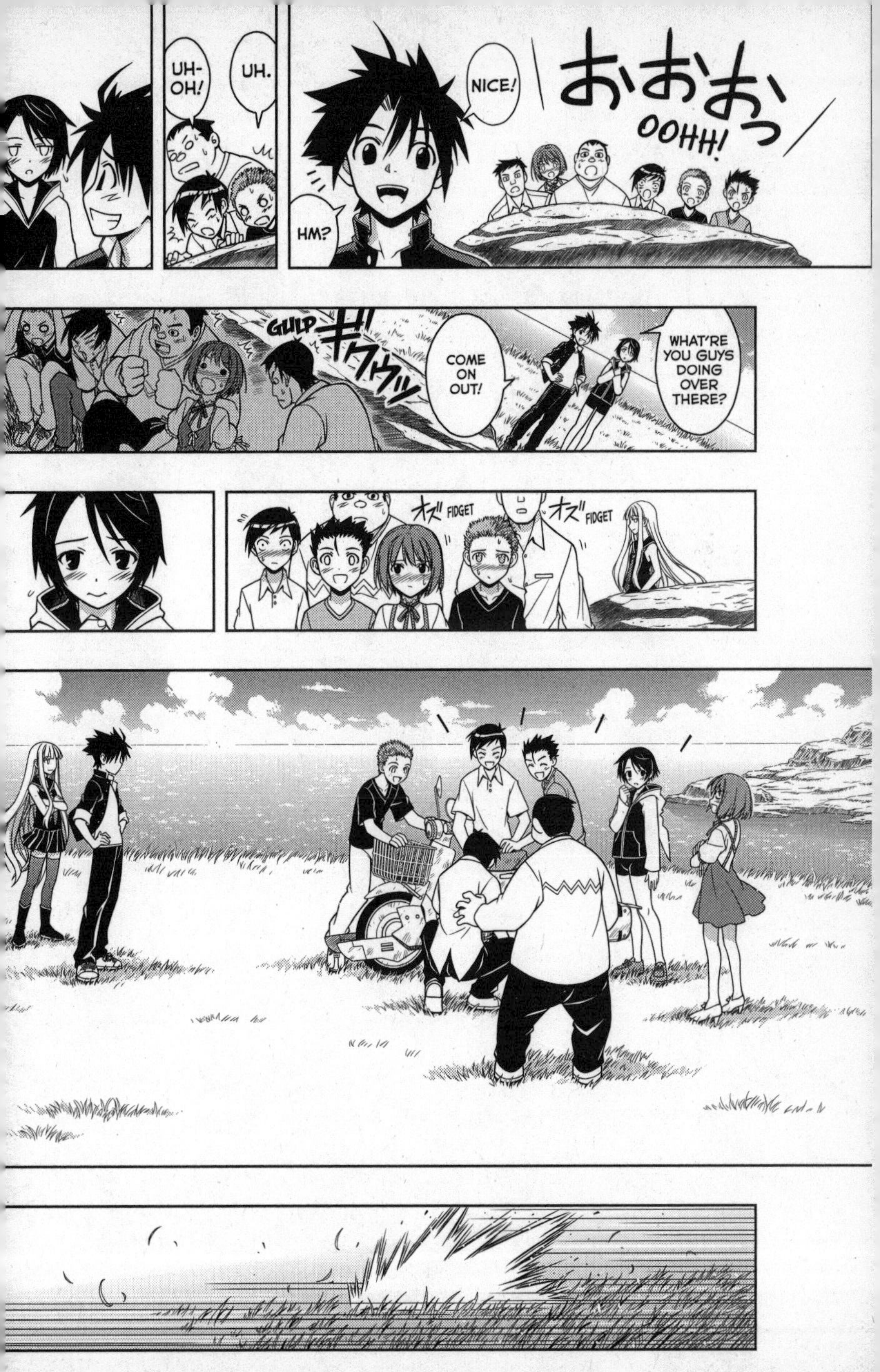
おおおっ
OOHH!
NICE!
HM?
UH.
UH-OH!
WHAT'RE YOU GUYS DOING OVER THERE?
COME ON OUT!
ギクウッ
GULP
オズ FIDGET
オズ FIDGET

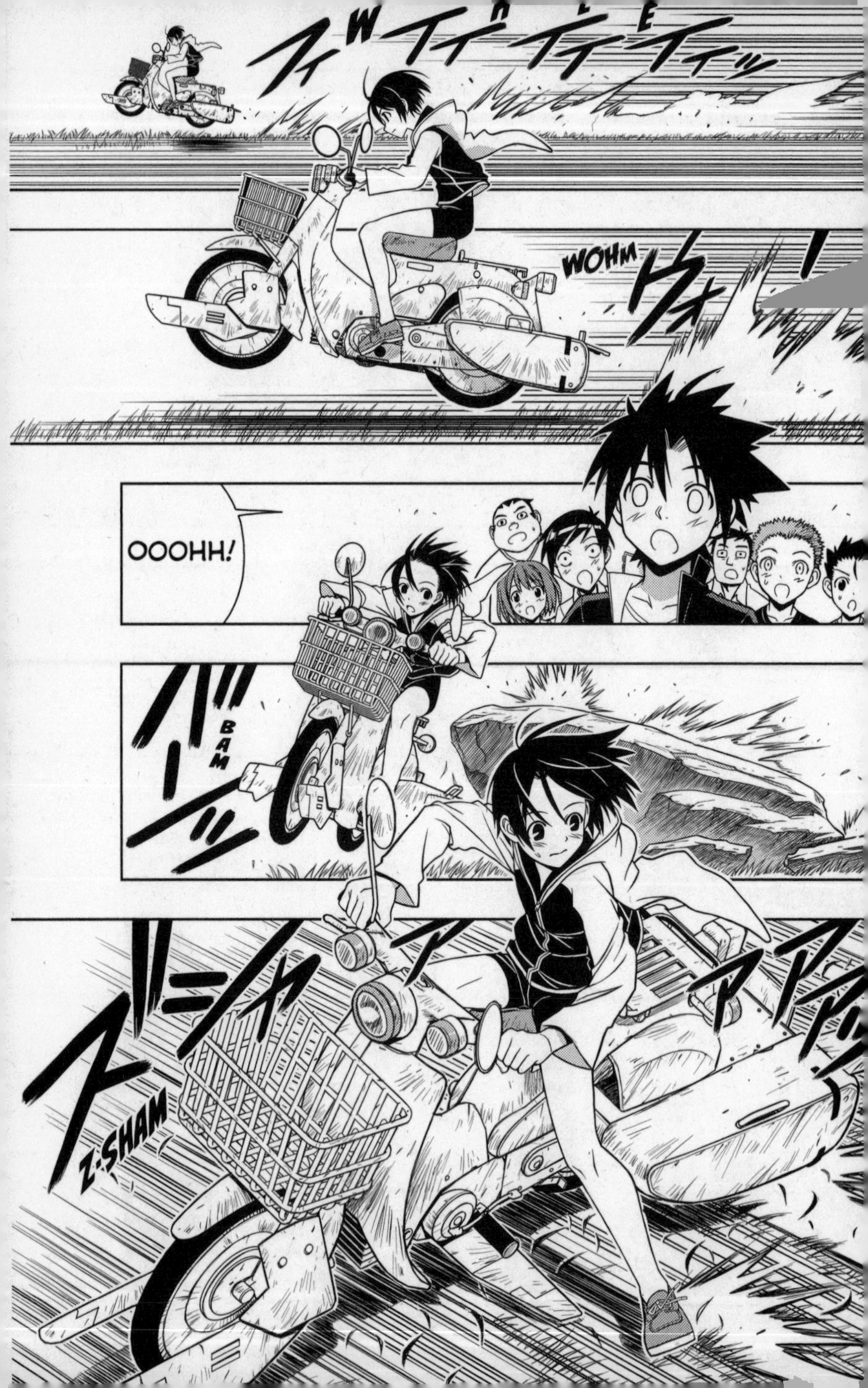
WOHM
OOOHH!
BAM
Z-SHAM

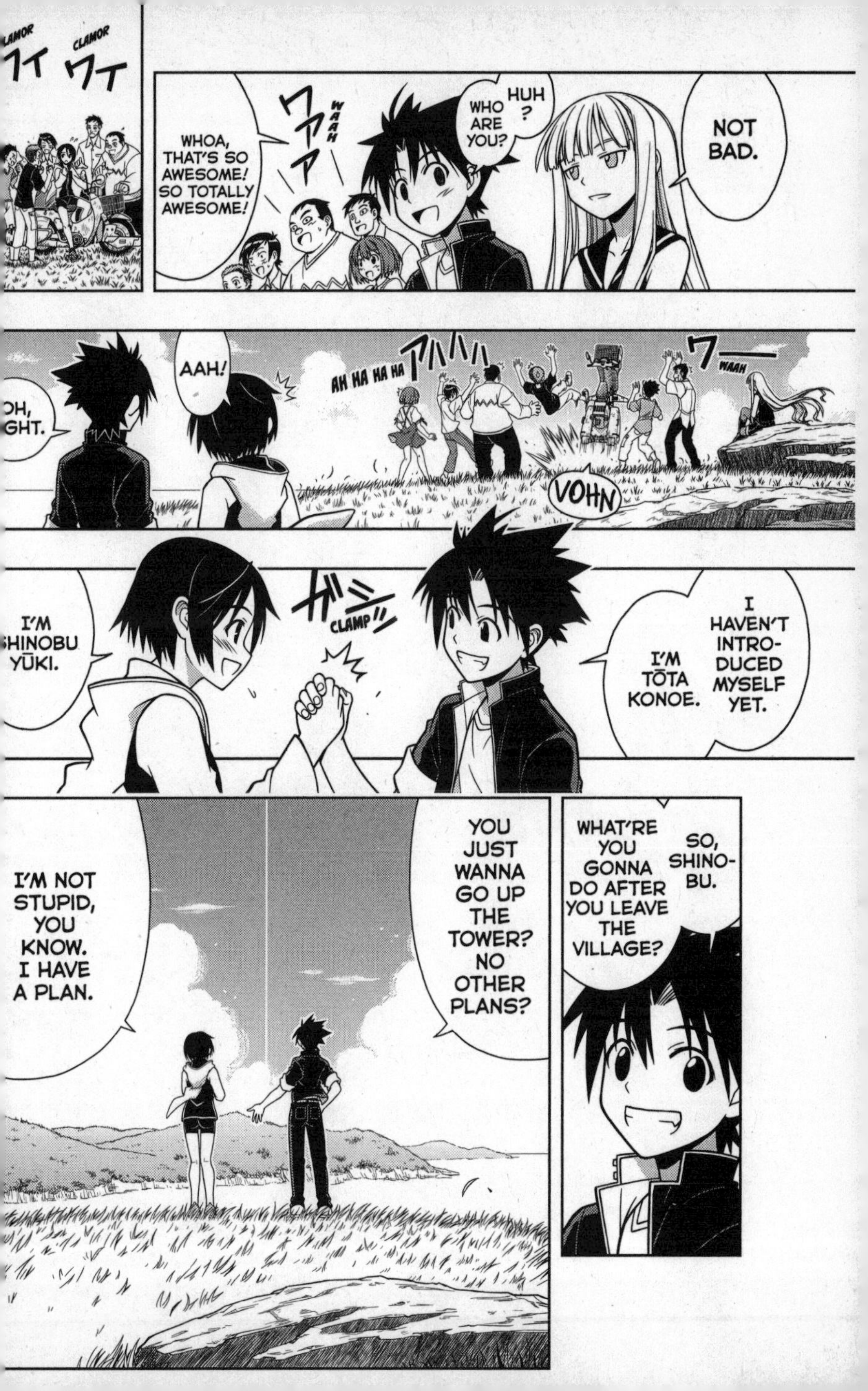
NOT BAD.
HUH? WHO ARE YOU?
ワァア WAAH
WHOA, THAT'S SO AWESOME! SO TOTALLY AWESOME!
CLAMOR ワイ CLAMOR ワイ
ワー WAAH
VOHN
アハハハ AH HA HA HA
AAH!
OH,
GHT.
I HAVEN'T INTRODUCED MYSELF YET.
I'M TŌTA KONOE.
CLAMP
I'M SHINOBU YŪKI.
SO, SHINOBU.
WHAT'RE YOU GONNA DO AFTER YOU LEAVE THE VILLAGE?
YOU JUST WANNA GO UP THE TOWER? NO OTHER PLANS?
I'M NOT STUPID, YOU KNOW. I HAVE A PLAN.

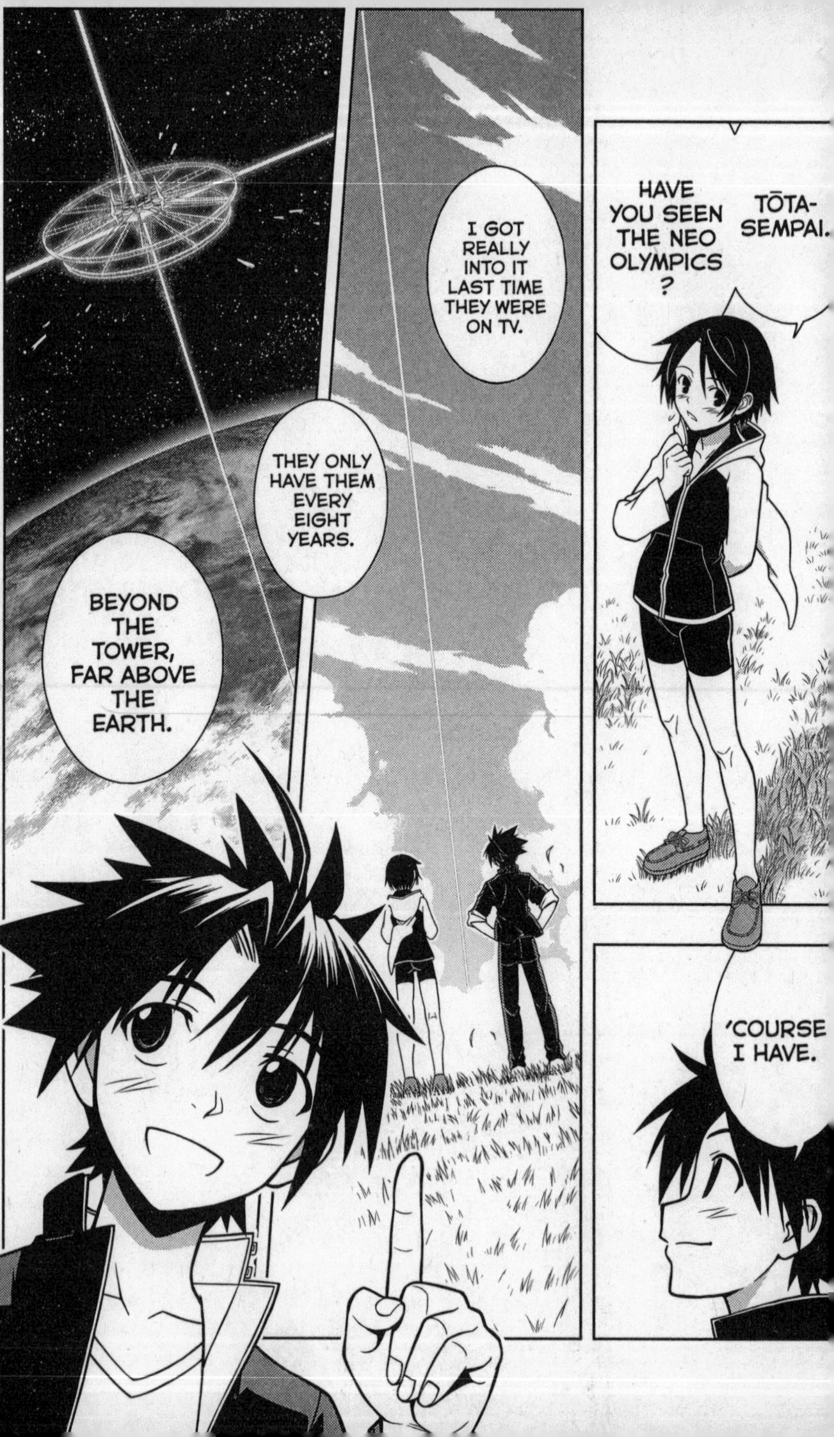
TŌTA-SEMPAI.
HAVE YOU SEEN THE NEO OLYMPICS?
'COURSE I HAVE.
I GOT REALLY INTO IT LAST TIME THEY WERE ON TV.
THEY ONLY HAVE THEM EVERY EIGHT YEARS.
BEYOND THE TOWER, FAR ABOVE THE EARTH.

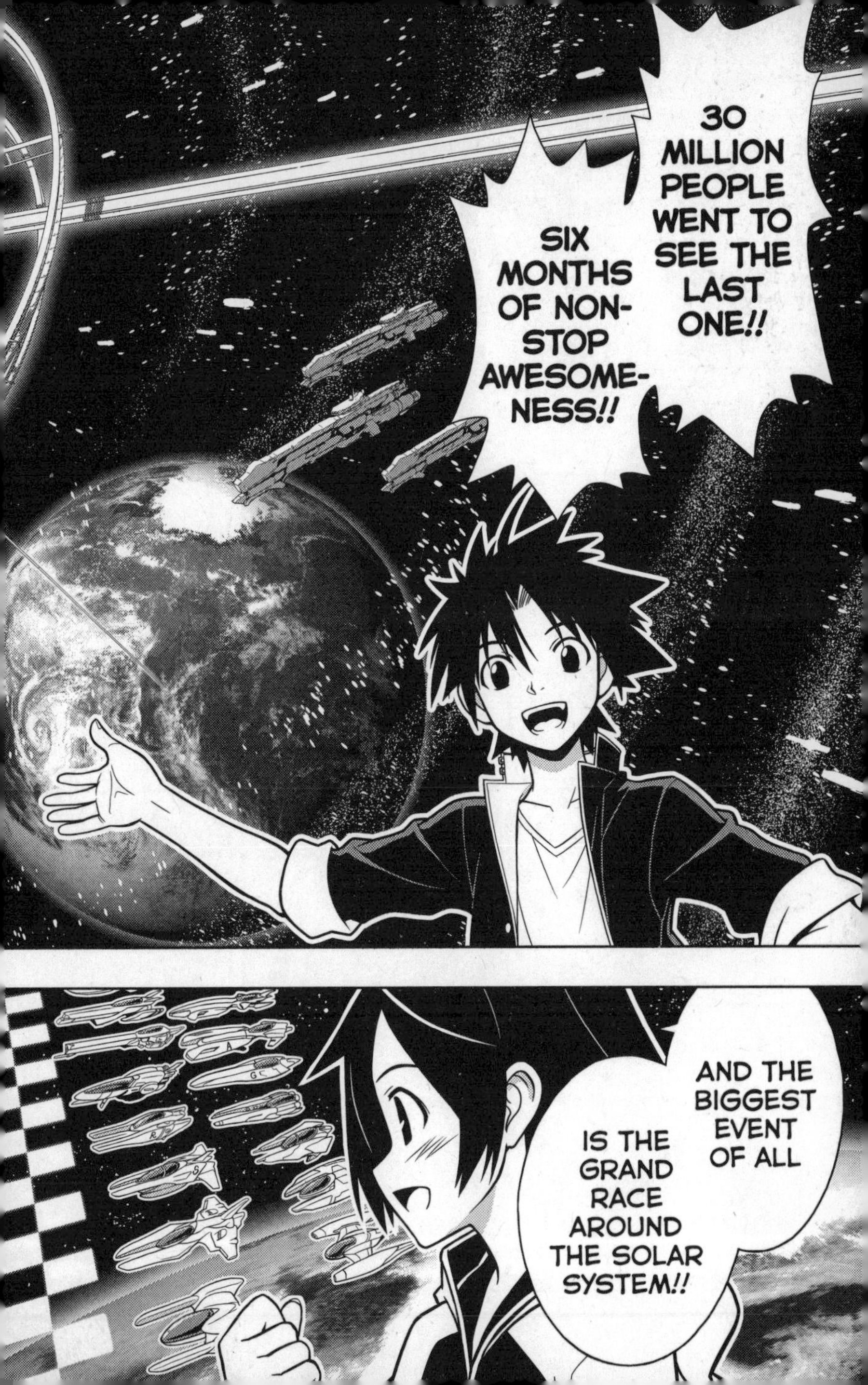
30 MILLION PEOPLE WENT TO SEE THE LAST ONE!!
SIX MONTHS OF NON-STOP AWESOMENESS!!
AND THE BIGGEST EVENT OF ALL
IS THE GRAND RACE AROUND THE SOLAR SYSTEM!!

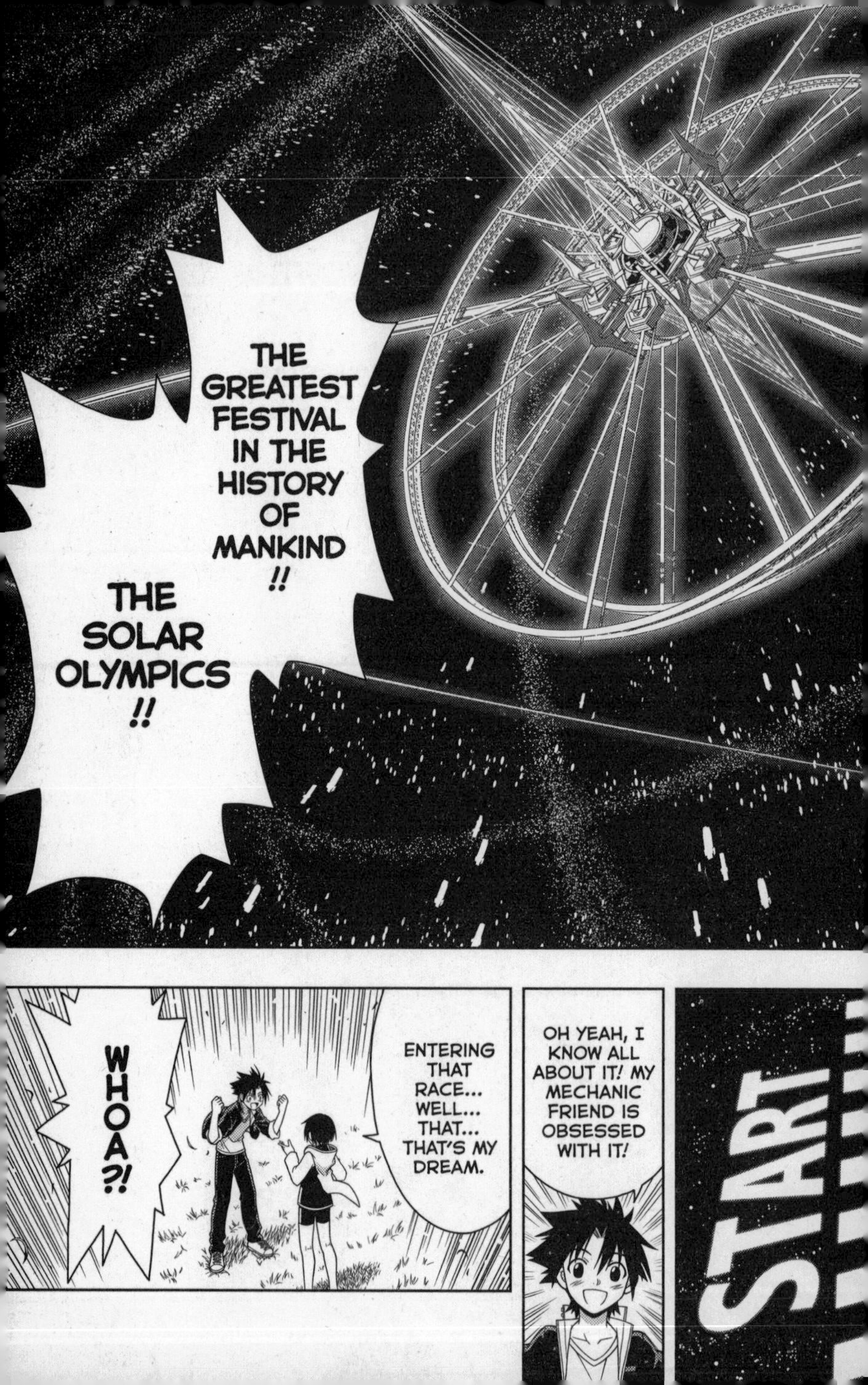
THE GREATEST FESTIVAL IN THE HISTORY OF MANKIND !!
THE SOLAR OLYMPICS !!
START
OH YEAH, I KNOW ALL ABOUT IT! MY MECHANIC FRIEND IS OBSESSED WITH IT!
ENTERING THAT RACE... WELL... THAT... THAT'S MY DREAM.
WHOA?!

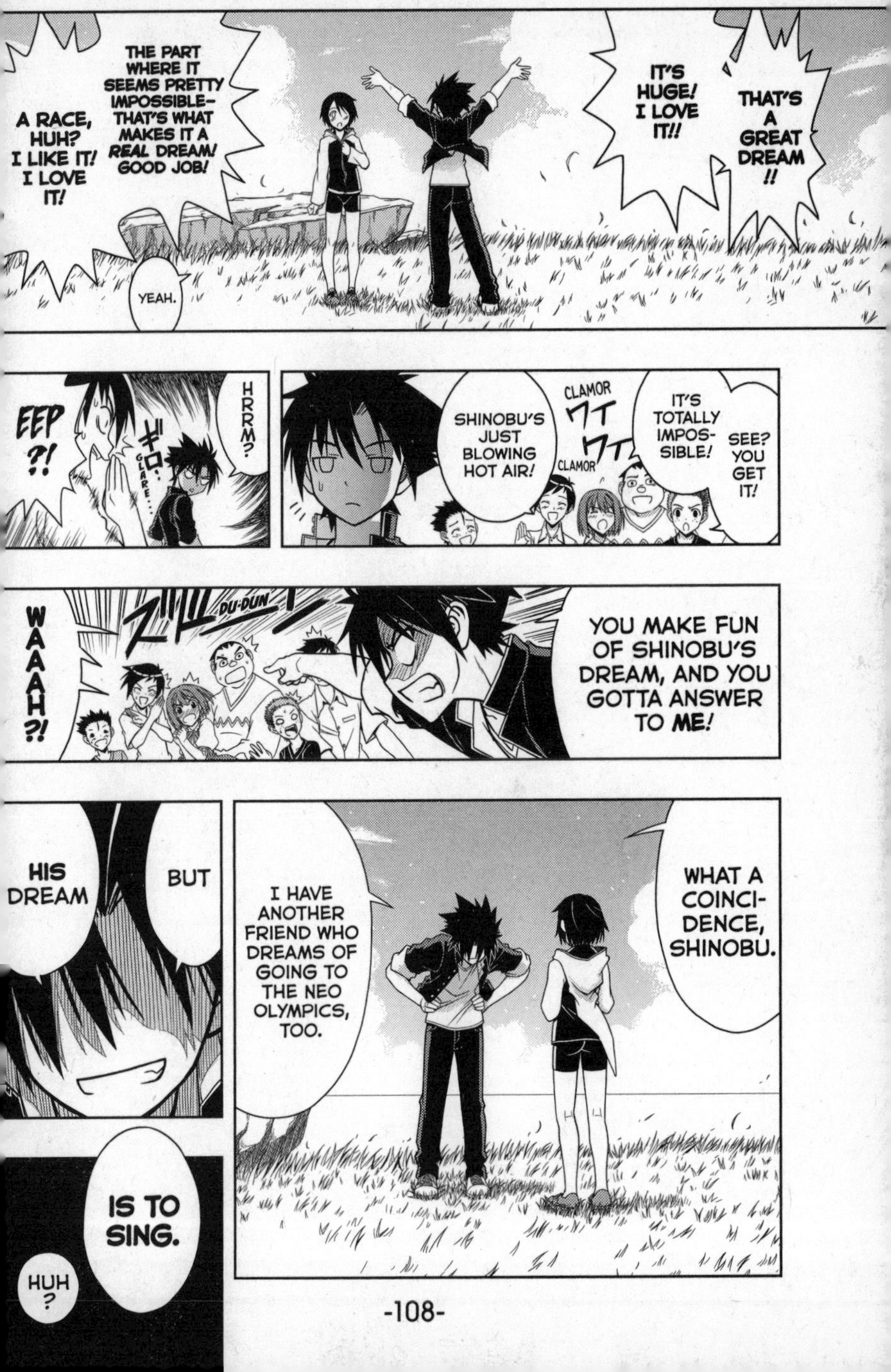
THAT'S A GREAT DREAM!!
IT'S HUGE! I LOVE IT!!
THE PART WHERE IT SEEMS PRETTY IMPOSSIBLE— THAT'S WHAT MAKES IT A REAL DREAM! GOOD JOB!
A RACE, HUH? I LIKE IT! I LOVE IT!
YEAH.
SEE? YOU GET IT!
IT'S TOTALLY IMPOS-SIBLE!
CLAMOR ワイ
ワイ CLAMOR
SHINOBU'S JUST BLOWING HOT AIR!
HRRM?
ギロ GLARE...
EEP?!
YOU MAKE FUN OF SHINOBU'S DREAM, AND YOU GOTTA ANSWER TO ME!
DU-DUN
WAAAAH?!
WHAT A COINCI-DENCE, SHINOBU.
I HAVE ANOTHER FRIEND WHO DREAMS OF GOING TO THE NEO OLYMPICS, TOO.
BUT
HIS DREAM
IS TO SING.
HUH?

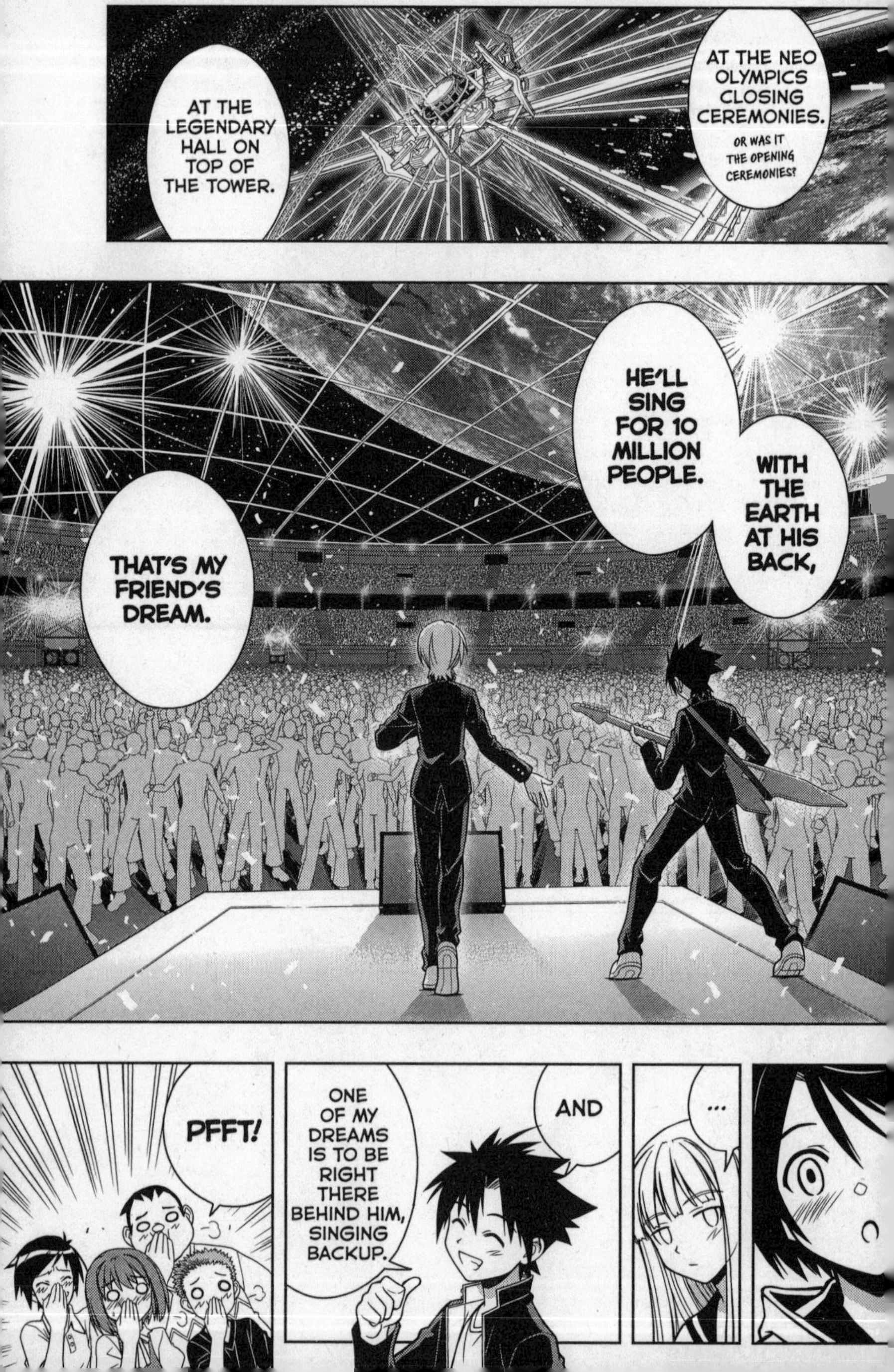

AT THE NEO OLYMPICS CLOSING CEREMONIES.
OR WAS IT THE OPENING CEREMONIES?
AT THE LEGENDARY HALL ON TOP OF THE TOWER.
WITH THE EARTH AT HIS BACK,
HE'LL SING FOR 10 MILLION PEOPLE.
THAT'S MY FRIEND'S DREAM.
...
AND
ONE OF MY DREAMS IS TO BE RIGHT THERE BEHIND HIM, SINGING BACKUP.
PFFT!

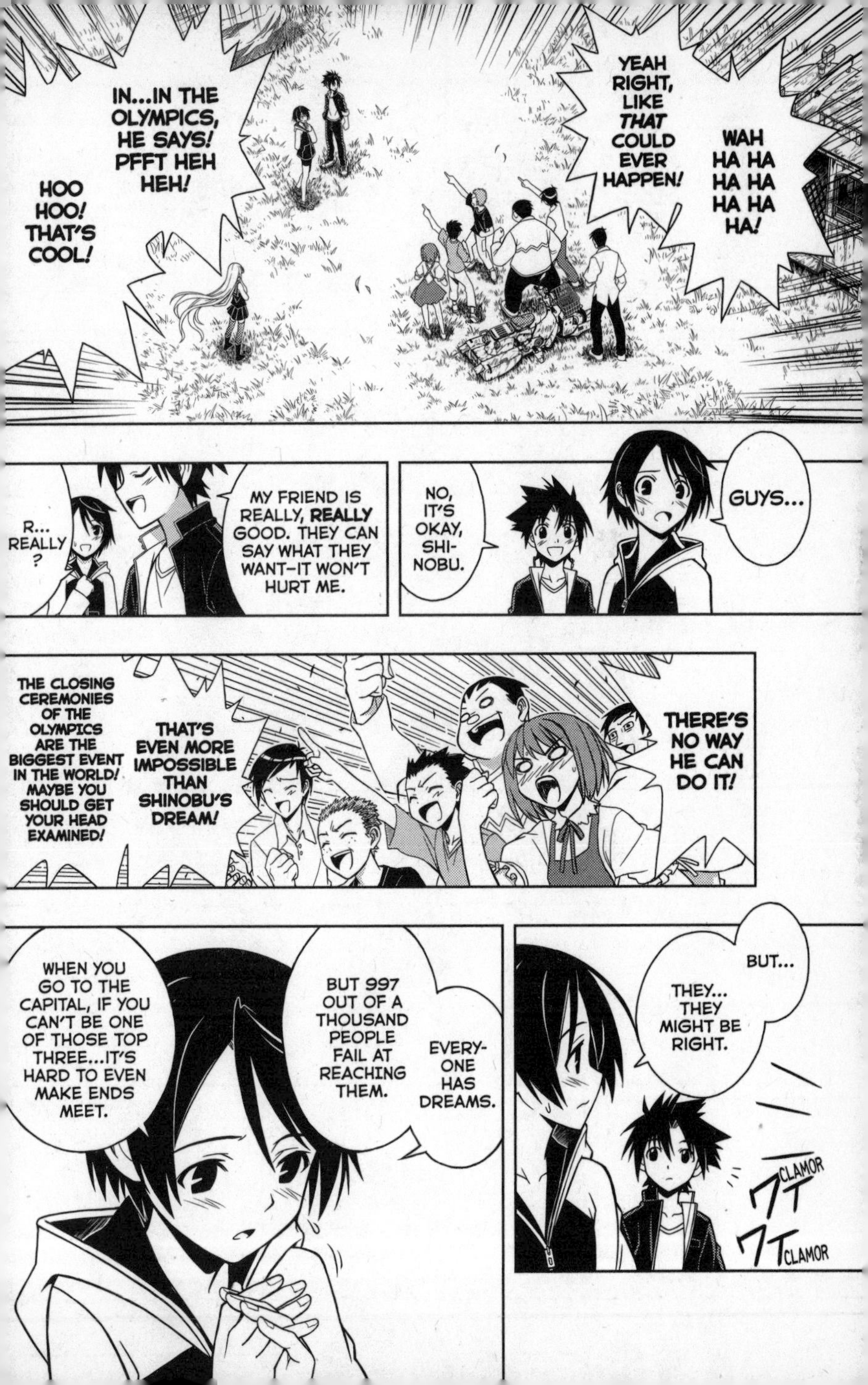
WAH HA HA HA HA HA HA HA!
YEAH RIGHT, LIKE *THAT* COULD EVER HAPPEN!
IN...IN THE OLYMPICS, HE SAYS! PFFT HEH HEH!
HOO HOO! THAT'S COOL!
GUYS...
NO, IT'S OKAY, SHINOBU.
MY FRIEND IS REALLY, **REALLY** GOOD. THEY CAN SAY WHAT THEY WANT–IT WON'T HURT ME.
R... REALLY?
THERE'S NO WAY HE CAN DO IT!
THAT'S EVEN MORE IMPOSSIBLE THAN SHINOBU'S DREAM!
THE CLOSING CEREMONIES OF THE OLYMPICS ARE THE BIGGEST EVENT IN THE WORLD! MAYBE YOU SHOULD GET YOUR HEAD EXAMINED!
BUT...
THEY... THEY MIGHT BE RIGHT.
CLAMOR
CLAMOR
EVERY-ONE HAS DREAMS.
BUT 997 OUT OF A THOUSAND PEOPLE FAIL AT REACHING THEM.
WHEN YOU GO TO THE CAPITAL, IF YOU CAN'T BE ONE OF THOSE TOP THREE...IT'S HARD TO EVEN MAKE ENDS MEET.

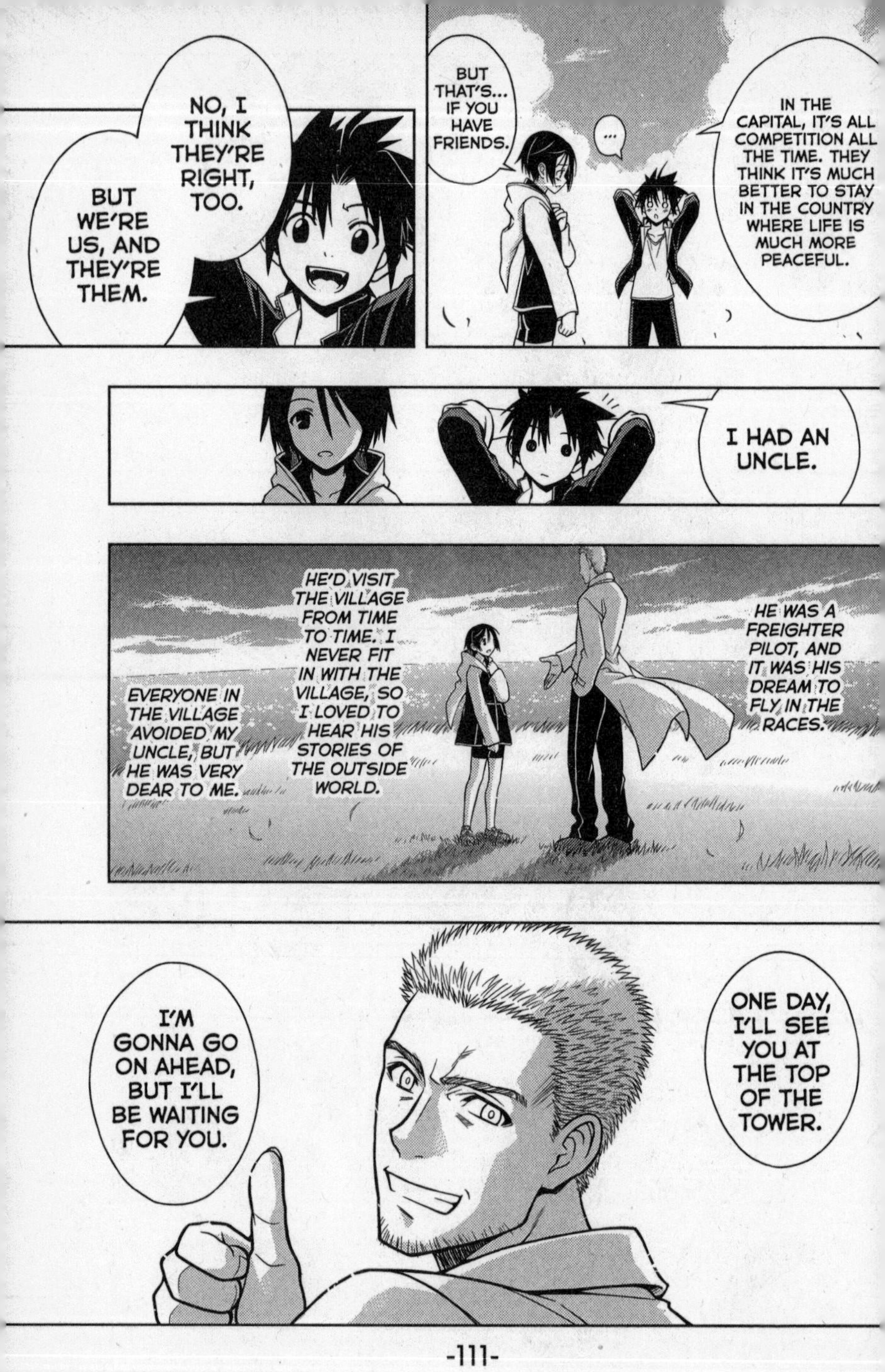
IN THE CAPITAL, IT'S ALL COMPETITION ALL THE TIME. THEY THINK IT'S MUCH BETTER TO STAY IN THE COUNTRY WHERE LIFE IS MUCH MORE PEACEFUL.
...
BUT THAT'S... IF YOU HAVE FRIENDS.
NO, I THINK THEY'RE RIGHT, TOO.
BUT WE'RE US, AND THEY'RE THEM.
I HAD AN UNCLE.
HE WAS A FREIGHTER PILOT, AND IT WAS HIS DREAM TO FLY IN THE RACES.
HE'D VISIT THE VILLAGE FROM TIME TO TIME. I NEVER FIT IN WITH THE VILLAGE, SO I LOVED TO HEAR HIS STORIES OF THE OUTSIDE WORLD.
EVERYONE IN THE VILLAGE AVOIDED MY UNCLE, BUT HE WAS VERY DEAR TO ME.
ONE DAY, I'LL SEE YOU AT THE TOP OF THE TOWER.
I'M GONNA GO ON AHEAD, BUT I'LL BE WAITING FOR YOU.

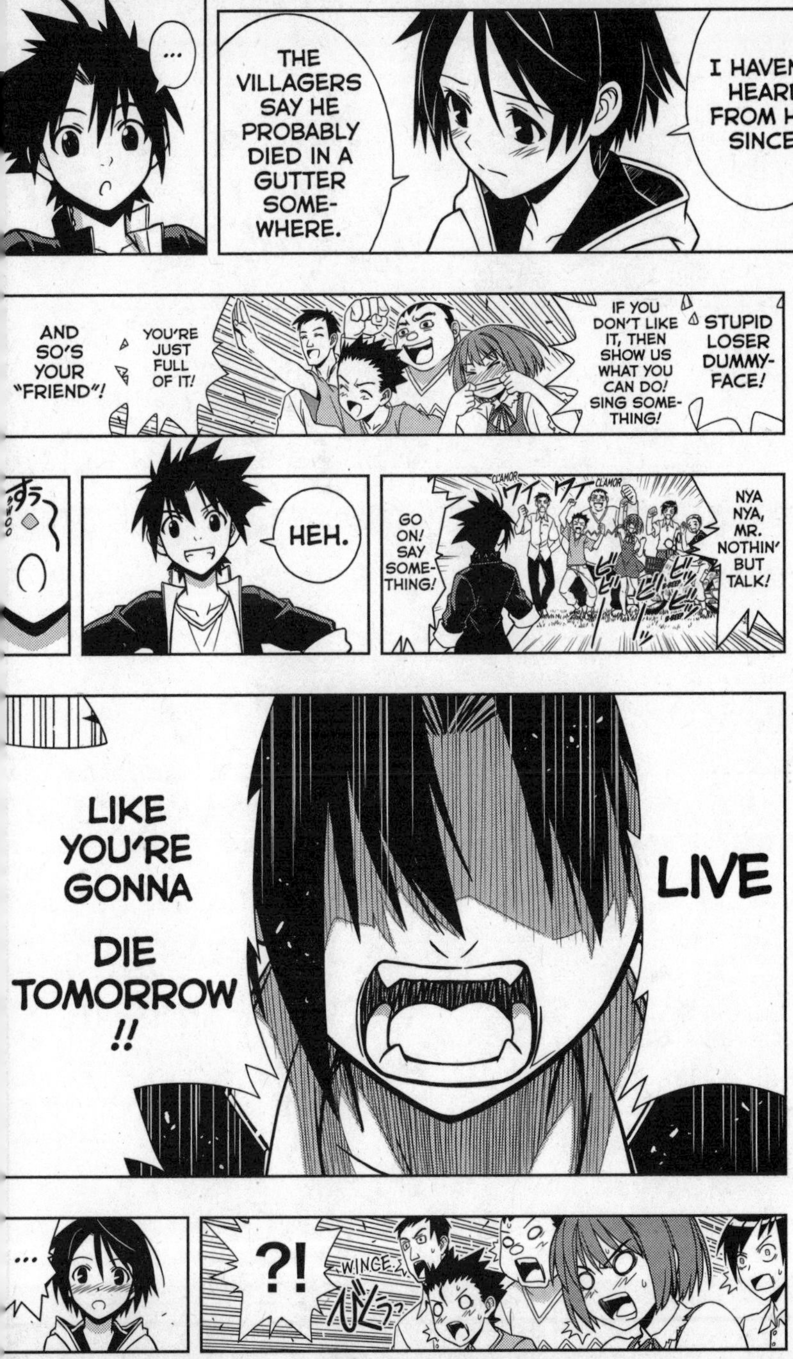
I HAVEN'T HEARD FROM HIM SINCE.
THE VILLAGERS SAY HE PROBABLY DIED IN A GUTTER SOMEWHERE.
...
STUPID LOSER DUMMY-FACE!
IF YOU DON'T LIKE IT, THEN SHOW US WHAT YOU CAN DO! SING SOMETHING!
YOU'RE JUST FULL OF IT!
AND SO'S YOUR "FRIEND"!
NYA NYA, MR. NOTHIN' BUT TALK!
CLAMOR
CLAMOR
GO ON! SAY SOMETHING!
HEH.
LIVE
LIKE YOU'RE GONNA DIE TOMORROW!!
?!
WINCE
...

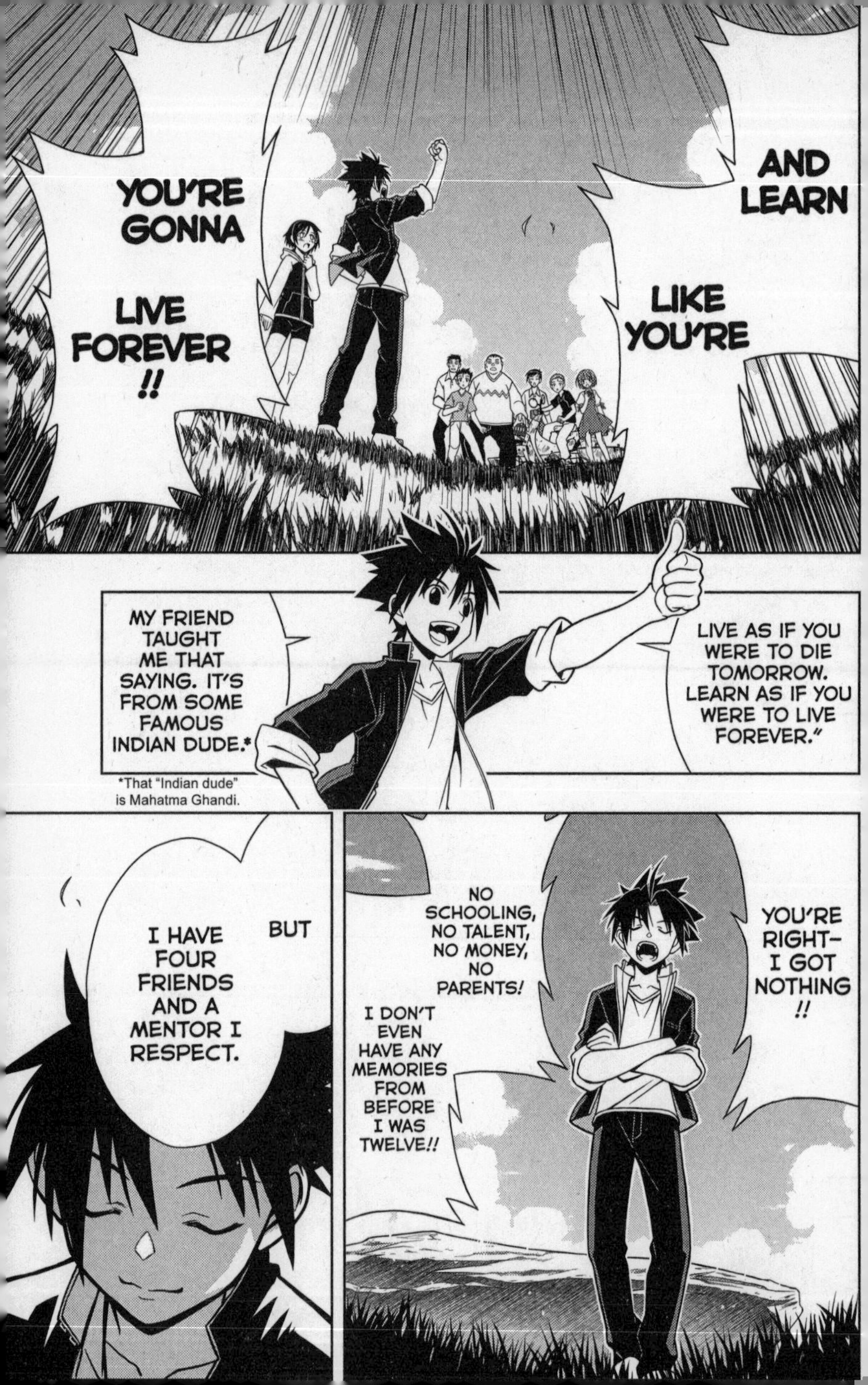
AND LEARN LIKE YOU'RE
YOU'RE GONNA LIVE FOREVER!!
LIVE AS IF YOU WERE TO DIE TOMORROW. LEARN AS IF YOU WERE TO LIVE FOREVER."
MY FRIEND TAUGHT ME THAT SAYING. IT'S FROM SOME FAMOUS INDIAN DUDE.*
YOU'RE RIGHT– I GOT NOTHING!!
NO SCHOOLING, NO TALENT, NO MONEY, NO PARENTS!
I DON'T EVEN HAVE ANY MEMORIES FROM BEFORE I WAS TWELVE!!
BUT
I HAVE FOUR FRIENDS AND A MENTOR I RESPECT.

*That "Indian dude" is Mahatma Ghandi.

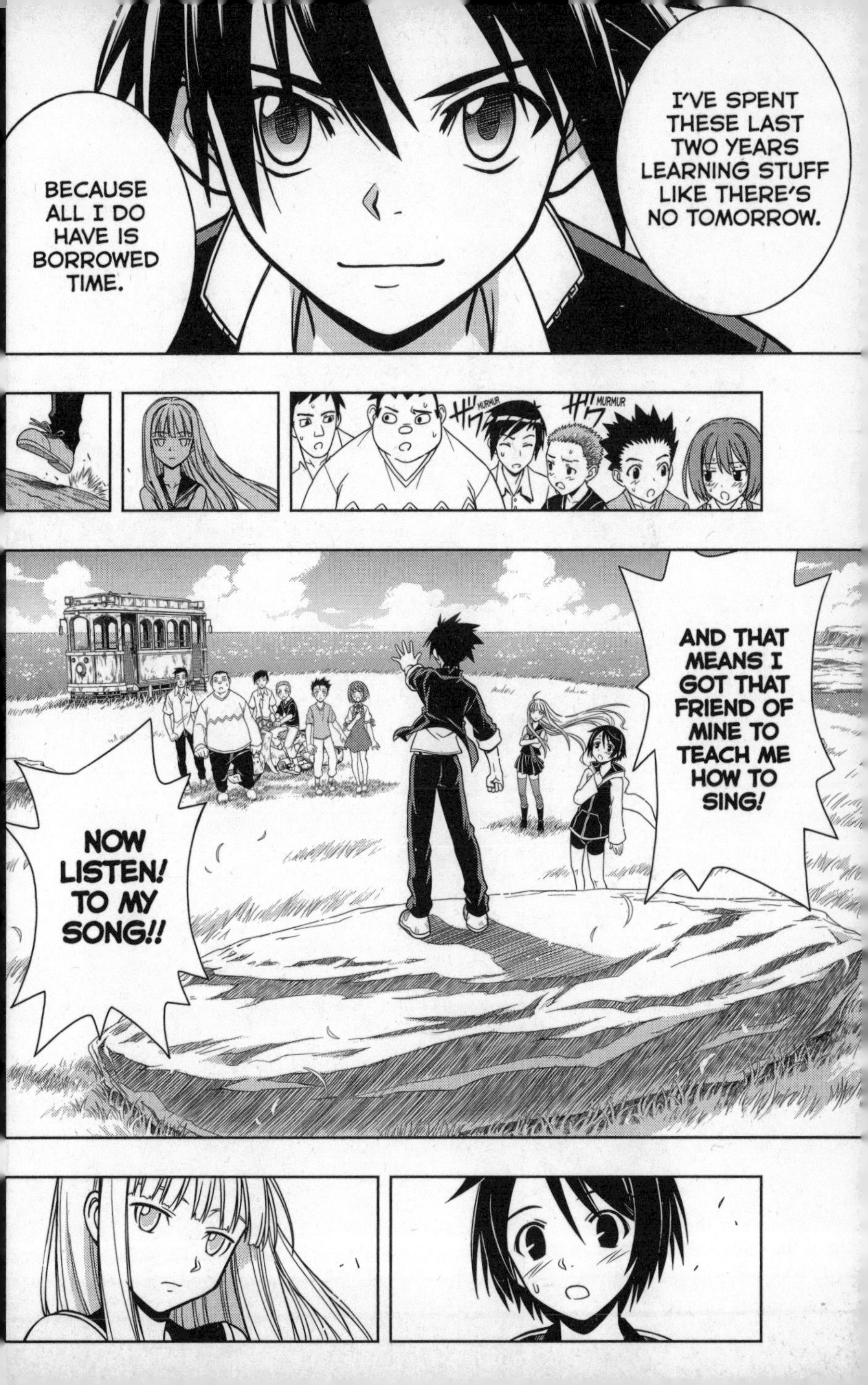
I'VE SPENT THESE LAST TWO YEARS LEARNING STUFF LIKE THERE'S NO TOMORROW.
BECAUSE ALL I DO HAVE IS BORROWED TIME.
MURMUR
MURMUR
AND THAT MEANS I GOT THAT FRIEND OF MINE TO TEACH ME HOW TO SING!
NOW LISTEN! TO MY SONG!!

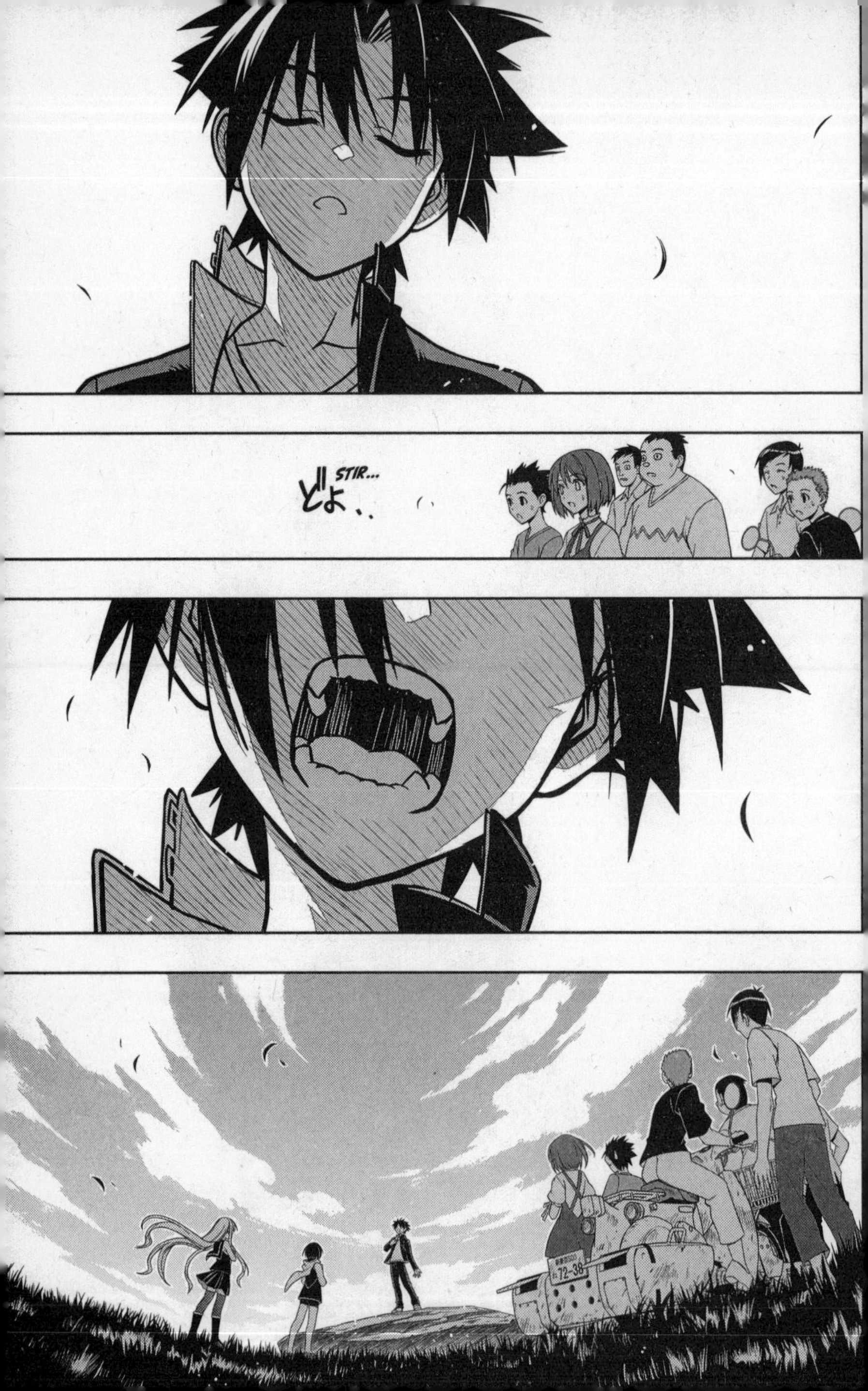
どよ‥
STIR...

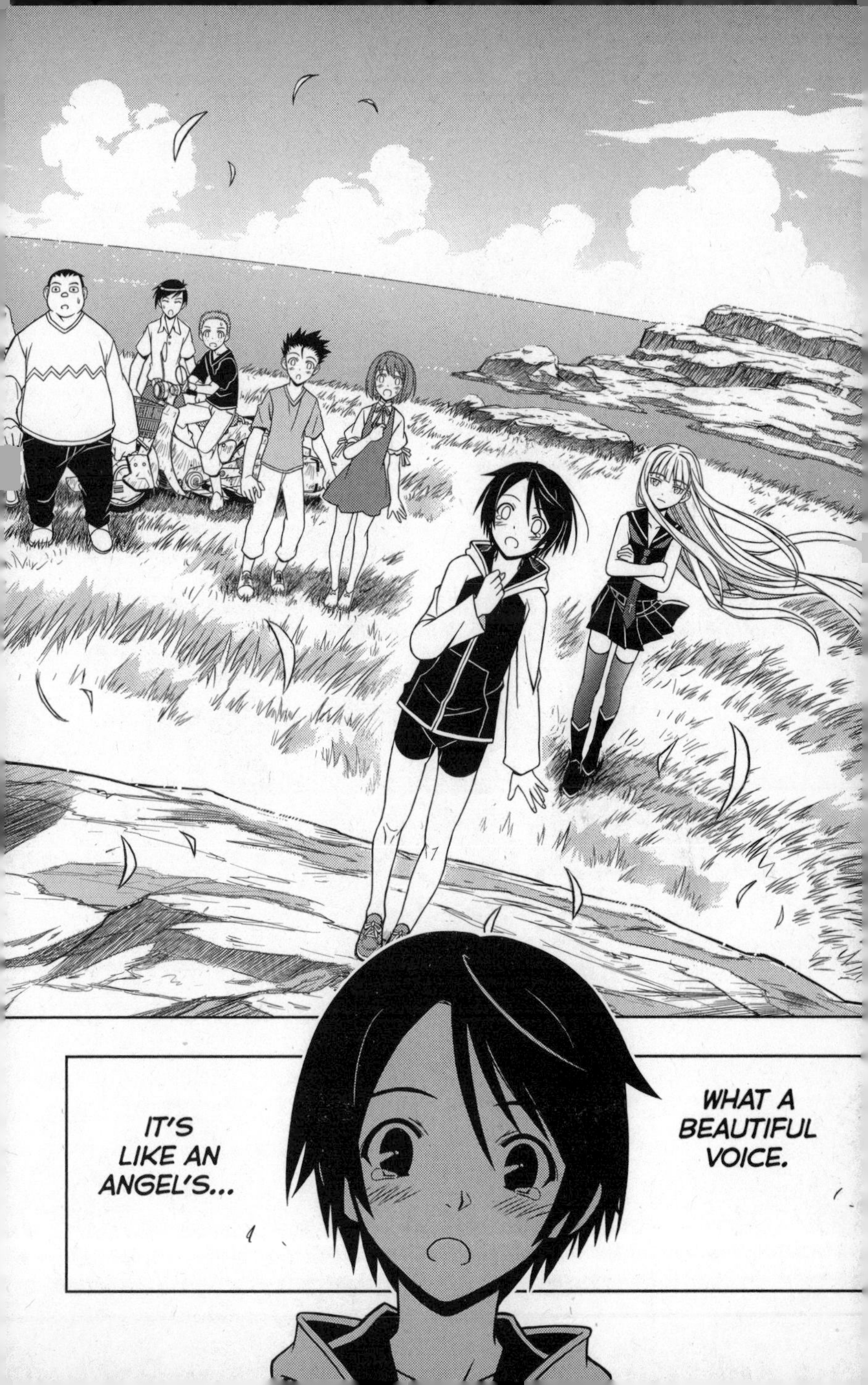
WHAT A BEAUTIFUL VOICE.
IT'S LIKE AN ANGEL'S...

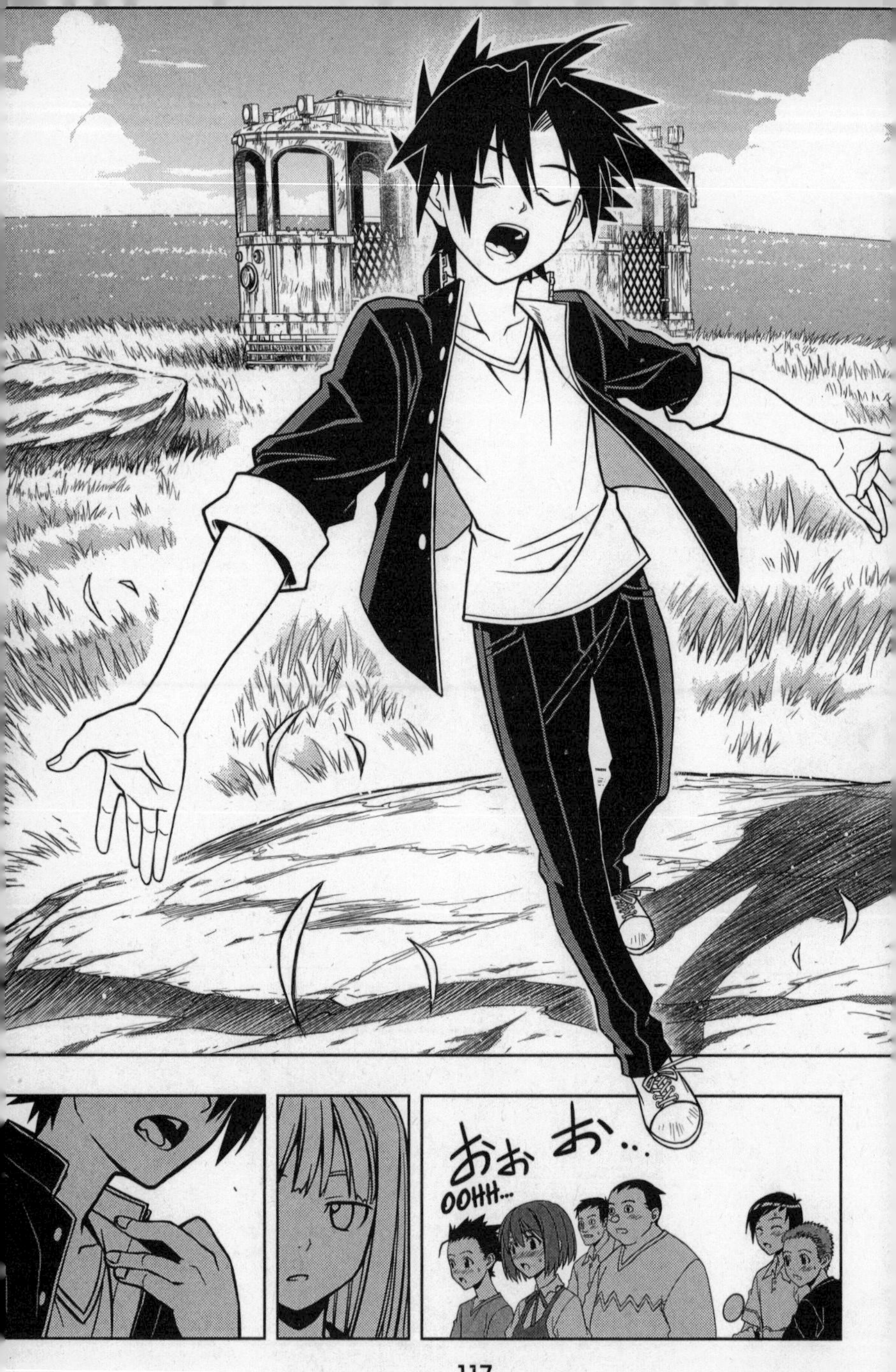
おぉ お…
OOHH...

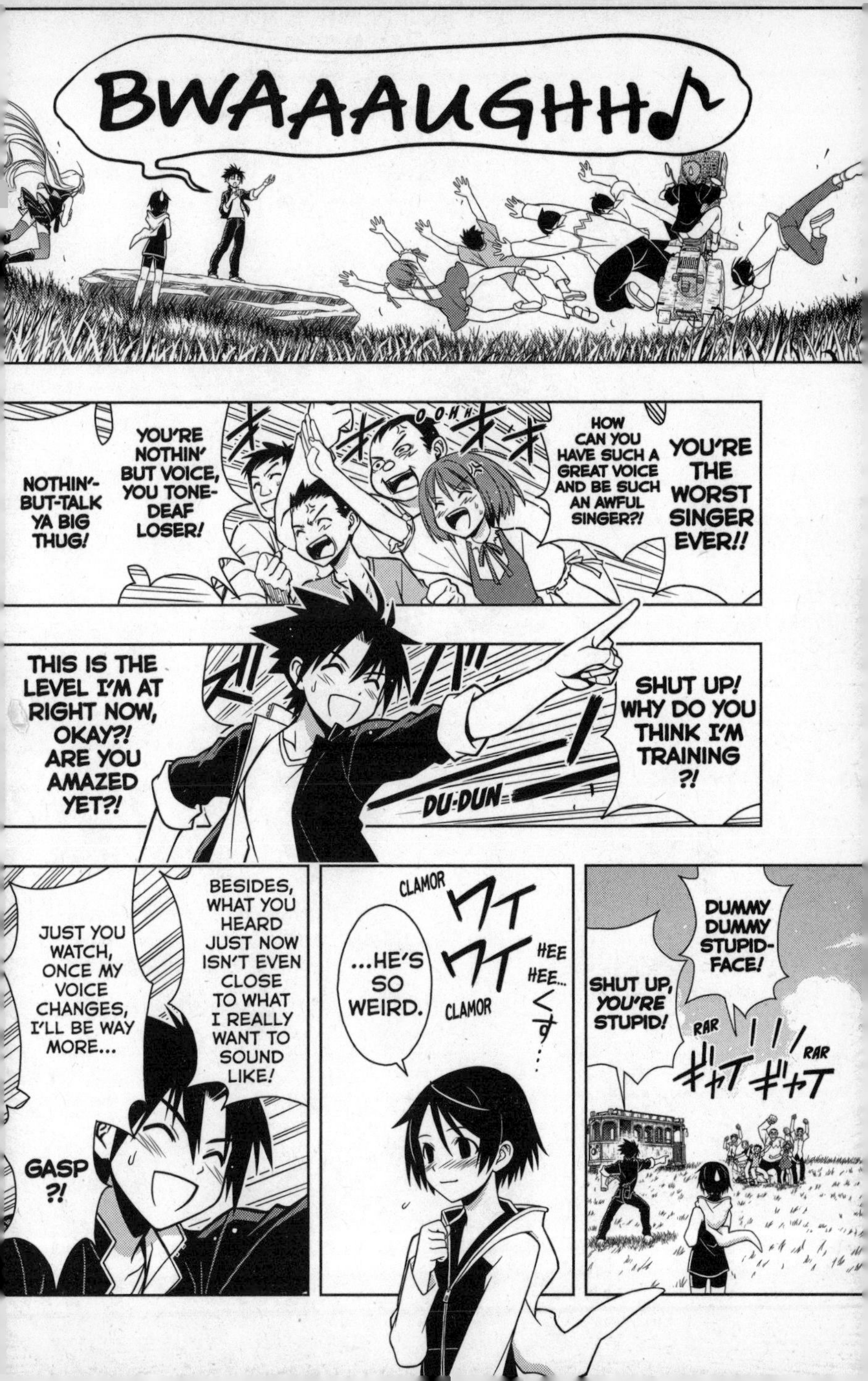
BWAAAUGHH♪
YOU'RE THE WORST SINGER EVER!!
HOW CAN YOU HAVE SUCH A GREAT VOICE AND BE SUCH AN AWFUL SINGER?!
OOHH
YOU'RE NOTHIN' BUT VOICE, YOU TONE-DEAF LOSER!
NOTHIN'-BUT-TALK YA BIG THUG!
SHUT UP! WHY DO YOU THINK I'M TRAINING?!
THIS IS THE LEVEL I'M AT RIGHT NOW, OKAY?! ARE YOU AMAZED YET?!
DU-DUN
DUMMY DUMMY STUPID-FACE!
SHUT UP, YOU'RE STUPID!
RAR
ギャアギャア
RAR
CLAMOR
ワイワイ
CLAMOR
HEE HEE...
くす…
...HE'S SO WEIRD.
BESIDES, WHAT YOU HEARD JUST NOW ISN'T EVEN CLOSE TO WHAT I REALLY WANT TO SOUND LIKE!
JUST YOU WATCH, ONCE MY VOICE CHANGES, I'LL BE WAY MORE...
GASP?!

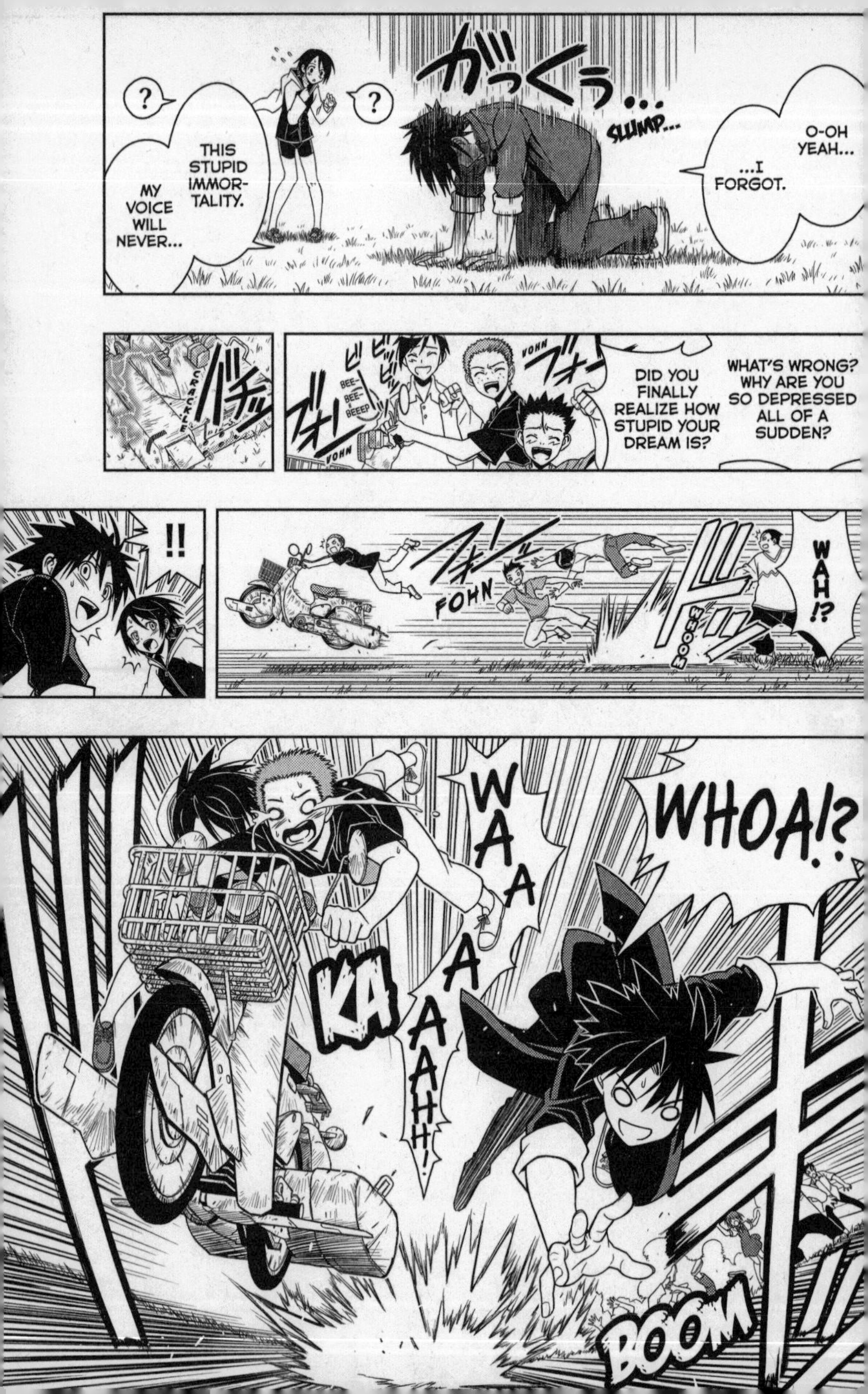

O-OH YEAH...
...I FORGOT.
がっくぅ...
SLUMP...
?
?
THIS STUPID IMMORTALITY.
MY VOICE WILL NEVER...
WHAT'S WRONG? WHY ARE YOU SO DEPRESSED ALL OF A SUDDEN?
DID YOU FINALLY REALIZE HOW STUPID YOUR DREAM IS?
VOHN
BEE-BEE-BEEEP
VOHN
CRACKLE
WAH!?
WHOOM
FOHN
!!
WHOA!?
WAAAAAAHH!
KA
BOOM

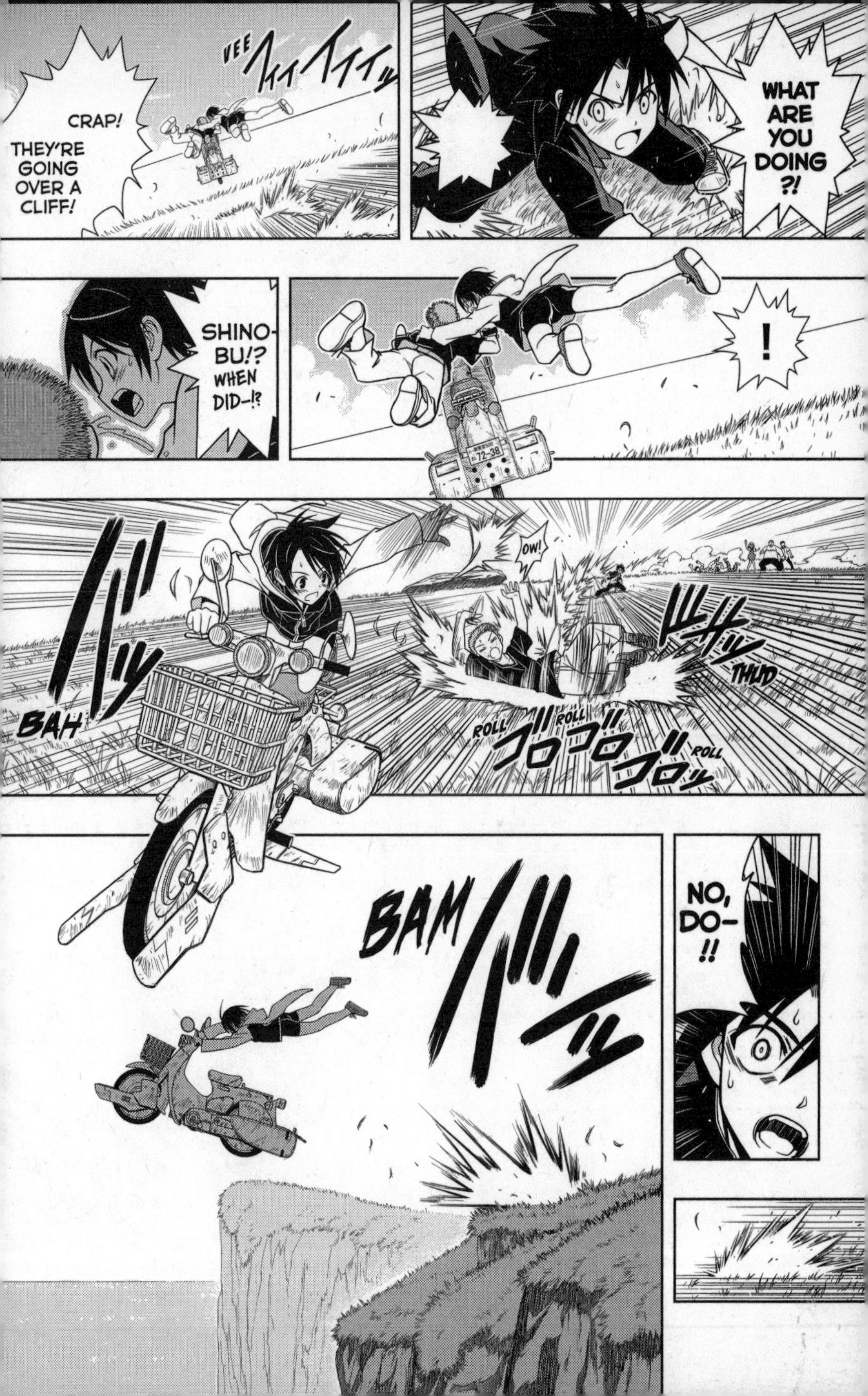
WHAT ARE YOU DOING ?!
VEE
CRAP!
THEY'RE GOING OVER A CLIFF!
!
SHINO-BU!? WHEN DID-!?
THUD
OW!
ROLL ROLL ROLL
BAH
NO, DO-!!
BAM

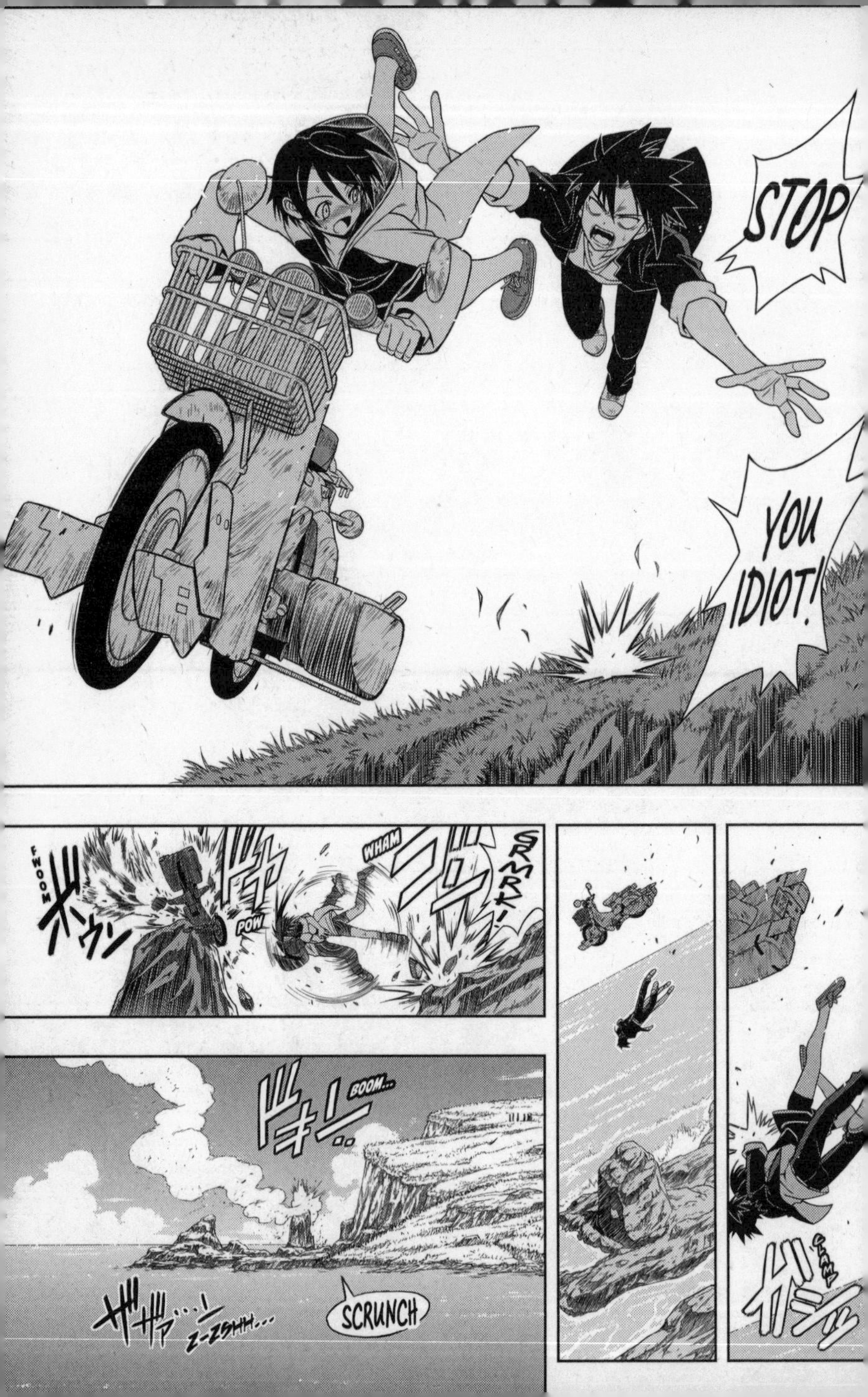
STOP
YOU IDIOT!
CLAMP
FWOOM
ボウン
ドカ
POW
WHAM
GRMRK!
BOOM...
SCRUNCH
ザザァ…ン
Z-ZSHH...

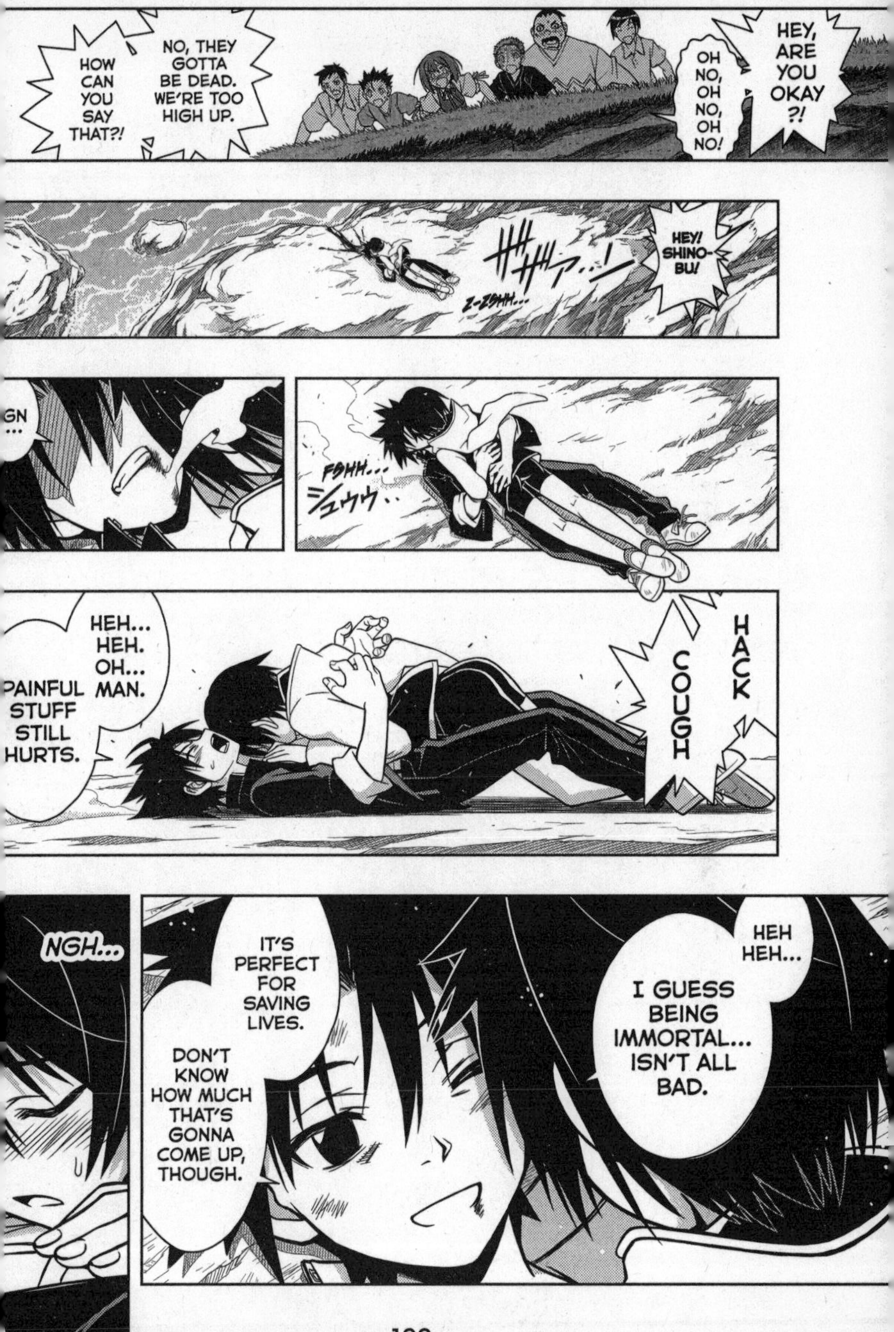
HEY, ARE YOU OKAY?!
OH NO, OH NO, OH NO!
NO, THEY GOTTA BE DEAD. WE'RE TOO HIGH UP.
HOW CAN YOU SAY THAT?!
HEY! SHINOBU!
ザザァ…!
Z-ZSHH...
FSHH...
シュウウ…
GN...
HACK
COUGH
HEH... HEH. OH... MAN.
PAINFUL STUFF STILL HURTS.
HEH HEH...
I GUESS BEING IMMORTAL... ISN'T ALL BAD.
IT'S PERFECT FOR SAVING LIVES.
DON'T KNOW HOW MUCH THAT'S GONNA COME UP, THOUGH.
NGH...

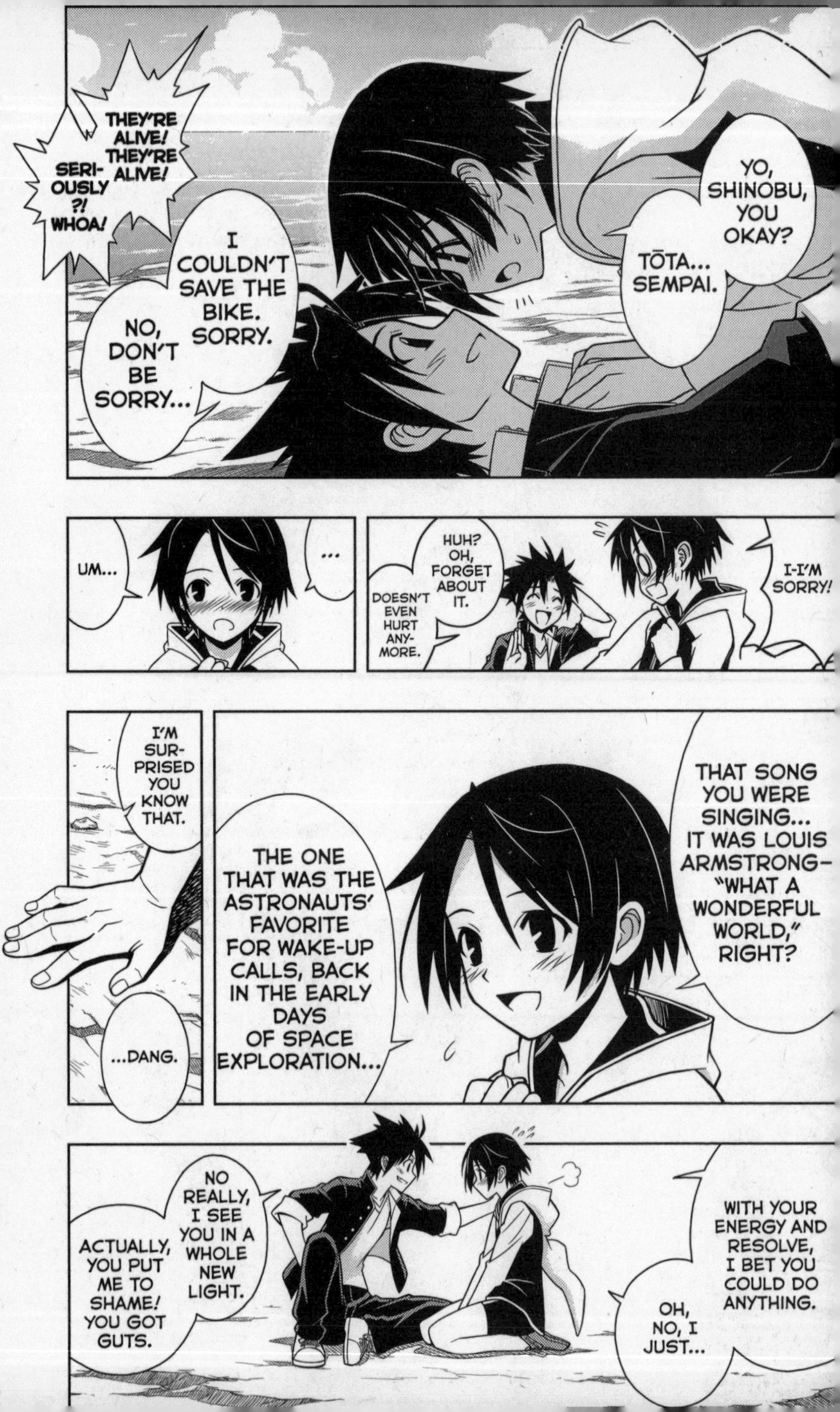
YO, SHINOBU, YOU OKAY?
TŌTA... SEMPAI.
I COULDN'T SAVE THE BIKE. SORRY.
NO, DON'T BE SORRY...
THEY'RE ALIVE! THEY'RE ALIVE!
SERIOUSLY ?! WHOA!
I-I'M SORRY!
HUH? OH, FORGET ABOUT IT.
DOESN'T EVEN HURT ANYMORE.
...
UM...
THAT SONG YOU WERE SINGING... IT WAS LOUIS ARMSTRONG—"WHAT A WONDERFUL WORLD," RIGHT?
THE ONE THAT WAS THE ASTRONAUTS' FAVORITE FOR WAKE-UP CALLS, BACK IN THE EARLY DAYS OF SPACE EXPLORATION...
I'M SURPRISED YOU KNOW THAT.
...DANG.
WITH YOUR ENERGY AND RESOLVE, I BET YOU COULD DO ANYTHING.
OH, NO, I JUST...
NO REALLY, I SEE YOU IN A WHOLE NEW LIGHT.
ACTUALLY, YOU PUT ME TO SHAME! YOU GOT GUTS.

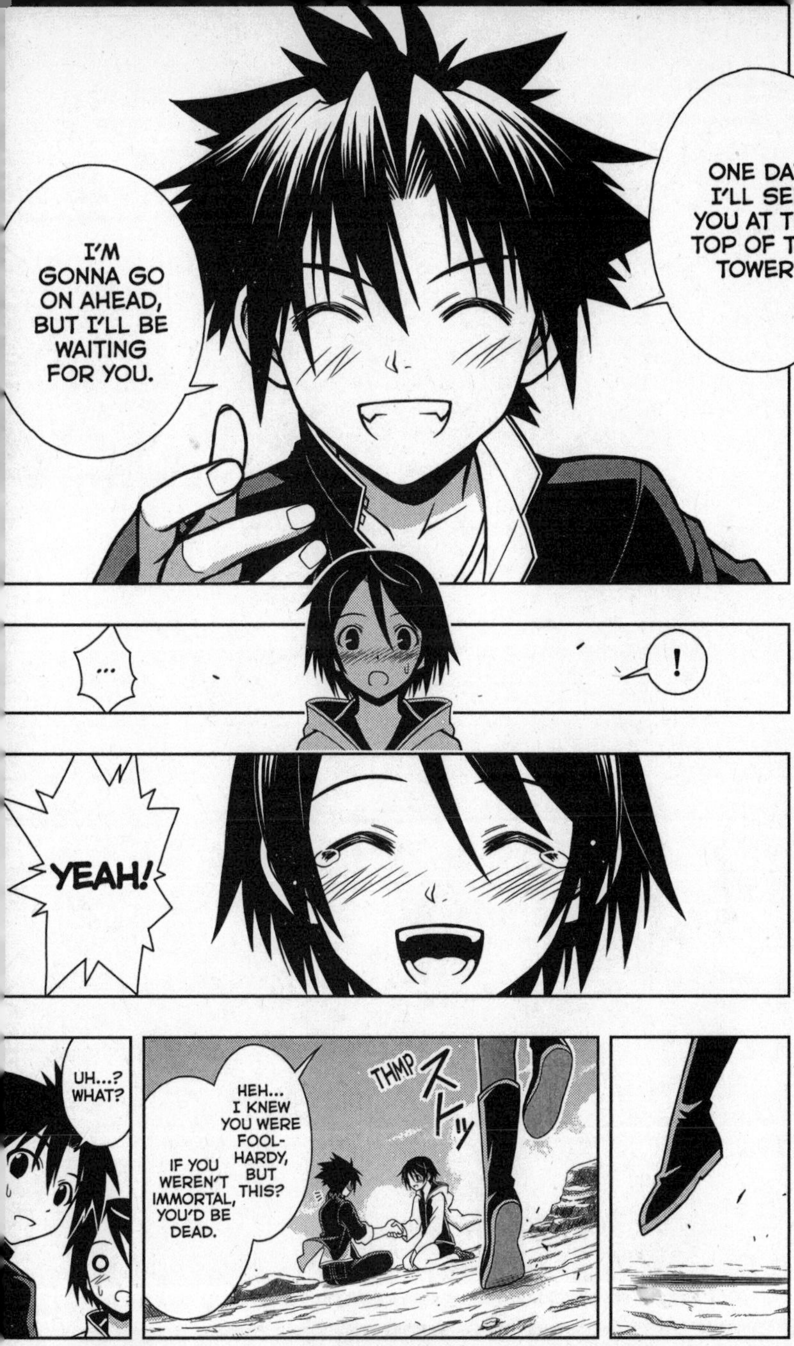
ONE DAY, I'LL SEE YOU AT THE TOP OF THE TOWER.
I'M GONNA GO ON AHEAD, BUT I'LL BE WAITING FOR YOU.
!
...
YEAH!
THMP
ストッ
HEH... I KNEW YOU WERE FOOL-HARDY, BUT THIS?
IF YOU WEREN'T IMMORTAL, YOU'D BE DEAD.
UH...? WHAT?

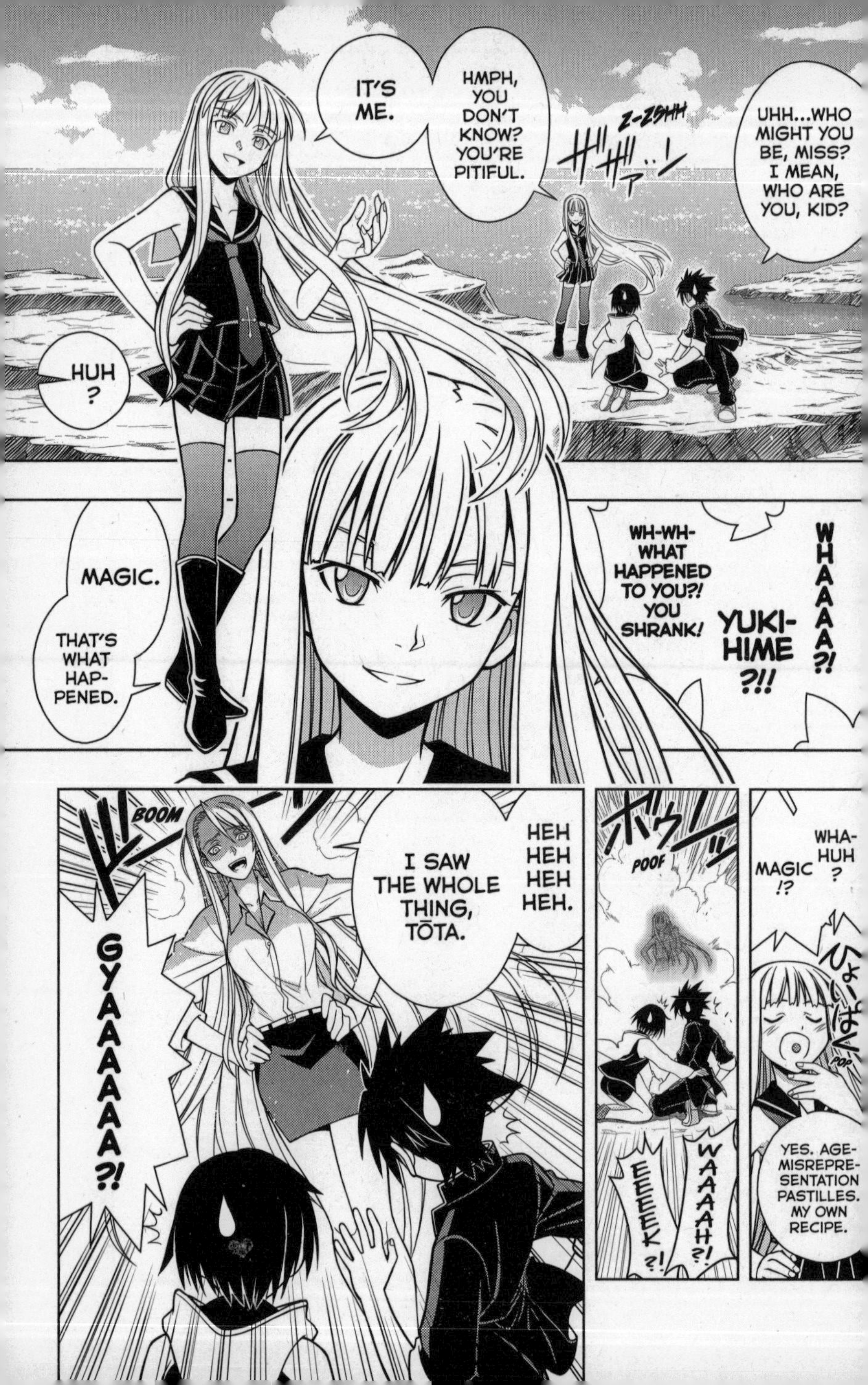
UHH...WHO MIGHT YOU BE, MISS? I MEAN, WHO ARE YOU, KID?
Z-ZSHH
HMPH, YOU DON'T KNOW? YOU'RE PITIFUL.
IT'S ME.
HUH ?
WHAAAAA?!
YUKI-HIME ?!!
WH-WH-WHAT HAPPENED TO YOU?! YOU SHRANK!
MAGIC.
THAT'S WHAT HAP-PENED.
WHA-HUH ?
MAGIC !?
POP
YES. AGE-MISREPRESENTATION PASTILLES. MY OWN RECIPE.
POOF
WAAAAAH?!
EEEEK ?!
HEH HEH HEH HEH.
I SAW THE WHOLE THING, TŌTA.
BOOM
GYAAAAAAA?!

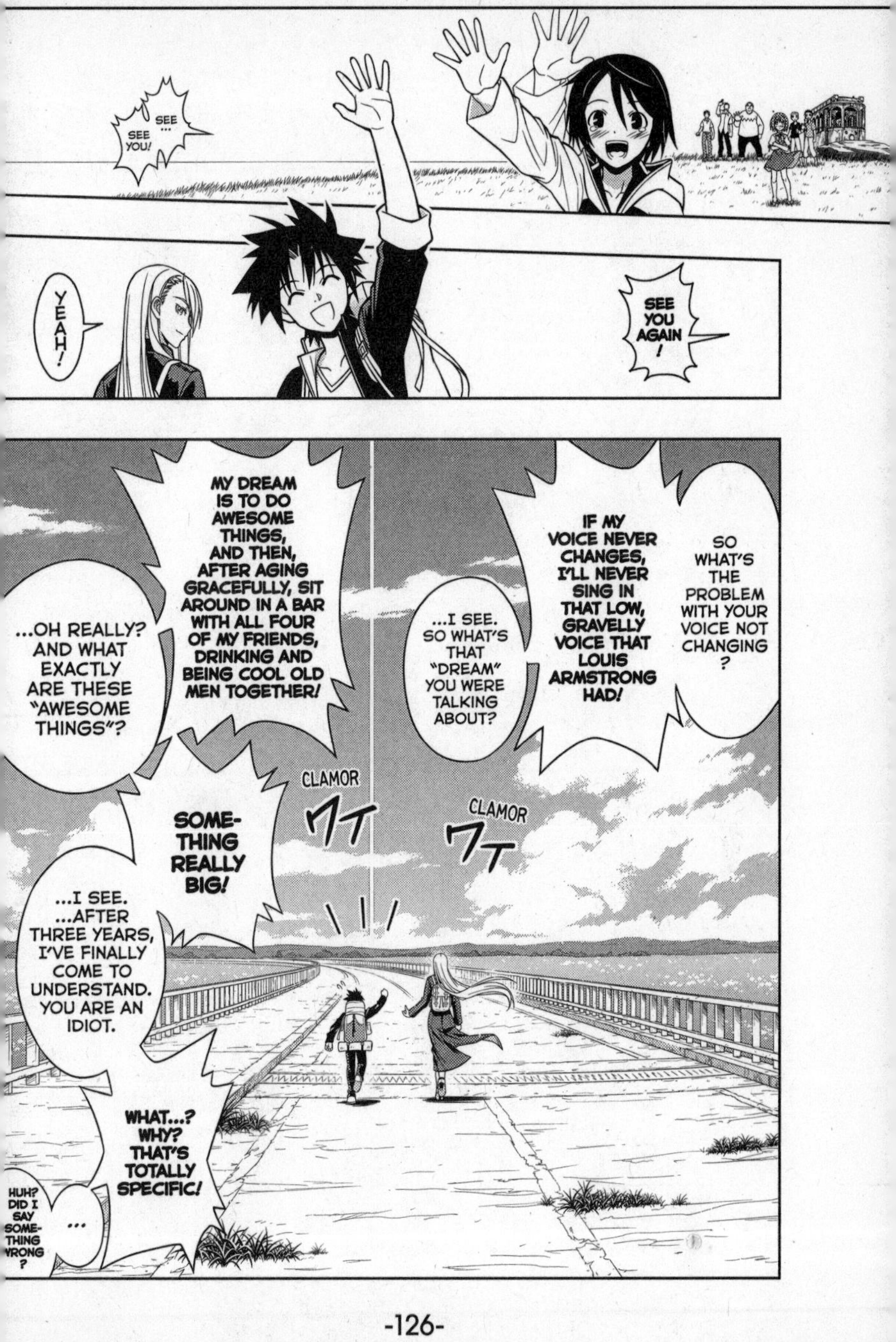
SEE... SEE YOU!
SEE YOU AGAIN!
YEAH!
SO WHAT'S THE PROBLEM WITH YOUR VOICE NOT CHANGING?
IF MY VOICE NEVER CHANGES, I'LL NEVER SING IN THAT LOW, GRAVELLY VOICE THAT LOUIS ARMSTRONG HAD!
...I SEE. SO WHAT'S THAT "DREAM" YOU WERE TALKING ABOUT?
MY DREAM IS TO DO AWESOME THINGS, AND THEN, AFTER AGING GRACEFULLY, SIT AROUND IN A BAR WITH ALL FOUR OF MY FRIENDS, DRINKING AND BEING COOL OLD MEN TOGETHER!
...OH REALLY? AND WHAT EXACTLY ARE THESE "AWESOME THINGS"?
CLAMOR
CLAMOR
SOME-THING REALLY BIG!
...I SEE. ...AFTER THREE YEARS, I'VE FINALLY COME TO UNDERSTAND. YOU ARE AN IDIOT.
WHAT...? WHY? THAT'S TOTALLY SPECIFIC!
...
HUH? DID I SAY SOME-THING WRONG?

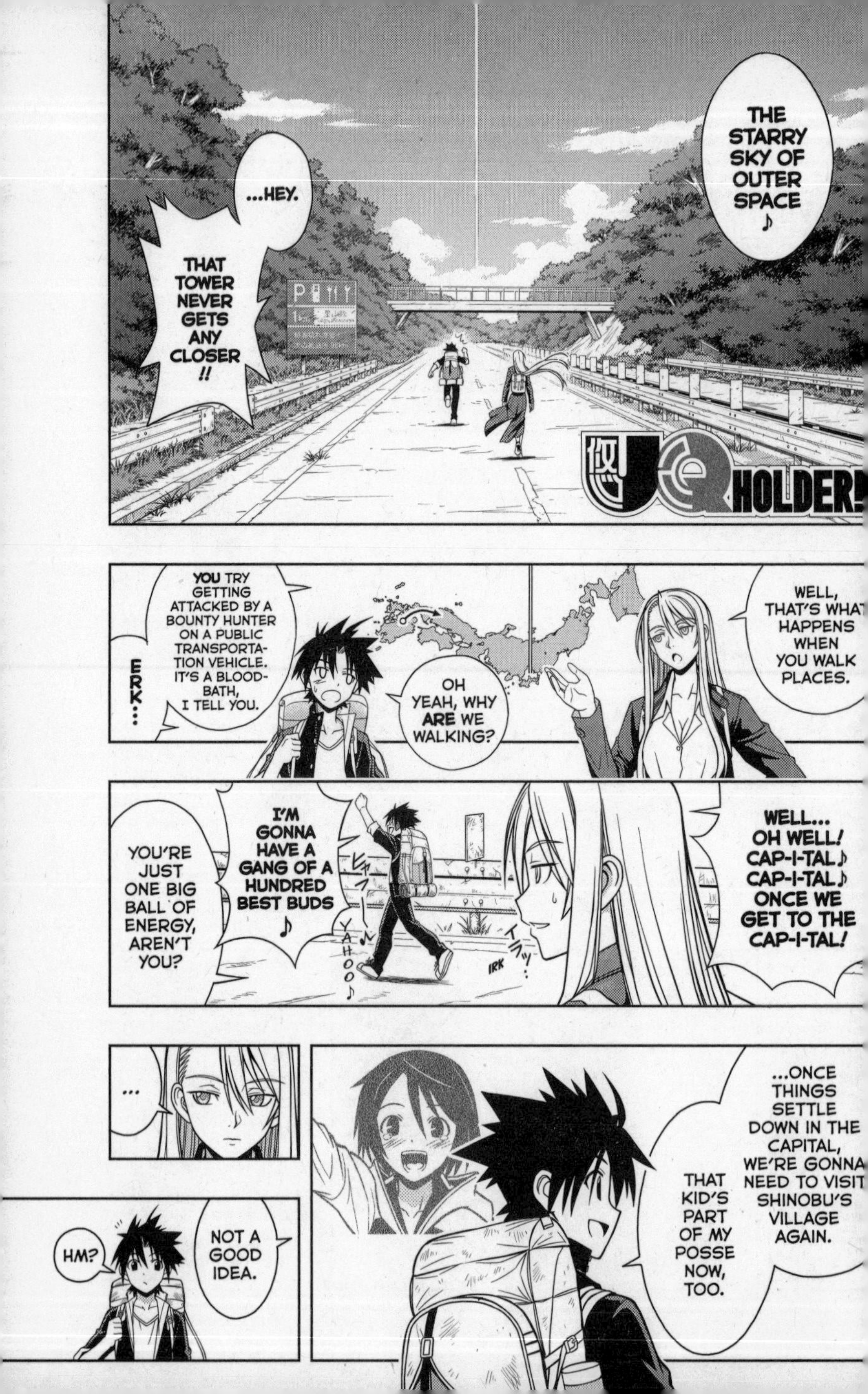
THE STARRY SKY OF OUTER SPACE ♪
...HEY.
THAT TOWER NEVER GETS ANY CLOSER !!
HOLDER!
WELL, THAT'S WHAT HAPPENS WHEN YOU WALK PLACES.
OH YEAH, WHY ARE WE WALKING?
YOU TRY GETTING ATTACKED BY A BOUNTY HUNTER ON A PUBLIC TRANSPORTATION VEHICLE. IT'S A BLOODBATH, I TELL YOU.
ERK...
WELL... OH WELL! CAP-I-TAL♪ CAP-I-TAL♪ ONCE WE GET TO THE CAP-I-TAL!
IRK
YAHOO♪
I'M GONNA HAVE A GANG OF A HUNDRED BEST BUDS ♪
YOU'RE JUST ONE BIG BALL OF ENERGY, AREN'T YOU?
...ONCE THINGS SETTLE DOWN IN THE CAPITAL, WE'RE GONNA NEED TO VISIT SHINOBU'S VILLAGE AGAIN.
THAT KID'S PART OF MY POSSE NOW, TOO.
...
NOT A GOOD IDEA.
HM?

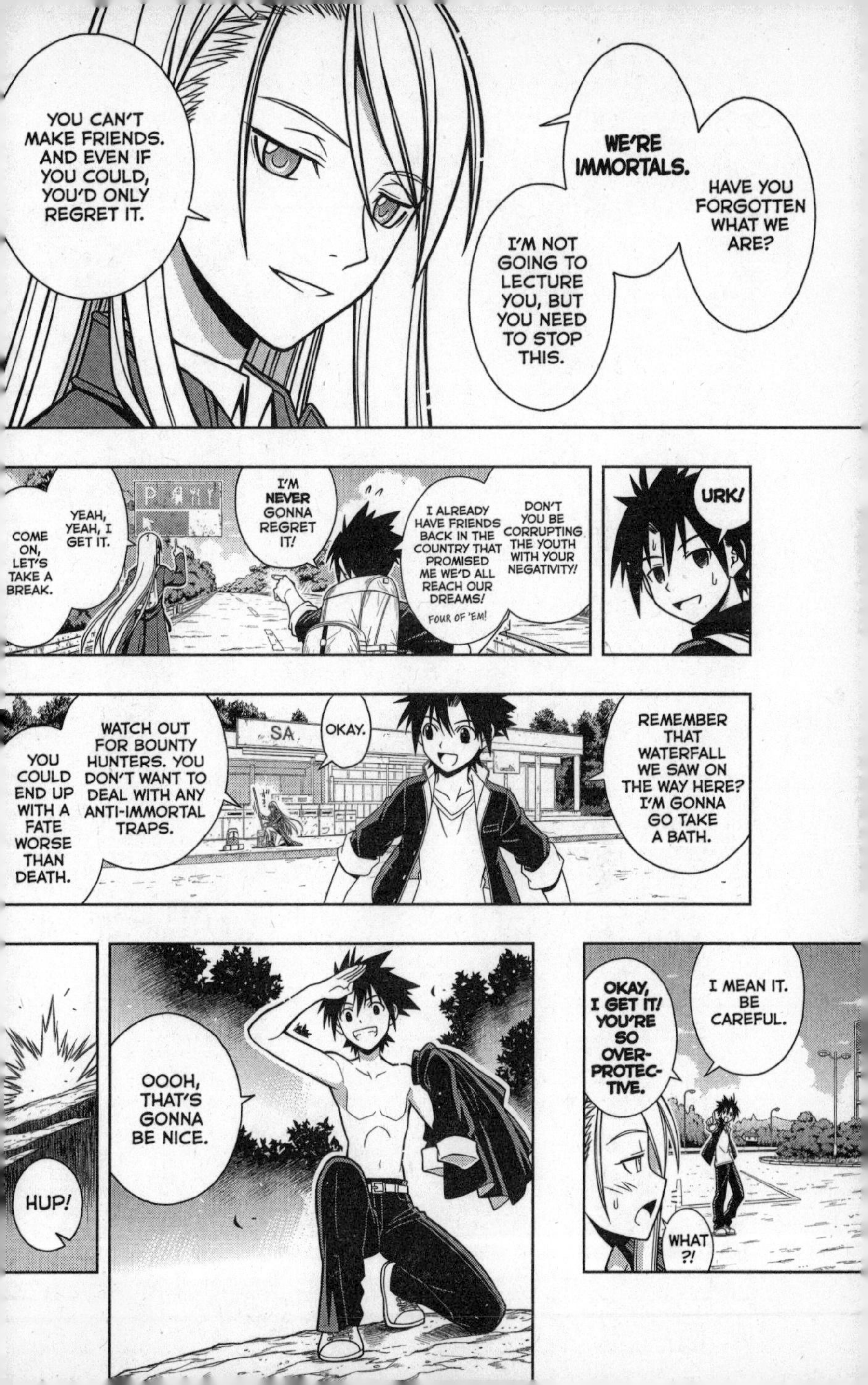

HAVE YOU FORGOTTEN WHAT WE ARE?
WE'RE IMMORTALS.
I'M NOT GOING TO LECTURE YOU, BUT YOU NEED TO STOP THIS.
YOU CAN'T MAKE FRIENDS. AND EVEN IF YOU COULD, YOU'D ONLY REGRET IT.
URK!
DON'T YOU BE CORRUPTING THE YOUTH WITH YOUR NEGATIVITY!
I ALREADY HAVE FRIENDS BACK IN THE COUNTRY THAT PROMISED ME WE'D ALL REACH OUR DREAMS!
FOUR OF 'EM!
I'M NEVER GONNA REGRET IT!
YEAH, YEAH, I GET IT.
COME ON, LET'S TAKE A BREAK.
REMEMBER THAT WATERFALL WE SAW ON THE WAY HERE? I'M GONNA GO TAKE A BATH.
OKAY.
SA
WATCH OUT FOR BOUNTY HUNTERS. YOU DON'T WANT TO DEAL WITH ANY ANTI-IMMORTAL TRAPS.
YOU COULD END UP WITH A FATE WORSE THAN DEATH.
I MEAN IT. BE CAREFUL.
OKAY, I GET IT! YOU'RE SO OVER-PROTECTIVE.
WHAT?!
OOOH, THAT'S GONNA BE NICE.
HUP!

STAGE 3: I THOUGHT WE COULD BE FRIENDS

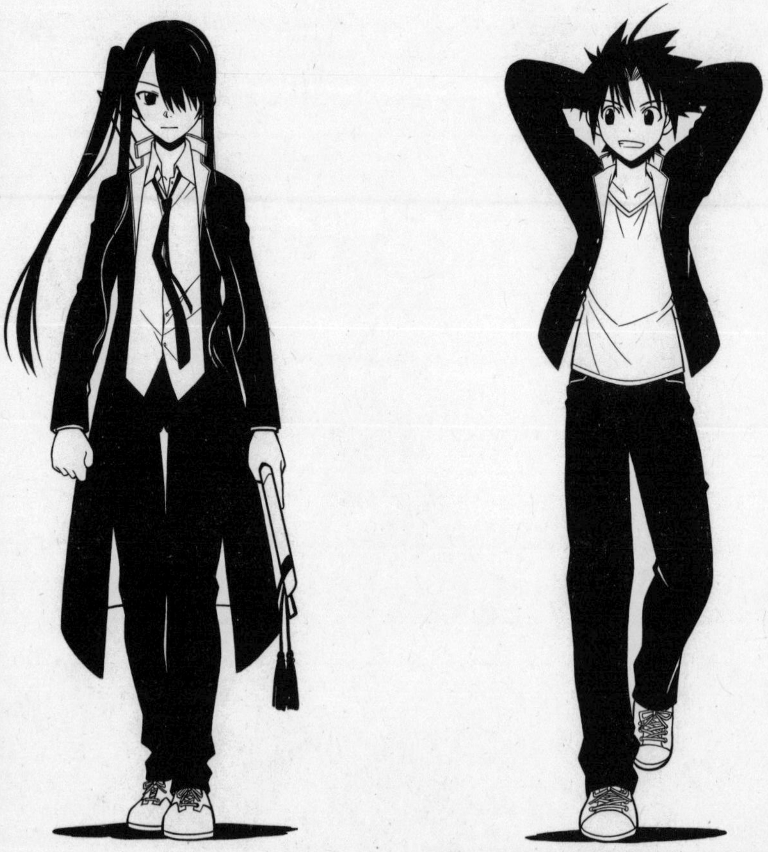

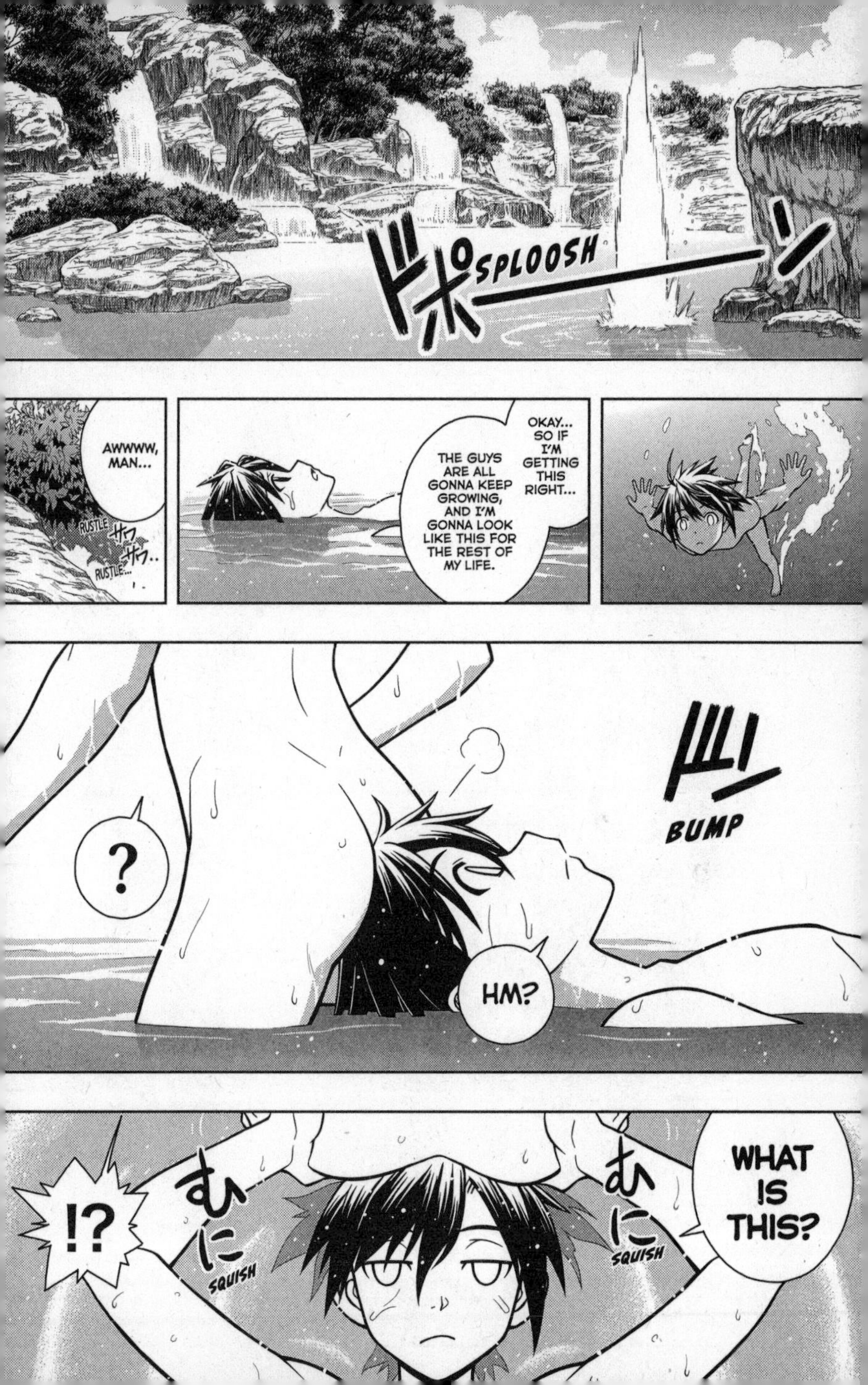
ドボ
SPLOOSH
ン
OKAY... SO IF I'M GETTING THIS RIGHT...
THE GUYS ARE ALL GONNA KEEP GROWING, AND I'M GONNA LOOK LIKE THIS FOR THE REST OF MY LIFE.
AWWWW, MAN...
サワ
RUSTLE
サワ..
RUSTLE...
ドン
BUMP
?
HM?
WHAT IS THIS?
むに
SQUISH
むに
SQUISH
!?

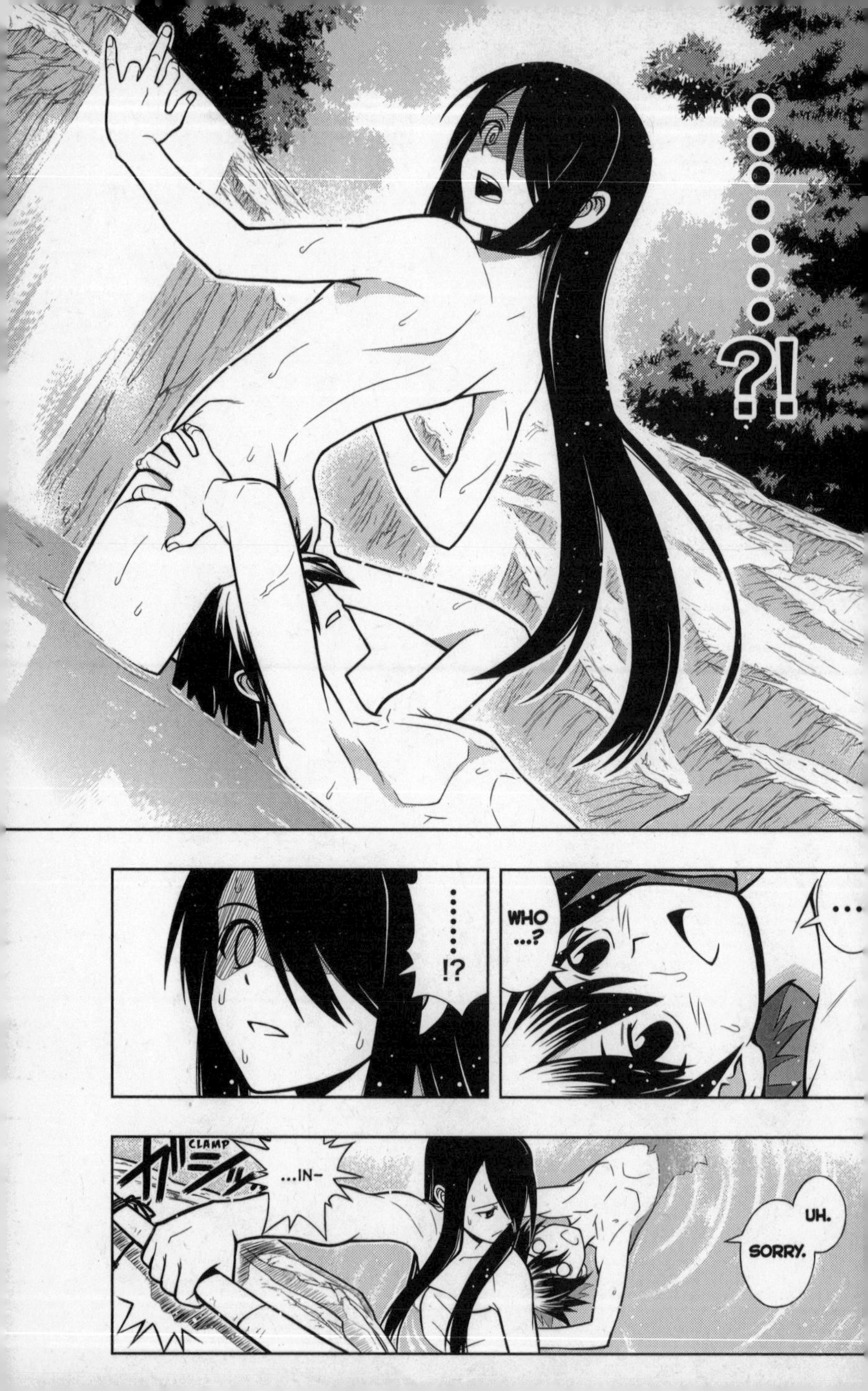

.........?!
...
WHO ...?
......!?
UH. SORRY.
...IN-
CLAMP

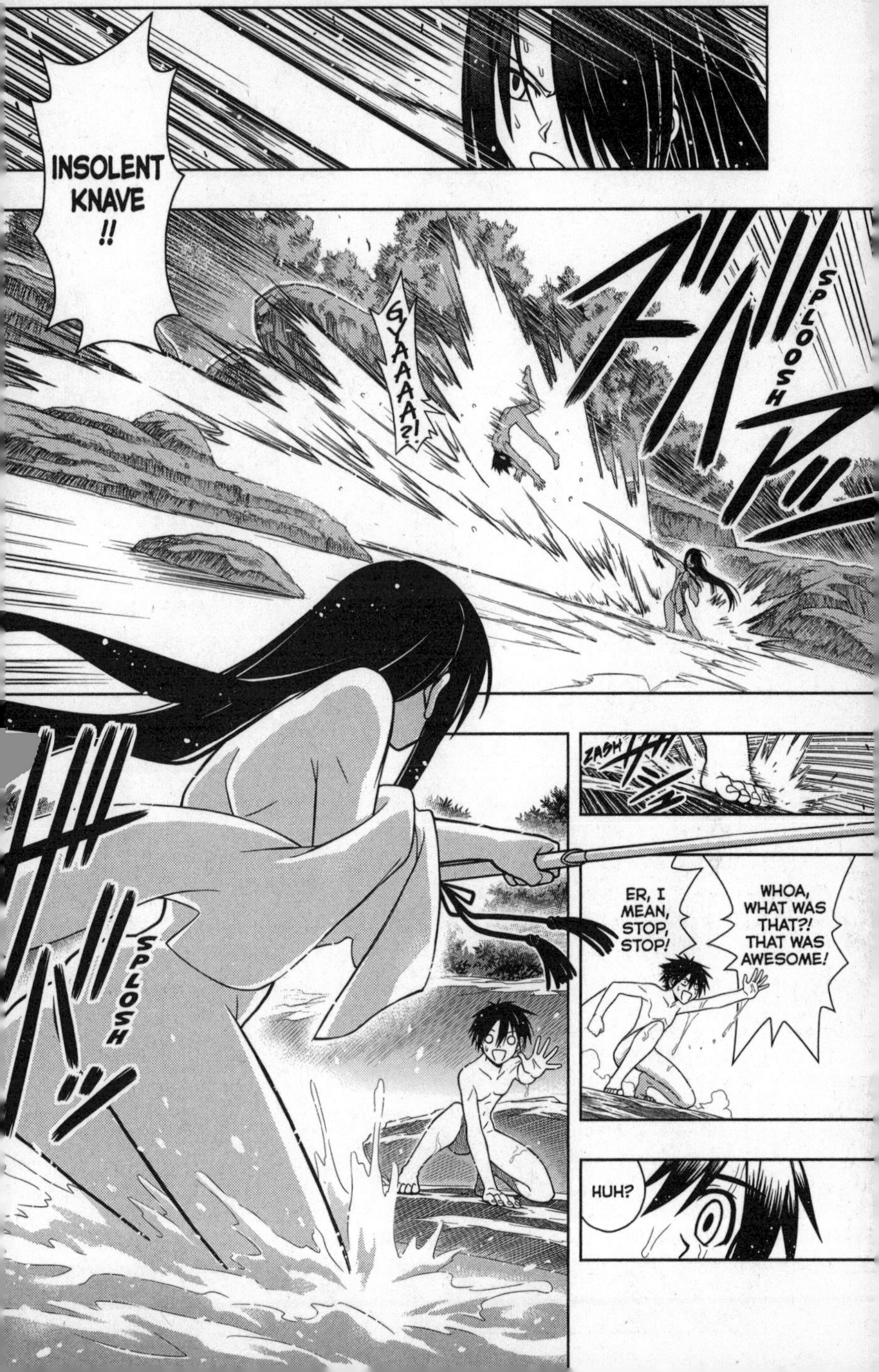
INSOLENT KNAVE !!
SPLOOSH
GYAAAAA?!
ZASH
WHOA, WHAT WAS THAT?! THAT WAS AWESOME!
ER, I MEAN, STOP, STOP!
HUH?
SPLOSH

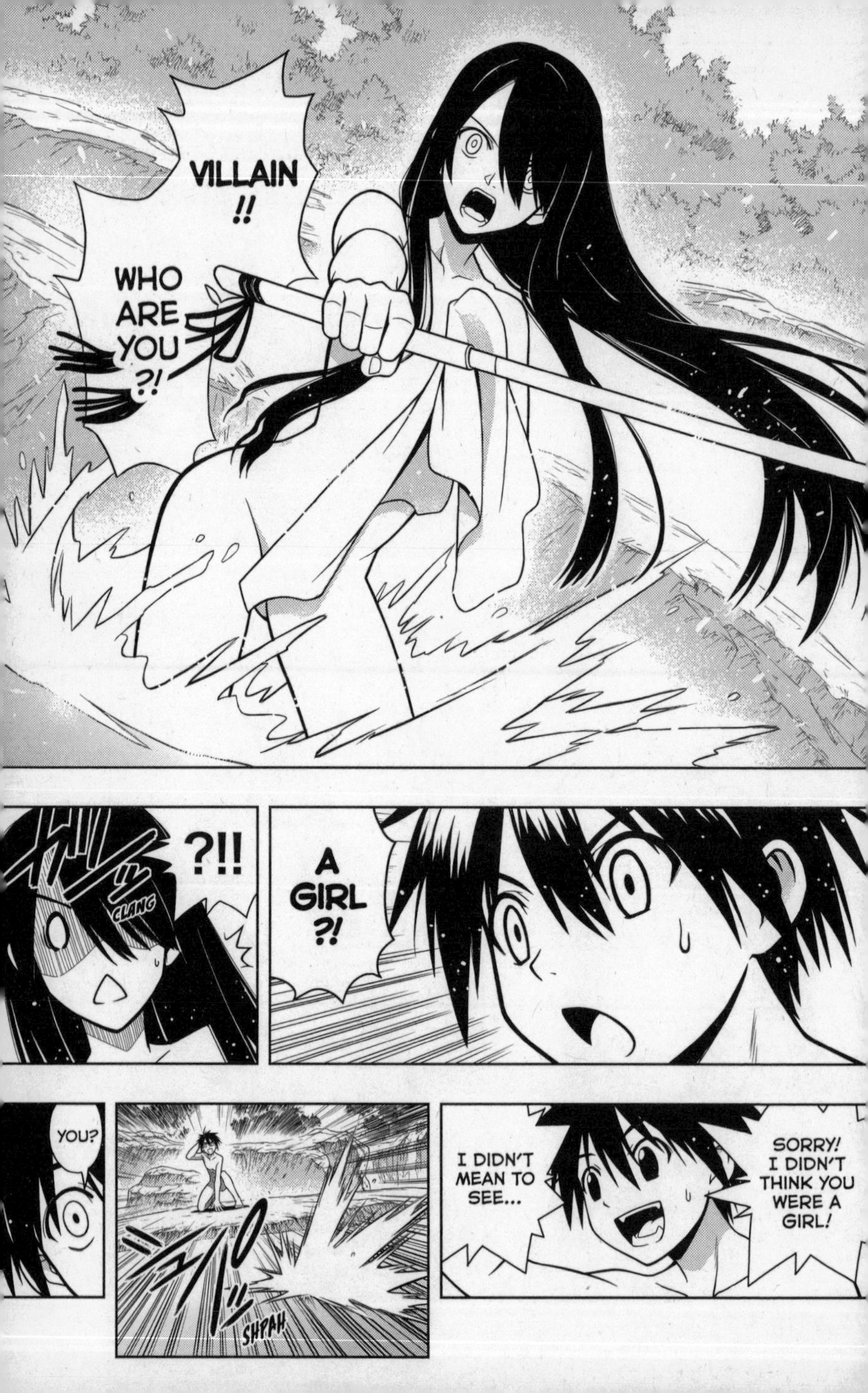
VILLAIN!!
WHO ARE YOU?!
A GIRL?!
?!!
CLANG
SORRY! I DIDN'T THINK YOU WERE A GIRL!
I DIDN'T MEAN TO SEE...
SHPAH
YOU?

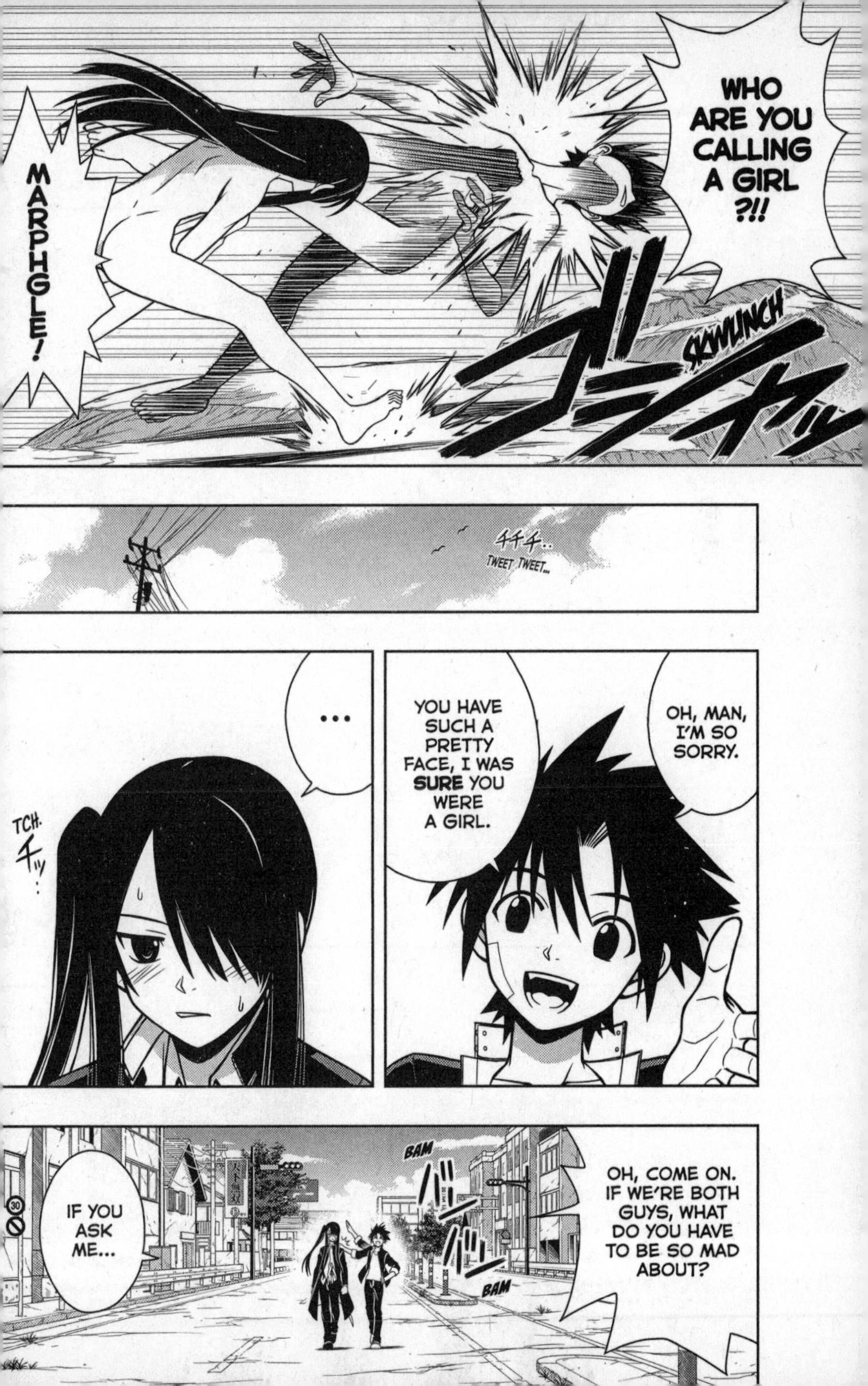
WHO ARE YOU CALLING A GIRL ?!!
SKWUNCH
MARPHGLE!
チチチ..
TWEET TWEET...
OH, MAN, I'M SO SORRY.
YOU HAVE SUCH A PRETTY FACE, I WAS **SURE** YOU WERE A GIRL.
...
TCH.
チッ
OH, COME ON. IF WE'RE BOTH GUYS, WHAT DO YOU HAVE TO BE SO MAD ABOUT?
BAM
BAM
IF YOU ASK ME...

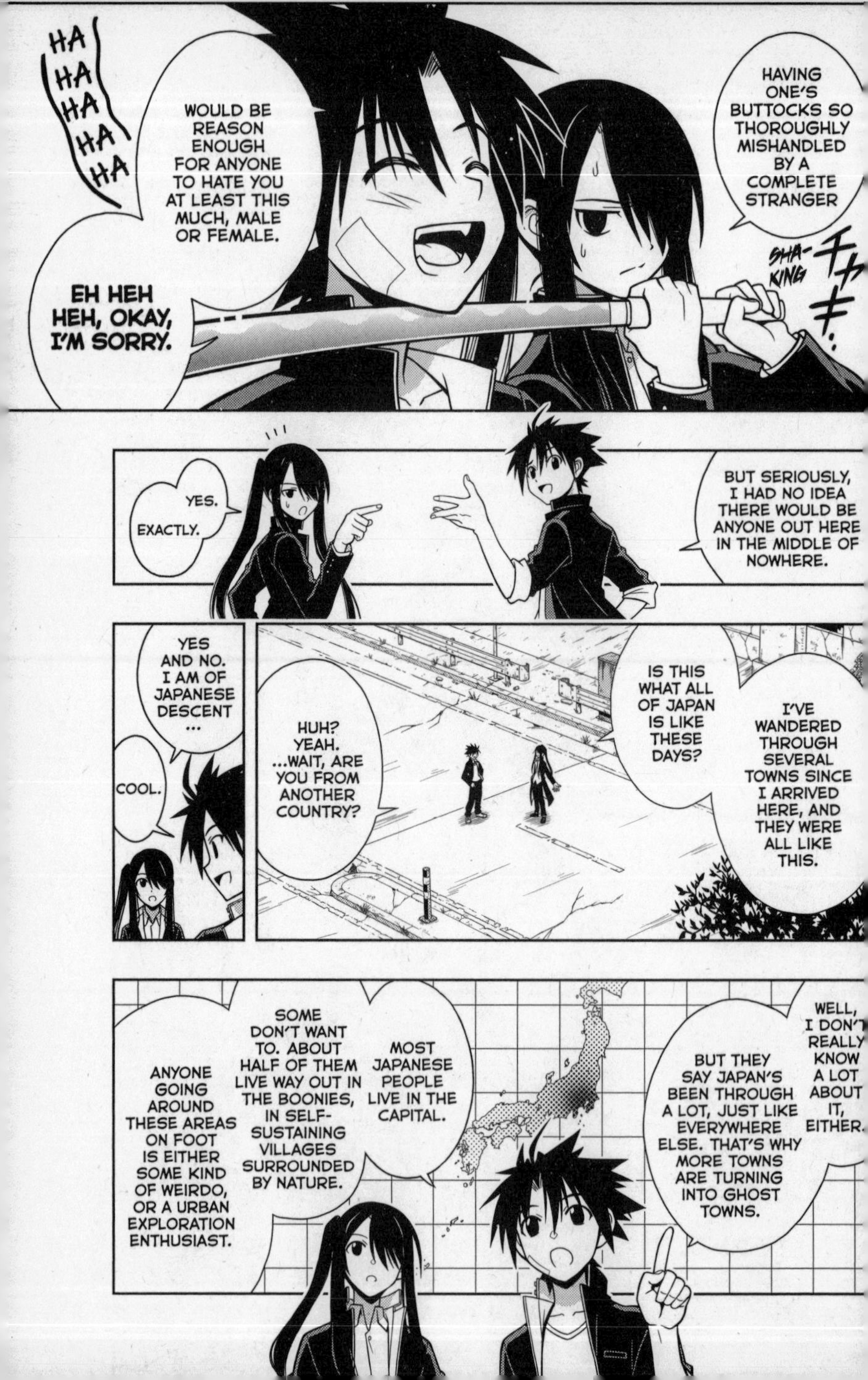
HAVING ONE'S BUTTOCKS SO THOROUGHLY MISHANDLED BY A COMPLETE STRANGER
SHA-KING
WOULD BE REASON ENOUGH FOR ANYONE TO HATE YOU AT LEAST THIS MUCH, MALE OR FEMALE.
HA HA HA HA HA
EH HEH HEH, OKAY, I'M SORRY.
BUT SERIOUSLY, I HAD NO IDEA THERE WOULD BE ANYONE OUT HERE IN THE MIDDLE OF NOWHERE.
YES. EXACTLY.
I'VE WANDERED THROUGH SEVERAL TOWNS SINCE I ARRIVED HERE, AND THEY WERE ALL LIKE THIS.
IS THIS WHAT ALL OF JAPAN IS LIKE THESE DAYS?
HUH? YEAH. ...WAIT, ARE YOU FROM ANOTHER COUNTRY?
YES AND NO. I AM OF JAPANESE DESCENT ...
COOL.
WELL, I DON'T REALLY KNOW A LOT ABOUT IT, EITHER.
BUT THEY SAY JAPAN'S BEEN THROUGH A LOT, JUST LIKE EVERYWHERE ELSE. THAT'S WHY MORE TOWNS ARE TURNING INTO GHOST TOWNS.
MOST JAPANESE PEOPLE LIVE IN THE CAPITAL.
SOME DON'T WANT TO. ABOUT HALF OF THEM LIVE WAY OUT IN THE BOONIES, IN SELF-SUSTAINING VILLAGES SURROUNDED BY NATURE.
ANYONE GOING AROUND THESE AREAS ON FOOT IS EITHER SOME KIND OF WEIRDO, OR A URBAN EXPLORATION ENTHUSIAST.

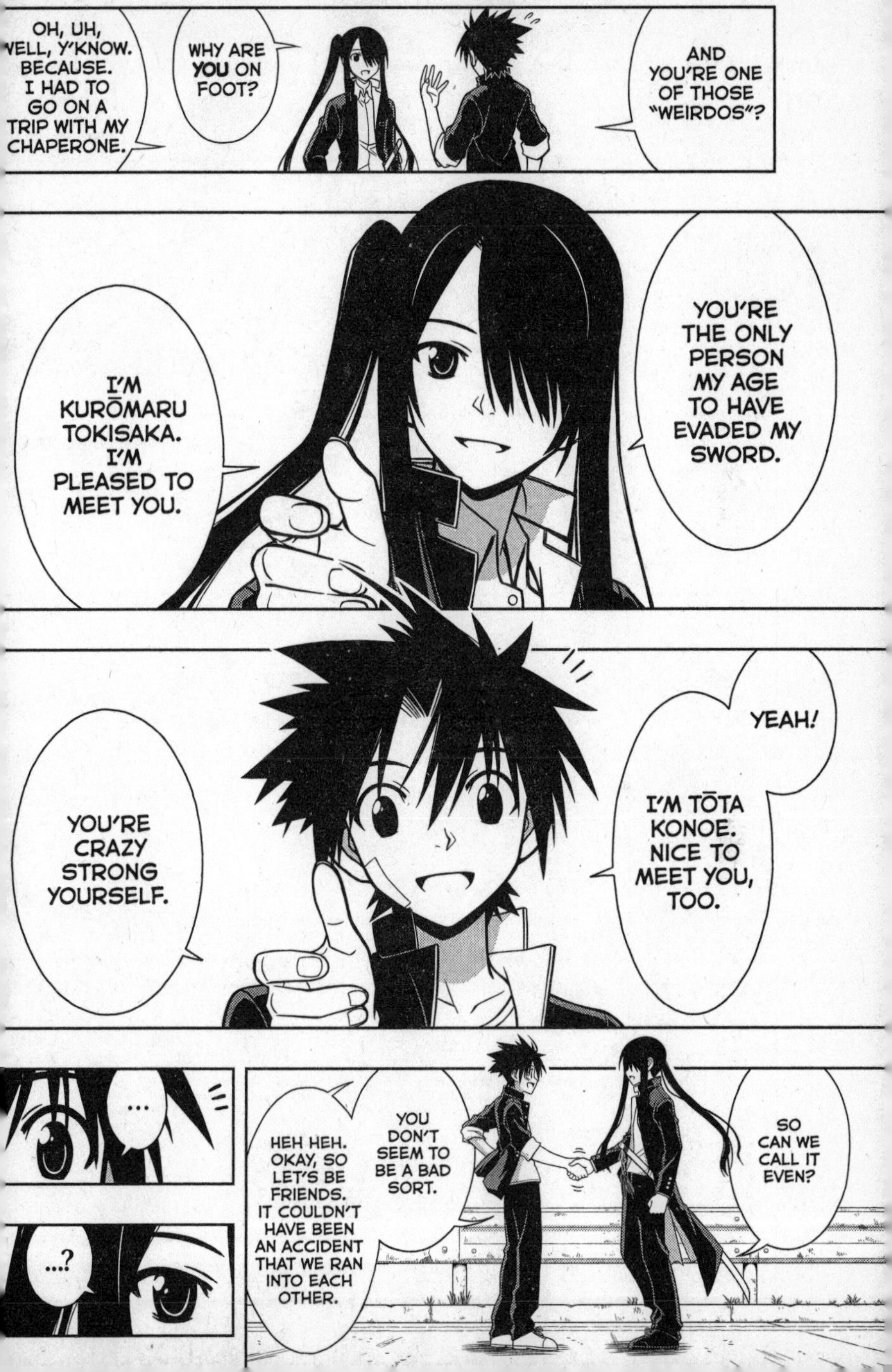
AND YOU'RE ONE OF THOSE "WEIRDOS"?
WHY ARE YOU ON FOOT?
OH, UH, WELL, Y'KNOW. BECAUSE. I HAD TO GO ON A TRIP WITH MY CHAPERONE.
YOU'RE THE ONLY PERSON MY AGE TO HAVE EVADED MY SWORD.
I'M KURŌMARU TOKISAKA. I'M PLEASED TO MEET YOU.
YEAH!
I'M TŌTA KONOE. NICE TO MEET YOU, TOO.
YOU'RE CRAZY STRONG YOURSELF.
SO CAN WE CALL IT EVEN?
YOU DON'T SEEM TO BE A BAD SORT.
HEH HEH. OKAY, SO LET'S BE FRIENDS. IT COULDN'T HAVE BEEN AN ACCIDENT THAT WE RAN INTO EACH OTHER.
...
...?

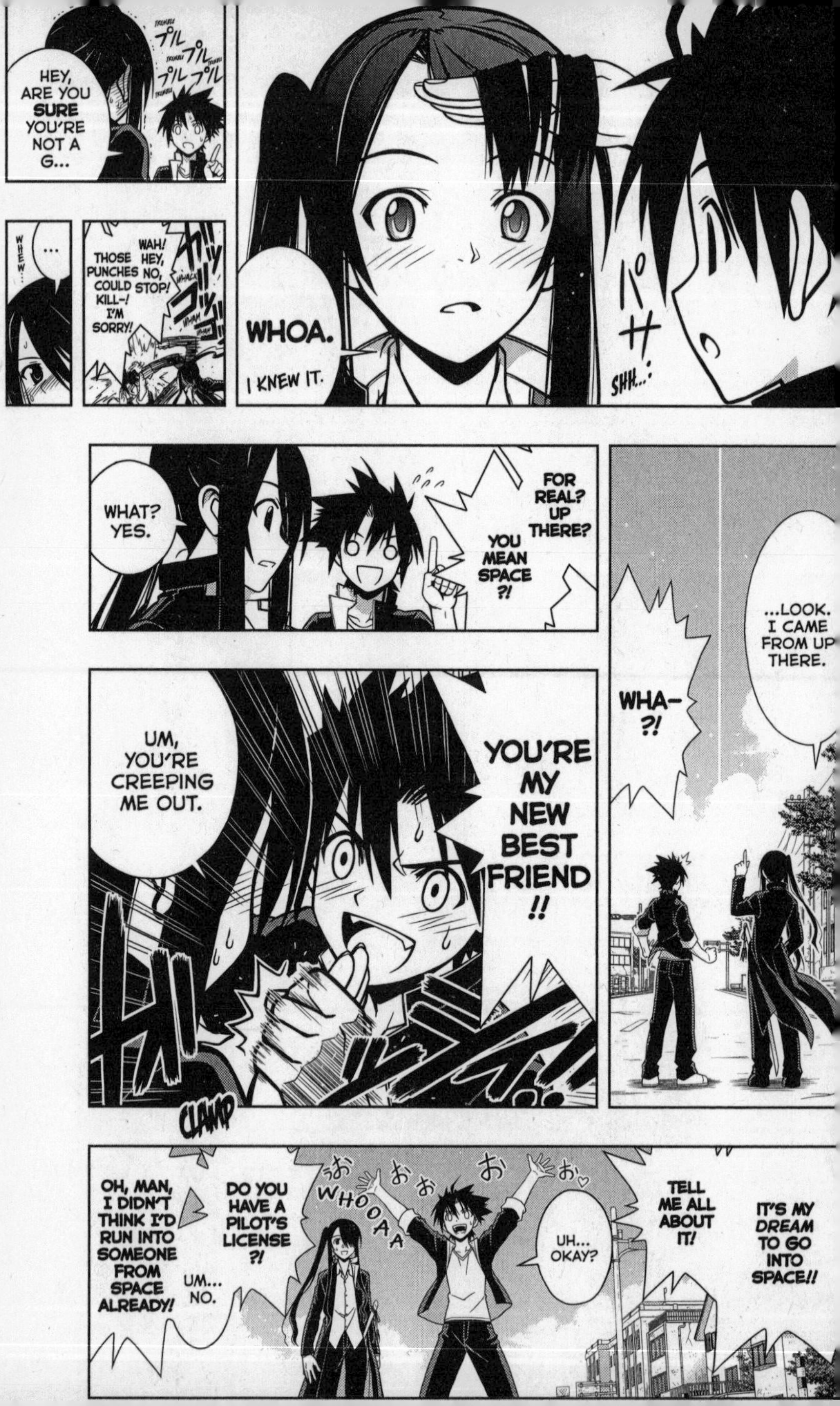
WHOA.
I KNEW IT.
SHH...
HEY, ARE YOU SURE YOU'RE NOT A G...
TREMBLE
WAH! HEY, NO, STOP!
THOSE PUNCHES COULD KILL-! I'M SORRY!
WHACK
WHAM
...
WHEW...
...LOOK. I CAME FROM UP THERE.
WHA-?!
FOR REAL? UP THERE?
YOU MEAN SPACE?!
WHAT? YES.
YOU'RE MY NEW BEST FRIEND!!
UM, YOU'RE CREEPING ME OUT.
CLAMP
IT'S MY DREAM TO GO INTO SPACE!!
TELL ME ALL ABOUT IT!
UH... OKAY?
WHOOAAA
DO YOU HAVE A PILOT'S LICENSE?!
UM... NO.
OH, MAN, I DIDN'T THINK I'D RUN INTO SOMEONE FROM SPACE ALREADY!

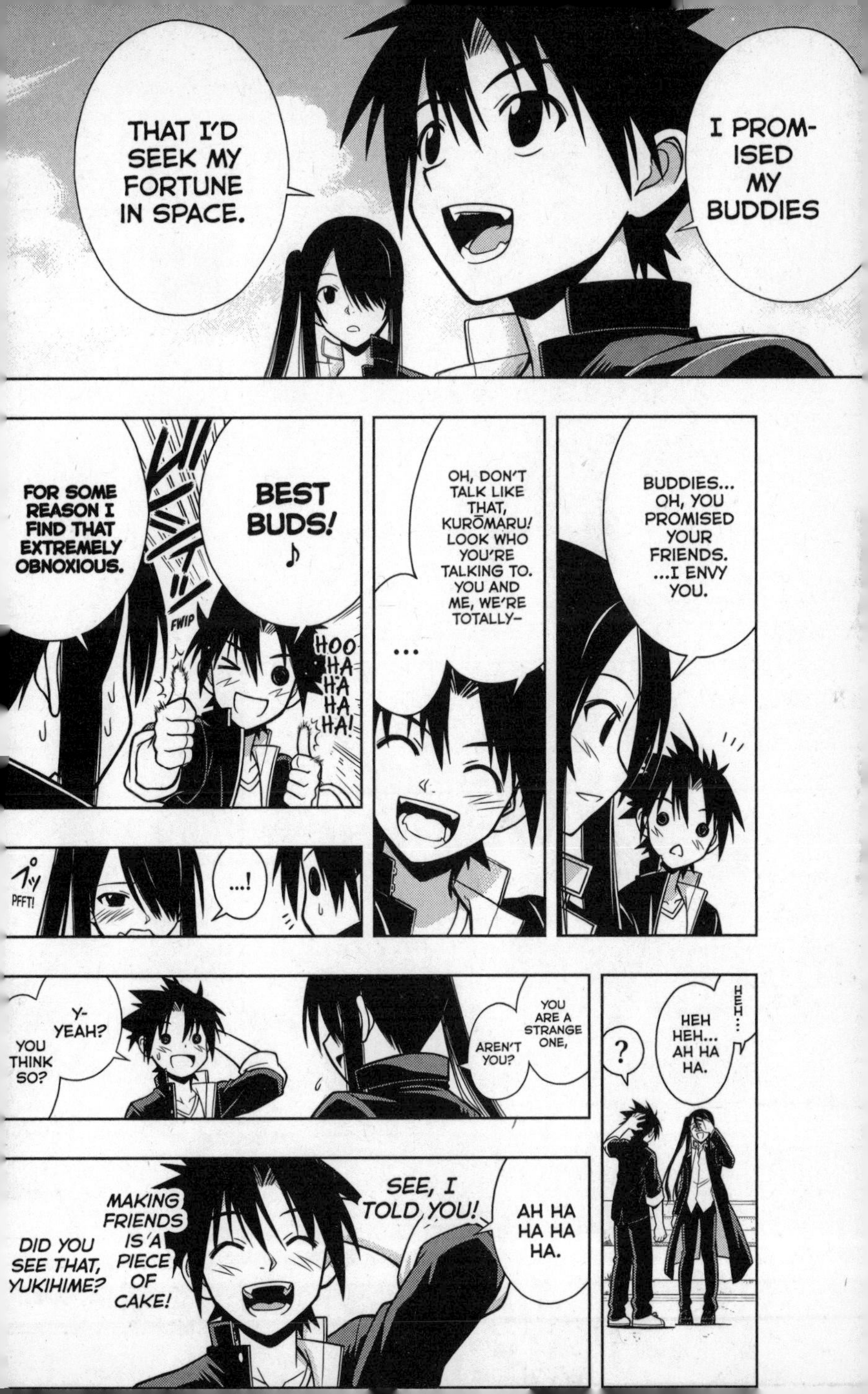
I PROMISED MY BUDDIES
THAT I'D SEEK MY FORTUNE IN SPACE.
BUDDIES... OH, YOU PROMISED YOUR FRIENDS. ...I ENVY YOU.
OH, DON'T TALK LIKE THAT, KURŌMARU! LOOK WHO YOU'RE TALKING TO. YOU AND ME, WE'RE TOTALLY–
...
BEST BUDS! ♪
HOO HA HA HA HA!
FWIP
FOR SOME REASON I FIND THAT EXTREMELY OBNOXIOUS.
...!
プッ PFFT!
HEH...
HEH HEH... AH HA HA.
?
YOU ARE A STRANGE ONE,
AREN'T YOU?
Y- YEAH?
YOU THINK SO?
AH HA HA HA HA.
SEE, I TOLD YOU!
MAKING FRIENDS IS A PIECE OF CAKE!
DID YOU SEE THAT, YUKIHIME?

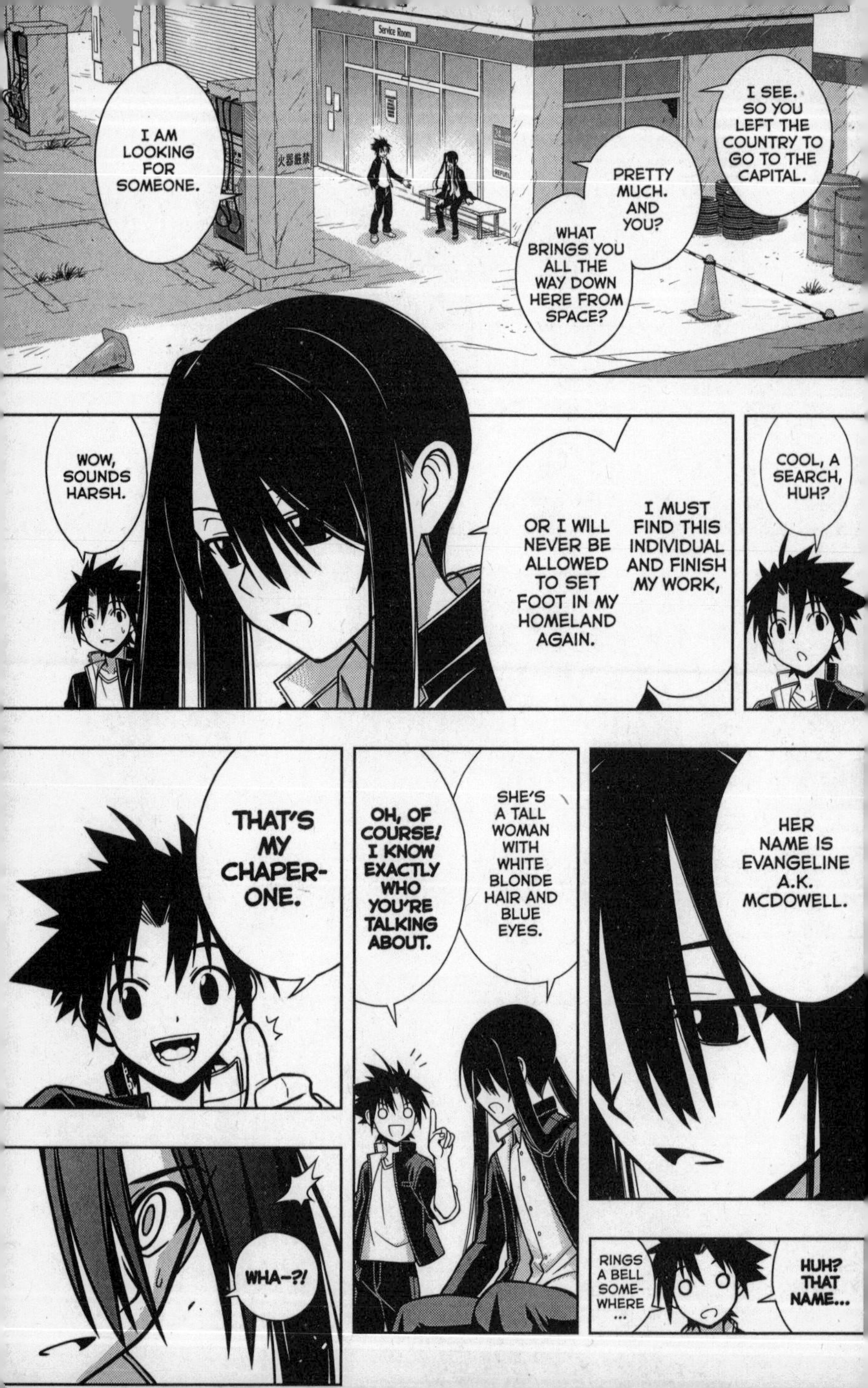
Service Room
火器厳禁
REFUEL
I SEE. SO YOU LEFT THE COUNTRY TO GO TO THE CAPITAL.
PRETTY MUCH. AND YOU?
WHAT BRINGS YOU ALL THE WAY DOWN HERE FROM SPACE?
I AM LOOKING FOR SOMEONE.
COOL, A SEARCH, HUH?
I MUST FIND THIS INDIVIDUAL AND FINISH MY WORK,
OR I WILL NEVER BE ALLOWED TO SET FOOT IN MY HOMELAND AGAIN.
WOW, SOUNDS HARSH.
HER NAME IS EVANGELINE A.K. MCDOWELL.
HUH? THAT NAME...
RINGS A BELL SOMEWHERE ...
SHE'S A TALL WOMAN WITH WHITE BLONDE HAIR AND BLUE EYES.
OH, OF COURSE! I KNOW EXACTLY WHO YOU'RE TALKING ABOUT.
THAT'S MY CHAPER-ONE.
WHA-?!

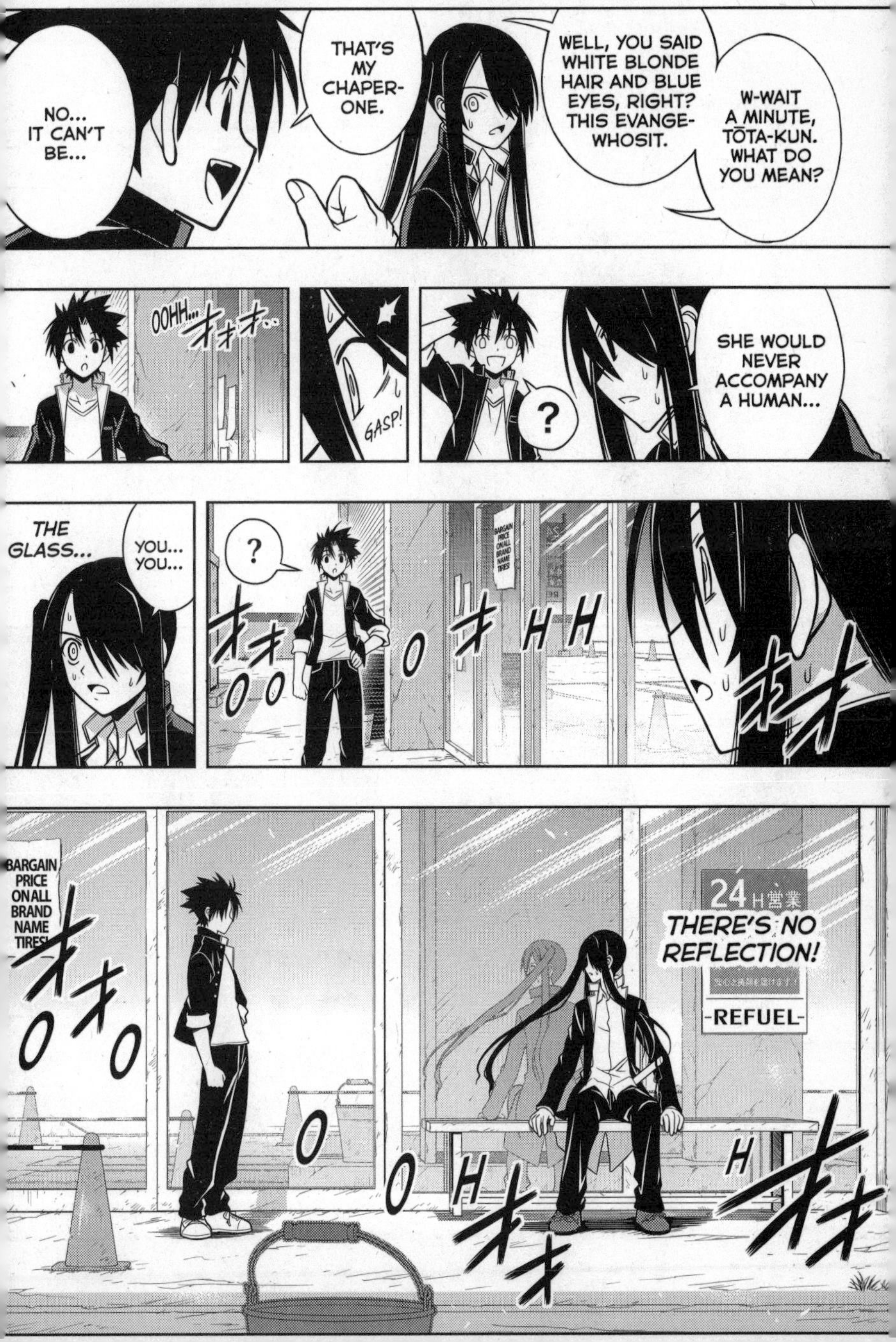
W-WAIT A MINUTE, TŌTA-KUN. WHAT DO YOU MEAN?
WELL, YOU SAID WHITE BLONDE HAIR AND BLUE EYES, RIGHT? THIS EVANGE-WHOSIT.
THAT'S MY CHAPER-ONE.
NO... IT CAN'T BE...
SHE WOULD NEVER ACCOMPANY A HUMAN...
?
GASP!
OOHH... オォォ..
オオ
BARGAIN PRICE ON ALL BRAND NAME TIRES!
O オ HH
?
オオ OO
YOU... YOU...
THE GLASS...
24H営業
THERE'S NO REFLECTION!
-REFUEL-
BARGAIN PRICE ONALL BRAND NAME TIRES!
オオ OO
OOHH
オオ

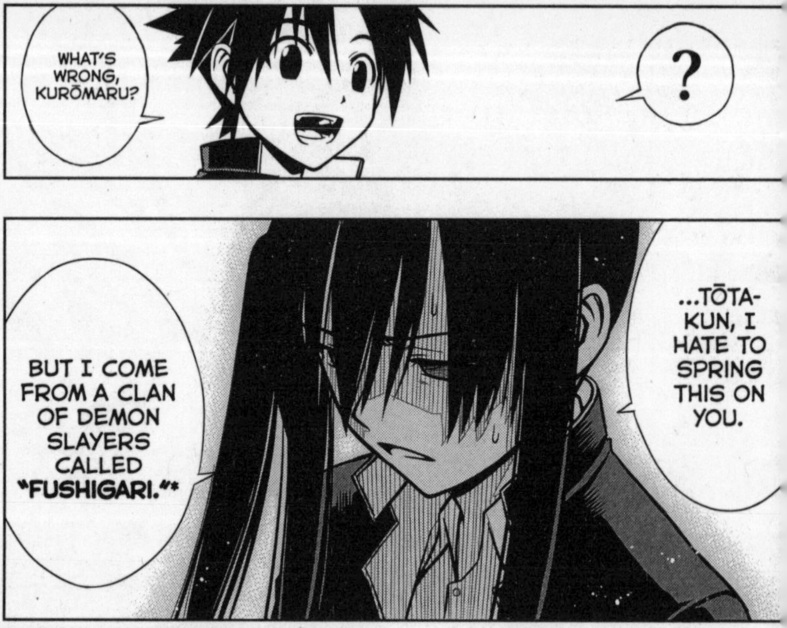
?
WHAT'S WRONG, KURŌMARU?
...TŌTA-KUN, I HATE TO SPRING THIS ON YOU.
BUT I COME FROM A CLAN OF DEMON SLAYERS CALLED "FUSHIGARI."*

*Japanese for "immortal hunters"

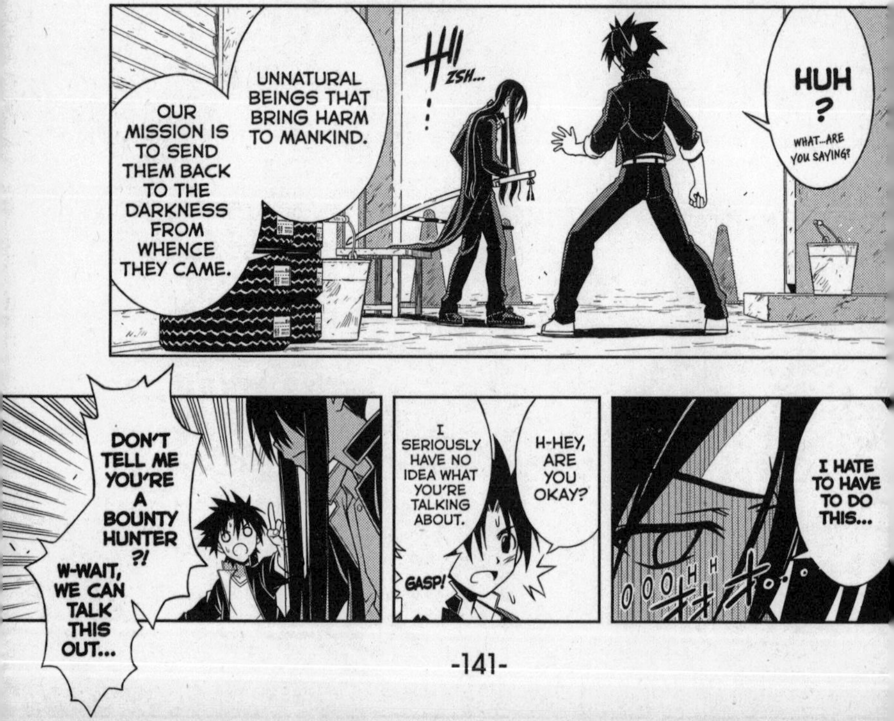
HUH? WHAT...ARE YOU SAYING?
ZSH...
UNNATURAL BEINGS THAT BRING HARM TO MANKIND.
OUR MISSION IS TO SEND THEM BACK TO THE DARKNESS FROM WHENCE THEY CAME.
I HATE TO HAVE TO DO THIS...
H-HEY, ARE YOU OKAY?
I SERIOUSLY HAVE NO IDEA WHAT YOU'RE TALKING ABOUT.
GASP!
DON'T TELL ME YOU'RE A BOUNTY HUNTER?!
W-WAIT, WE CAN TALK THIS OUT...

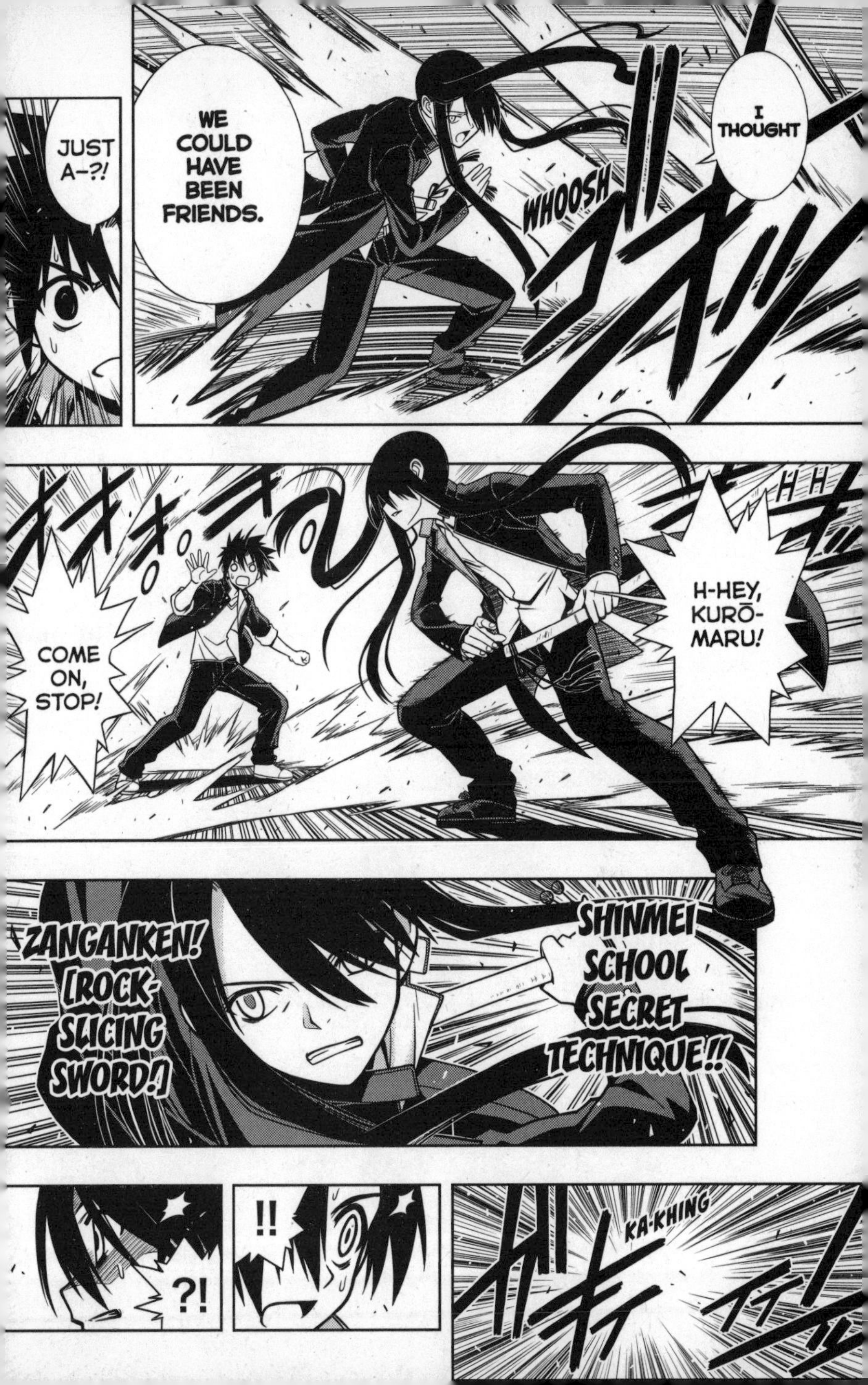
I THOUGHT
WHOOSH
WE COULD HAVE BEEN FRIENDS.
JUST A-?!
H-HEY, KURŌ-MARU!
COME ON, STOP!
SHINMEI SCHOOL SECRET TECHNIQUE!!
ZANGANKEN! [ROCK-SLICING SWORD!]
KA-KHING
!!
?!

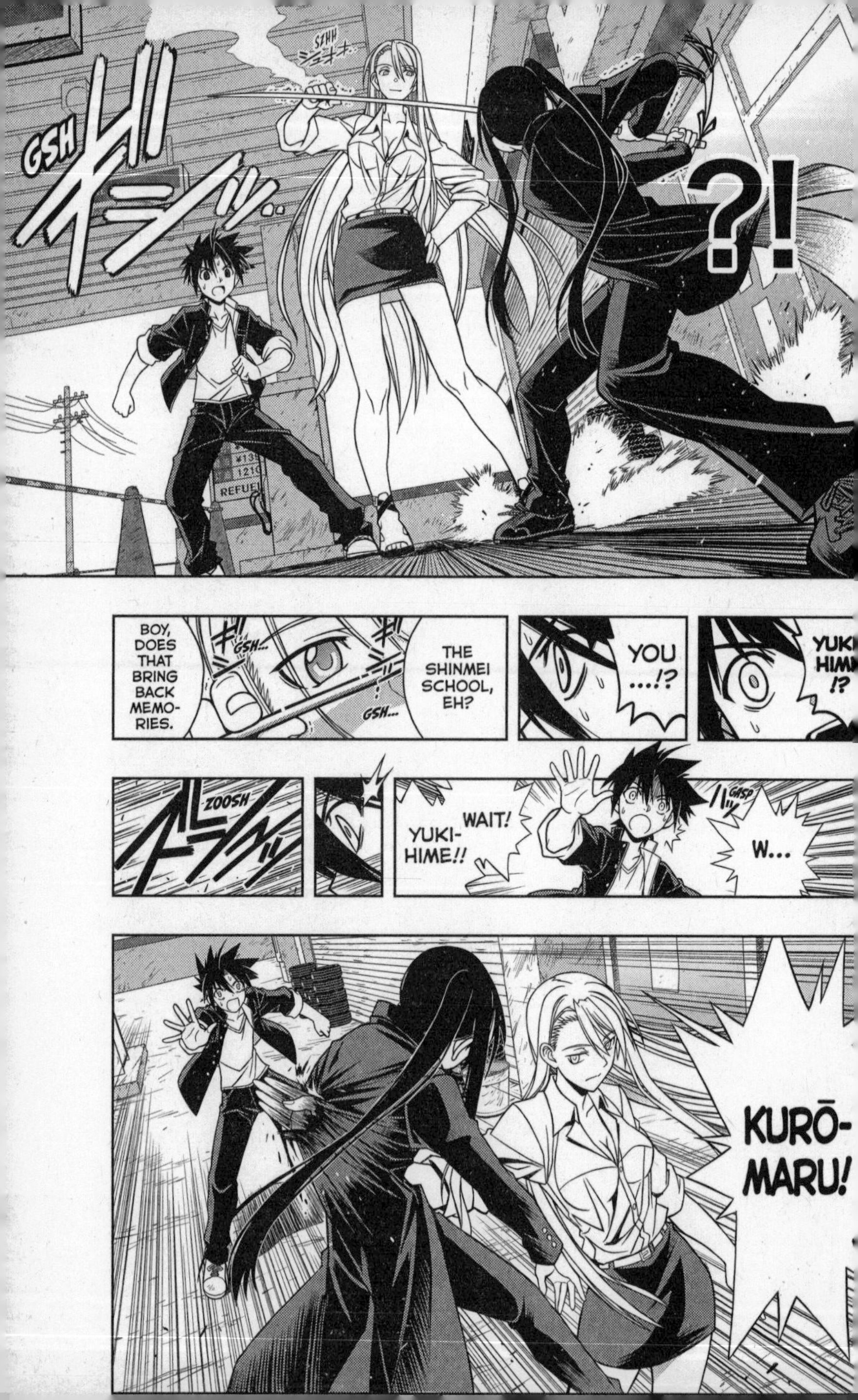

?!
SZHH
GSH
YUKI
HIM
!?
YOU
...!?
THE SHINMEI SCHOOL, EH?
GSH...
GSH...
BOY, DOES THAT BRING BACK MEMO-RIES.
GASP
W...
WAIT!
YUKI-HIME!!
ZOOSH
KURŌ-MARU!

UQ
HOLDER!

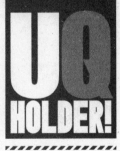

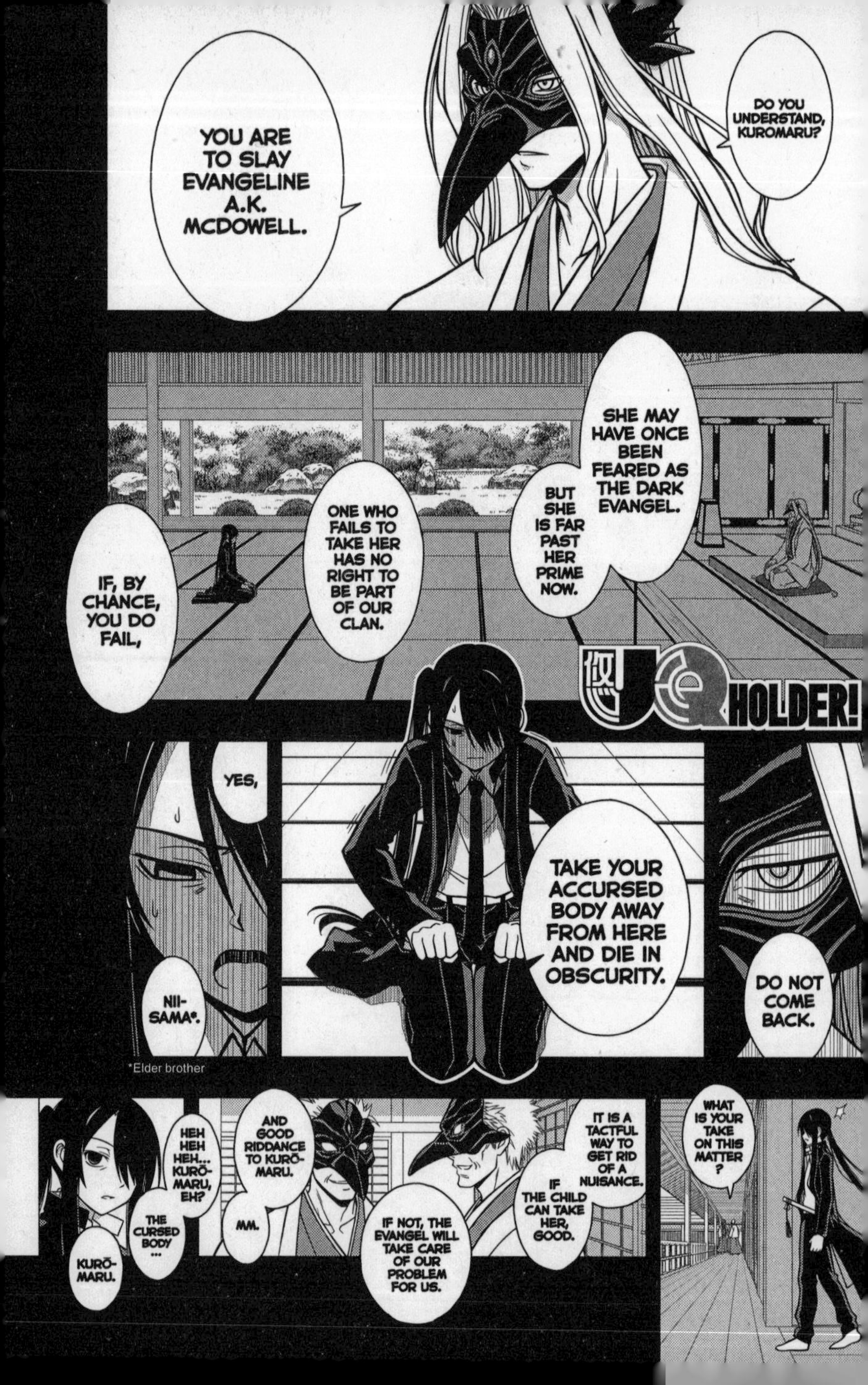
YOU ARE TO SLAY EVANGELINE A.K. MCDOWELL.
DO YOU UNDERSTAND, KUROMARU?
SHE MAY HAVE ONCE BEEN FEARED AS THE DARK EVANGEL.
BUT SHE IS FAR PAST HER PRIME NOW.
ONE WHO FAILS TO TAKE HER HAS NO RIGHT TO BE PART OF OUR CLAN.
IF, BY CHANCE, YOU DO FAIL,
UQ HOLDER!
DO NOT COME BACK.
TAKE YOUR ACCURSED BODY AWAY FROM HERE AND DIE IN OBSCURITY.
YES,
NII-SAMA*.
WHAT IS YOUR TAKE ON THIS MATTER?
IT IS A TACTFUL WAY TO GET RID OF A NUISANCE.
IF THE CHILD CAN TAKE HER, GOOD.
IF NOT, THE EVANGEL WILL TAKE CARE OF OUR PROBLEM FOR US.
AND GOOD RIDDANCE TO KURŌMARU.
MM.
HEH HEH HEH... KURŌMARU, EH?
THE CURSED BODY...
KURŌMARU.

*Elder brother

STAGE 4: TŌTA'S SCHEME

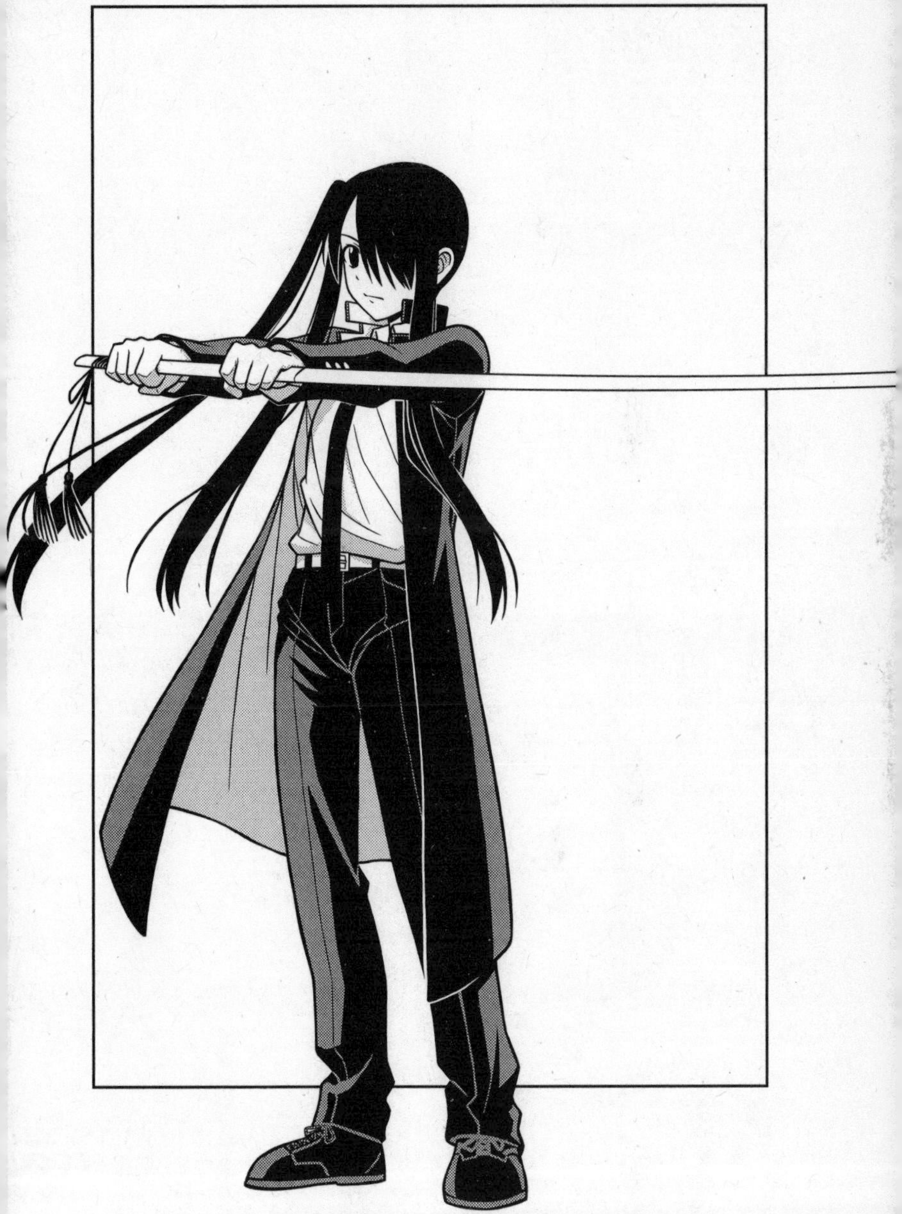

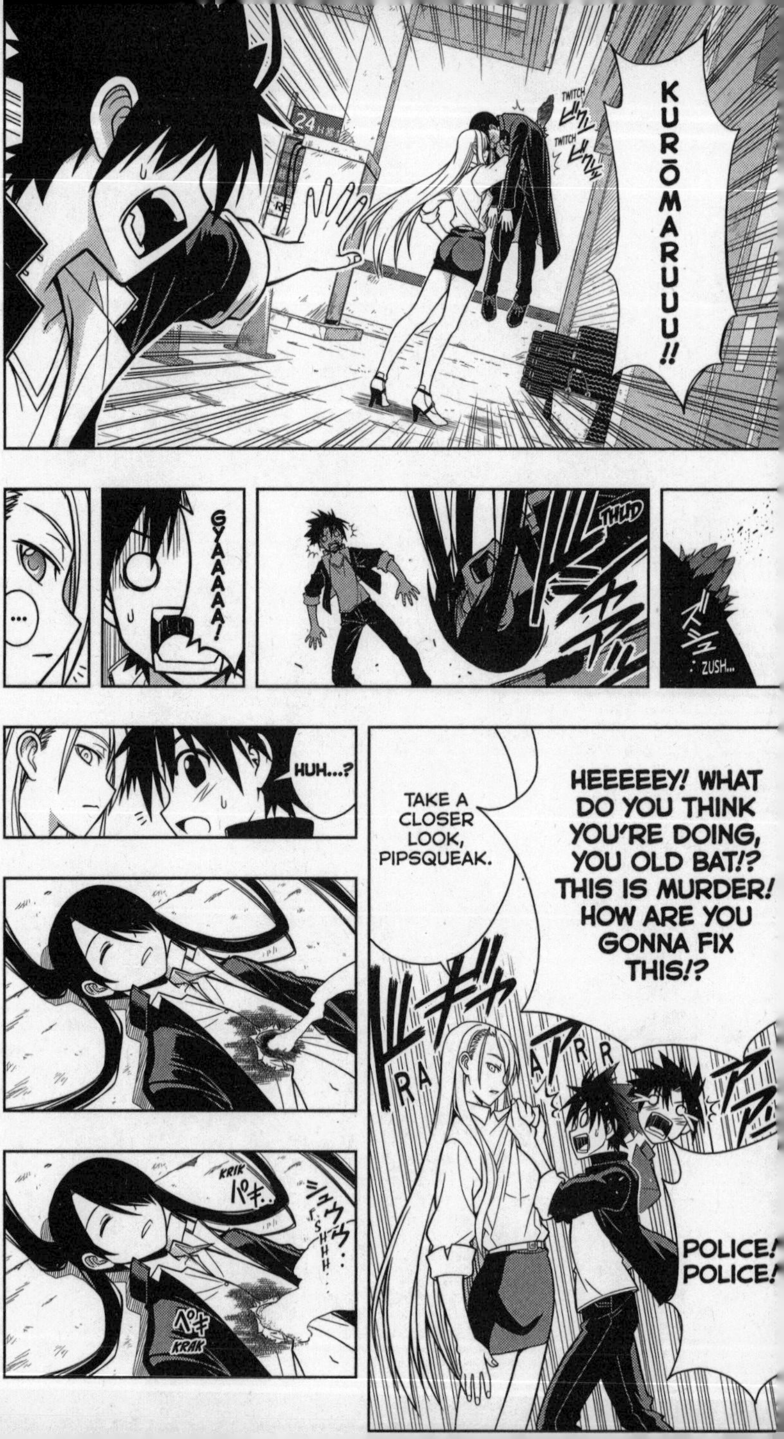
KURŌMARUUU!!
TWITCH
TWITCH
ZUSH...
THUD
GYAAAAA!
...
HEEEEEY! WHAT DO YOU THINK YOU'RE DOING, YOU OLD BAT!? THIS IS MURDER! HOW ARE YOU GONNA FIX THIS!?
TAKE A CLOSER LOOK, PIPSQUEAK.
RAARR
POLICE! POLICE!
HUH...?
KRIK
SHHH...
KRAK

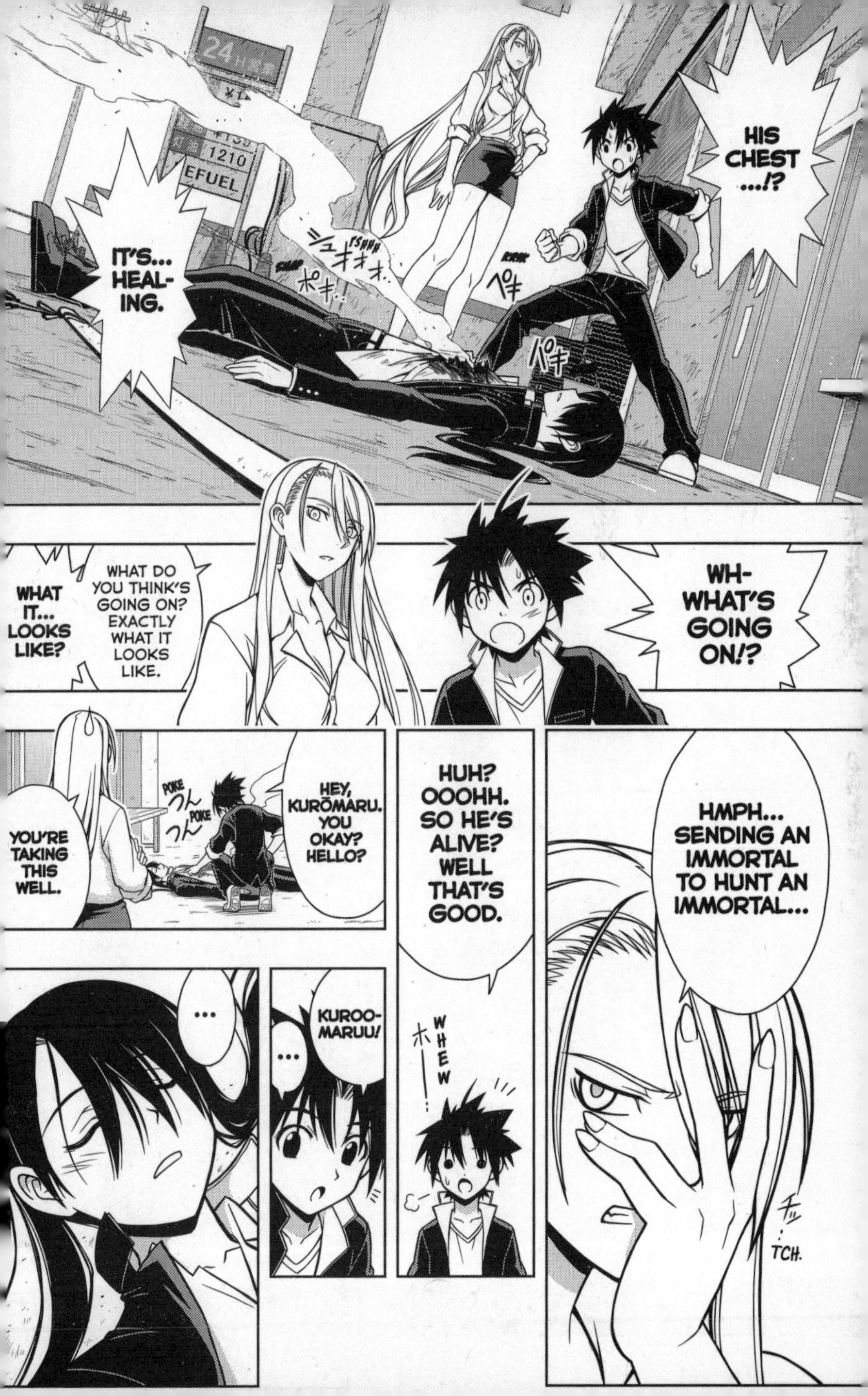
HIS CHEST ...!?
KRIK
FSHHH
SNAP
IT'S... HEAL-ING.
WH-WHAT'S GOING ON!?
WHAT DO YOU THINK'S GOING ON? EXACTLY WHAT IT LOOKS LIKE.
WHAT IT... LOOKS LIKE?
HMPH... SENDING AN IMMORTAL TO HUNT AN IMMORTAL...
TCH.
HUH? OOOHH. SO HE'S ALIVE? WELL THAT'S GOOD.
WHEW
HEY, KURŌMARU. YOU OKAY? HELLO?
POKE
POKE
YOU'RE TAKING THIS WELL.
KUROO-MARUU!
...
...

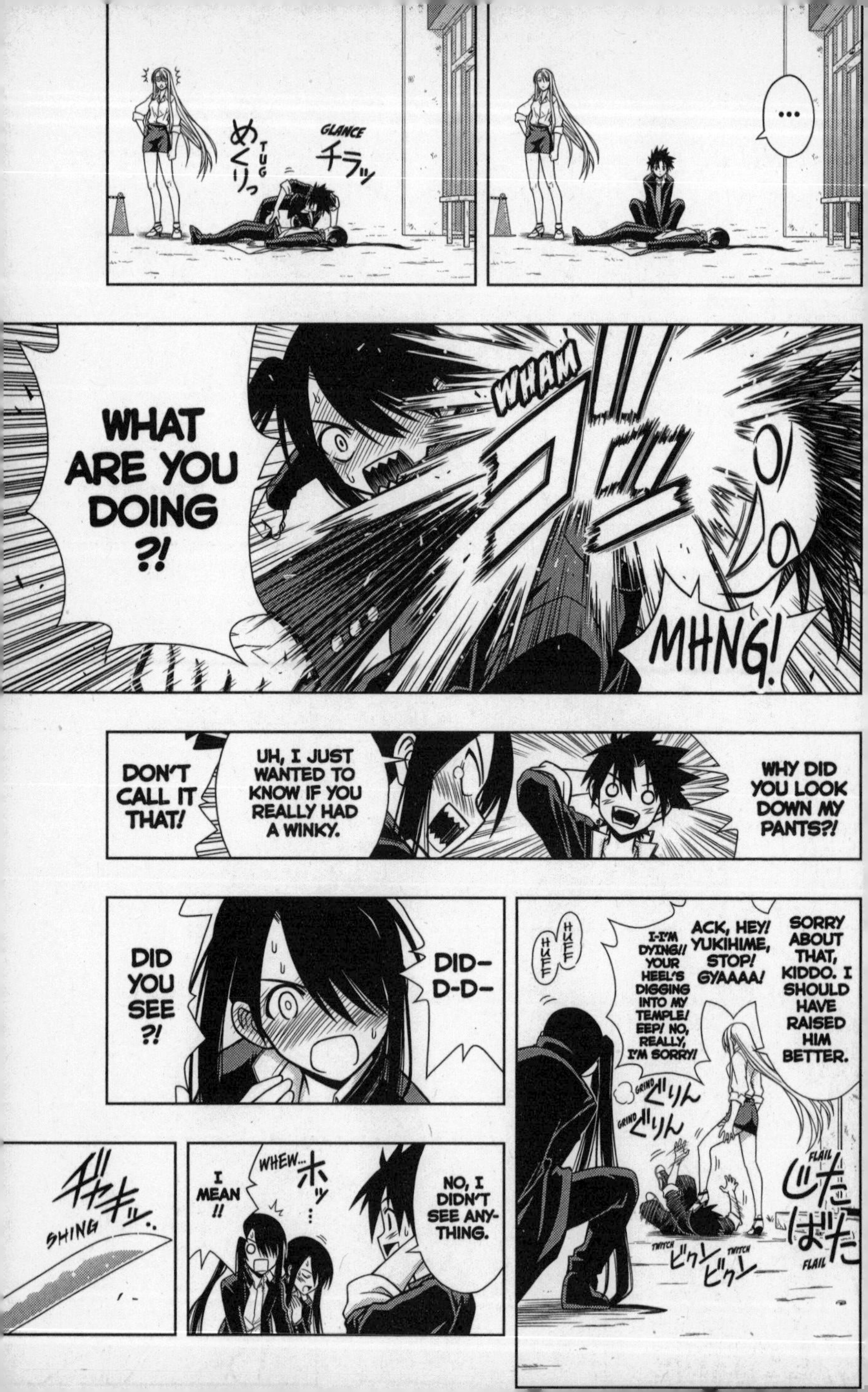

...
GLANCE
チラッ
TUG
めくりっ
WHAM
MHNG!
WHAT ARE YOU DOING?!
WHY DID YOU LOOK DOWN MY PANTS?!
UH, I JUST WANTED TO KNOW IF YOU REALLY HAD A WINKY.
DON'T CALL IT THAT!
SORRY ABOUT THAT, KIDDO. I SHOULD HAVE RAISED HIM BETTER.
ACK, HEY! YUKIHIME, STOP! GYAAAA!
I-I'M DYING!! YOUR HEEL'S DIGGING INTO MY TEMPLE! EEP! NO, REALLY, I'M SORRY!
HUFF HUFF
GRIND ぐりん
GRIND ぐりん
FLAIL じたばた FLAIL
TWITCH ビクン TWITCH ビクン
DID-D-D-
DID YOU SEE?!
NO, I DIDN'T SEE ANYTHING.
WHEW... ホッ...
I MEAN!!
SHING チャキッ..

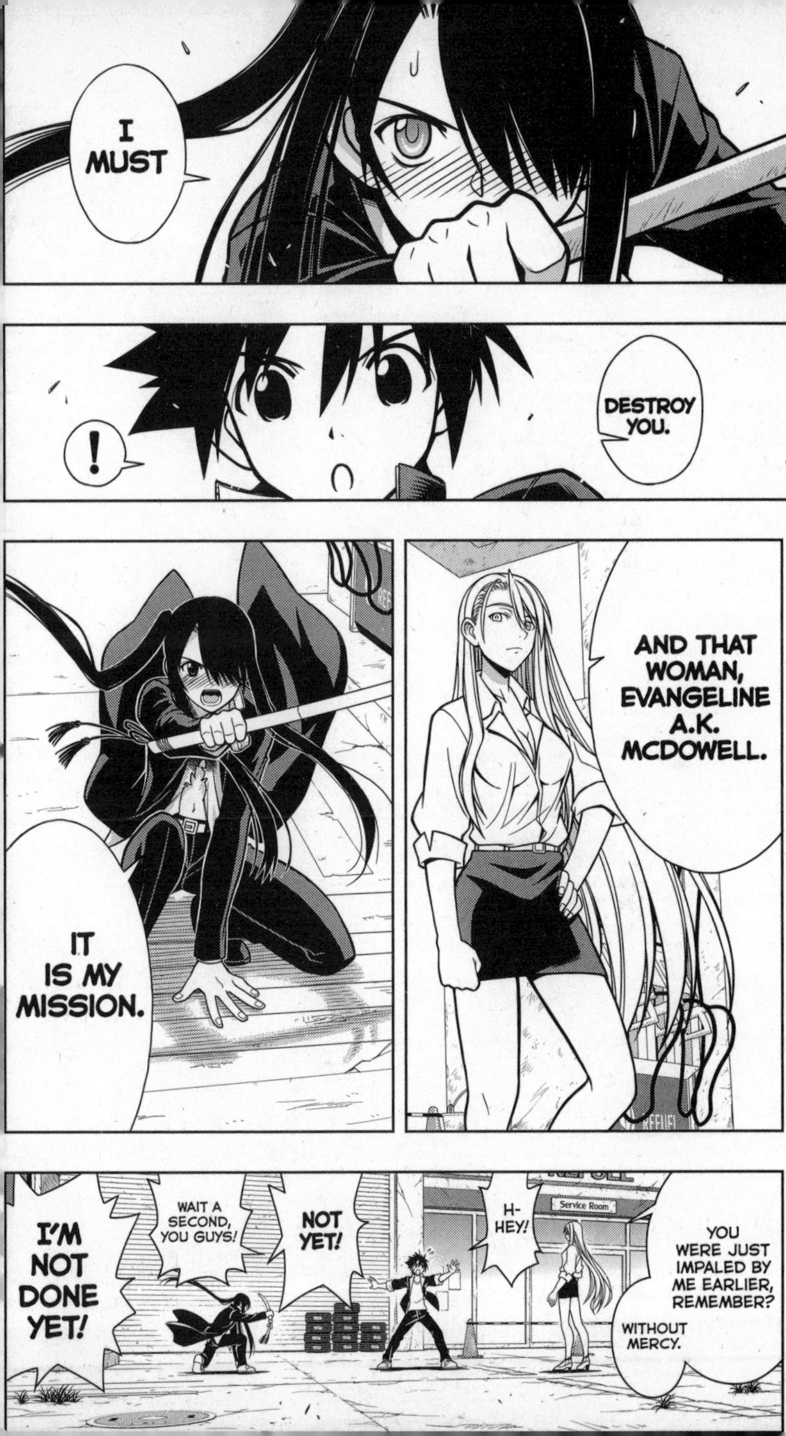
I MUST
DESTROY YOU.
!
AND THAT WOMAN, EVANGELINE A.K. MCDOWELL.
IT IS MY MISSION.
YOU WERE JUST IMPALED BY ME EARLIER, REMEMBER?
WITHOUT MERCY.
Service Room
H-HEY!
NOT YET!
WAIT A SECOND, YOU GUYS!
I'M NOT DONE YET!

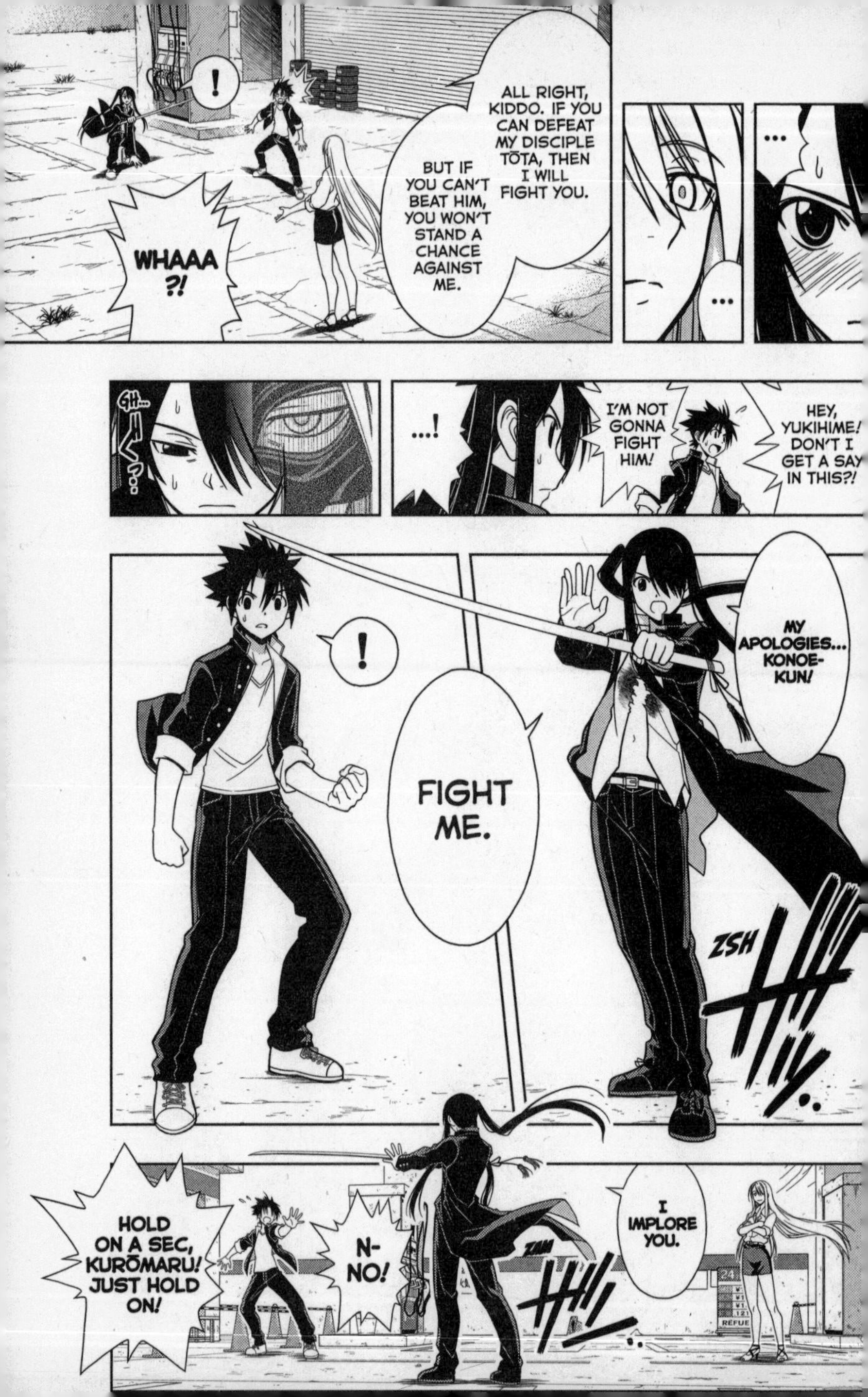
...
...
ALL RIGHT, KIDDO. IF YOU CAN DEFEAT MY DISCIPLE TŌTA, THEN I WILL FIGHT YOU.
BUT IF YOU CAN'T BEAT HIM, YOU WON'T STAND A CHANCE AGAINST ME.
!
WHAAA ?!
HEY, YUKIHIME! DON'T I GET A SAY IN THIS?!
I'M NOT GONNA FIGHT HIM!
...!
GH...
MY APOLOGIES... KONOE-KUN!
ZSH
FIGHT ME.
!
I IMPLORE YOU.
ZAM
N- NO!
HOLD ON A SEC, KURŌMARU! JUST HOLD ON!

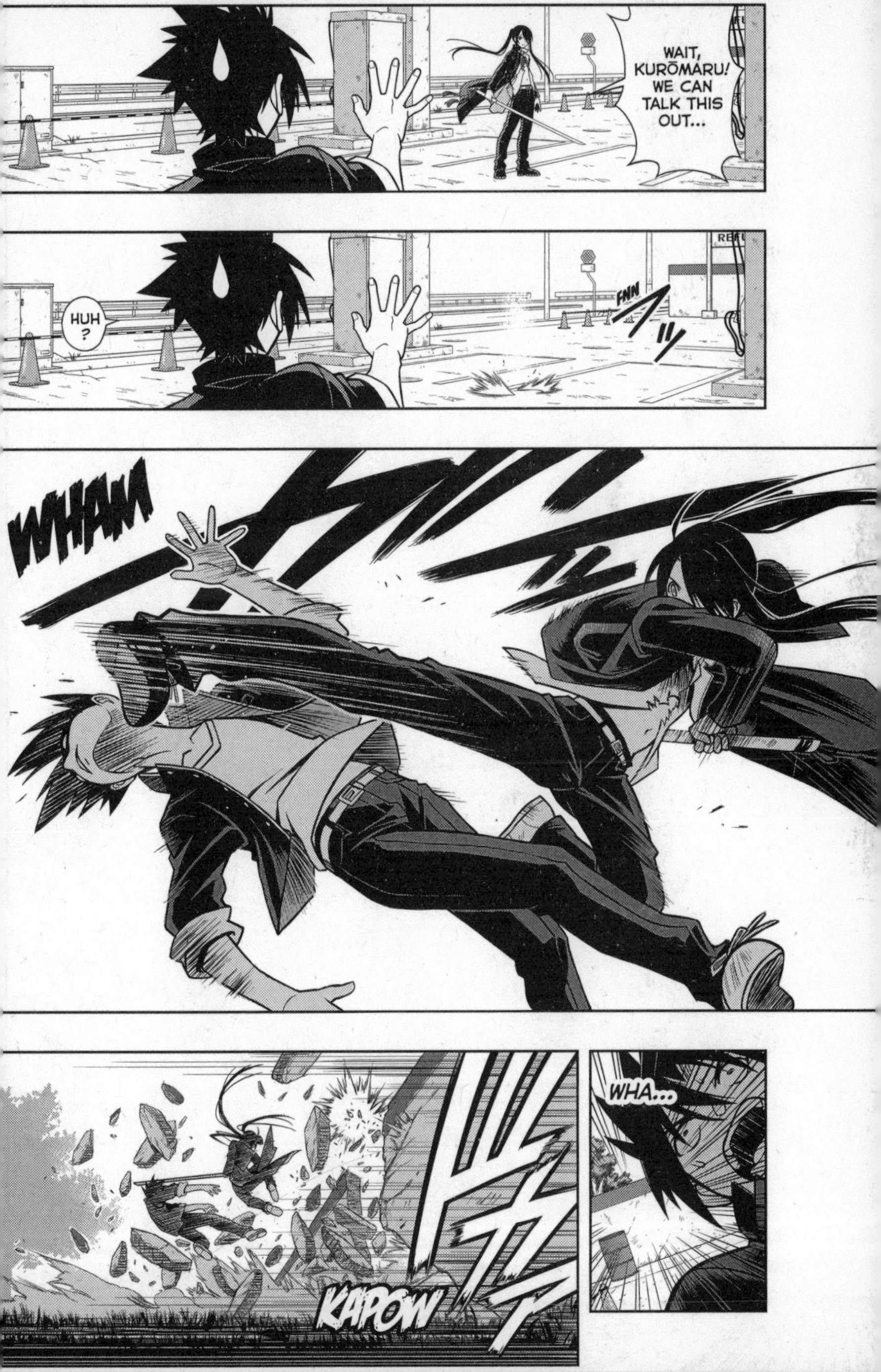
WAIT, KURŌMARU! WE CAN TALK THIS OUT...
FWN
HUH ?
WHAM
WHA...
KAPOW

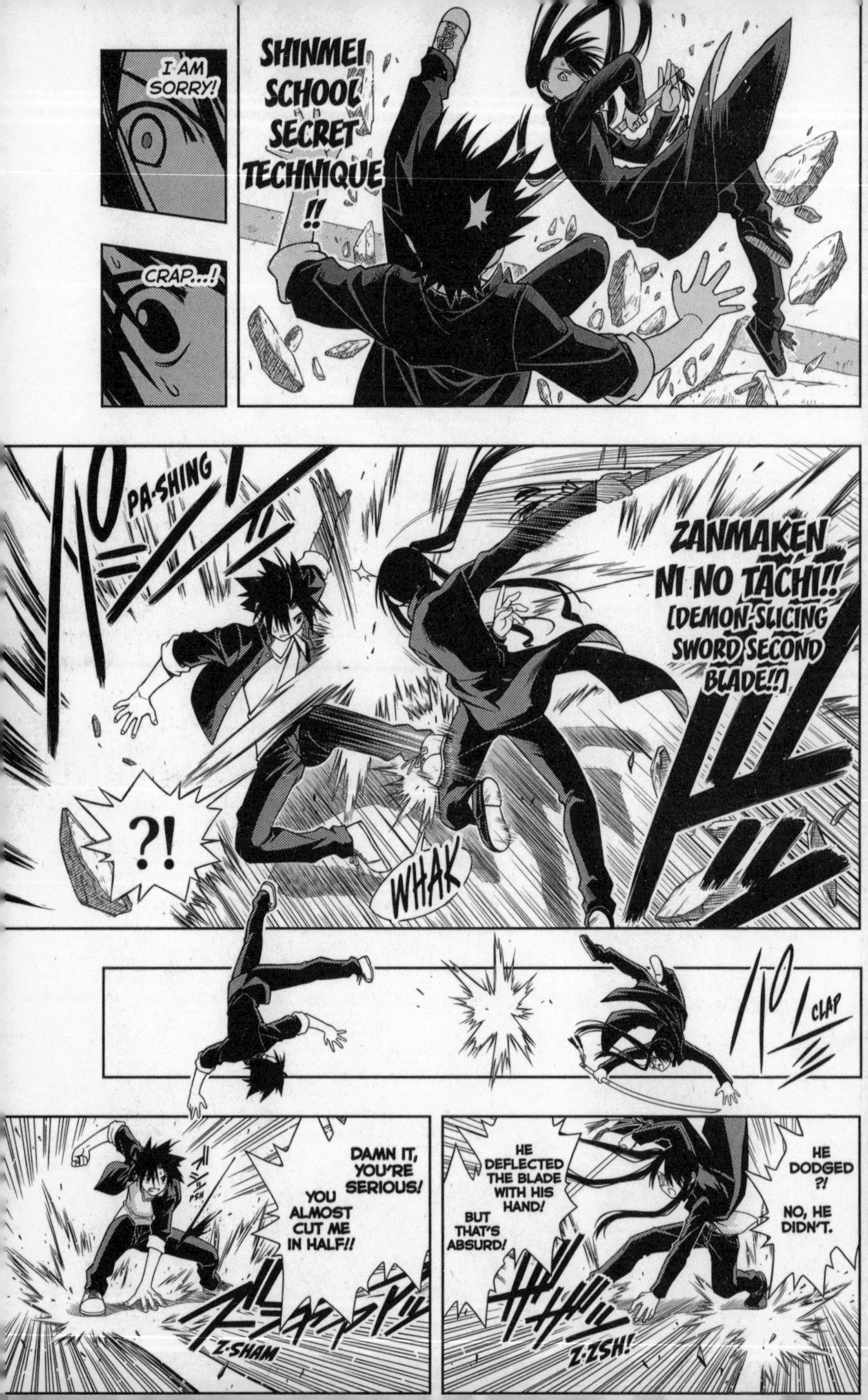
SHINMEI SCHOOL SECRET TECHNIQUE!!
I AM SORRY!
CRAP...!
ZANMAKEN NI NO TACHI!! [DEMON-SLICING SWORD SECOND BLADE!!]
PA-SHING
?!
WHAK
CLAP
HE DODGED?!
NO, HE DIDN'T.
HE DEFLECTED THE BLADE WITH HIS HAND!
BUT THAT'S ABSURD!
Z-ZSH!
DAMN IT, YOU'RE SERIOUS!
YOU ALMOST CUT ME IN HALF!!
PSH
Z-SHAM

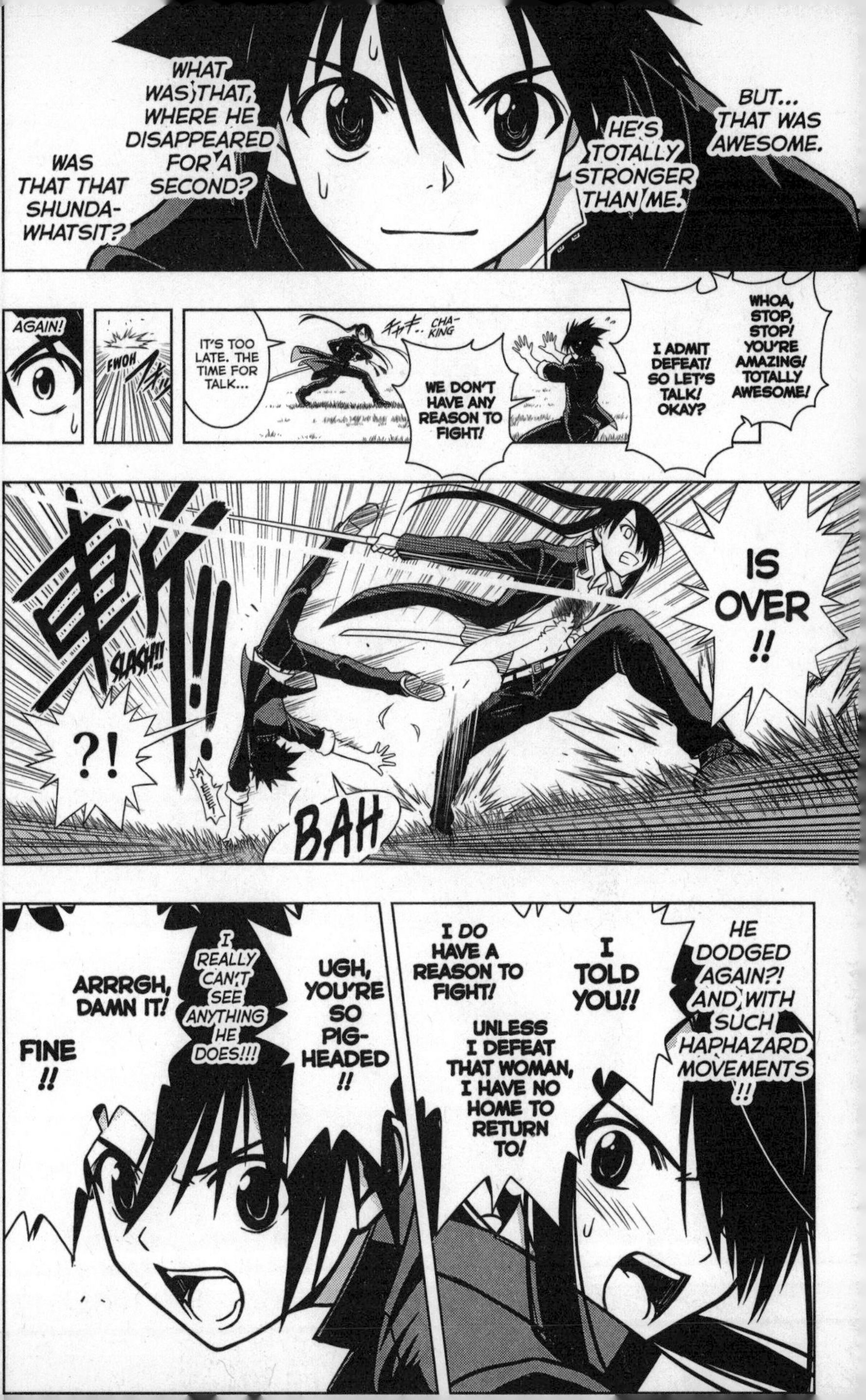
BUT... THAT WAS AWESOME.
HE'S TOTALLY STRONGER THAN ME.
WHAT WAS THAT, WHERE HE DISAPPEARED FOR A SECOND?
WAS THAT THAT SHUNDA-WHATSIT?
WHOA, STOP, STOP! YOU'RE AMAZING! TOTALLY AWESOME!
I ADMIT DEFEAT! SO LET'S TALK! OKAY?
WE DON'T HAVE ANY REASON TO FIGHT!
CHA-KING
IT'S TOO LATE. THE TIME FOR TALK...
FWOH
AGAIN!
IS OVER !!
SLASH!!
?!
BAH
HE DODGED AGAIN?! AND WITH SUCH HAPHAZARD MOVEMENTS !!
I TOLD YOU!!
I DO HAVE A REASON TO FIGHT!
UNLESS I DEFEAT THAT WOMAN, I HAVE NO HOME TO RETURN TO!
UGH, YOU'RE SO PIG-HEADED !!
I REALLY CAN'T SEE ANYTHING HE DOES!!!
ARRRGH, DAMN IT!
FINE !!

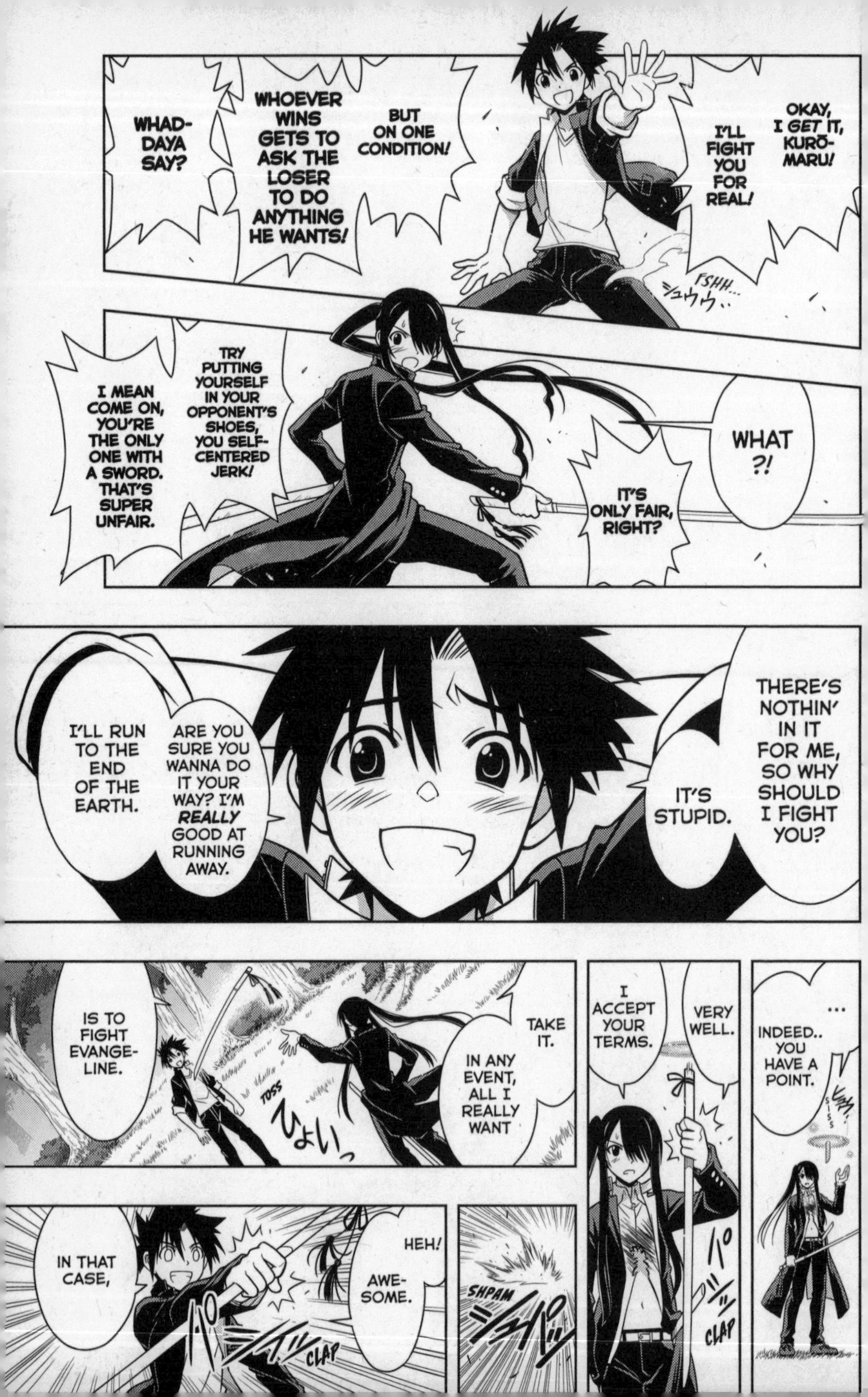

OKAY, I GET IT, KURŌ-MARU!
I'LL FIGHT YOU FOR REAL!
FSHH...
シュウウ...
BUT ON ONE CONDITION!
WHOEVER WINS GETS TO ASK THE LOSER TO DO ANYTHING HE WANTS!
WHAD-DAYA SAY?
WHAT?!
IT'S ONLY FAIR, RIGHT?
TRY PUTTING YOURSELF IN YOUR OPPONENT'S SHOES, YOU SELF-CENTERED JERK!
I MEAN COME ON, YOU'RE THE ONLY ONE WITH A SWORD. THAT'S SUPER UNFAIR.
THERE'S NOTHIN' IN IT FOR ME, SO WHY SHOULD I FIGHT YOU?
IT'S STUPID.
ARE YOU SURE YOU WANNA DO IT YOUR WAY? I'M *REALLY* GOOD AT RUNNING AWAY.
I'LL RUN TO THE END OF THE EARTH.
...
INDEED.. YOU HAVE A POINT.
SISS
VERY WELL.
I ACCEPT YOUR TERMS.
パ
CLAP
TAKE IT.
IN ANY EVENT, ALL I REALLY WANT
IS TO FIGHT EVANGE-LINE.
TOSS
ひょいっ
SHPAM
シュパッ
HEH!
AWE-SOME.
IN THAT CASE,
パシ
CLAP

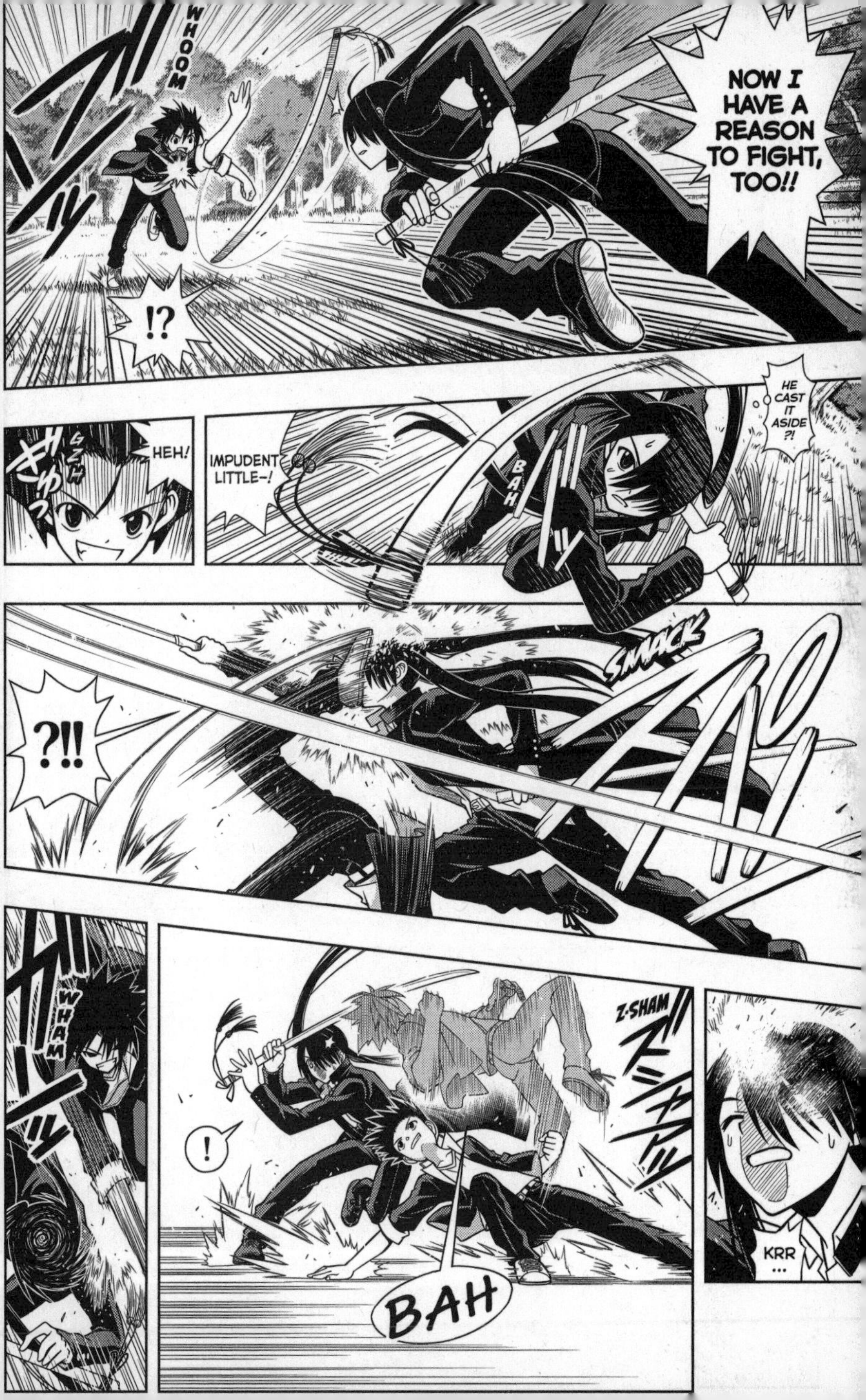
NOW I HAVE A REASON TO FIGHT, TOO!!
WHOOM
!?
HE CAST IT ASIDE?!
BAH
IMPUDENT LITTLE-!
HEH!
GZH
SMACK
?!!
KRR...
Z-SHAM
!
BAH
WHAM

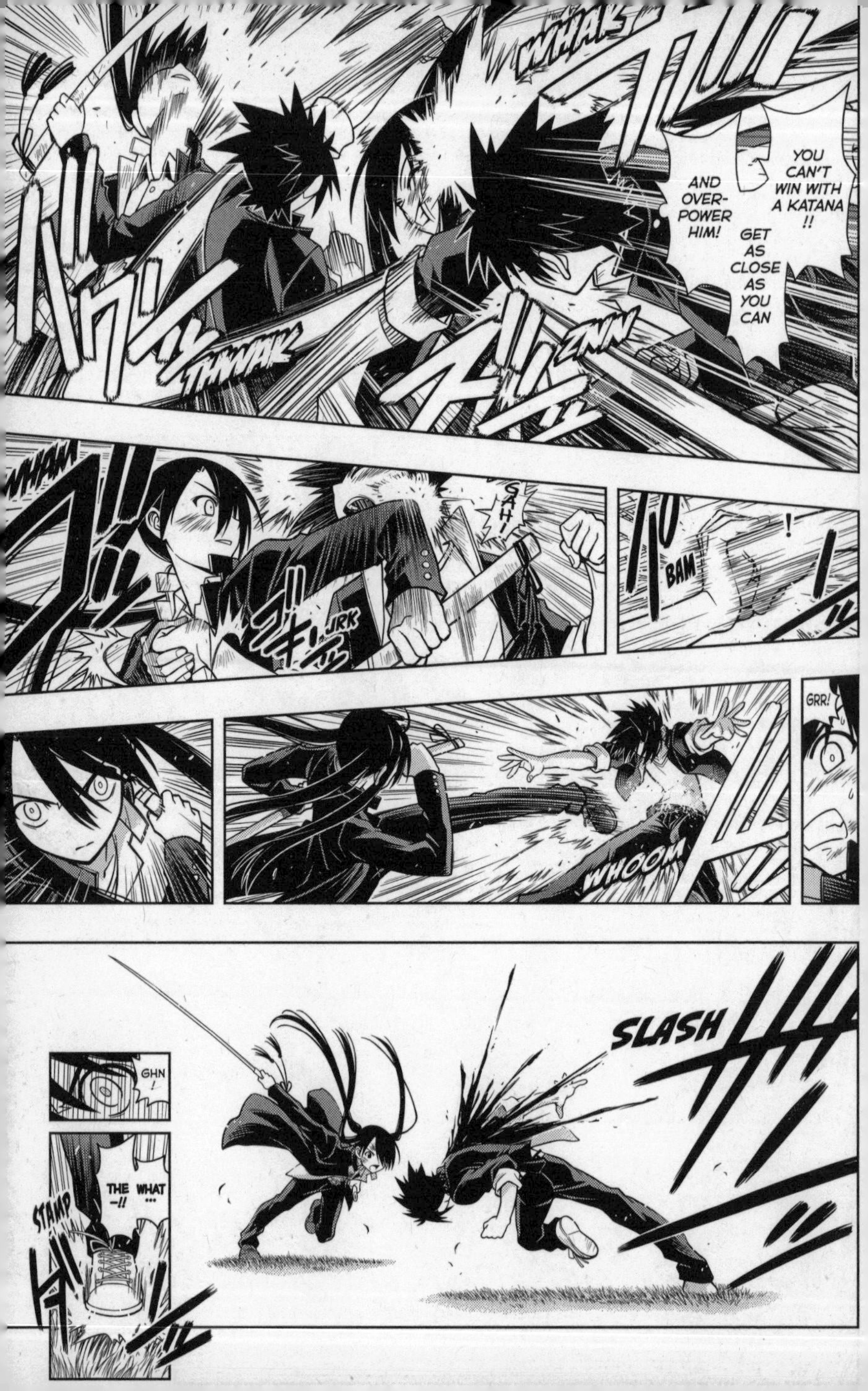
WHAK
YOU CAN'T WIN WITH A KATANA !!
GET AS CLOSE AS YOU CAN
AND OVER-POWER HIM!
ZNN
THWAK
!
BAM
GAH!
JRK
WHAM
GRR!
WHOOM
SLASH
GHN!
THE WHAT —!! ...
STAMP

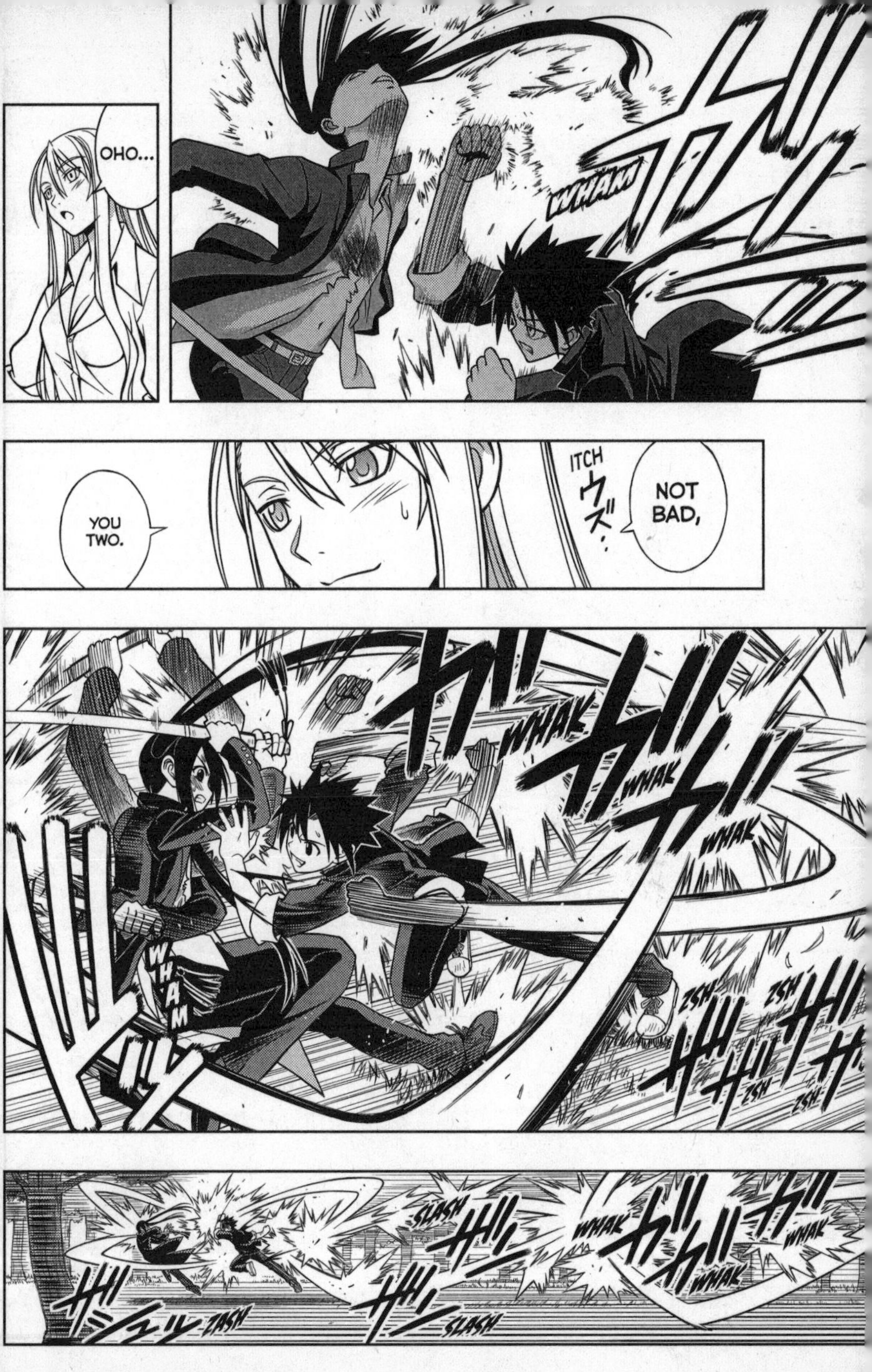
WHAM
OHO...
NOT BAD,
ITCH
ウズ
YOU TWO.
WHAK
WHAK
WHAK
WHAM
ZSH
ZSH
ZSH
ZSH
WHAK
WHAK
WHAK
SLASH
SLASH
ZASH

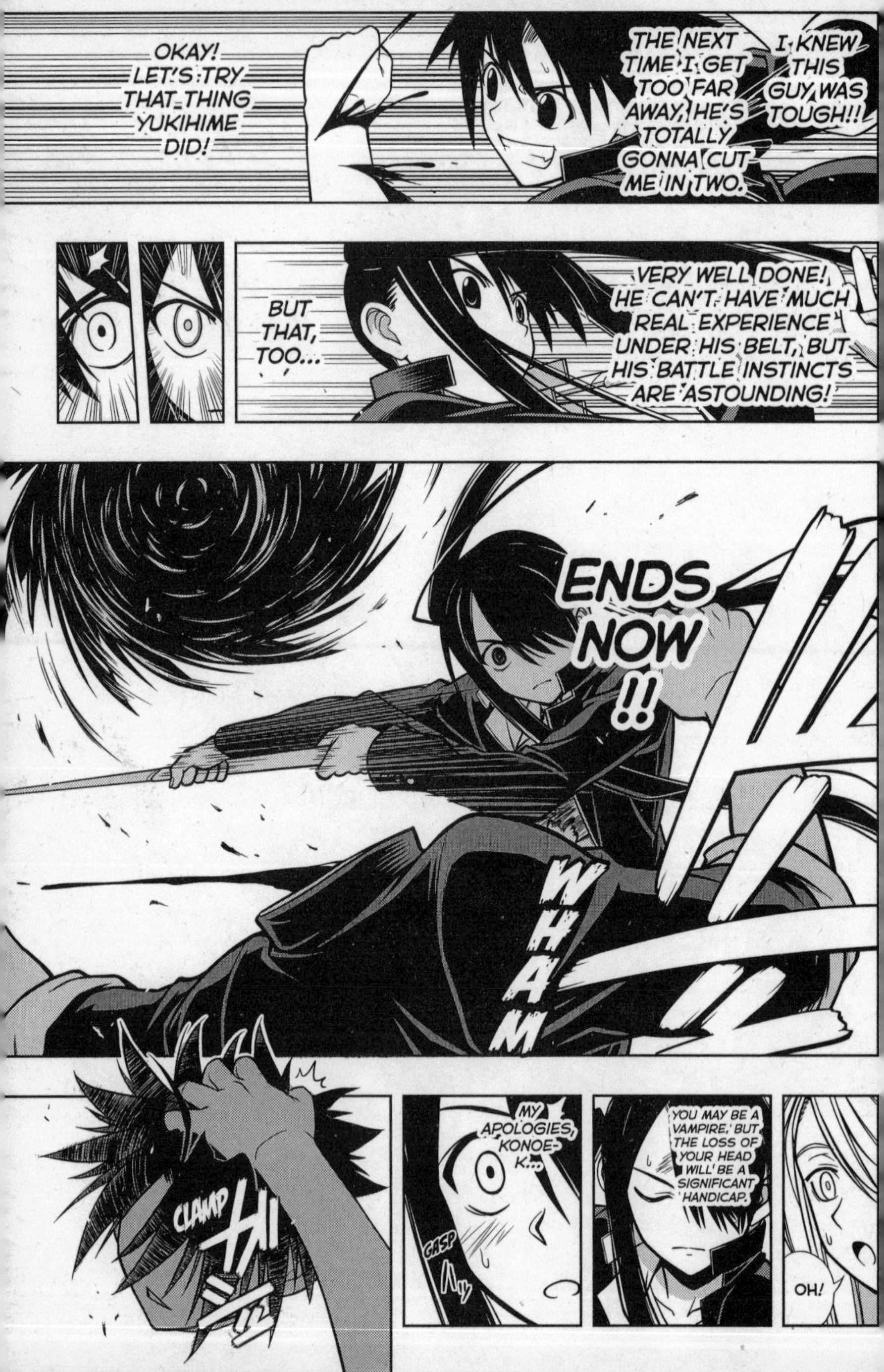
I KNEW THIS GUY WAS TOUGH!!
THE NEXT TIME I GET TOO FAR AWAY, HE'S TOTALLY GONNA CUT ME IN TWO.
OKAY! LET'S TRY THAT THING YUKIHIME DID!
VERY WELL DONE! HE CAN'T HAVE MUCH REAL EXPERIENCE UNDER HIS BELT, BUT HIS BATTLE INSTINCTS ARE ASTOUNDING!
BUT THAT, TOO...
ENDS NOW!!
WHAM
OH!
YOU MAY BE A VAMPIRE, BUT THE LOSS OF YOUR HEAD WILL BE A SIGNIFICANT HANDICAP.
MY APOLOGIES, KONOE-K...
GASP
CLAMP

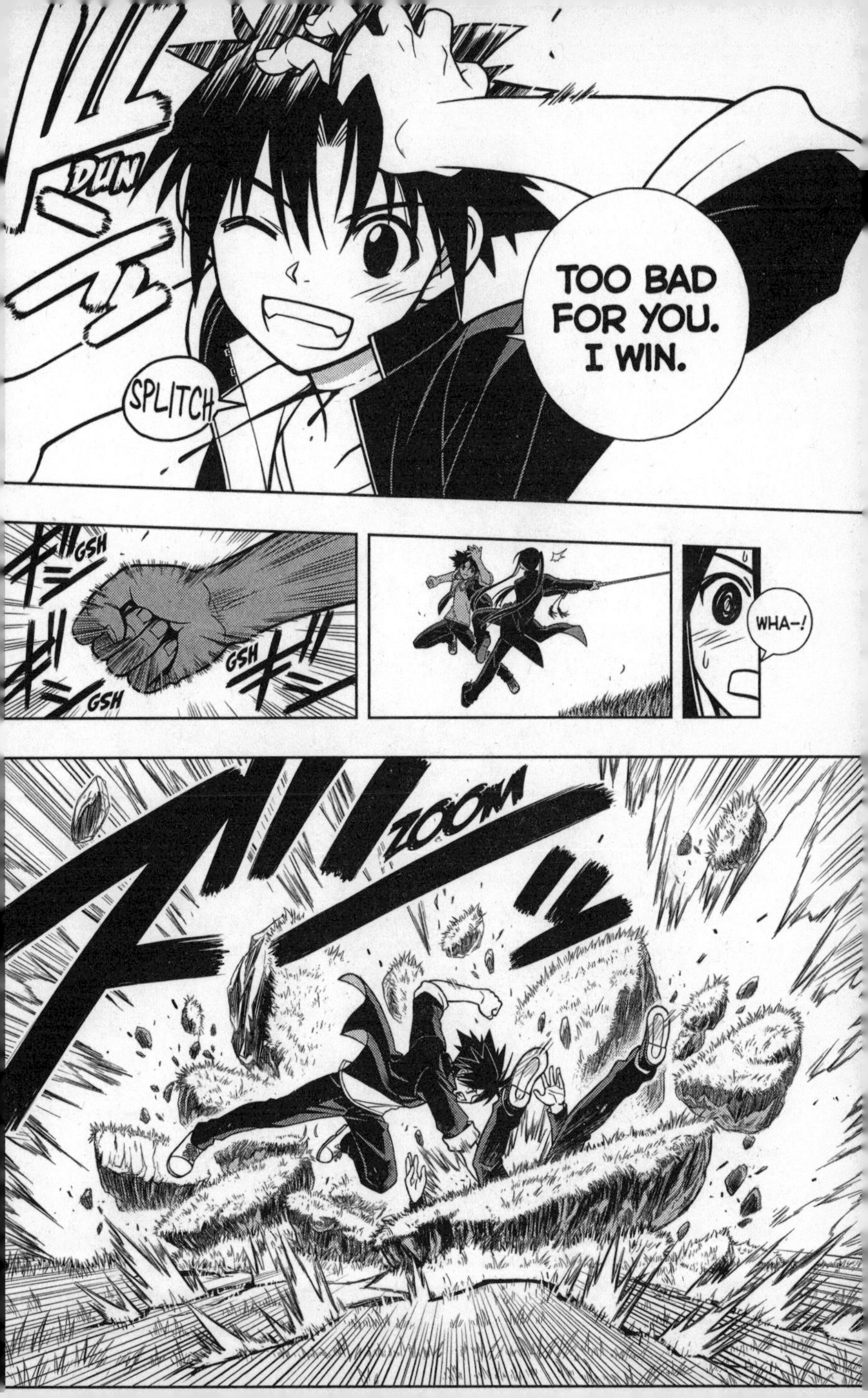
TOO BAD FOR YOU. I WIN.
SPLITCH
DUN
WHA-!
GSH
GSH
GSH
ZOOM

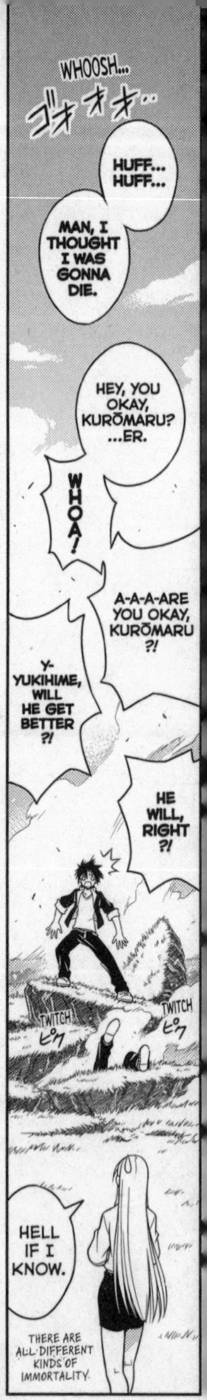
WHOOSH...
ゴオオオ..
HUFF... HUFF...
MAN, I THOUGHT I WAS GONNA DIE.
HEY, YOU OKAY, KURŌMARU? ...ER.
WHOA!
A-A-A-ARE YOU OKAY, KURŌMARU?!
Y-YUKIHIME, WILL HE GET BETTER?!
HE WILL, RIGHT?!
TWITCH
ピク
TWITCH
ピク
HELL IF I KNOW.
THERE ARE ALL DIFFERENT KINDS OF IMMORTALITY.

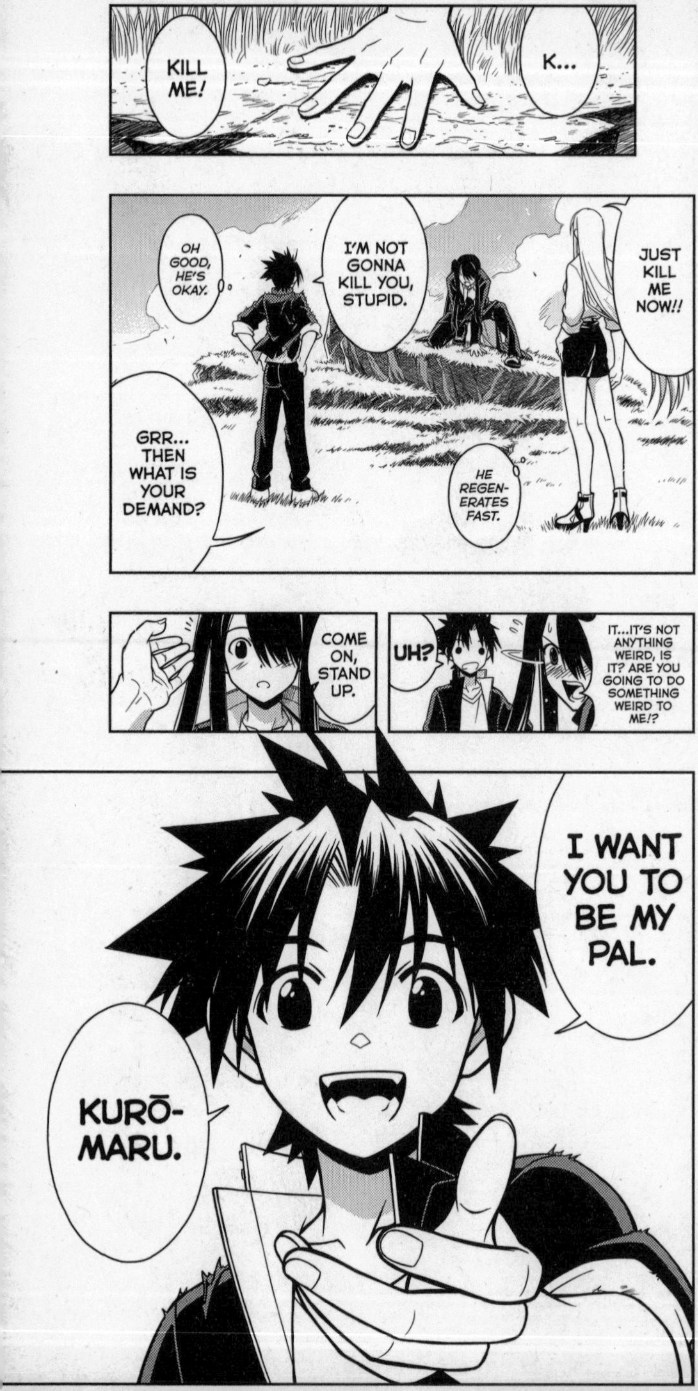
K...
KILL ME!
JUST KILL ME NOW!!
I'M NOT GONNA KILL YOU, STUPID.
OH GOOD, HE'S OKAY.
HE REGENERATES FAST.
GRR... THEN WHAT IS YOUR DEMAND?
IT...IT'S NOT ANYTHING WEIRD, IS IT? ARE YOU GOING TO DO SOMETHING WEIRD TO ME!?
UH?
COME ON, STAND UP.
I WANT YOU TO BE MY PAL.
KURŌ-MARU.

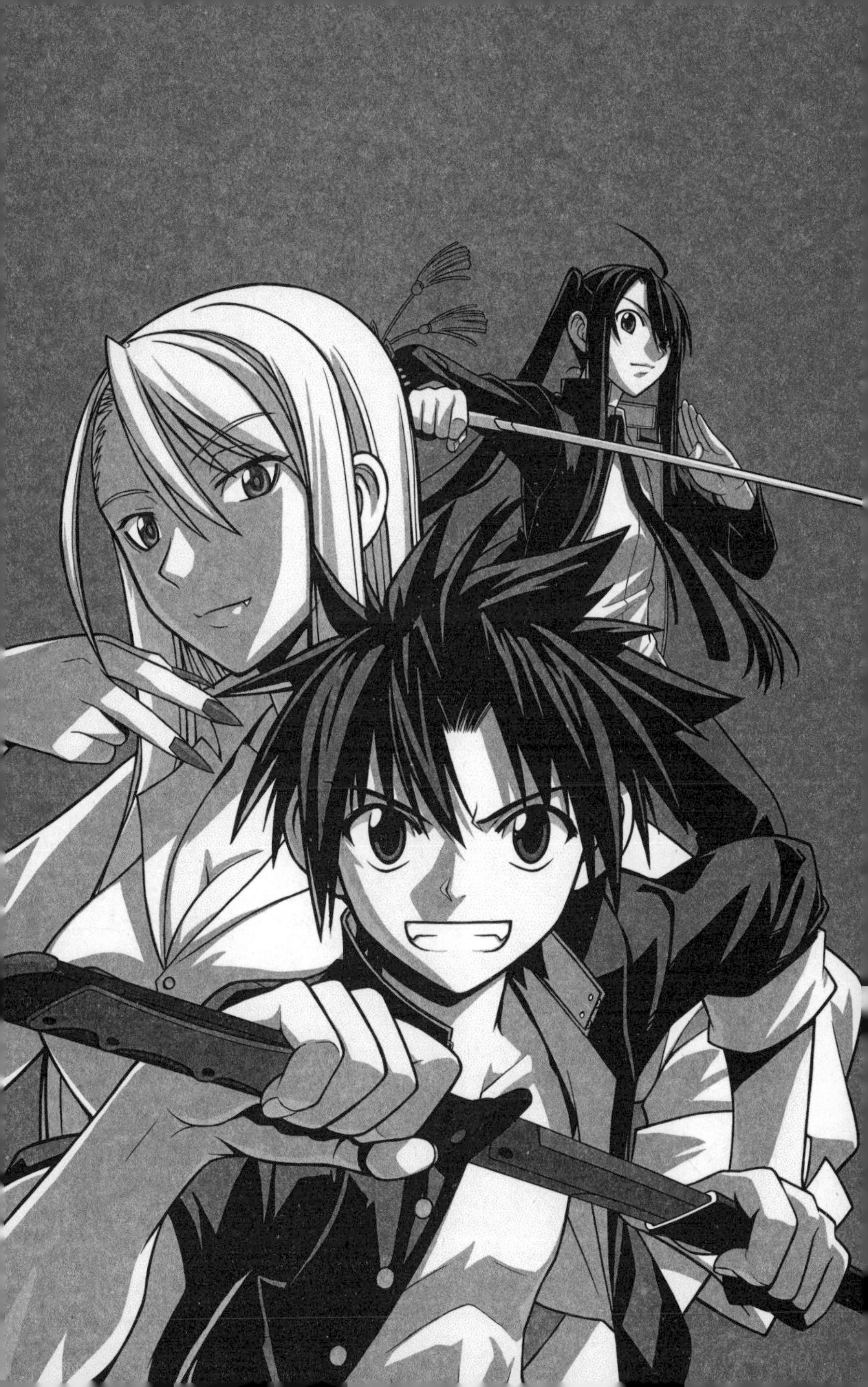

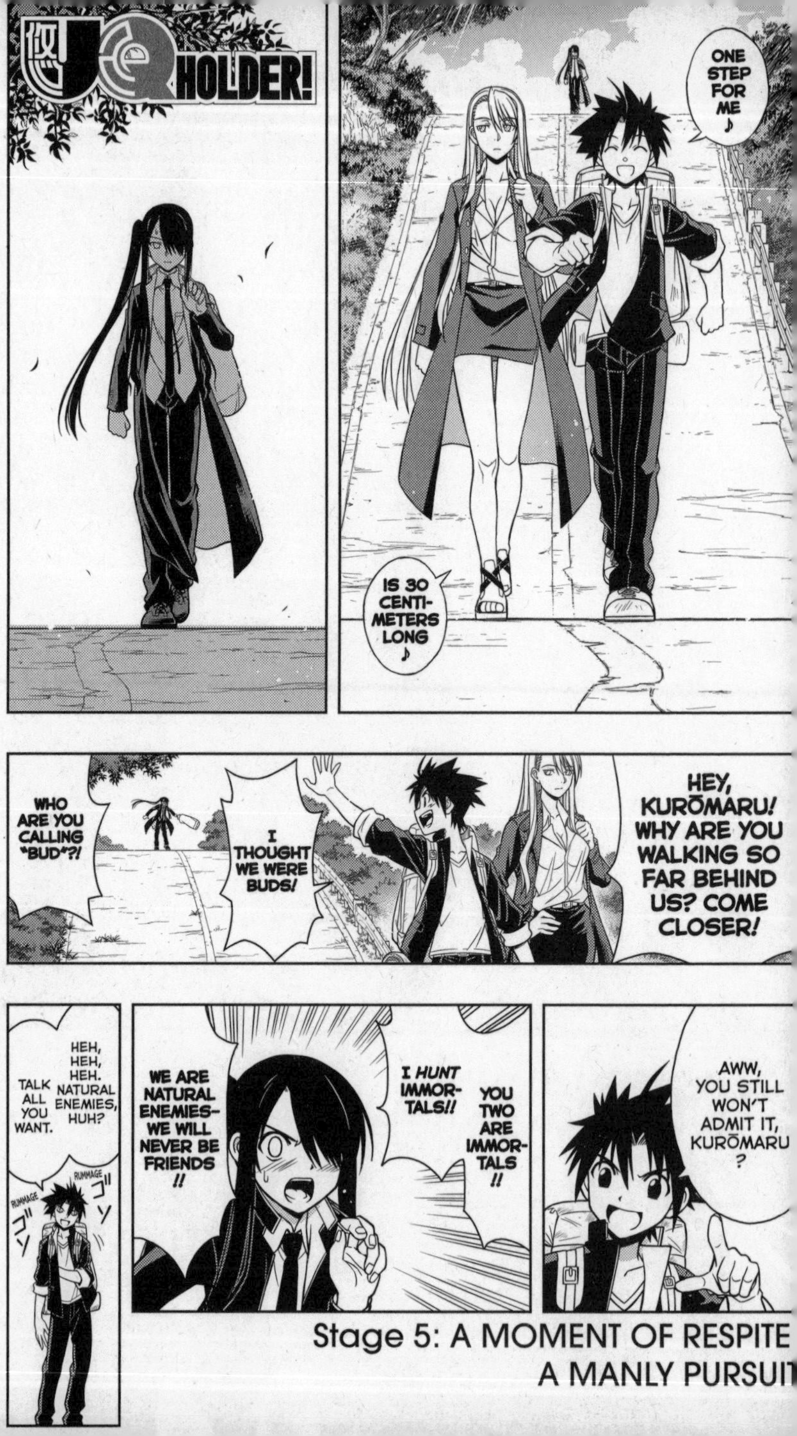
ONE STEP FOR ME ♪
IS 30 CENTIMETERS LONG ♪
HEY, KURŌMARU! WHY ARE YOU WALKING SO FAR BEHIND US? COME CLOSER!
I THOUGHT WE WERE BUDS!
WHO ARE YOU CALLING "BUD"?!
AWW, YOU STILL WON'T ADMIT IT, KURŌMARU?
YOU TWO ARE IMMORTALS!!
I HUNT IMMORTALS!!
WE ARE NATURAL ENEMIES— WE WILL NEVER BE FRIENDS!!
HEH, HEH, HEH. NATURAL ENEMIES, HUH?
TALK ALL YOU WANT.
RUMMAGE
RUMMAGE

Stage 5: A MOMENT OF RESPITE A MANLY PURSUIT

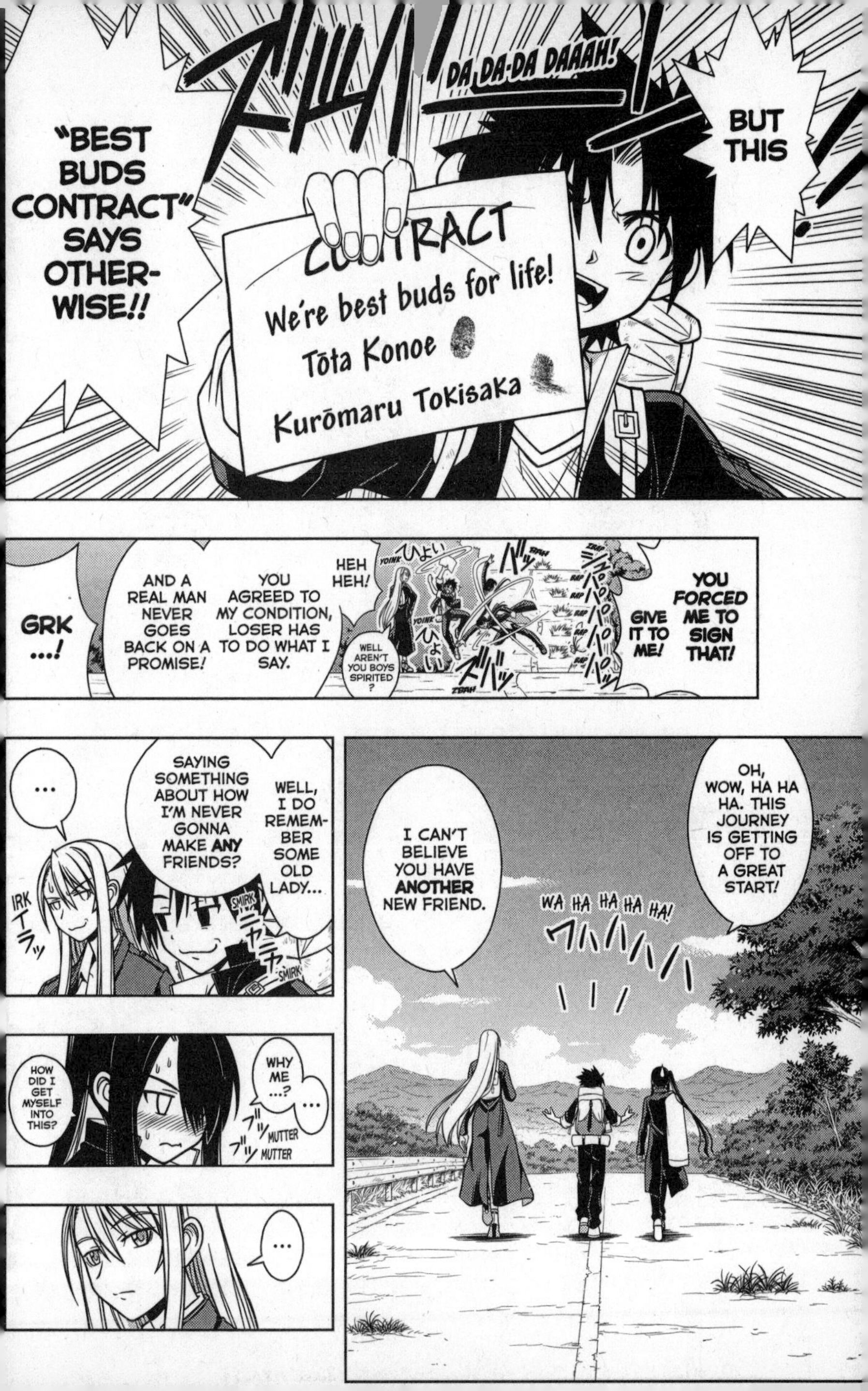
DA DA-DA DAAAH!
BUT THIS
CONTRACT
We're best buds for life!
Tōta Konoe
Kurōmaru Tokisaka
"BEST BUDS CONTRACT" SAYS OTHER-WISE!!
YOU FORCED ME TO SIGN THAT!
GIVE IT TO ME!
ZBAH
YOINK
YOINK
WELL AREN'T YOU BOYS SPIRITED?
HEH HEH!
YOU AGREED TO MY CONDITION, LOSER HAS TO DO WHAT I SAY.
AND A REAL MAN NEVER GOES BACK ON A PROMISE!
GRK ...!
OH, WOW, HA HA HA. THIS JOURNEY IS GETTING OFF TO A GREAT START!
WA HA HA HA HA!
I CAN'T BELIEVE YOU HAVE ANOTHER NEW FRIEND.
WELL, I DO REMEMBER SOME OLD LADY...
SAYING SOMETHING ABOUT HOW I'M NEVER GONNA MAKE ANY FRIENDS?
...
SMIRK
SMIRK
IRK
WHY ME ...?
...
MUTTER
MUTTER
HOW DID I GET MYSELF INTO THIS?
...

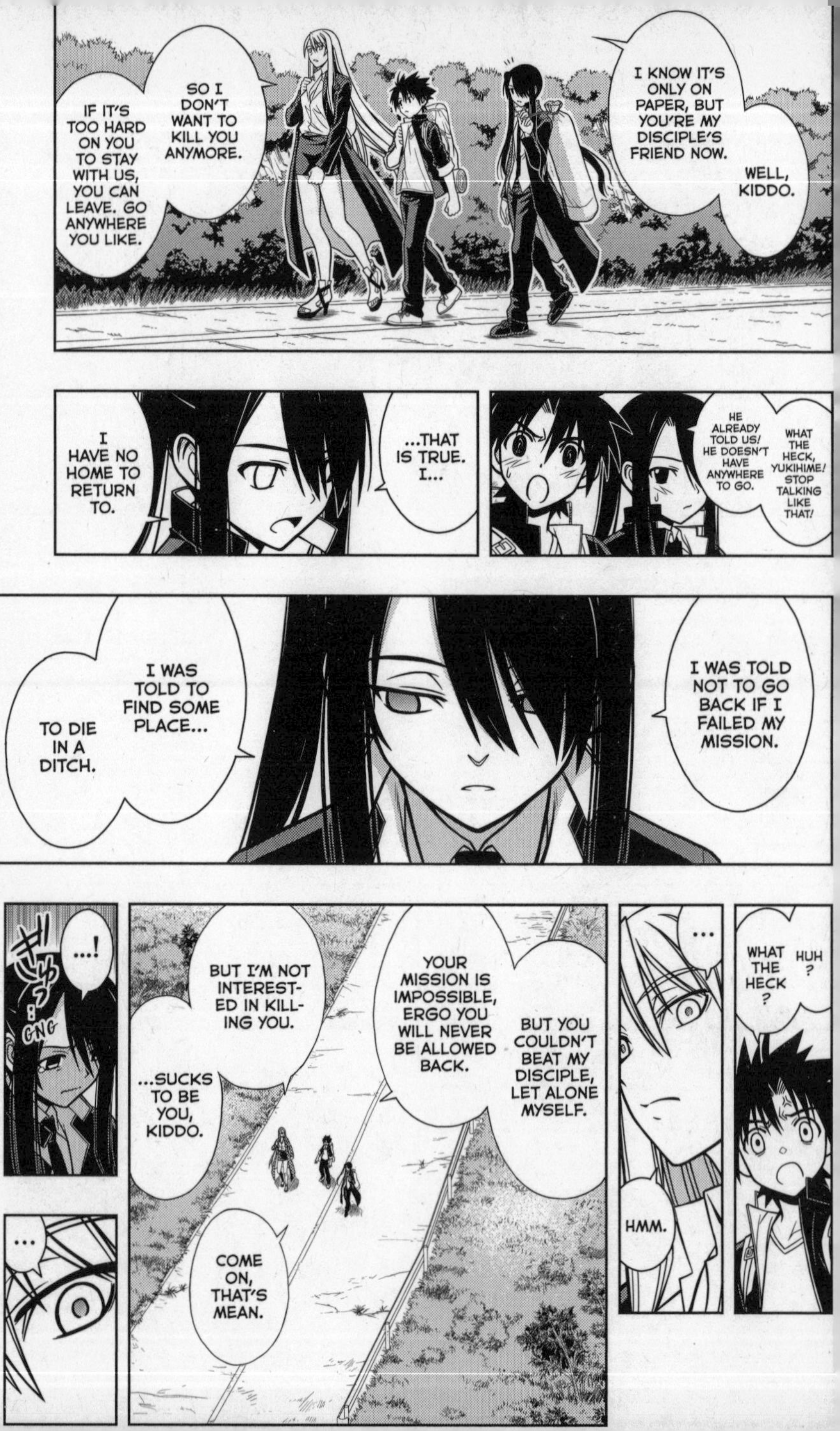
WELL, KIDDO.
I KNOW IT'S ONLY ON PAPER, BUT YOU'RE MY DISCIPLE'S FRIEND NOW.
SO I DON'T WANT TO KILL YOU ANYMORE.
IF IT'S TOO HARD ON YOU TO STAY WITH US, YOU CAN LEAVE. GO ANYWHERE YOU LIKE.
WHAT THE HECK, YUKIHIME! STOP TALKING LIKE THAT!
HE ALREADY TOLD US! HE DOESN'T HAVE ANYWHERE TO GO.
...THAT IS TRUE. I...
I HAVE NO HOME TO RETURN TO.
I WAS TOLD NOT TO GO BACK IF I FAILED MY MISSION.
I WAS TOLD TO FIND SOME PLACE...
TO DIE IN A DITCH.
HUH?
WHAT THE HECK?
...
HMM.
YOUR MISSION IS IMPOSSIBLE, ERGO YOU WILL NEVER BE ALLOWED BACK.
BUT YOU COULDN'T BEAT MY DISCIPLE, LET ALONE MYSELF.
BUT I'M NOT INTEREST-ED IN KILL-ING YOU.
...SUCKS TO BE YOU, KIDDO.
COME ON, THAT'S MEAN.
...!
GNG
...

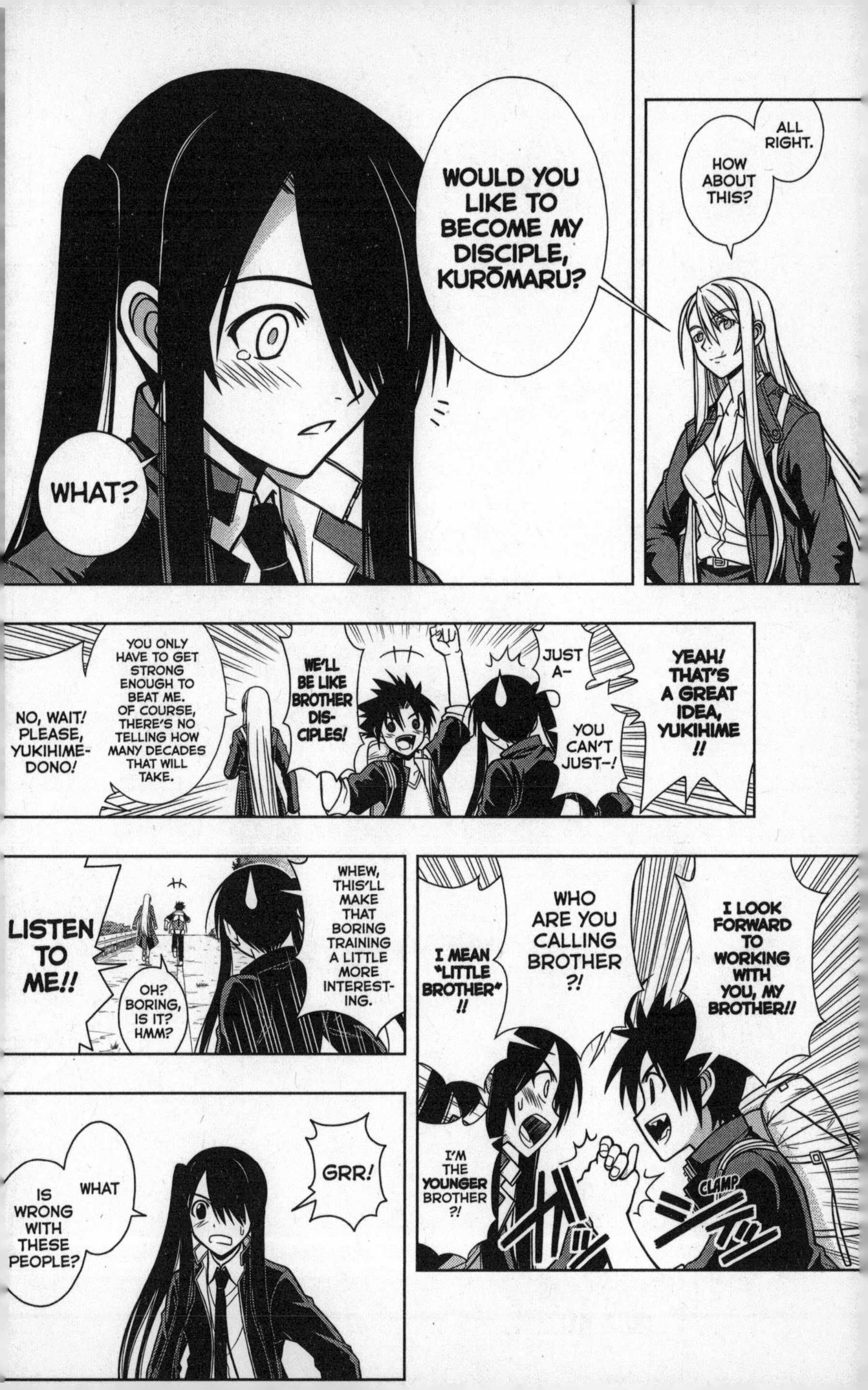
ALL RIGHT.
HOW ABOUT THIS?
WOULD YOU LIKE TO BECOME MY DISCIPLE, KURŌMARU?
WHAT?
YEAH! THAT'S A GREAT IDEA, YUKIHIME!!
JUST A-
YOU CAN'T JUST-!
WE'LL BE LIKE BROTHER DIS-CIPLES!
YOU ONLY HAVE TO GET STRONG ENOUGH TO BEAT ME. OF COURSE, THERE'S NO TELLING HOW MANY DECADES THAT WILL TAKE.
NO, WAIT! PLEASE, YUKIHIME-DONO!
I LOOK FORWARD TO WORKING WITH YOU, MY BROTHER!!
WHO ARE YOU CALLING BROTHER?!
I MEAN "LITTLE BROTHER"!!
I'M THE YOUNGER BROTHER?!
CLAMP
WHEW, THIS'LL MAKE THAT BORING TRAINING A LITTLE MORE INTEREST-ING.
OH? BORING, IS IT? HMM?
LISTEN TO ME!!
GRR!
WHAT IS WRONG WITH THESE PEOPLE?

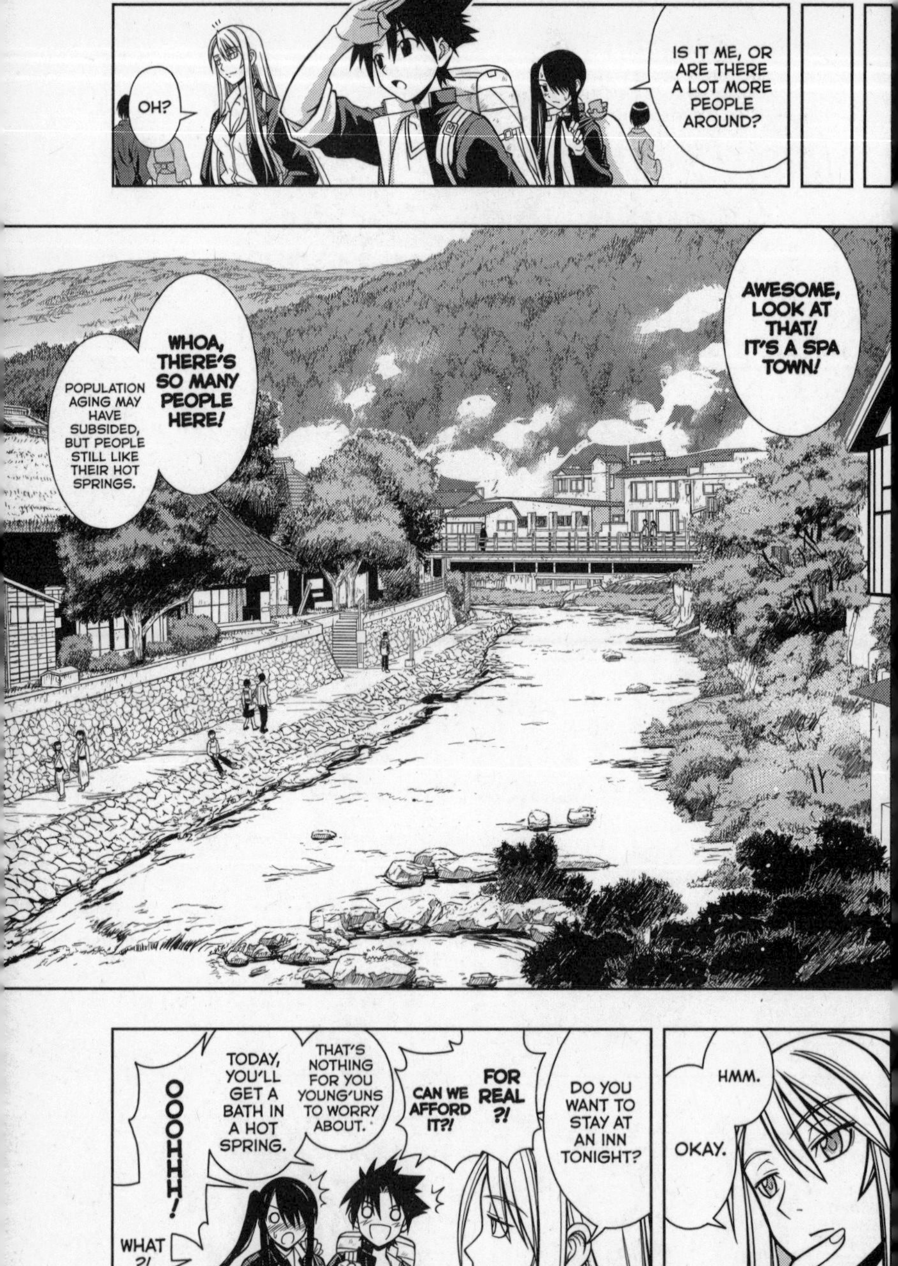
IS IT ME, OR ARE THERE A LOT MORE PEOPLE AROUND?
OH?
AWESOME, LOOK AT THAT! IT'S A SPA TOWN!
WHOA, THERE'S SO MANY PEOPLE HERE!
POPULATION AGING MAY HAVE SUBSIDED, BUT PEOPLE STILL LIKE THEIR HOT SPRINGS.
HMM.
OKAY.
DO YOU WANT TO STAY AT AN INN TONIGHT?
FOR REAL ?!
CAN WE AFFORD IT?!
THAT'S NOTHING FOR YOU YOUNG'UNS TO WORRY ABOUT.
TODAY, YOU'LL GET A BATH IN A HOT SPRING.
OOOHHH!
WHAT ?!

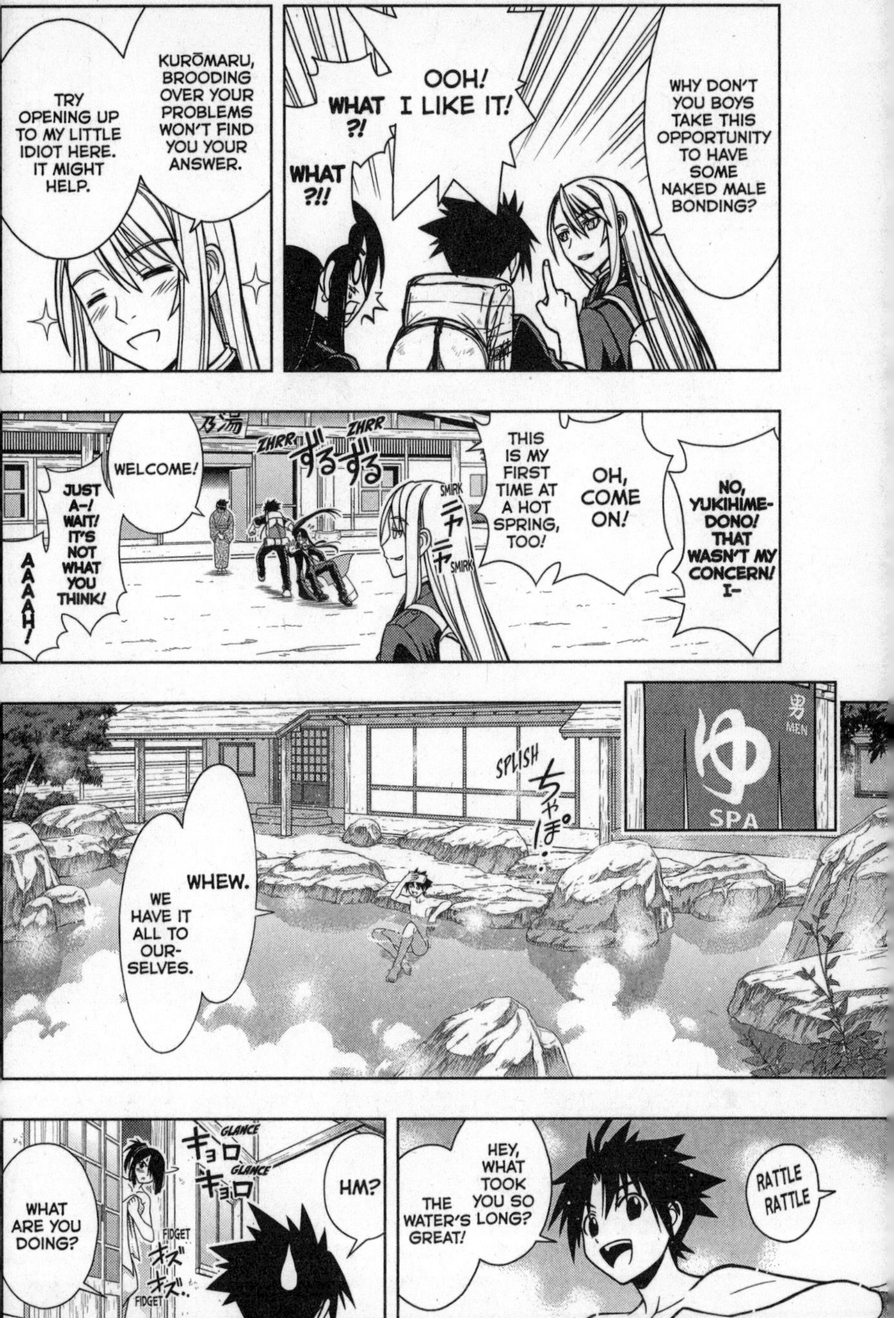
WHY DON'T YOU BOYS TAKE THIS OPPORTUNITY TO HAVE SOME NAKED MALE BONDING?
OOH! I LIKE IT!
WHAT ?!
WHAT ?!!
KURŌMARU, BROODING OVER YOUR PROBLEMS WON'T FIND YOU YOUR ANSWER.
TRY OPENING UP TO MY LITTLE IDIOT HERE. IT MIGHT HELP.
NO, YUKIHIME-DONO! THAT WASN'T MY CONCERN! I-
OH, COME ON!
THIS IS MY FIRST TIME AT A HOT SPRING, TOO!
SMIRK
ニヤニヤ
SMIRK
ZHRR
ずるずる
ZHRR
WELCOME!
JUST A-! WAIT! IT'S NOT WHAT YOU THINK!
AAAAH!
男
MEN
ゆ
SPA
SPLISH
ちゃぽ…
WHEW.
WE HAVE IT ALL TO OUR-SELVES.
RATTLE RATTLE
HEY, WHAT TOOK YOU SO LONG?
THE WATER'S GREAT!
HM?
GLANCE
キョロキョロ
GLANCE
WHAT ARE YOU DOING?
FIDGET
オズオズ…
FIDGET

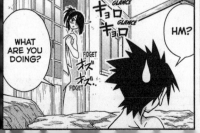

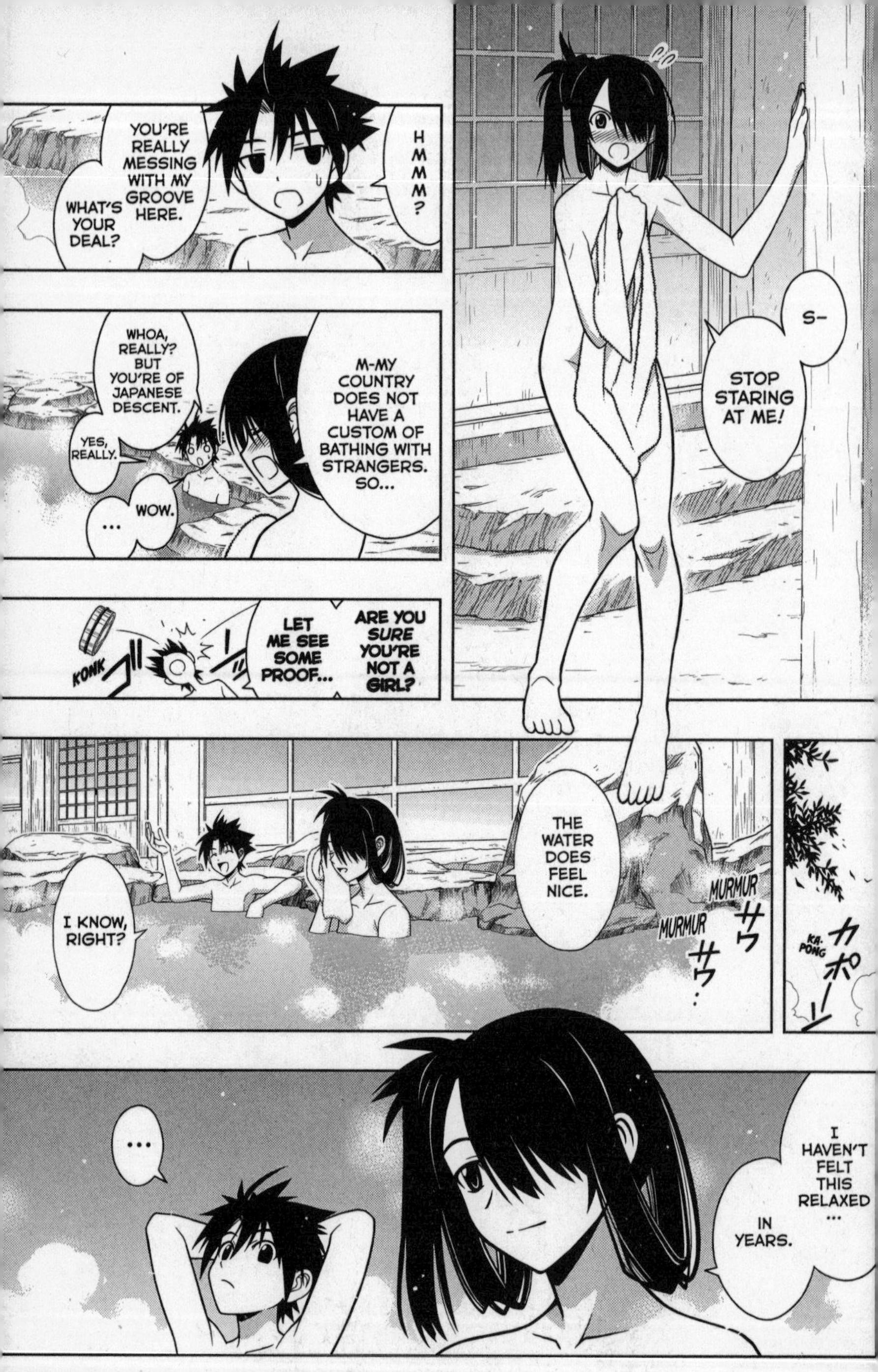
S–
STOP STARING AT ME!
HMMMM?
YOU'RE REALLY MESSING WITH MY GROOVE HERE.
WHAT'S YOUR DEAL?
M-MY COUNTRY DOES NOT HAVE A CUSTOM OF BATHING WITH STRANGERS. SO...
WHOA, REALLY? BUT YOU'RE OF JAPANESE DESCENT.
YES, REALLY.
... WOW.
ARE YOU *SURE* YOU'RE NOT A GIRL?
LET ME SEE SOME PROOF...
KONK
KA-PONG
MURMUR
MURMUR
THE WATER DOES FEEL NICE.
I KNOW, RIGHT?
I HAVEN'T FELT THIS RELAXED ...
IN YEARS.
...

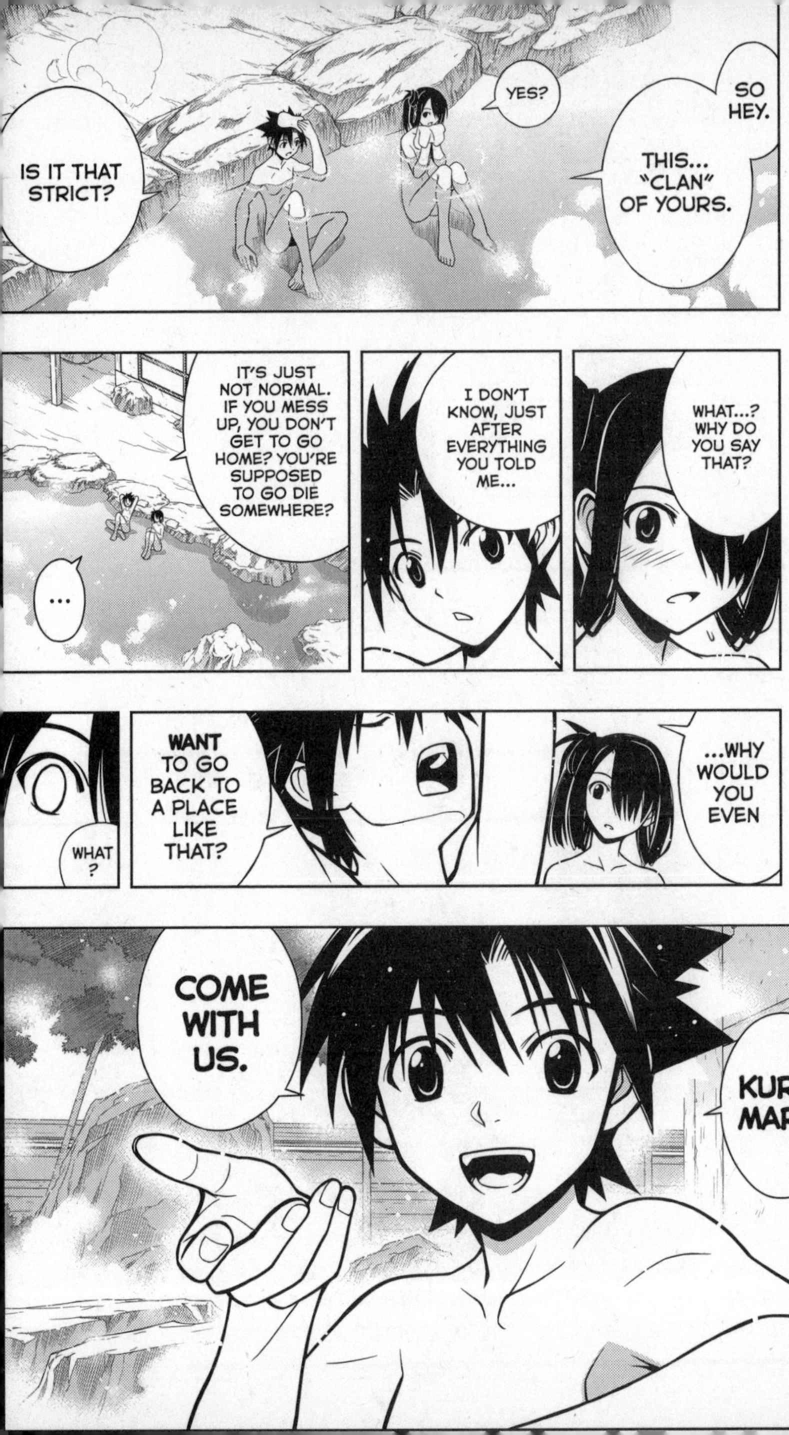
SO HEY.
THIS... "CLAN" OF YOURS.
YES?
IS IT THAT STRICT?
WHAT...? WHY DO YOU SAY THAT?
I DON'T KNOW, JUST AFTER EVERYTHING YOU TOLD ME...
IT'S JUST NOT NORMAL. IF YOU MESS UP, YOU DON'T GET TO GO HOME? YOU'RE SUPPOSED TO GO DIE SOMEWHERE?
...
...WHY WOULD YOU EVEN
WANT TO GO BACK TO A PLACE LIKE THAT?
WHAT?
KURŌ-MARU.
COME WITH US.

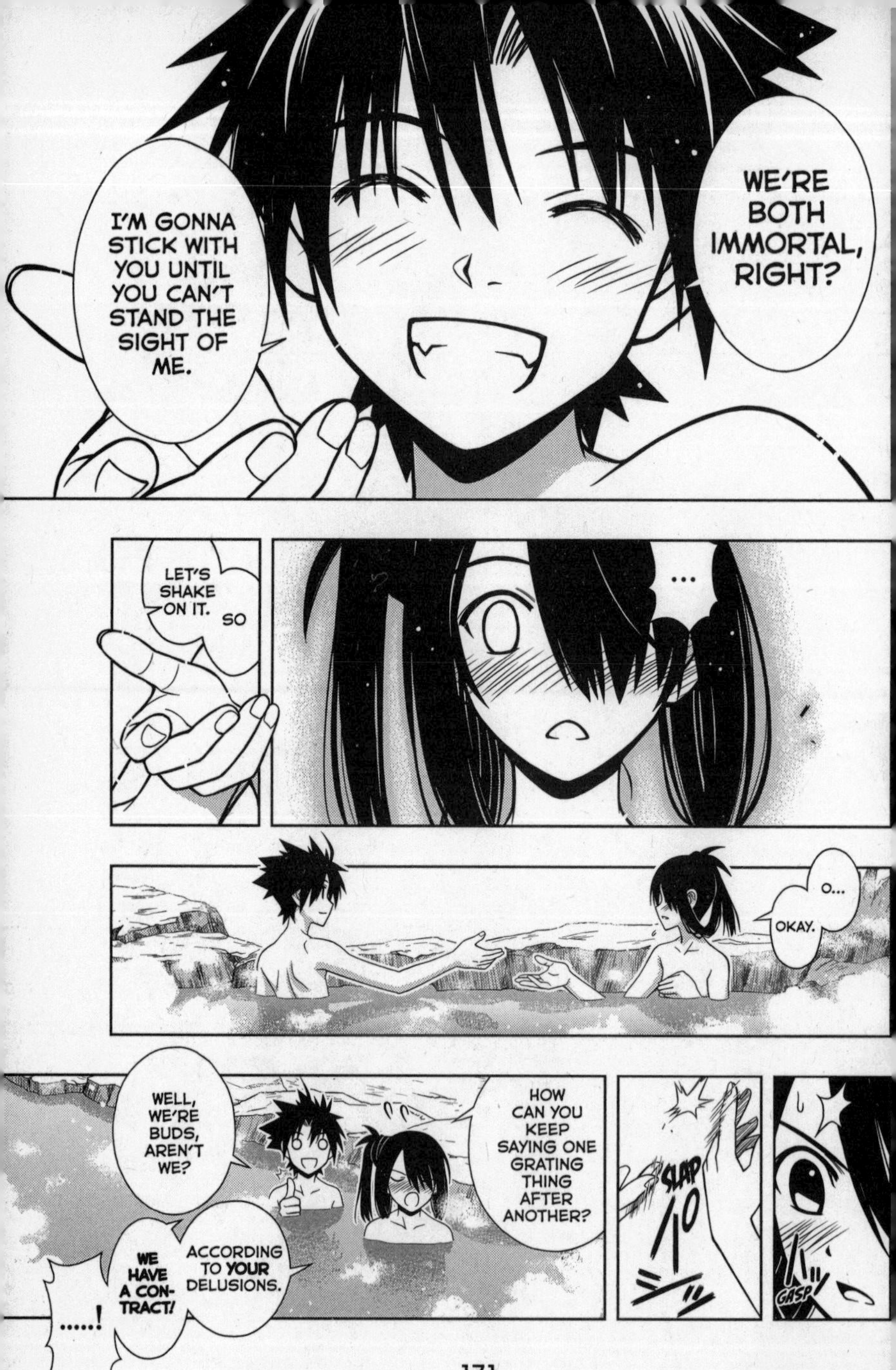

WE'RE BOTH IMMORTAL, RIGHT?
I'M GONNA STICK WITH YOU UNTIL YOU CAN'T STAND THE SIGHT OF ME.
...
SO
LET'S SHAKE ON IT.
O... OKAY.
GASP!
SLAP
HOW CAN YOU KEEP SAYING ONE GRATING THING AFTER ANOTHER?
WELL, WE'RE BUDS, AREN'T WE?
ACCORDING TO **YOUR** DELUSIONS.
WE HAVE A CONTRACT!
.....!

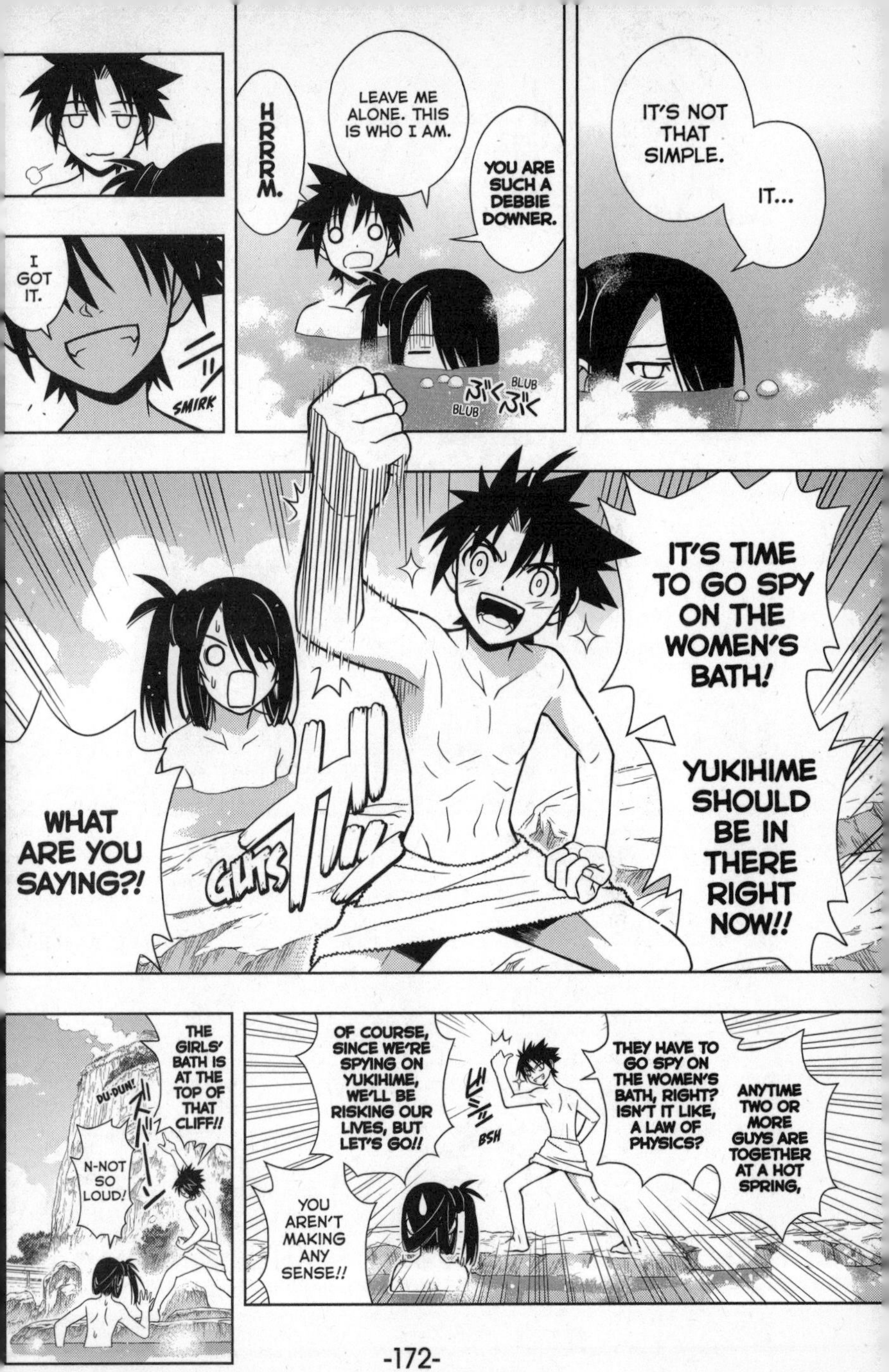
IT'S NOT THAT SIMPLE.
IT...
YOU ARE SUCH A DEBBIE DOWNER.
LEAVE ME ALONE. THIS IS WHO I AM.
HRRRM.
ぶくぶく
BLUB BLUB
I GOT IT.
SMIRK
IT'S TIME TO GO SPY ON THE WOMEN'S BATH!
YUKIHIME SHOULD BE IN THERE RIGHT NOW!!
GUTS
WHAT ARE YOU SAYING?!
ANYTIME TWO OR MORE GUYS ARE TOGETHER AT A HOT SPRING,
THEY HAVE TO GO SPY ON THE WOMEN'S BATH, RIGHT? ISN'T IT LIKE, A LAW OF PHYSICS?
BSH
OF COURSE, SINCE WE'RE SPYING ON YUKIHIME, WE'LL BE RISKING OUR LIVES, BUT LET'S GO!!
YOU AREN'T MAKING ANY SENSE!!
THE GIRLS' BATH IS AT THE TOP OF THAT CLIFF!!
DU-DUN!
N-NOT SO LOUD!

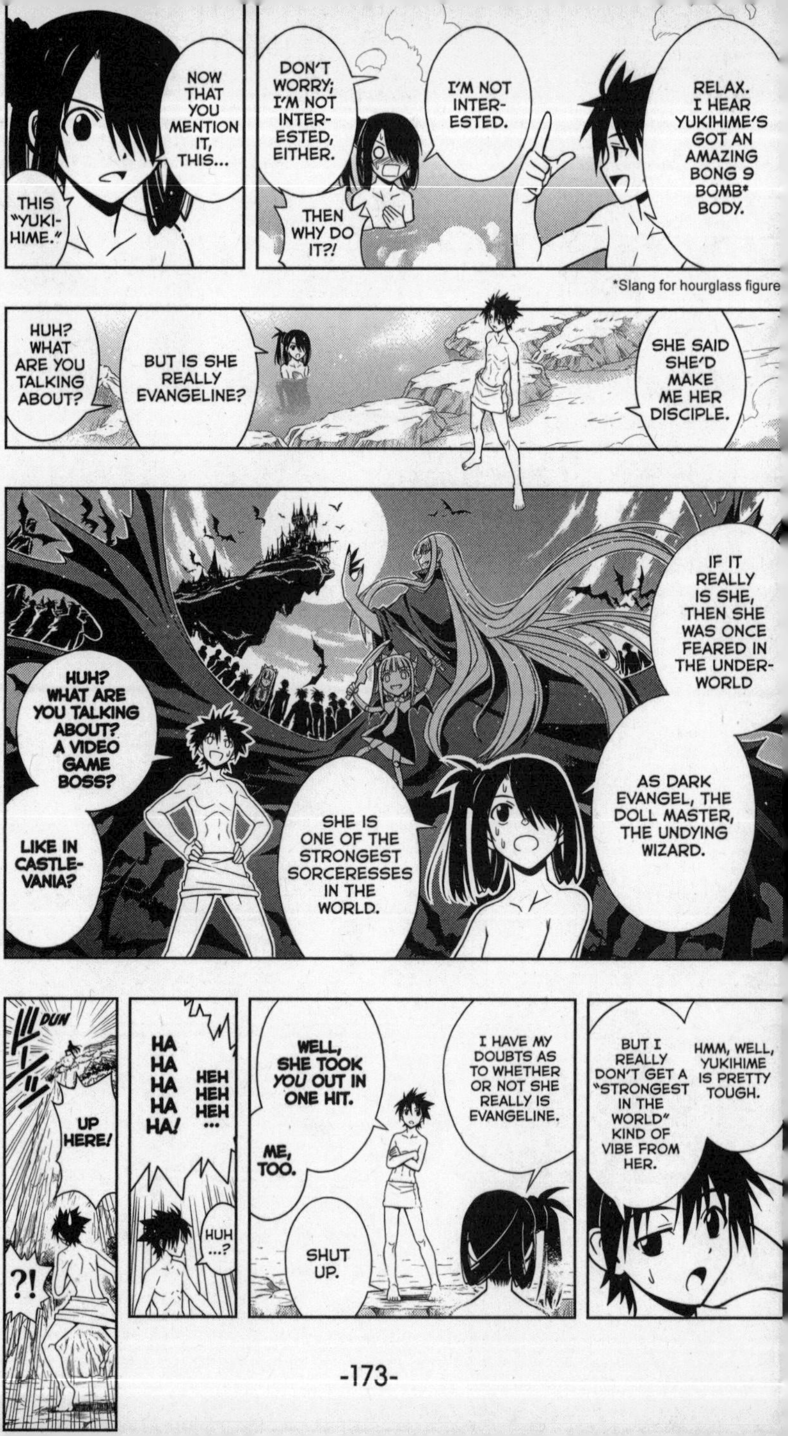
RELAX. I HEAR YUKIHIME'S GOT AN AMAZING BONG 9 BOMB* BODY.
I'M NOT INTERESTED.
DON'T WORRY; I'M NOT INTERESTED, EITHER.
THEN WHY DO IT?!
NOW THAT YOU MENTION IT, THIS...
THIS "YUKIHIME."
SHE SAID SHE'D MAKE ME HER DISCIPLE.
BUT IS SHE REALLY EVANGELINE?
HUH? WHAT ARE YOU TALKING ABOUT?
IF IT REALLY IS SHE, THEN SHE WAS ONCE FEARED IN THE UNDERWORLD
AS DARK EVANGEL, THE DOLL MASTER, THE UNDYING WIZARD.
SHE IS ONE OF THE STRONGEST SORCERESSES IN THE WORLD.
HUH? WHAT ARE YOU TALKING ABOUT? A VIDEO GAME BOSS?
LIKE IN CASTLEVANIA?
HMM, WELL, YUKIHIME IS PRETTY TOUGH.
BUT I REALLY DON'T GET A "STRONGEST IN THE WORLD" KIND OF VIBE FROM HER.
I HAVE MY DOUBTS AS TO WHETHER OR NOT SHE REALLY IS EVANGELINE.
WELL, SHE TOOK *YOU* OUT IN ONE HIT.
ME, TOO.
SHUT UP.
HA HA HA HA HA!
HEH HEH HEH...
HUH ...?
DUN
UP HERE!
?!

*Slang for hourglass figure

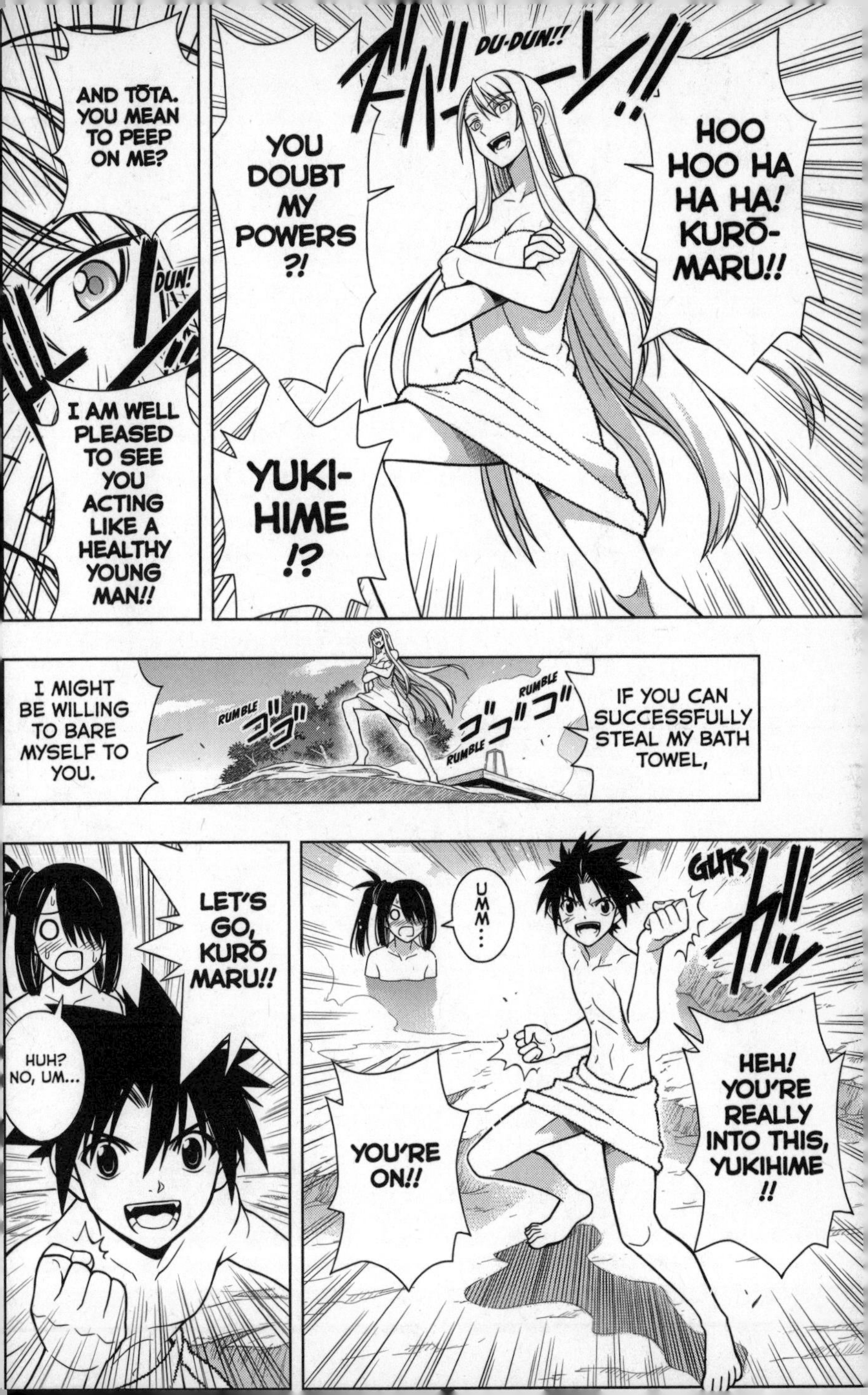
DU-DUN!!
HOO HOO HA HA HA! KURŌ-MARU!!
YOU DOUBT MY POWERS?!
YUKI-HIME!?
AND TŌTA. YOU MEAN TO PEEP ON ME?
DUN!
I AM WELL PLEASED TO SEE YOU ACTING LIKE A HEALTHY YOUNG MAN!!
IF YOU CAN SUCCESSFULLY STEAL MY BATH TOWEL,
RUMBLE
RUMBLE
RUMBLE
I MIGHT BE WILLING TO BARE MYSELF TO YOU.
GUTS
HEH! YOU'RE REALLY INTO THIS, YUKIHIME!!
UMM...
YOU'RE ON!!
LET'S GO, KURŌ MARU!!
HUH? NO, UM...

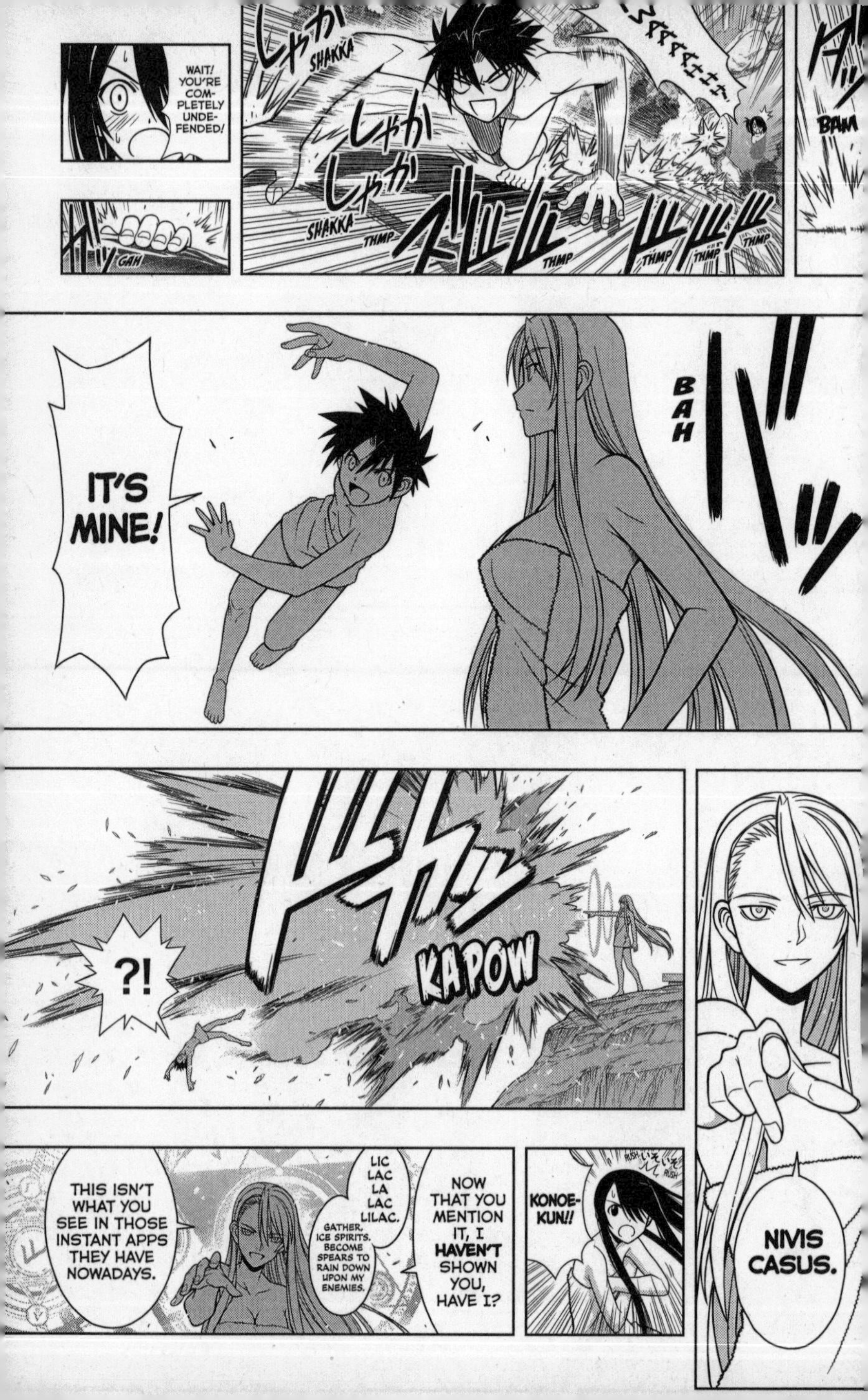
BAM
SHAKKA
SHAKKA
THMP
THMP
THMP
THMP
THMP
WAIT! YOU'RE COMPLETELY UNDEFENDED!
GAH
BAH
IT'S MINE!
NIVIS CASUS.
KAPOW
?!
RUSH
RUSH
KONOE-KUN!!
NOW THAT YOU MENTION IT, I HAVEN'T SHOWN YOU, HAVE I?
LIC LAC LA LAC LILAC.
GATHER, ICE SPIRITS. BECOME SPEARS TO RAIN DOWN UPON MY ENEMIES.
THIS ISN'T WHAT YOU SEE IN THOSE INSTANT APPS THEY HAVE NOWADAYS.

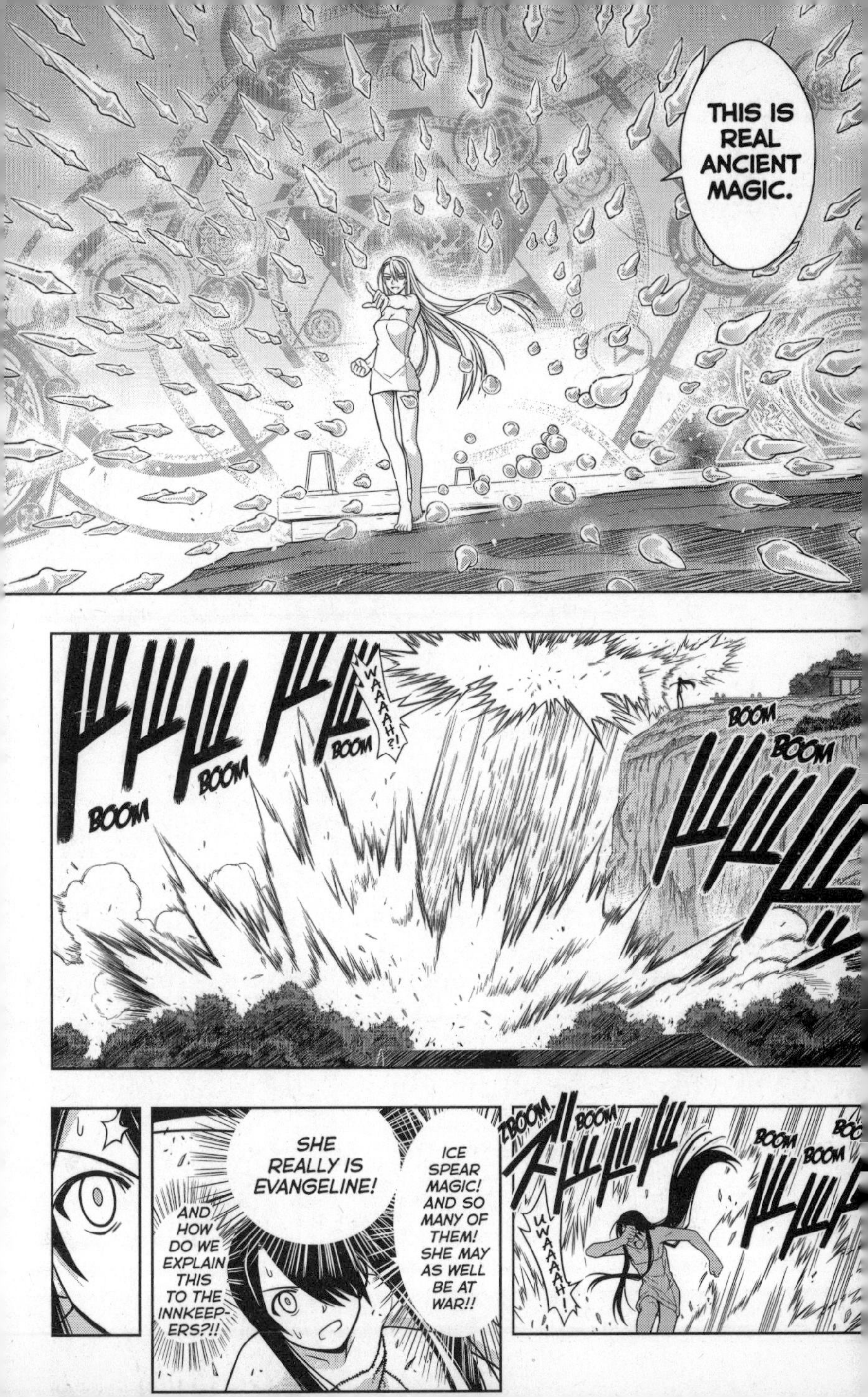
THIS IS REAL ANCIENT MAGIC.
BOOM
BOOM
WAAAAAH?!
BOOM
BOOM
BOOM
BOOM
BOOM
BOOM
ZBOOM
UWAAAAAH!
ICE SPEAR MAGIC! AND SO MANY OF THEM! SHE MAY AS WELL BE AT WAR!!
SHE REALLY IS EVANGELINE!
AND HOW DO WE EXPLAIN THIS TO THE INNKEEPERS?!!

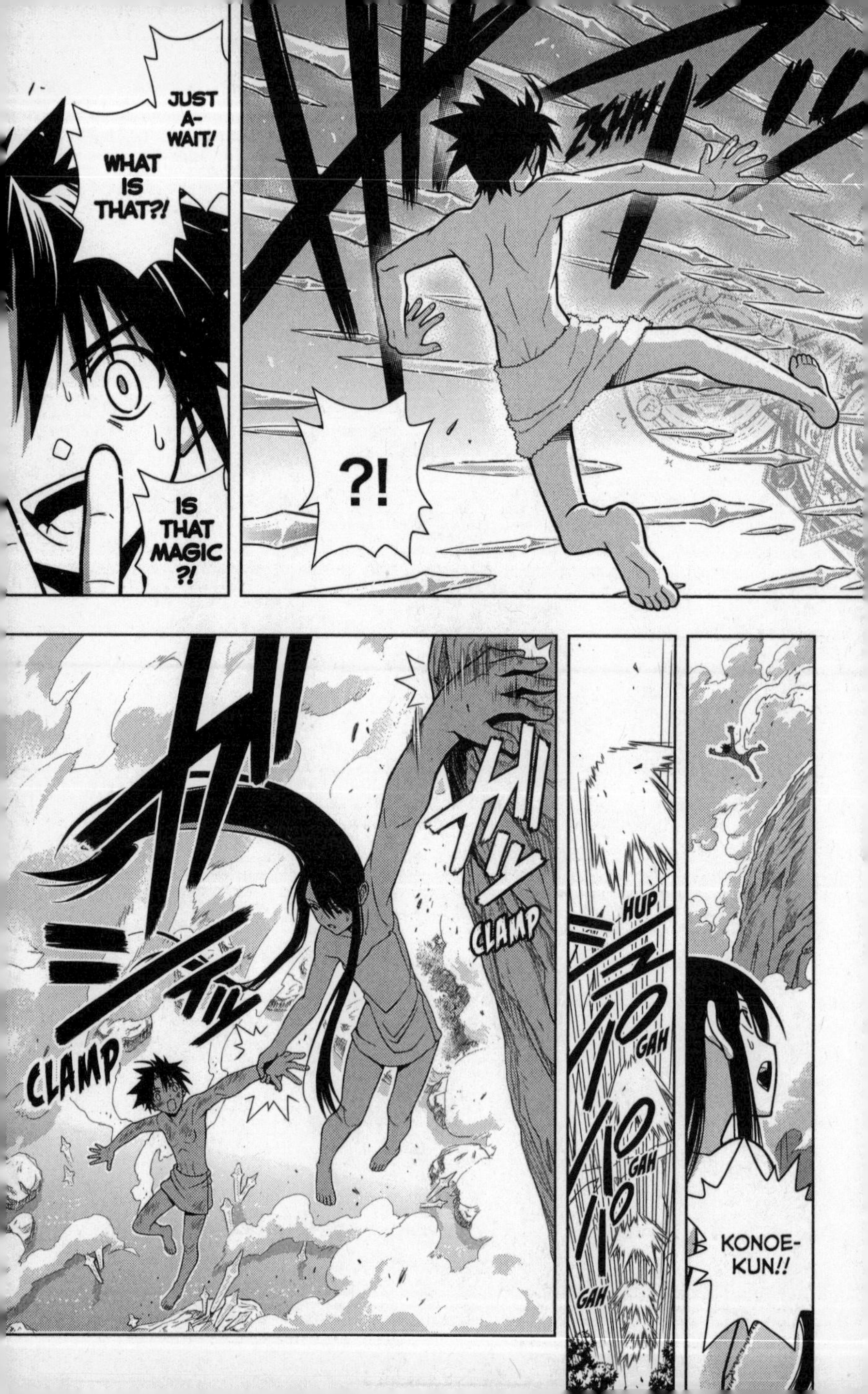
ZSHHH
?!
JUST A-WAIT!
WHAT IS THAT?!
IS THAT MAGIC?!
KONOE-KUN!!
HUP
GAH
GAH
GAH
CLAMP
CLAMP

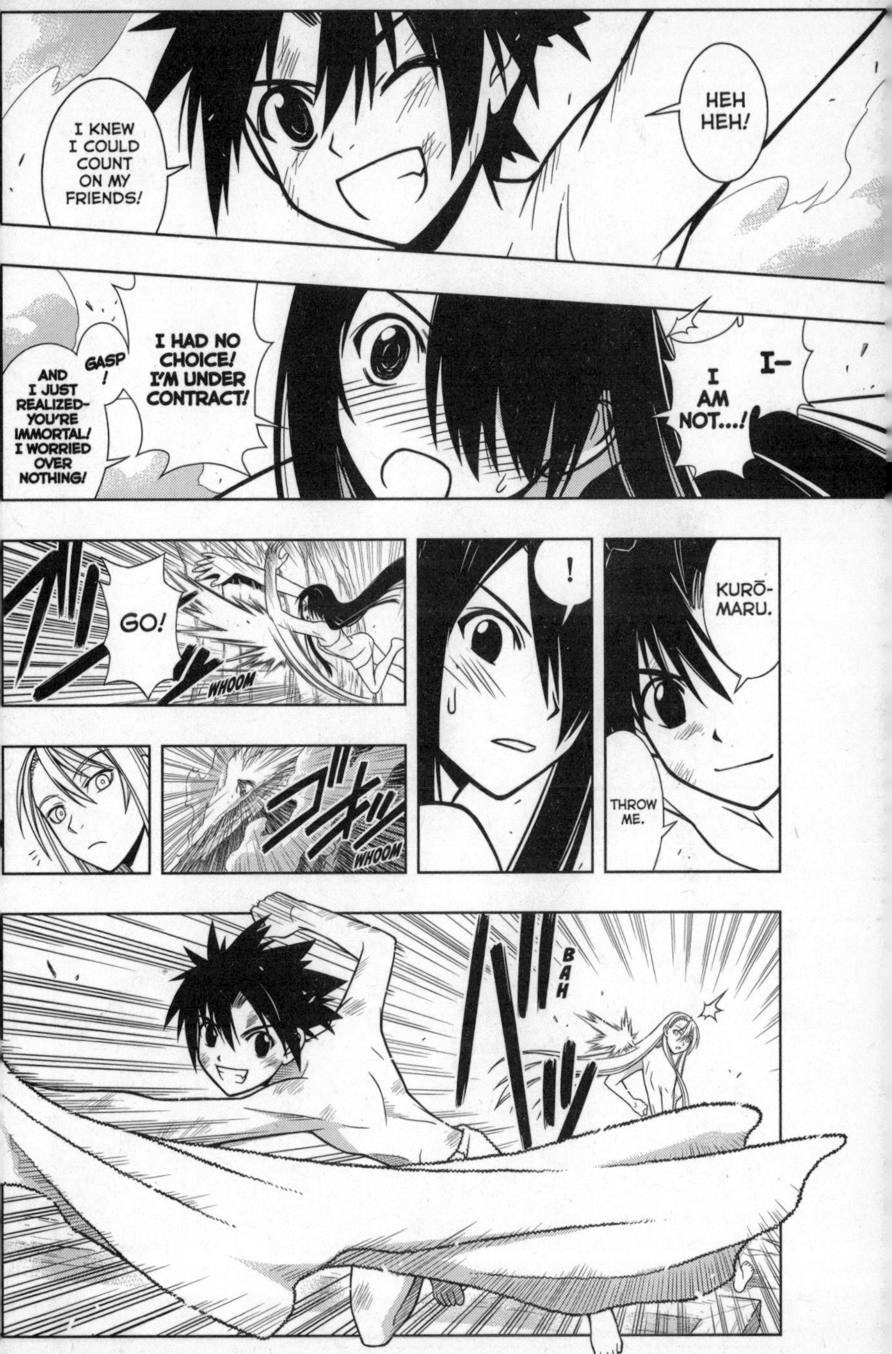
HEH HEH!
I KNEW I COULD COUNT ON MY FRIENDS!
I—
I AM NOT...!
I HAD NO CHOICE! I'M UNDER CONTRACT!
GASP!
AND I JUST REALIZED- YOU'RE IMMORTAL! I WORRIED OVER NOTHING!
KURŌ-MARU.
THROW ME.
!
GO!
WHOOM
WHOOM
BAH

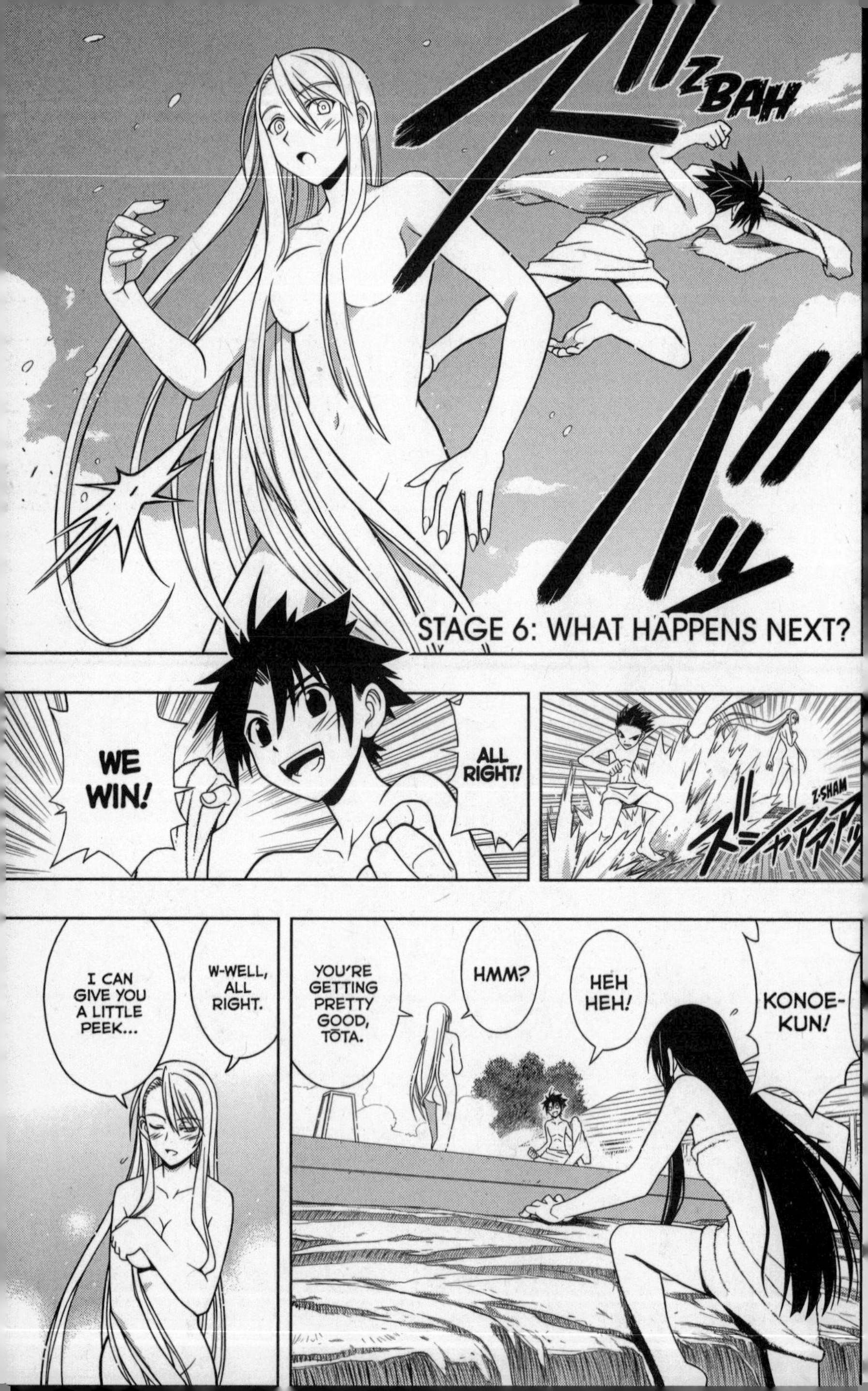
ZBAH
STAGE 6: WHAT HAPPENS NEXT?
Z-SHAM
ALL RIGHT!
WE WIN!
KONOE-KUN!
HEH HEH!
HMM?
YOU'RE GETTING PRETTY GOOD, TŌTA.
W-WELL, ALL RIGHT.
I CAN GIVE YOU A LITTLE PEEK...

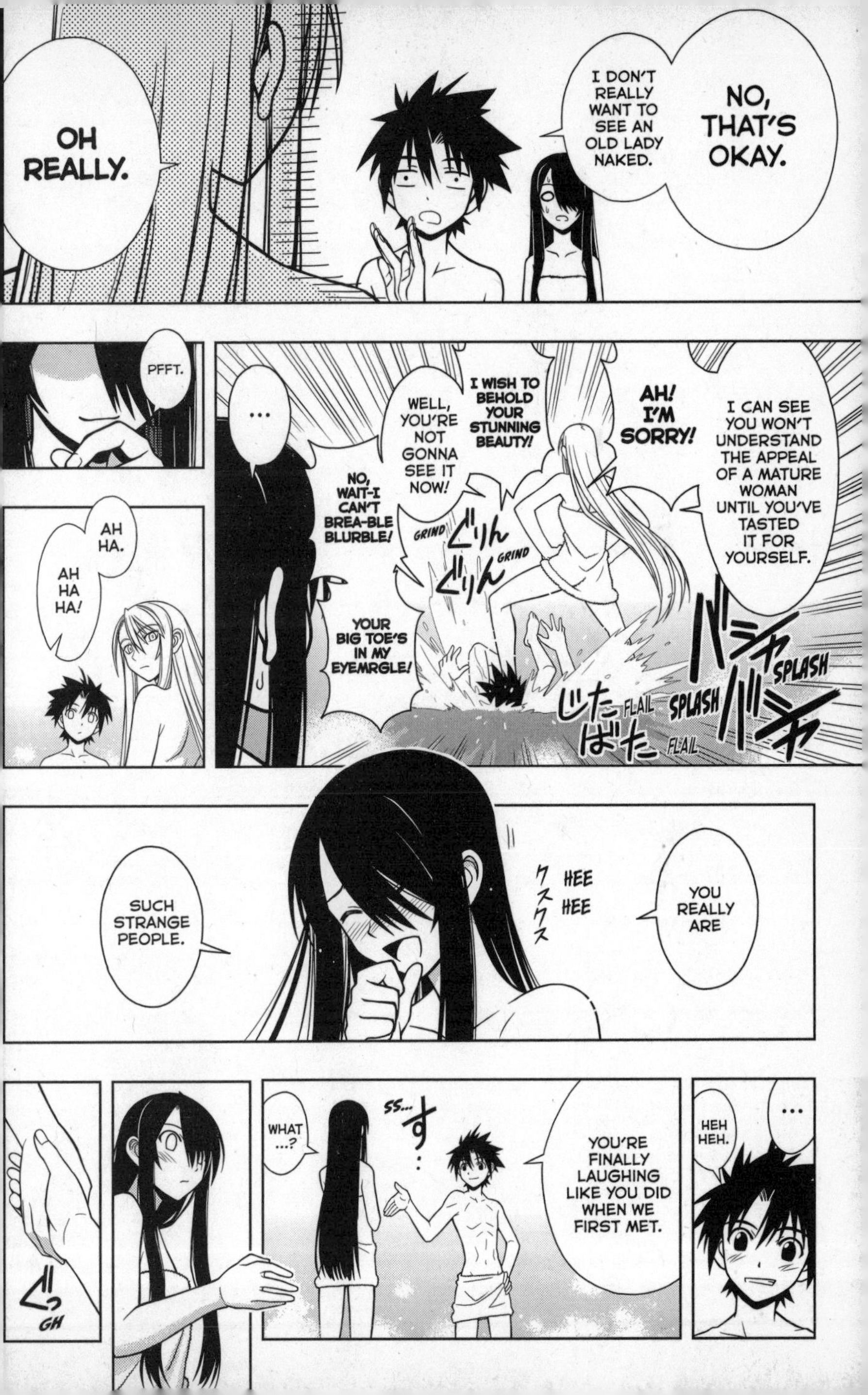

NO, THAT'S OKAY.
I DON'T REALLY WANT TO SEE AN OLD LADY NAKED.
OH REALLY.
I CAN SEE YOU WON'T UNDERSTAND THE APPEAL OF A MATURE WOMAN UNTIL YOU'VE TASTED IT FOR YOURSELF.
AH! I'M SORRY!
I WISH TO BEHOLD YOUR STUNNING BEAUTY!
WELL, YOU'RE NOT GONNA SEE IT NOW!
NO, WAIT-I CAN'T BREA-BLE BLURBLE!
YOUR BIG TOE'S IN MY EYEMRGLE!
...
バシャ SPLASH
バシャ SPLASH
じたばた FLAIL FLAIL
ぐりん GRIND
ぐりん GRIND
PFFT.
AH HA.
AH HA HA!
YOU REALLY ARE
クスクス HEE HEE
SUCH STRANGE PEOPLE.
...
HEH HEH.
YOU'RE FINALLY LAUGHING LIKE YOU DID WHEN WE FIRST MET.
す SS...
WHAT ...?
ぐっ GH

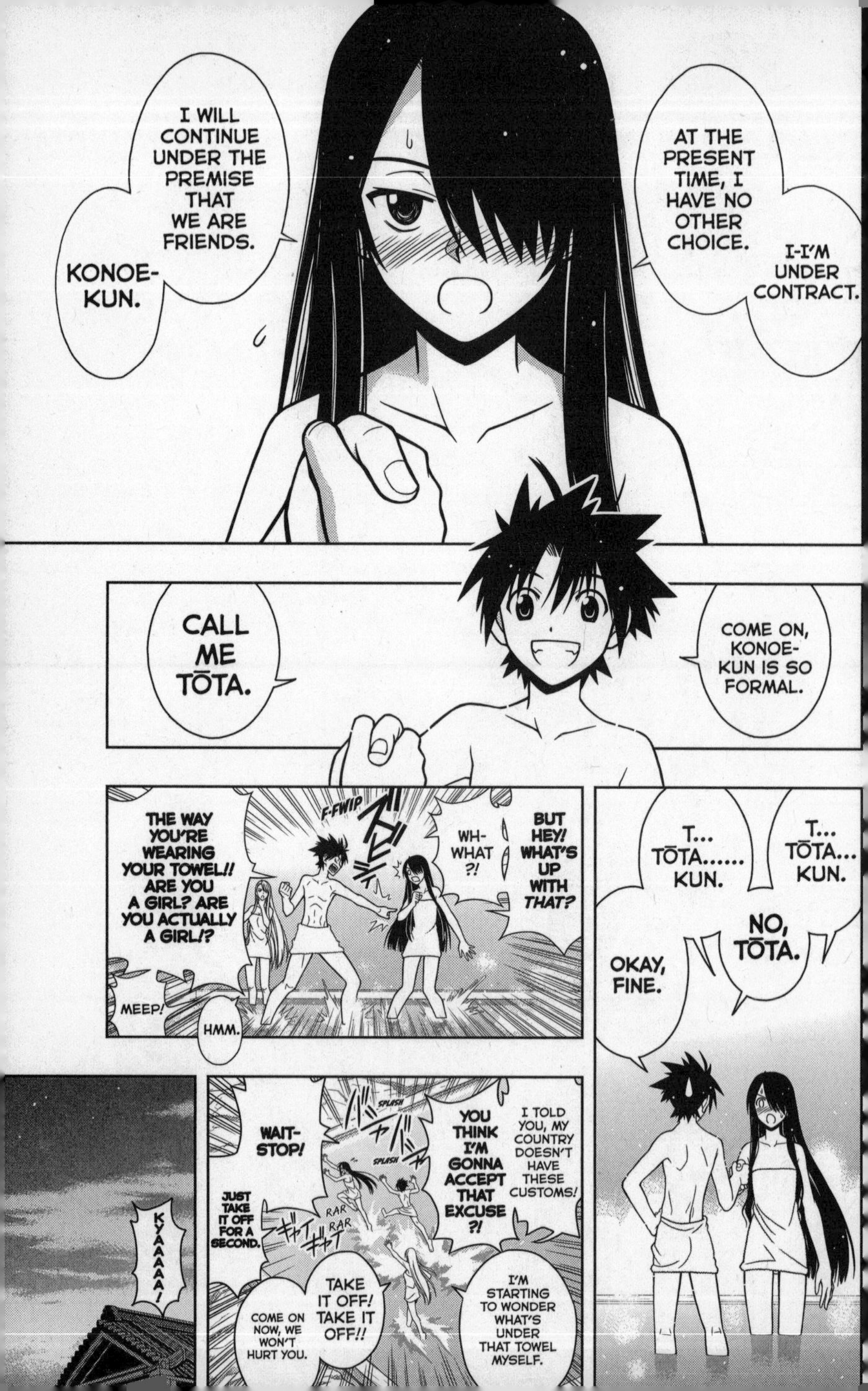
AT THE PRESENT TIME, I HAVE NO OTHER CHOICE.
I-I'M UNDER CONTRACT.
I WILL CONTINUE UNDER THE PREMISE THAT WE ARE FRIENDS.
KONOE-KUN.
COME ON, KONOE-KUN IS SO FORMAL.
CALL ME TŌTA.
T... TŌTA... KUN.
NO, TŌTA.
T... TŌTA...... KUN.
OKAY, FINE.
BUT HEY! WHAT'S UP WITH *THAT?*
WH-WHAT?!
F-FWIP
THE WAY YOU'RE WEARING YOUR TOWEL!! ARE YOU A GIRL? ARE YOU ACTUALLY A GIRL!?
HMM.
MEEP!
I TOLD YOU, MY COUNTRY DOESN'T HAVE THESE CUSTOMS!
YOU THINK I'M GONNA ACCEPT THAT EXCUSE?!
SPLASH
SPLASH
WAIT-STOP!
RAR RAR
JUST TAKE IT OFF FOR A SECOND.
I'M STARTING TO WONDER WHAT'S UNDER THAT TOWEL MYSELF.
TAKE IT OFF! TAKE IT OFF!!
COME ON NOW, WE WON'T HURT YOU.
KYAAAAA!

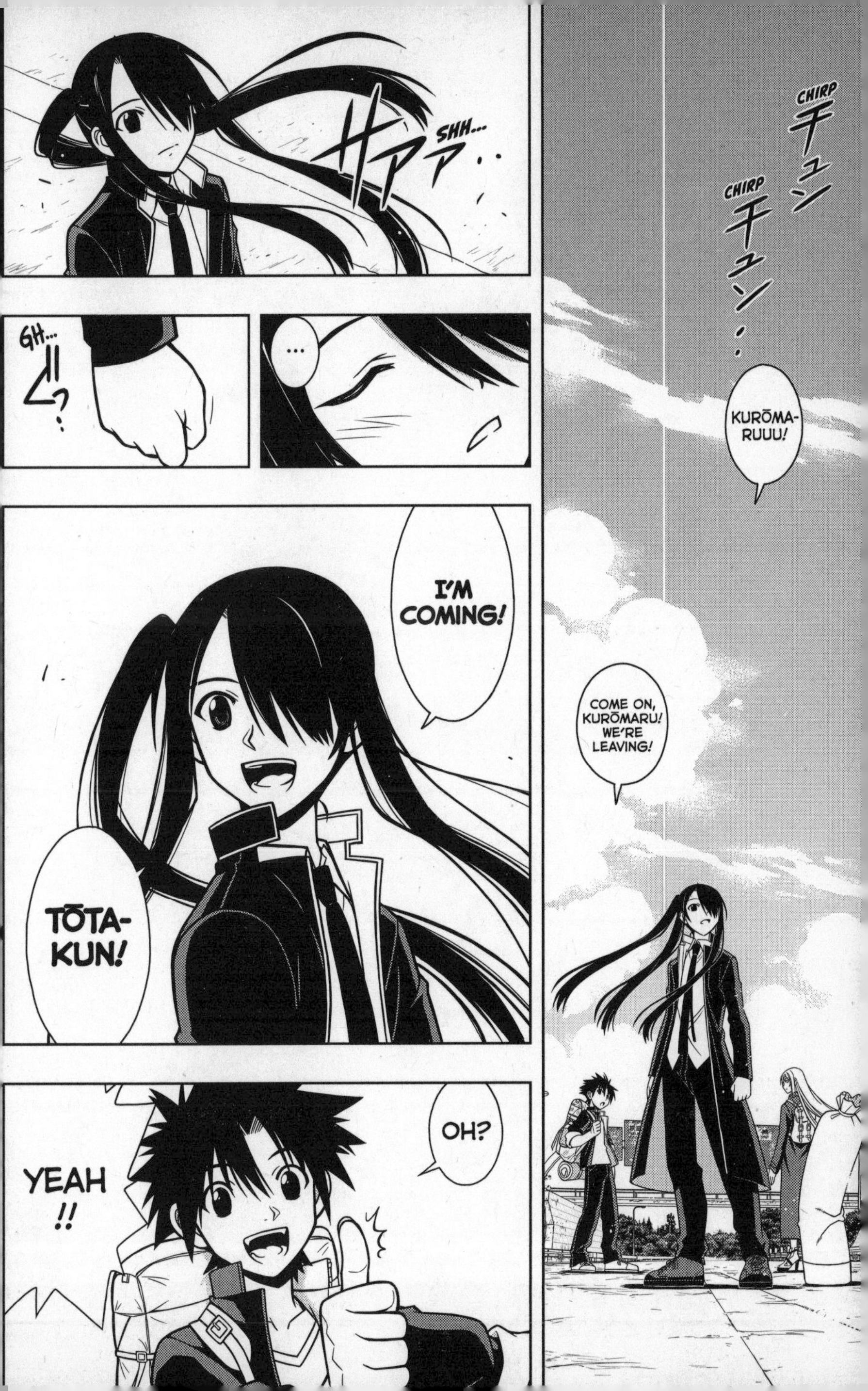
CHIRP
チュン
CHIRP
チュン・・
KURŌMA-RUUU!
COME ON, KURŌMARU! WE'RE LEAVING!
SHH...
サァァ
...
GH...
I'M COMING!
TŌTA-KUN!
OH?
YEAH!!

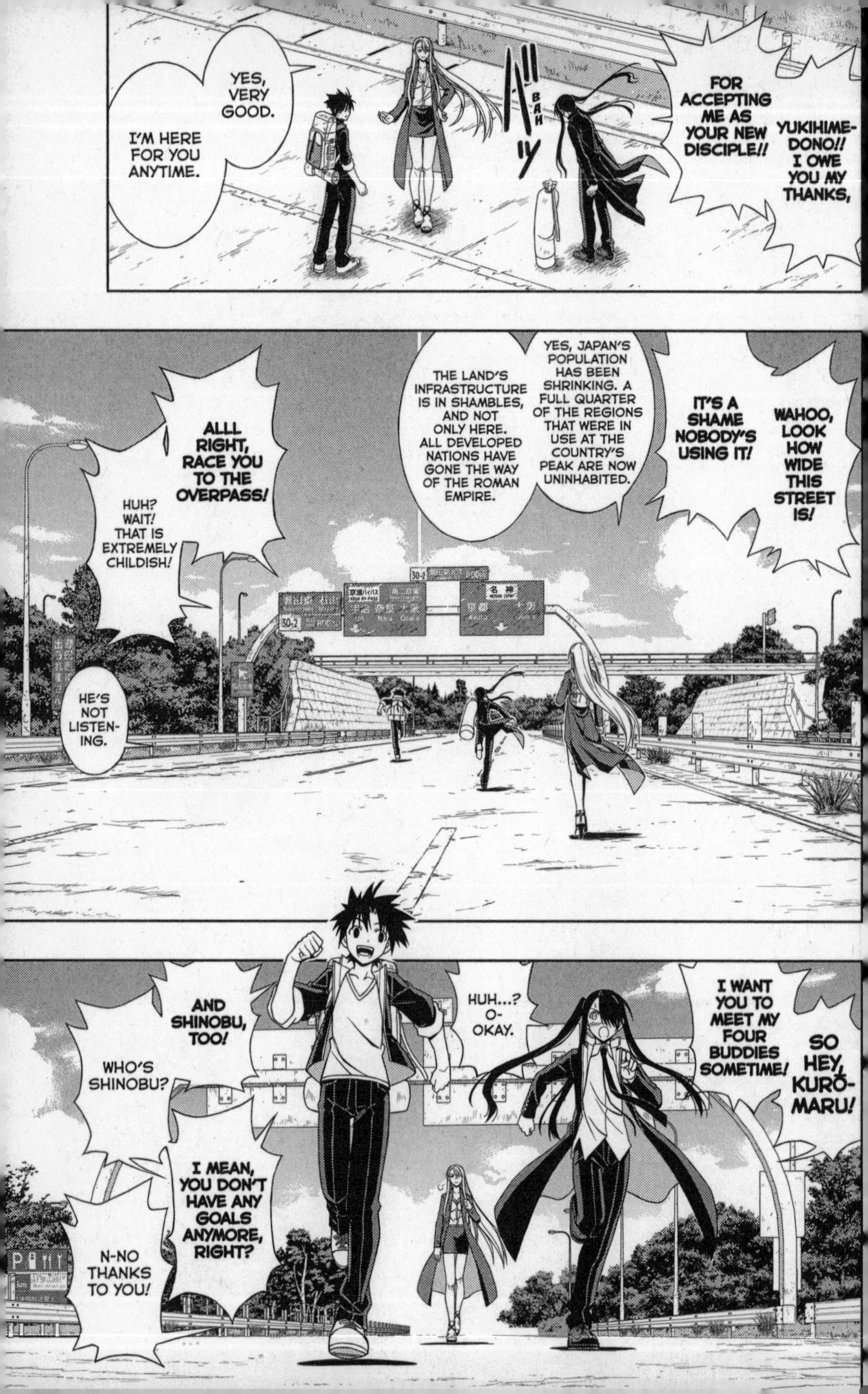
YUKIHIME-DONO!! I OWE YOU MY THANKS,
FOR ACCEPTING ME AS YOUR NEW DISCIPLE!!
BAH
YES, VERY GOOD.
I'M HERE FOR YOU ANYTIME.
WAHOO, LOOK HOW WIDE THIS STREET IS!
IT'S A SHAME NOBODY'S USING IT!
YES, JAPAN'S POPULATION HAS BEEN SHRINKING. A FULL QUARTER OF THE REGIONS THAT WERE IN USE AT THE COUNTRY'S PEAK ARE NOW UNINHABITED.
THE LAND'S INFRASTRUCTURE IS IN SHAMBLES, AND NOT ONLY HERE. ALL DEVELOPED NATIONS HAVE GONE THE WAY OF THE ROMAN EMPIRE.
ALLL RIGHT, RACE YOU TO THE OVERPASS!
HUH? WAIT! THAT IS EXTREMELY CHILDISH!
HE'S NOT LISTEN-ING.
SO HEY, KURŌMARU!
I WANT YOU TO MEET MY FOUR BUDDIES SOMETIME!
HUH...? O-OKAY.
AND SHINOBU, TOO!
WHO'S SHINOBU?
I MEAN, YOU DON'T HAVE ANY GOALS ANYMORE, RIGHT?
N-NO THANKS TO YOU!

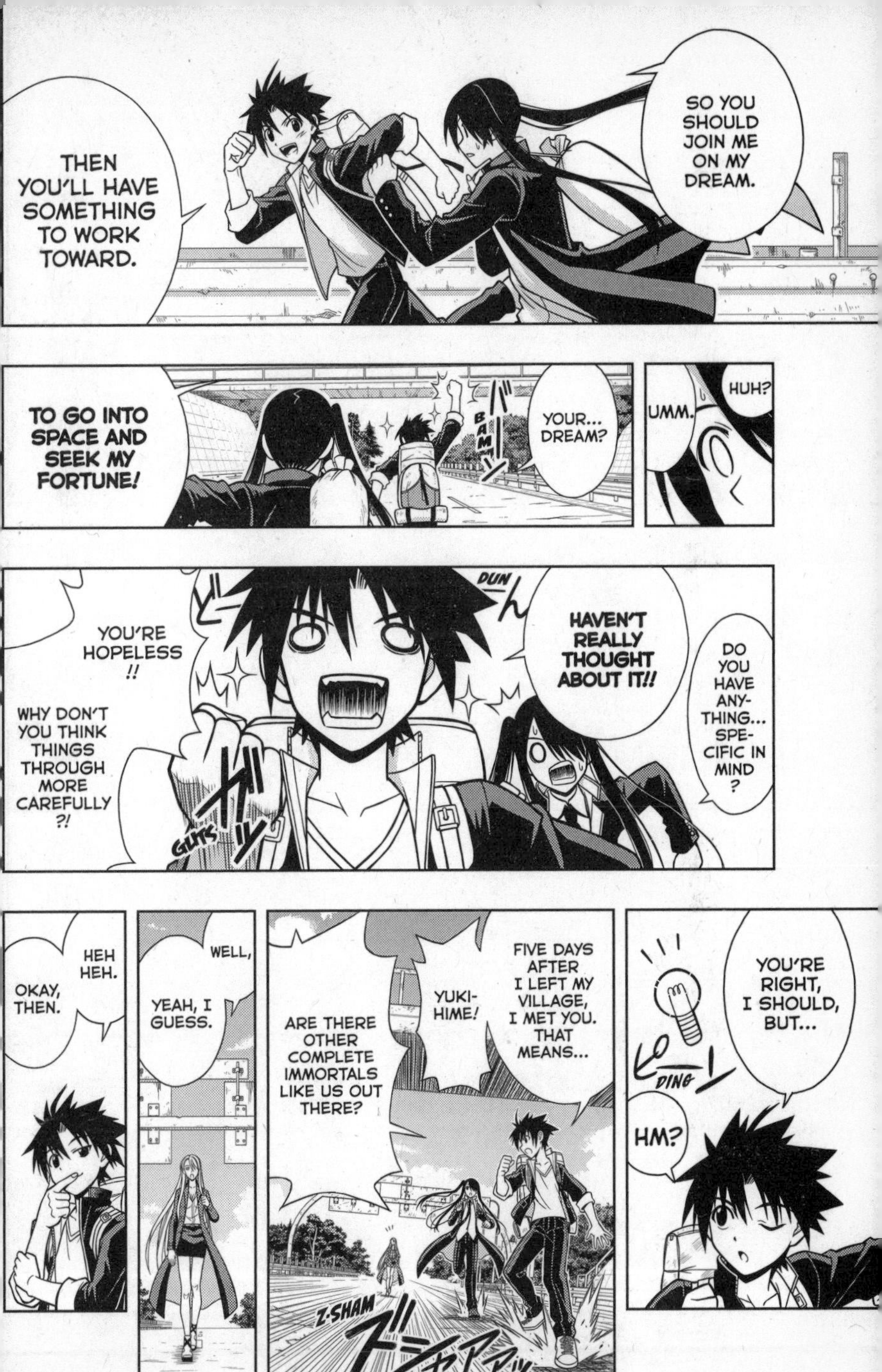
SO YOU SHOULD JOIN ME ON MY DREAM.
THEN YOU'LL HAVE SOMETHING TO WORK TOWARD.
HUH?
UMM.
YOUR... DREAM?
BAM
TO GO INTO SPACE AND SEEK MY FORTUNE!
DO YOU HAVE ANYTHING... SPECIFIC IN MIND?
HAVEN'T REALLY THOUGHT ABOUT IT!!
DUN
YOU'RE HOPELESS!!
WHY DON'T YOU THINK THINGS THROUGH MORE CAREFULLY?!
GUTS
YOU'RE RIGHT, I SHOULD, BUT...
DING
HM?
FIVE DAYS AFTER I LEFT MY VILLAGE, I MET YOU. THAT MEANS...
YUKI-HIME!
ARE THERE OTHER COMPLETE IMMORTALS LIKE US OUT THERE?
Z-SHAM
WELL,
YEAH, I GUESS.
HEH HEH.
OKAY, THEN.

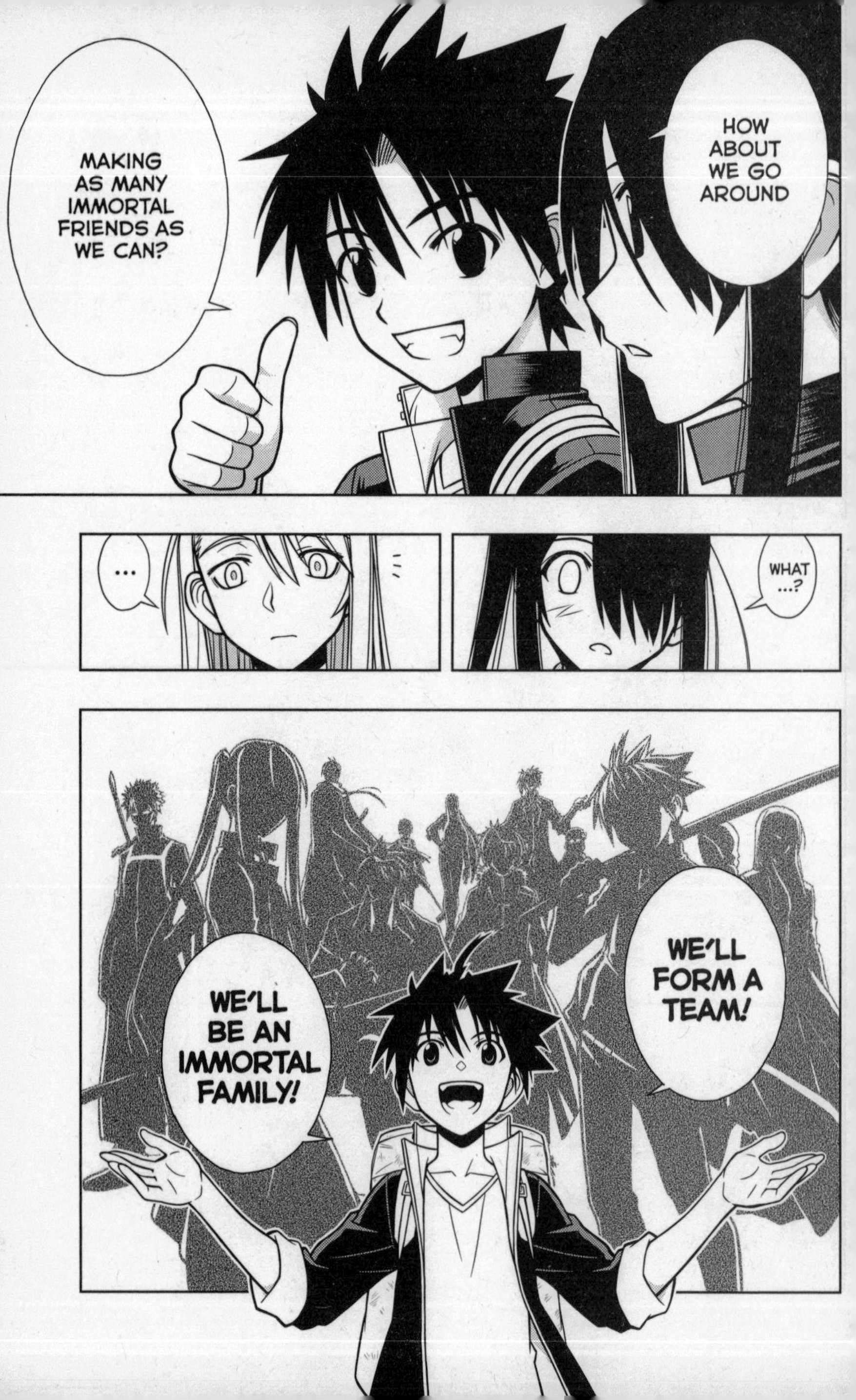
HOW ABOUT WE GO AROUND
MAKING AS MANY IMMORTAL FRIENDS AS WE CAN?
WHAT ...?
...
WE'LL FORM A TEAM!
WE'LL BE AN IMMORTAL FAMILY!

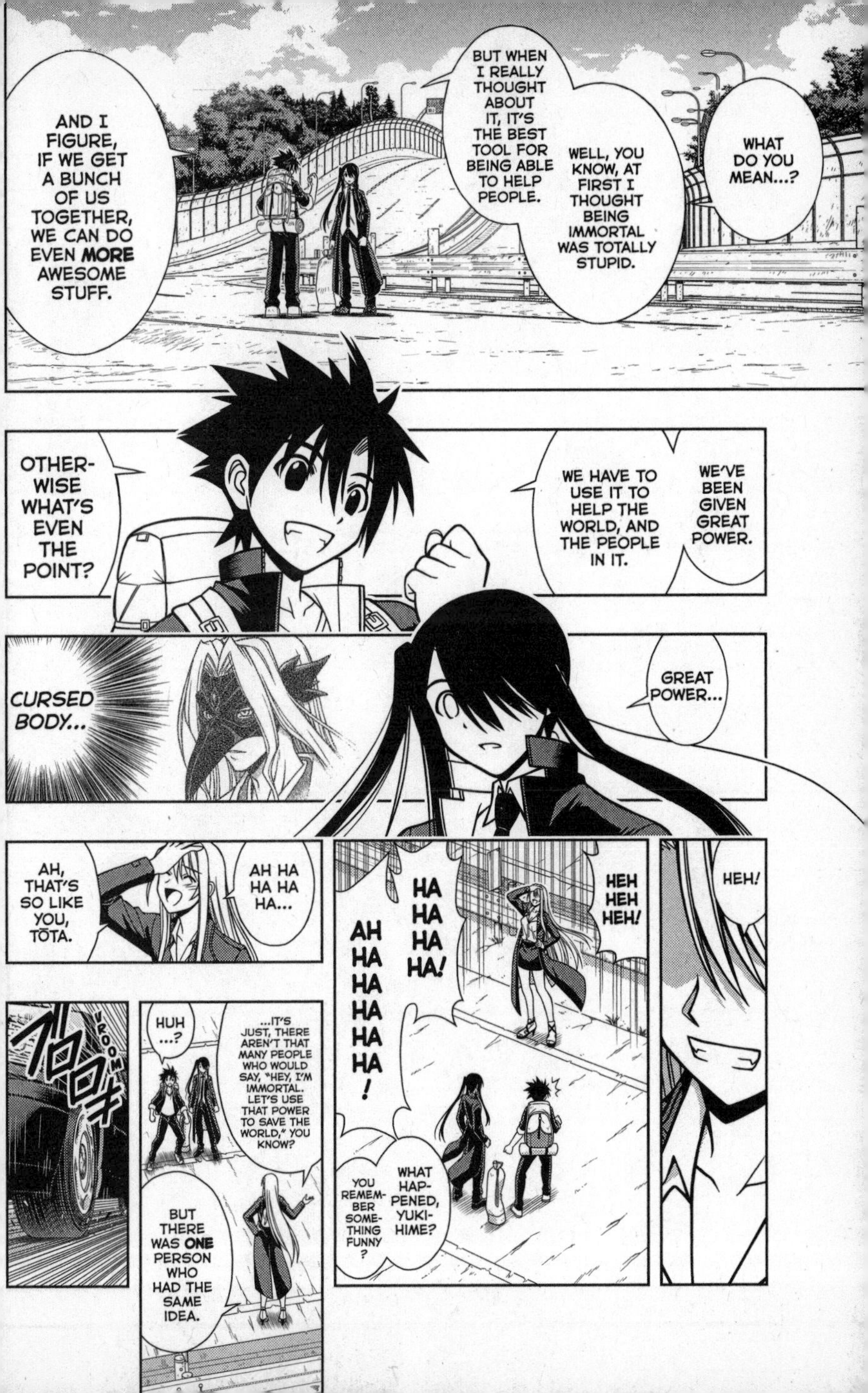
WHAT DO YOU MEAN...?
WELL, YOU KNOW, AT FIRST I THOUGHT BEING IMMORTAL WAS TOTALLY STUPID.
BUT WHEN I REALLY THOUGHT ABOUT IT, IT'S THE BEST TOOL FOR BEING ABLE TO HELP PEOPLE.
AND I FIGURE, IF WE GET A BUNCH OF US TOGETHER, WE CAN DO EVEN **MORE** AWESOME STUFF.
WE'VE BEEN GIVEN GREAT POWER.
WE HAVE TO USE IT TO HELP THE WORLD, AND THE PEOPLE IN IT.
OTHER-WISE WHAT'S EVEN THE POINT?
GREAT POWER...
CURSED BODY...
HEH!
HEH HEH HEH!
HA HA HA HA!
AH HA HA HA HA HA HA !
WHAT HAP-PENED, YUKI-HIME?
YOU REMEM-BER SOME-THING FUNNY ?
AH HA HA HA HA...
AH, THAT'S SO LIKE YOU, TŌTA.
...IT'S JUST, THERE AREN'T THAT MANY PEOPLE WHO WOULD SAY, "HEY, I'M IMMORTAL. LET'S USE THAT POWER TO SAVE THE WORLD," YOU KNOW?
HUH ...?
BUT THERE WAS **ONE** PERSON WHO HAD THE SAME IDEA.
VROOM

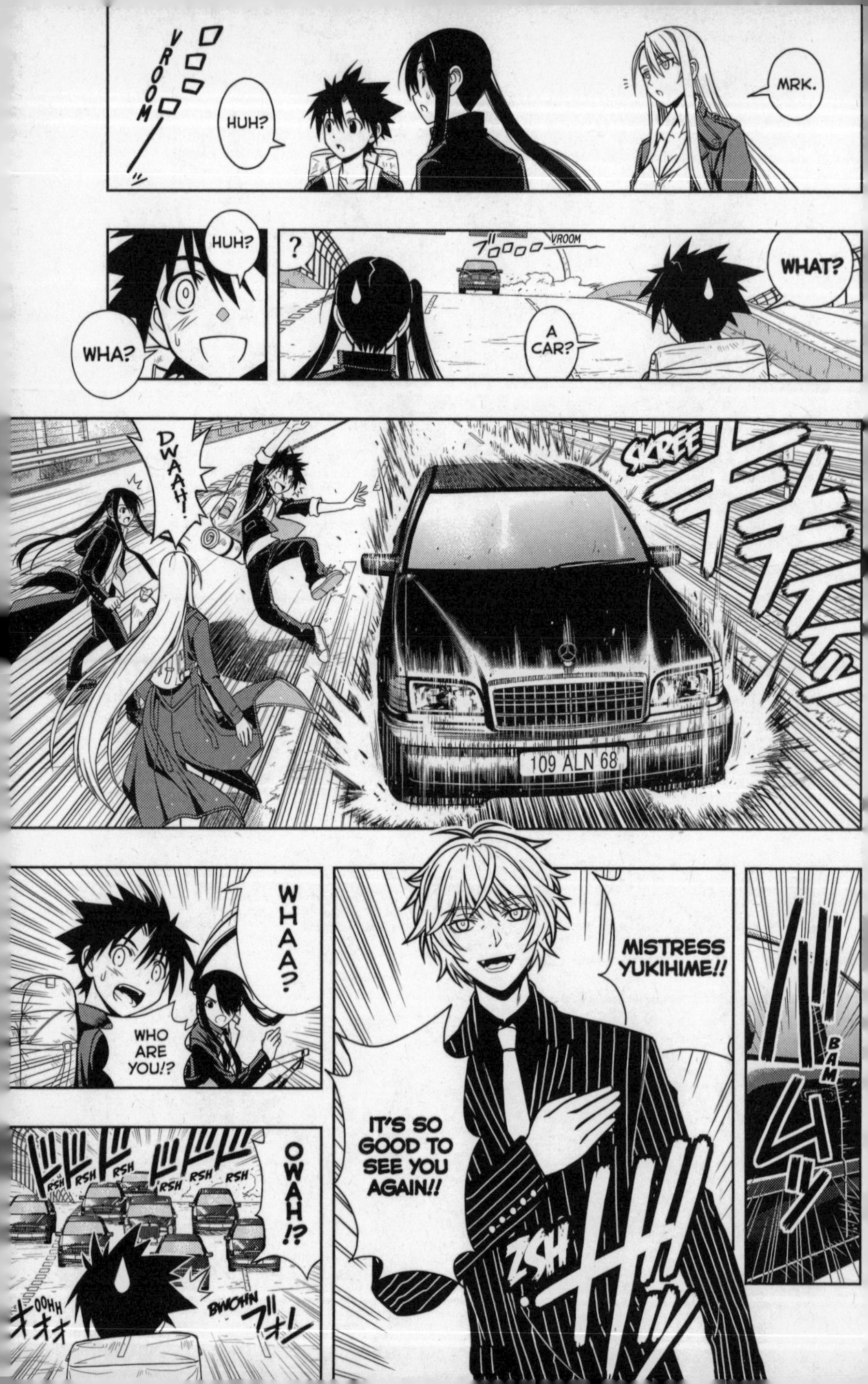
MRK.
HUH?
VROOM
WHAT?
A CAR?
?
VROOM
HUH?
WHA?
SKREE
109 ALN 68
DWAAH!
BAM
MISTRESS YUKIHIME!!
IT'S SO GOOD TO SEE YOU AGAIN!!
ZSH
WHAAA?
WHO ARE YOU!?
OWAH!?
RSH RSH RSH RSH RSH RSH
BWOHN
OOHH

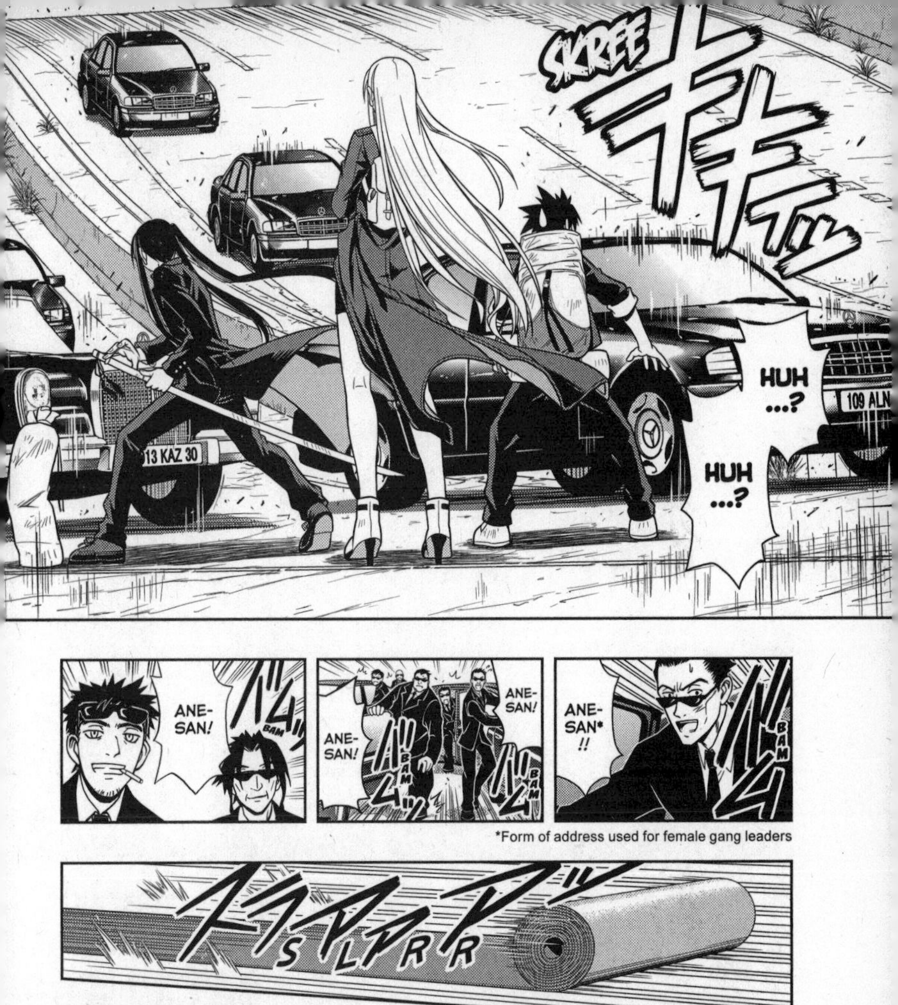
SKREE
HUH ...?
HUH ...?
ANE-SAN* !!
BAM
ANE-SAN!
ANE-SAN!
BAM
BAM
ANE-SAN!
BAM

*Form of address used for female gang leaders

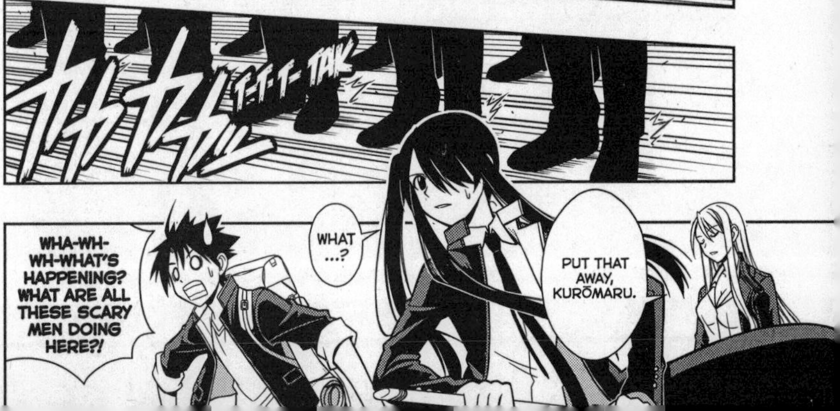
SLRRR
T-T-T-TAK
PUT THAT AWAY, KURŌMARU.
WHAT ...?
WHA-WH-WH-WHAT'S HAPPENING? WHAT ARE ALL THESE SCARY MEN DOING HERE?!

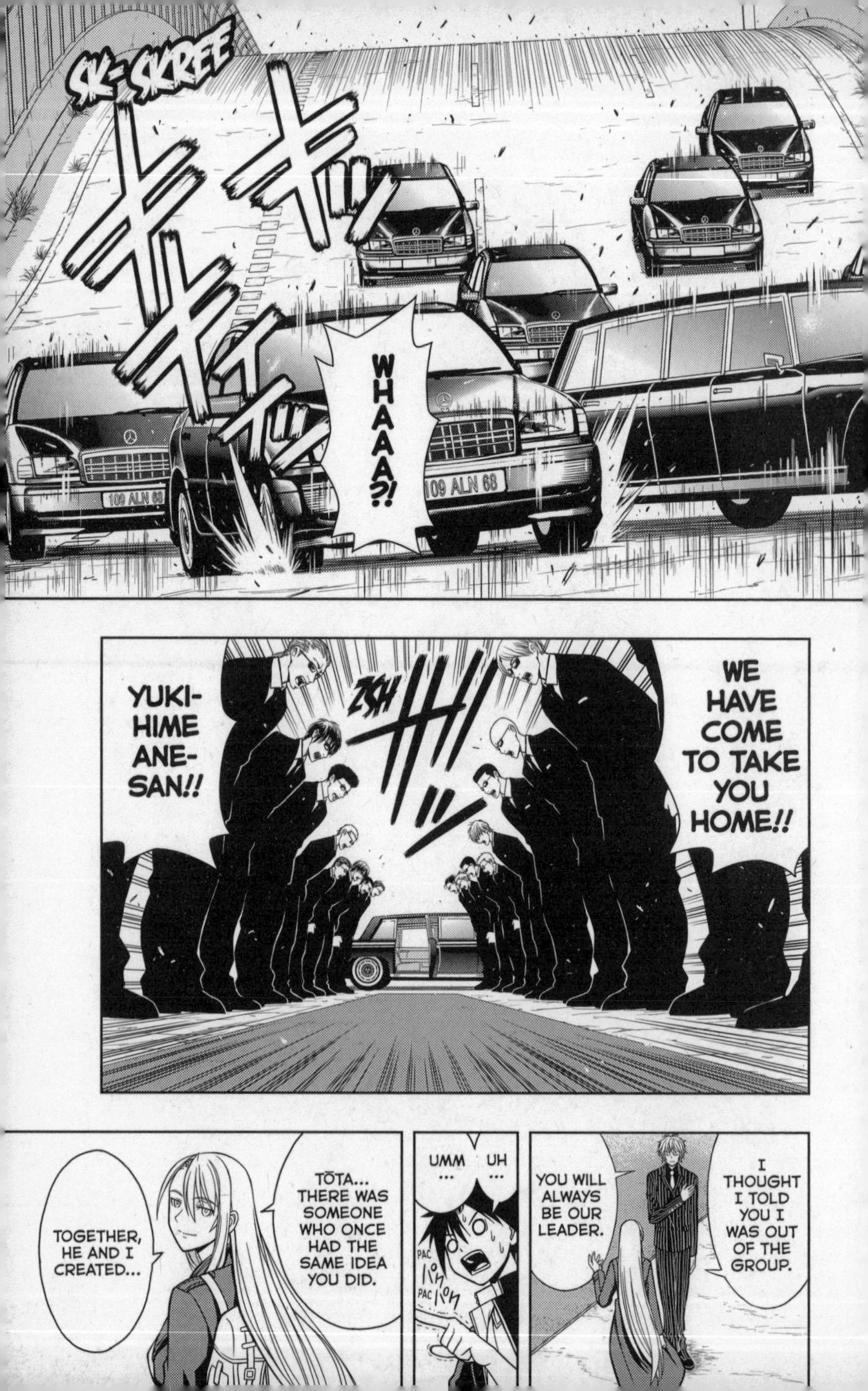
SK-SKREE
WHAAAA?!
WE HAVE COME TO TAKE YOU HOME!!
YUKI-HIME ANE-SAN!!
ZSH
I THOUGHT I TOLD YOU I WAS OUT OF THE GROUP.
YOU WILL ALWAYS BE OUR LEADER.
UH...
UMM...
PAC
PAC
TŌTA... THERE WAS SOMEONE WHO ONCE HAD THE SAME IDEA YOU DID.
TOGETHER, HE AND I CREATED...

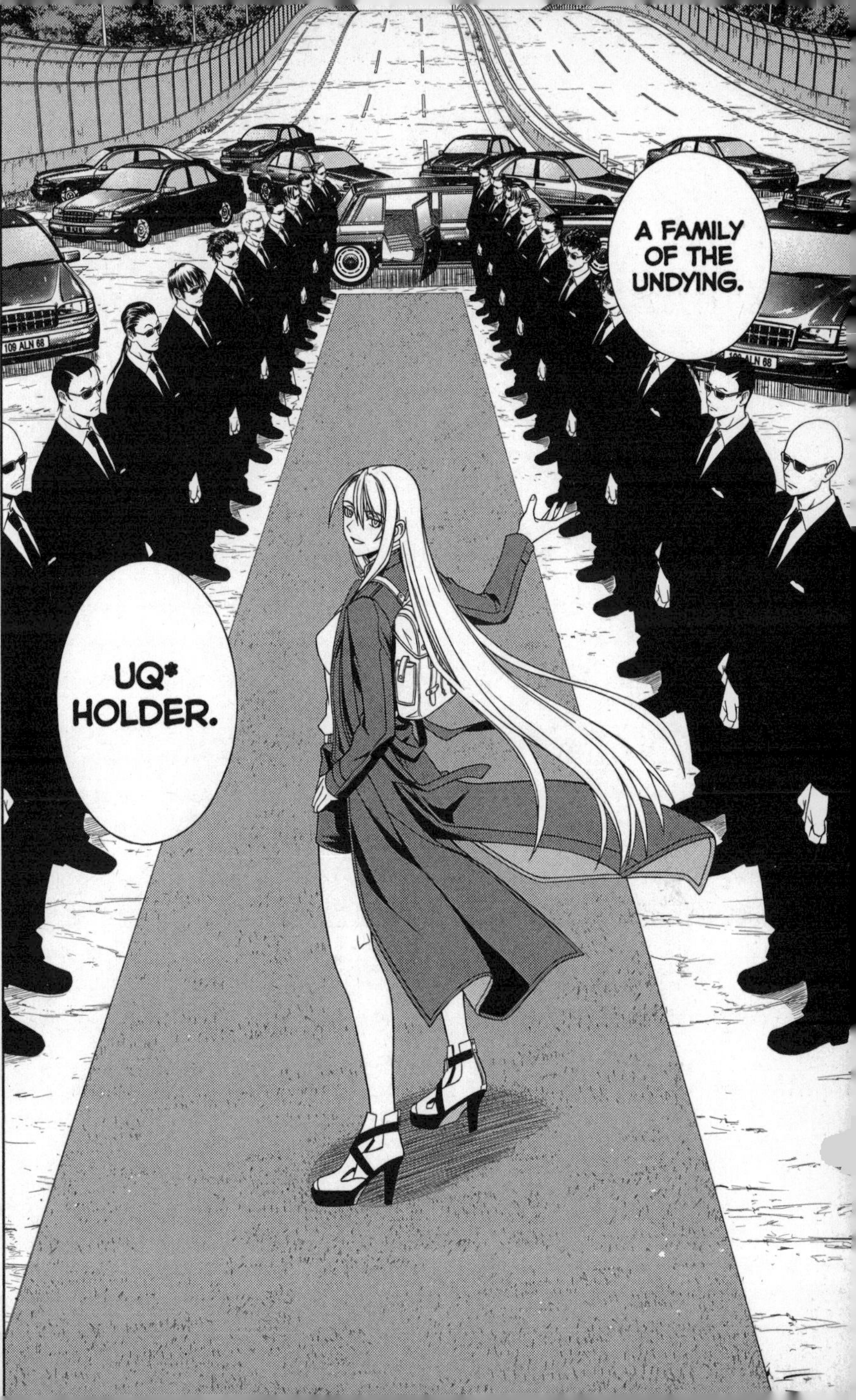
A FAMILY OF THE UNDYING.
UQ* HOLDER.

*UQ in Japanese sounds the same as 悠久, which means "everlasting"

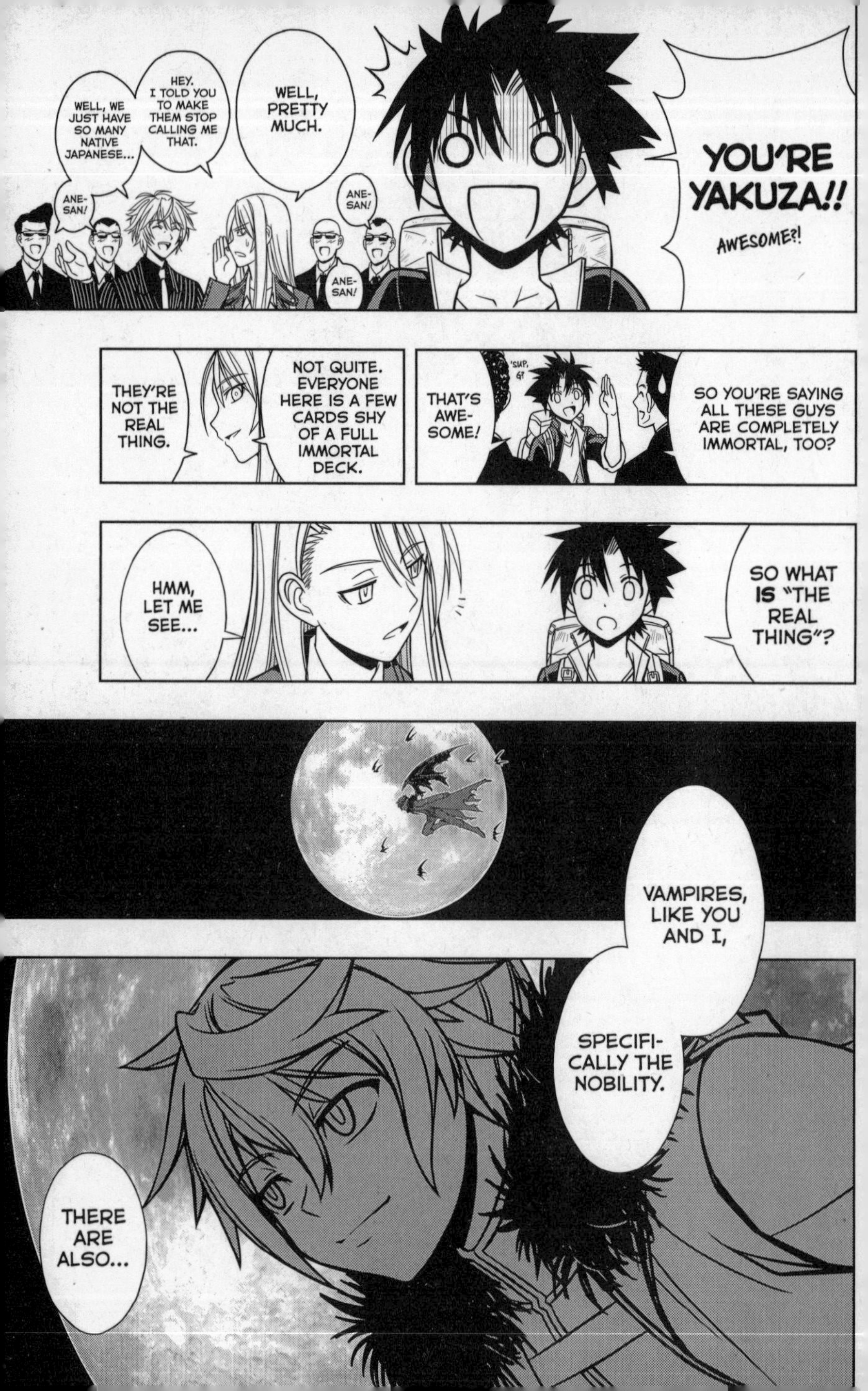
YOU'RE YAKUZA!!
AWESOME?!
WELL, PRETTY MUCH.
ANE-SAN!
ANE-SAN!
HEY. I TOLD YOU TO MAKE THEM STOP CALLING ME THAT.
WELL, WE JUST HAVE SO MANY NATIVE JAPANESE...
ANE-SAN!
SO YOU'RE SAYING ALL THESE GUYS ARE COMPLETELY IMMORTAL, TOO?
'SUP, G?
THAT'S AWESOME!
NOT QUITE. EVERYONE HERE IS A FEW CARDS SHY OF A FULL IMMORTAL DECK.
THEY'RE NOT THE REAL THING.
SO WHAT IS "THE REAL THING"?
HMM, LET ME SEE...
VAMPIRES, LIKE YOU AND I,
SPECIFICALLY THE NOBILITY.
THERE ARE ALSO...

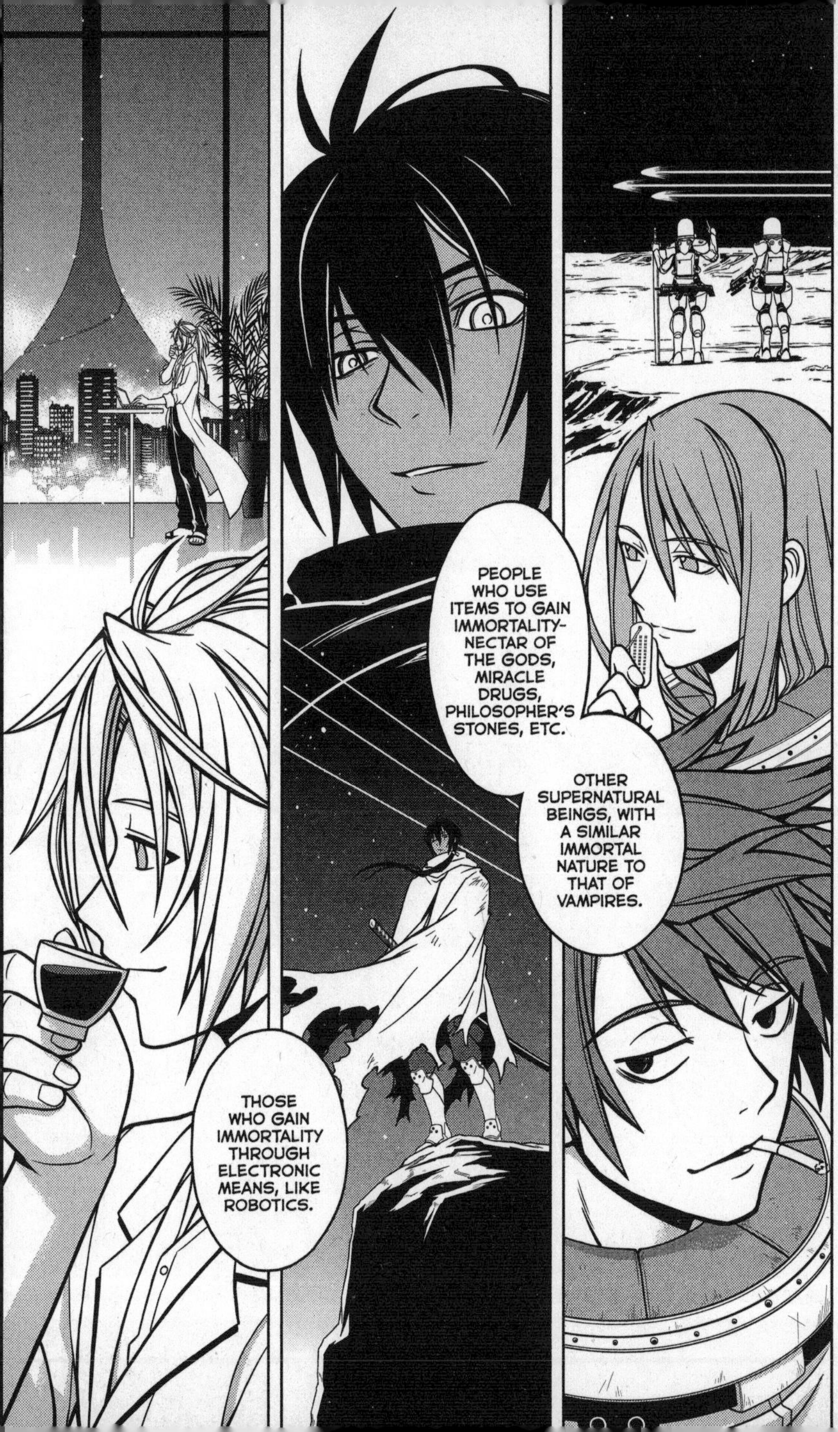
PEOPLE WHO USE ITEMS TO GAIN IMMORTALITY- NECTAR OF THE GODS, MIRACLE DRUGS, PHILOSOPHER'S STONES, ETC.
OTHER SUPERNATURAL BEINGS, WITH A SIMILAR IMMORTAL NATURE TO THAT OF VAMPIRES.
THOSE WHO GAIN IMMORTALITY THROUGH ELECTRONIC MEANS, LIKE ROBOTICS.

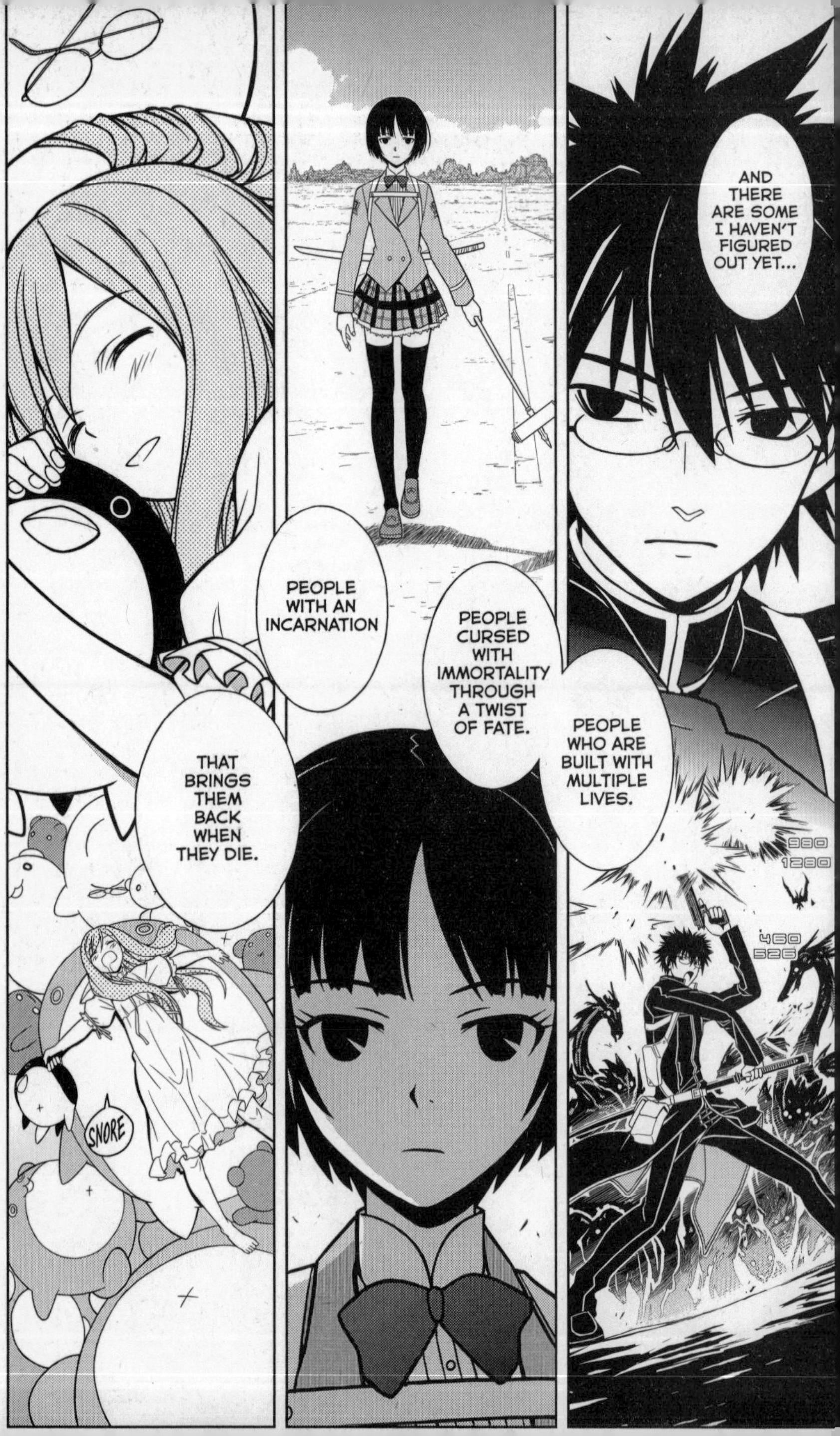
AND THERE ARE SOME I HAVEN'T FIGURED OUT YET...
PEOPLE WHO ARE BUILT WITH MULTIPLE LIVES.
980
1280
460
526
PEOPLE CURSED WITH IMMORTALITY THROUGH A TWIST OF FATE.
PEOPLE WITH AN INCARNATION
THAT BRINGS THEM BACK WHEN THEY DIE.
SNORE

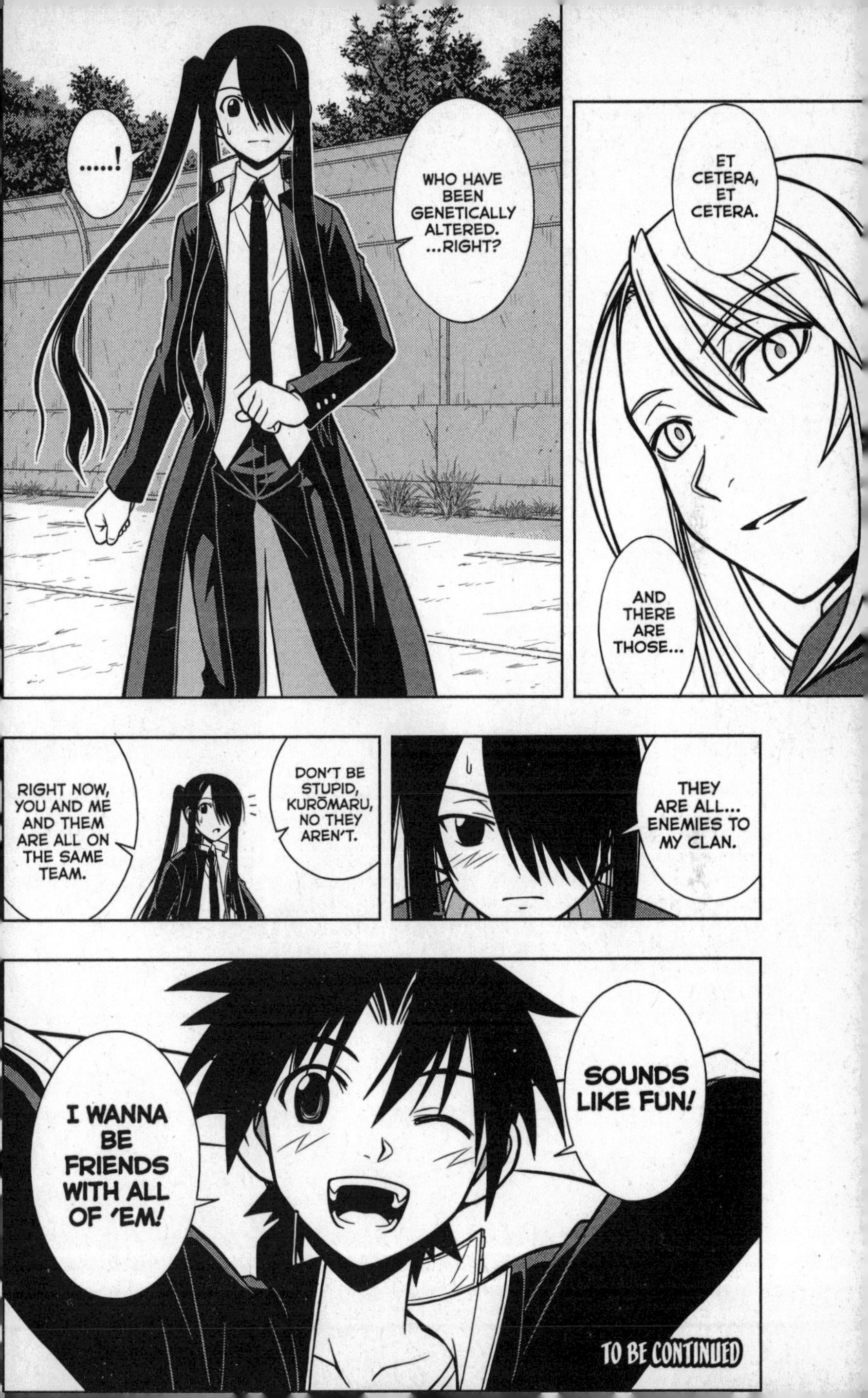
ET CETERA, ET CETERA.
AND THERE ARE THOSE...
WHO HAVE BEEN GENETICALLY ALTERED. ...RIGHT?
......!
THEY ARE ALL... ENEMIES TO MY CLAN.
DON'T BE STUPID, KURŌMARU, NO THEY AREN'T.
RIGHT NOW, YOU AND ME AND THEM ARE ALL ON THE SAME TEAM.
SOUNDS LIKE FUN!
I WANNA BE FRIENDS WITH ALL OF 'EM!
TO BE CONTINUED

UQ HOLDER!

STAFF

Ken Akamatsu

Takashi Takemoto

Kenichi Nakamura

Keiichi Yamashita

Tohru Mitsuhashi

Susumu Kuwabara

Thanks to Ran Ayanaga

FROM HIRO MASHIMA,
CREATOR OF **RAVE MASTER**

Lucy has always dreamed of joining the Fairy Tail, a club for the most powerful sorcerers in the land. But once she becomes a member, the fun really starts!

Special extras in each volume! Read them all!

RATING T AGES 13+

SHERLOCK BONES

DEDUCTIVE DOG DETECTIVE

When Takeru adopts a new pet, he's in for a surprise—the dog is none other than the reincarnation of Sherlock Holmes. With no one else able to communicate with Holmes, Takeru is roped into becoming Sherdog's assistant, John Watson. Using his sleuthing skills, Holmes uncovers clues to solve the trickiest crimes.

BY MAKOTO RAIKU

In a world of animals, where the strong eat the weak, Monoko the tanuki stumbles across a strange creature the likes of which has never been seen before–a human baby! While the newborn has no claws or teeth to protect itself, it does have the special ability to speak to and understand all different animals. Can the gift of speech between species change the balance of power in a land where the weak must always fear the strong?

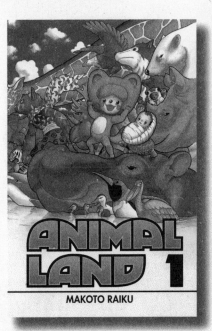

Ages 13+

VISIT KODANSHACOMICS.COM TO:
- View release date calendars for upcoming volumes
- Find out the latest about upcoming Kodansha Comics series